A Game of Life and Death

"You begin, Willi, dear," said Nina. "You go first." She was leaning forward, and her blue eyes seemed very bright. "I've been wondering since I saw the Strangler interviewed on *Sixty Minutes*. He *was* yours, Willi?"

"*Ja, ja*, he was mine. He was the gardener of a neighbor of mine. I left him alive so that the police could question him. He will hang himself in his cell next month. But this is more interesting. Look at this." Willi slid across several glossy black-and-white photographs. The NBC executive had murdered the five members of his family and drowned a visiting soap-opera actress in his pool. He had then stabbed himself repeatedly and written 50 SHARE in blood on the wall of the bathhouse.

"I think it should receive points for irony," Willi said. "The girl had been scheduled to drown on the program. It was already in the script."

"Did you have to repeat the contact?"

Willi frowned at me. "*Ja, ja*, I saw him twice more."

"Points for irony," said Nina. "But you lose points for repeated contact. What else do you have?"

He had his usual assortment. Pathetic skid-row murders. Two domestic slayings. A highway collision that turned into a fatal shooting. "I was in the crowd," said Willi. "I made contact. He had a gun in the glove compartment."

When he was finished, the three of us went through the ritual of assigning points. Willi went from being sullen to expansive to sullen again. His eyes were small, red embers in a bloody mask.

"Forty-one," said Nina at last and showed the calculator. "I count forty-one points. It's your turn, Melanie."

Books by Dan Simmons

Prayers
to
Broken
Stones

A Collection By
Dan Simmons

Introduction by Harlan Ellison

BANTAM BOOKS
NEW YORK · TORONTO · LONDON · SYDNEY · AUCKLAND

This edition contains the complete text
of the original hardcover edition.
NOT ONE WORD HAS BEEN OMITTED.

PRAYERS TO BROKEN STONES

A Bantam Spectra Book / published by arrangement with the author

PRINTING HISTORY
Dark Harvest edition published 1990
Bantam edition / May 1992

SPECTRA and the portrayal of a boxed "s" are trademarks of Bantam Books, a division of Bantam Doubleday Dell Publishing Group, Inc.

Grateful acknowledgment is made for permission to reprint the following: "The River Styx Runs Upstream" Copyright © Dan Simmons; first appeared in *Rod Serling's The Twilight Zone Magazine* April, 1982. "Eyes I Dare Not Meet in Dreams" Copyright © Dan Simmons; first appeared in *OMNI Magazine* September, 1982. "Vanni Fucci is Alive and Well and Living in Hell" Copyright © Dan Simmons; first appeared in *Night Visions 5* from Dark Harvest 1988. "Vexed to Nightmare by a Rocking Cradle" Copyright © Dan Simmons; first appeared in *Mile High Futures* November, 1985. "Remembering Siri" Copyright © Dan Simmons; first appeared in *Isaac Asimov's Science Fiction Magazine* December, 1983. "Metastasis" Copyright © Dan Simmons; first appeared in *Night Visions 5* from Dark Harvest 1988. "The Offering" (teleplay) Copyright © Laurel EFX 1989; first appeared on the syndicated television show *Monsters* 1990. "E-Ticket to 'Namland" Copyright © Dan Simmons; first appeared in *OMNI Magazine* November, 1987. "Iverson's Pits" Copyright © Dan Simmons; first appeared in *Night Visions 5* from Dark Harvest 1988. "Shave and a Haircut, Two Bites" Copyright © Dan Simmons; first appeared in *Masques III*, edited by J.N. Williamson 1989. "The Death of the Centaur" Copyright © Dan Simmons 1990. "Two Minutes Forty-Five Seconds" Copyright © Dan Simmons; first appeared in *OMNI Magazine* April, 1988. "Carrion Comfort" Copyright © Dan Simmons; first appeared in *OMNI Magazine* Sept.–Oct. 1983.

ISBN 0-553-29665-5

Published simultaneously in the United States and Canada

Bantam Books are published by Bantam Books, a division of Bantam Doubleday Dell Publishing Group, Inc. Its trademark, consisting of the words "Bantam Books" and the portrayal of a rooster, is Registered in U.S. Patent and Trademark Office and in other countries. Marca Registrada. Bantam Books, 666 Fifth Avenue, New York, New York 10103.

This is for Karen, with love.

TABLE OF CONTENTS

Introduction

Harlan Ellison

Then the time comes when it is clear nothing new or important will be done; and one draws out the ledger and begins to itemize what there is, of value, that can be offered to posterity. And here a good deed, and there an act of courage; during this year one worthy story was told, during that decade involvement in an important social movement. If there are babies, that is logged in. If there are books, they are noted. Loving friends. Wives and husbands. Kindness to small animals. A hill bearing your name. But the laurels you counted on, they've turned to dust.

Cultural amnesia. Yesterday is buried. Who ever heard of Crispus Attucks or Edward Yashinsky, Bettie Page or Wendell Willkie, Preacher Roe or Memphis Minnie Douglas? Seven people in all the world remember them. Just you and I, and five others.

The tusks that clashed in mighty brawls
Of mastodons, are billiard balls.

The sword of Charlemagne the Just
Is ferric oxide, known as rust.

The grizzly bear whose potent hug
Was feared by all, is now a rug.

Introduction

Great Caesar's bust is on the shelf,
And I don't feel so well myself.

ON THE VANITY OF EARTHLY GREATNESS
by Arthur Guiterman

It is certain no one will remember, when I am gone, that I was a man who first published Lenny Bruce; that I saved two hundred acres of watershed land from developers; that I once singlehandedly caught a car thief and on another occasion deduced the identity of a cat burglar and was instrumental in his capture; that I corresponded with the mysterious B. Traven and published his first book of short stories; that it was I who manipulated Mystery Writers of America into paying authors and editors who contributed to their anthologies.

These things are important to me; but when I go . . . that they ever happened will pass from the world. The awards won, the escapades mythologized, the love spent so unwisely . . . it all grows clouded in the mirror, and the mirror is covered with a white sheet, and the ancient furniture is stored away, and one night when it gets cold the old furniture is broken up for kindling. Then who is to say what was important when this one lived, or that one made his mark?

In the ocean of time it is merest chance that saves the handful from oblivion.

It is my ever growing sense that of all the chances thrown to me, lifelines in the ocean of time, that my best chunk of flotsam is that I discovered Dan Simmons.

Oh, yes, that's the correct word. I *discovered* him.

There is a wonderful record album that Stan Freberg put together, titled *The United States of America* (Volume One: The Early Years). And one of the shticks on that album has Columbus meeting some Indians on the beach, and he tells them, "I've found you!" To which they reply, "We weren't lost. *We* knew we were here." So Columbus amends his declaration and says, "Well, at least I discovered you here on the beach," and they kind of agree that it's pretty dopey, but what the hell.

In much the same way I *discovered* Dan Simmons. All pink and cranky, there on the beach.

It is a story worth telling, for there is an important lesson to be learned from this bit of incidental literary history. And if I set it down, posterity may take note.

The catalyst was Ed Bryant, now a close friend of Dan's, but unknown to him at the time. Ed and I had been chums for a long stretch; I suppose that's why I allowed him to enlist me as one of the visiting authors to the Colorado Mountain College "Writers' Conference in the Rockies." It was the summer of 1981, it was hot and moist, and I dreaded having to workshop the stories of a group of aspiring authors who seemed more dilettante than the talented people I'd worked with at various Clarion conferences.

The physical set-up of the workshop sessions was hardly conducive to establishing rapport with the students: it was a stuffy classroom, with tablet-top chairs; the uncomfortable, hard-seat kind you suffered with in the third grade. Arranged in rows. There was a step-up platform where the "instructor" sat, facing the assemblage. From on high, one supposes, words of auctorial wisdom were intended to shower down on the groundlings.

Compared to the efficient and reassuring circle of sofas and comfy chairs at a Clarion Workshop, where everyone has a clear view of everyone else's face, where the group leader has no greater position of authority than each student ... this was a nightmare. And the group was too large to service everyone.

When I had arrived, the evening before, I'd been given a stack of manuscripts that needed to be workshopped, but no advisement was forthcoming as to the order in which the stories would be discussed. So I'd read at random, not much impressed by the quality of the material, hoping I'd hit the ones that would be up first. Naturally, I spent the night reading exactly the ones for later in the week.

So when I got to the foyer of the building next morning, with everyone mingling and doing bagels and doughnuts and coffee, I checked the list. Imagine my pleasure at discovering I hadn't even glanced at the first three or four scheduled for discussion.

Hurriedly, I grabbed copies of the unread stories from the stacks, found myself a far corner of the library, and began to catch up. The first three were undistinguished, but competent. The fourth was just plain awful. I didn't get to the fifth story ... the call for beginning the session was delivered by a staff liaison.

I entered the classroom, saw the rows filled, saw the empty chair on the low platform, waiting for me as if I were some stump revivalist minister come to preach The Word. My heart sank, and I knew this was going to be an extremely difficult morning.

Understand: I do not believe "anyone can write." That is to say, anyone can slap together words in some coherent sequence if s/he had done even a modicum of reading, and has at least a bare grasp of how to use language. Which is talent enough for writing letters, or doctoral theses, or amusing oneself with "creative endeavors." But to be a *writer*—not an "author" like such ongoing tragedies as Judith Krantz, Eric Segal, V.C. Andrews, Sidney Sheldon, and hordes of others I leave to you to name—one must hear the music. I cannot explicate it better than that. One need only hear the music. The syntax may be spavined, the spelling dyslectic, the subject matter dyspeptic. But you can tell there has been a writer at work. It fills the page, that music, however halting and rife with improper choices. And only amateurs or the counterproductively soft-hearted think it should be otherwise.

When I am hired to ramrod a workshop, I take it as my bond to be absolutely honest about the work. I may personally feel compassion for someone struggling toward the dream of being a writer, who doesn't hear the music, but if I were to take the easy way out, merely to avoid "hurting someone's feelings"—not the least of which are my own, because nobody likes to be thought of as an insensitive monster—I would be betraying my craft, as well as my employers. As well as the best interests of the students themselves. Lying to someone who, in my opinion (which can certainly be wrong, even as yours), doesn't have the stuff, is mendacious in the extreme. It is cowardly, not merely dishonest. Flannery O'Connor once said, "Every-where I go I'm asked if I think the university stifles writers. My opinion is that they don't stifle enough of them. There's many a bestseller that could have been prevented by a good teacher."

Similarly, I take it as my chore to discourage as many "aspiring authors" as I possibly can.

Because you *cannot* discourage a real writer. I've said it a hundred times in print. Break a real writer's hands, and s/he will tap out a story with feet or nose.

That was my attitude when I took my seat before the wary eyes of young and old men, young and old women, all of them assembled in hopes of having some guru tell them they had a chance. (I have virtually given up doing workshops. I cannot bear the pain I cause in the name of the holy task that is writing well. Let someone else do it.)

One of the writers whose manuscript was early on the list was elsewhere, in a poetry section, I believe. So we talked about the second story, and we went around the room asking for the opinions of the other workshoppers, before I spoke to the work at hand. The comments weren't particularly scintillant. The usual "I liked it a lot" or "I'd give it an 86, it has a good beat, and you can dance to it" but nothing very deep, and nothing very deep needed: it was an okay piece of writing, but no more than that.

Same for the third story. But then we came to the fourth; a truly amateurish hodge-podge of incomprehensible clichés presented without grace, virtually every word misspelled, and festooned with all of the worst bad habits indulged in by those who (in Stanley Ellin's words) "mistake a love of reading for a talent for writing." I knew this was going to be an unlovely interlude.

Comments around the room were sparse. Most of the people there had at least enough ability to recognize plain awful writing when they encountered it. So they lay back, and as I asked for more opinions, and didn't get them, a sense of genuine uneasiness filled the room. The tension that precedes the high wire aerialists attempting for the first time the death-defying simultaneous three-person triple somersault.

I asked for the gentleman who had written this story to

identify himself. If I was to do it, at least let me be brave enough to look the man in the eye.

An elderly man, tall and thin, looking weathered but very kind, raised his hand. I cannot remember his name.

And I told him. I told him that insofar as I was equipped, by years as an editor and critic and workshop attendee or instructor, by a lifetime of reading and struggling to overcome the flaws in my own writing, by everything I knew or believed or suspected about good writing, that he seemed—in my view—to possess no talent for writing. Not a small, but serviceable, talent. No talent at all. I was not insulting or disputatious, but I was sincerely firm in giving it to him straight.

As I spoke, the room grew tenebrous. Some of the attendees slumped far down in their chairs, as if trying to vanish from my sight. Others turned away, using one hand as blinder. On the faces of some of them I saw a look that must parallel that worn by soldiers in combat when they see, with guilt and human relief, that the bullet has struck the next man in the trench.

There was no way of stopping without explaining, page by page, the utter tone-deafness and ineptitude of what he had done.

Finally, I stopped. Then I asked him if this was his first story, or if he had ever submitted anything for publication.

He was a nice man, a very decent man, and he answered me without rancor. He said, "I've written sixty-four novels. I've never been published." My heart broke for him. But what was I to do? I said, "Perhaps you might better spend your time at a craft, or an art, for which you have a greater aptitude."

He shook his head. No one else but us in that room. Just that fine old man and I, joined at the hip forever. "I appreciate what you've said," he told me, with a strong voice. "I think you're being honest and saying what you believe. But it won't deter me. I want to write, and I'll keep at it. But I thank you." I think about that man whose name I cannot recall almost every week. Whenever I sit down to work, I think of him.

But it was clear we had to have a break right then.

We couldn't continue without a pause. It had to settle to its own level of acceptance in each of them. So I told them we would reassemble in fifteen minutes. The room emptied in an instant; and no one came out of the group to speak to me, or to ask a question. I feared I had been destructive, no matter how deeply I believed it was my obligation to be candid.

It was not in me to join the students in the corridor. I knew they hated the thought of returning, probably for more of the same; and wishing they had chosen one of the other visiting instructors' section. I couldn't blame them. It had been a horrorshow.

So I picked up the fifth story, now at the top of the stack. No matter how awful I felt, it was my job to get it read before the fifteen minute break was up. But the room, and my outlook, was dolorous. Pity the poor sonofabitch who had written that fifth manuscript. I began to read.

It bore a mundane title, but the opening sentences were strong and written well. *Thank goodness*, I remember thinking. At least we won't have another bloodbath.

And I read on.

It occurred to me, somewhere along about the middle of the story, that I was crying. And when I finished the story, I had been touched, had been manipulated as all excellent writing turns and bends us, had truly experienced that *frisson* we seek in everything we read.

I found my way into the corridor, needing air. The story had really gotten to me. And all down the hall, I saw others from the section, sitting on the floor, crying; holding onto the wall for support, crying; standing in small groups outside, many of them crying. Clearly, this was more than merely competent work. We had been reached by a real writer; a writer with a helluva gift.

When the section reassembled, I called out the title of the story, and said we would now open for discussion.

Very few hands were raised to offer comments. But the few who did speak, all praised the story. Then, as if the floodgates had been opened, others began speaking without taking turns, just tumbling over each other to say how deeply they had been affected by this wonderful, wonderful story.

Then it came my turn to offer a critique. And they looked up at me with some uneasiness. Would this awful man savage even this exemplary piece of work, was he merely acid-tongued and snide, did he *enjoy* hurting these delicate souls?

I said, "Who among you is Dan Simmons?"

A quiet man whom I hadn't even noticed, in the third or fourth row, raised his hand. He seemed to be in his early thirties, physically average, a plain man with nothing bizarre or even out of the ordinary about him. He looked at me squarely.

I only remember, in specific, some of the things I said to him. Dan remembers most of it accurately. But the *essence* of what I said was this:

"This is not just a good story, or a competent story, or an original story. It is a magnificent story. What you have created here is a wonder. It is what writers mean when they say 'this is what good writing is all about.'

"The writing is extraordinarily adept, a level of craft that comes to writers only after years of trial and error. The story is original, and it is filled with humanity. What you have created here is something that never existed in the world before you dreamed the dream."

The section was stunned. Fifteen minutes earlier they had seen a poor guy eviscerated, and now they were seeing some other guy raised as a symbol of everything they hungered to possess. (Had I planned the encounter as a demonstration of the two edges of a sword, I could not have put it together more perfectly. In real life, one does not encounter these neat, symbolic scenes of contrast. In real life it's messy, and rarely plotted for the epiphany. But here I had stumbled into just such a set-piece.)

Then I said, "Now, having said that to you, I will change your life forever.

"Mr. Simmons, you are a writer.

"You will always be a writer, even if you never set down another word. There may be another writer among this crowd, but I think it unlikely that anyone else here is as totally and correctly and impressively a writer as are you. But now that I've told you that, I must tell you this: you will never, not *ever* be allowed to turn away from that.

Now that you have the knowledge, you are doomed to spend the rest of your life working at this lonely and holy profession. Your relationships will suffer; your wife and family—if you have them—will inevitably hate you; any woman you come to love will despise that part of you for whom the writing is irreconcilable mistress; movies you will miss because you have a deadline; nights you will go without peace or sleep because the story doesn't work; financial woes forever, because writers don't usually make enough to pay the rent, allow the spouse to quit a second job, buy a kid a toy.

"And the most awful part about this, is that most of you think I dumped on *that* man . . ." and I pointed to the kindly old gentleman I'd savaged, ". . . but I've crowned with laurels *this* man. But the truth of it, is that I was trying to save *his* life, and I've just sentenced Simmons to a life of unending labor, probably very little recognition, and a curse that will not be lifted, even after death!

"You are a *writer*, Mr. Simmons. And you know how you can make book on that? You know you're a writer, when a *writer* says you're a writer.

"May I enter your story in the *Twilight Zone* magazine short story competition?" And everyone in the room fainted.

Dan can tell of all this better than I. His memory of that morning in the Rockies is near letter-perfect. But what he *cannot* tell you, is the look on his face as I spoke. It was amazement, and pleasure, and stunned silence, and fear. It was the moment in which the poor dirty stablehand learns he is the Lost Prince of Dimension Exotica.

He won the contest, of course. (On a technicality it was actually a tie with another yarn for first place, but each of the judges—including Peter Straub, Robert Bloch and Richard Matheson—went nuts for the piece.) Out of *thousands* of submissions, Dan Simmons took first place. The story was "The River Styx Runs Upstream" and it was only the first of many works that were to follow along the trail of awards.

Dan told me that he had been trying to sell fiction for

three years, with very little success. He had sold a story to
Galaxy, and the magazine had folded before it could see
print. He sold a story to *Galileo,* and the magazine folded
before it could see print. He had been batting his head
against the market for three years, while he earned a living
as an elementary school teacher, a specialist in gifted and
talented education.

He told me that he had come to this workshop as a last
chance. It was clear to Dan, and to Karen, that with a child
on the way, he had to make a commitment that could in-
sure their security. Karen's faith in Dan's talent never wavered, but she could see he was torn, and tormented. So
she urged him to go to the workshop. And Dan said to her,
"If I don't get some small reinforcement that I have talent,
I'll pack it in. This will be the watershed for me."

And he won the contest. And he sold a novella to
Omni. And he got an agent, and the agent sold SONG OF
KALI, and SONG OF KALI became the first first-novel
ever to win the World Fantasy Award for best novel. And
HYPERION came out, and HYPERION won the Hugo.
And I spoke to Dan one night late, he in Longmont, me in
L.A., and I said to him, "I once told you a true thing that
I said would change your life completely and forever. Did
you believe me, then?"

"Yes."

"Will you believe me now, when I tell you another true
thing that will alter your life again?".

"Yes."

Across the night that separated us I said as quietly as
I could, "Dan, you are going to become famous. Not just
wealthy; that's the easy part. You will become one of the
most important writers of our time. Strangers will know
your name, and recognize you on the street. People will
seek your advice, and businessmen will try to attach themselves to you. What I'm telling you is not just that you
will be a great writer, but more: you will become a famous
writer. You'd better know it now, because it'll all be coming faster than you can take note of it. And you'd damned
well better start arming yourself now, because they'll be
on you in a trice, kiddo, and you won't have time then to
figure out where survival lies."

I have been where Dan Simmons is now, and I have been where he will be soon enough. I may be there now, and I may be there again. But this I know: if I stand a chance of being remembered, it may well be that it will come to me because I "discovered" Dan Simmons. Now ain't *that* a pisser!

Introduction to
"The River Styx Runs Upstream"

It's a cliché that writing fiction is a bit like having children. As with most clichés, there's a base of truth there. Having the idea for a story or novel—that moment of pure inspiration and conception—is as close to ecstasy as writing offers. The actual writing, especially of a novel, runs about the length of a human gestation period and is a time of some discomfort, frequent queasiness, and the absolute assurance of difficult labor before the thing is born. Finally, the stories or books take on a definite life of their own once published and soon are out of the writer's control completely; they travel far, visiting countries that the writer may never see, learning to express themselves fluently in languages the author will never begin to master, gaining the ear of readers with levels of affluence and education far beyond those of their progenitor, and—perhaps the most galling of all—living on long after the author is dust and a forgotten footnote.

And the ungrateful whelps don't even write home.

"The River Styx Runs Upstream" was conceived on a beautiful August morning in 1979, in the summerhouse behind my wife's parents' home in Kenmore, New York. I remember typing the first paragraph, pausing, and thinking—*This will be my first story to be published.*

It was, but not before two and a half years and a myriad of misadventures had passed.

A week after I'd finished writing the first draft of "The River Styx ..." I drove from western New York to

Rockport, Maine, to pick up my wife Karen after her stay at the Maine Photographic Workshop. Along the way, I spent a day in Exeter, New Hampshire, meeting and talking to a respected writer whom I'd previously only corresponded with. His advice: submit to the "little magazines," spend years—perhaps decades—building a reputation in these limited-circulation, contributor-copy-in-lieu-of-pay markets before even *thinking* about trying a novel, and then spend more years producing these small books from little-known publishers, reaching only a thousand or so readers but trying to acquire some critical underpinning.

I picked up Karen in Rockport and we began the long drive back to our home in Colorado. I was silent much of the time, pondering the writer's advice. It was sage advice—only one would-be writer in hundreds, perhaps thousands, achieves publication. Of those who publish, a scant few manage to make a living at it . . . even a "living" below the poverty line. The statistical chances of becoming a "bestselling author" are approximately the same as being struck by lightning while simultaneously being attacked by a great white shark.

So between Rockport, Maine, and the front range of Colorado, I pondered, decided that the advice was undoubtedly sound, realized that the "little magazine route" was almost certainly the wise way to go, and began to understand that it was a sign of maturity to realize that the quest for being a widely read author, a "mass market" writer of quality tales, was a chimera . . . something to be given up.

And then, about the time I saw the Rocky Mountains rising from the plains ahead of us, I said, "Nahhh." Perversely, I decided to go for the widest audience possible.

Cut to the summer of 1981, two years later. Dispirited, discouraged, all but broken on the wheel of rejections, chastened by reality, I "gave up" writing for publication and did something I'd sworn I would never do: I went off to a writers' conference. *Paid* to go to a writers' conference. A "how-to", "this is the way to prepare your manuscript", "sit-in-the-circle and we'll critique it" kind of writers' conference. It was my swan song. I went to hear and see the writers present and to begin to view writing as a hobby rather than obsession.

Then I met Harlan Ellison.

I won't bore you with the details of that meeting. I won't describe the carnage that acted as prelude as the legendary *enfant terrible* beheaded, disemboweled, and generally dismembered the unfortunate would-be writers who had submitted stories for his critical approval.

Between story critiques, while Harlan Ellison rested and sipped Perrier, officials of the workshop rushed into the seminar room, carried out the scattered body parts, hosed down the walls, spread sawdust on the carpet, and generally made ready for the next sacrifice.

As it turned out, *I* was the next sacrifice.

"Who is this *Simmons?*" bellowed Ellison. "Stand up, wave your hand, *show* yourself, goddammit. What egomaniacal monstrosity has the fucking *gall*, the unmitigated *hubris* to inflict a story of *five thousand fucking words* on this workshop? *Show yourself, Simmons!*"

In one of the braver (read 'insane') moments of my life, I waggled my fingers. Stood.

Ellison stared at me over the top of his glasses. "At this length, it had better be *good*, Simmons . . . no, it had better be fucking *brilliant*, or you will not leave this room alive. *Comprende? Capish?*"

I left the room alive. In fact, I left it more alive than I had been in some years. It was not merely that Ellison had liked it. He . . . he and Ed Bryant and several of the other writers there . . . had found every flaw in the story, had revealed every false note and fake wall, had honed in on the places where I'd tapdanced fast rather than do the necessary work, had pulled the curtain off every crippled sentence and humbug phrase. *But they had taken the story seriously.*

Harlan Ellison did more than that. He told me what I had known for years but had lost the nerve to believe—he told me that I had no choice but to continue writing, whether anything was ever published or not. He told me that few heard the music but those who did had no choice but to follow the piper. He told me that if I didn't get back to the typewriter and keep working that he would fly to Colorado and rip my fucking nose off.

I went back to the typewriter. Ed Bryant was generous enough to allow me to become the first unpublished writer to attend the Milford Writers' Conference . . . where I learned to play pool with the big boys.

That autumn, I submitted the revised "The River Styx Runs Upstream" to *Twilight Zone Magazine* for their first annual contest for unpublished writers. According to the folks at *TZ*, more than nine thousand stories came in over the transom and had to be read and judged. "The River Styx . . ." tied for first place with a story by W.G. Norris.

Thus, my first published story reached the stands on February 15, 1982. It happened to be the same day that our daughter, Jane, was born.

It was some time before anyone, even I, really noticed that I'd been published. Analogies are fine and the similarities between being published and pregnancy are clever enough, but when it comes to being born—babies are the real thing.

And so, submitted for your approval (as a certain gentleman once said)—a story about love, and loss, and about the sad necessity sometimes to surrender what thou lov'st well . . .

The River Styx
Runs Upstream

What thou lovest well remains
    the rest is dross
What thou lov'st well shall not be reft
    from thee
What thou lov'st well is thy
    true heritage . . .

—*Ezra Pound*
Canto LXXXI

I loved my mother very much. After her funeral, after the coffin was lowered, the family went home and waited for her return.

I was only eight at the time. Of the required ceremony I remember little. I recall that the collar of the previous year's shirt was far too tight and that the unaccustomed tie was like a noose around my neck. I remember that the June day was too beautiful for such a solemn gathering. I remember Uncle Will's heavy drinking that morning and the bottle of Jack Daniels he pulled out as we drove home from the funeral. I remember my father's face.

The afternoon was too long. I had no role to play in

the family's gathering that day, and the adults ignored me. I found myself wandering from room to room with a warm glass of Kool-Aid, until finally I escaped to the backyard. Even that familiar landscape of play and seclusion was ruined by the glimpse of pale, fat faces staring out from the neighbor's windows. They were waiting. Hoping for a glimpse. I felt like shouting, throwing rocks at them. Instead I sat down on the old tractor tire we used as a sandbox. Very deliberately I poured the red Kool-Aid into the sand and watched the spreading stain digging a small pit.

They're digging her *up now.*

I ran to the swing set and angrily began to pump my legs against the bare soil. The swing creaked with rust, and one leg of the frame rose out of the ground.

No, they've already done that, stupid. Now they're hooking her up to big machines. Will they pump the blood back into her?

I thought of bottles hanging. I remembered the fat, red ticks that clung to our dog in the summer. Angry, I swung high, kicking up hard even when there was no more height to be gained.

Do her fingers twitch first? Or do her eyes just slide open like an owl waking up?

I reached the high point of my arc and jumped. For a second I was weightless and I hung above the earth like Superman, like a spirit flying from its body. Then gravity claimed me and I fell heavily on my hands and knees. I had scraped my palms and put grass stain on my right knee. Mother would be angry.

She's being walked around now. Maybe they're dressing her like one of the mannikins in Mr. Feldman's store window.

My brother Simon came out to the backyard. Although he was only two years older, Simon looked like an adult to me that afternoon. An old adult. His blond hair, as recently cut as mine, hung down in limp bangs across a pale forehead. His eyes looked tired. Simon almost never yelled at me. But he did that day.

"Get in here. It's almost time."

I followed him through the back porch. Most of the relatives had left, but from the living room we could hear

Uncle Will. He was shouting. We paused in the hallway to listen.

"For Chrissakes, Les, there's still time. You just can't do this."

"It's already done."

"Think of the . . . Jesus Christ . . . think of the kids."

We could hear the slur of the voices and knew that Uncle Will had been drinking more. Simon put his finger to his lips. There was a silence.

"Les, think about just the money side of it. What's . . . how much . . . it's twenty-five percent of everything you have. For how many years, Les? Think of the kids. What'll that do to—"

"It's *done*, Will."

We had never heard that tone from Father before. It was not argumentative—the way it was when he and Uncle Will used to argue politics late at night. It was not sad like the time he talked to Simon and me after he had brought Mother home from the hospital the first time. It was just final.

There was more talk. Uncle Will started shouting. Even the silences were angry. We went to the kitchen to get a Coke. When we came back down the hallway, Uncle Will almost ran over us in his rush to leave. The door slammed behind him. He never entered our home again.

They brought Mother home just after dark. Simon and I were looking out the picture window and we could feel the neighbors watching. Only Aunt Helen and a few of our closest relatives had stayed. I felt Father's surprise when he saw the car. I don't know what we'd been expecting— maybe a long black hearse like the one that had carried Mother to the cemetery that morning.

They drove up in a yellow Toyota. There were four men in the car with Mother. Instead of dark suits like the one Father was wearing, they had on pastel, short-sleeved shirts. One of the men got out of the car and offered his hand to Mother.

I wanted to rush to the door and down the sidewalk to her, but Simon grabbed my wrist and we stood back in the hallway while Father and the other grownups opened the door.

They came up the sidewalk in the glow of the gaslight on the lawn. Mother was between the two men, but they were not really helping her walk, just guiding her a little. She wore the light blue dress she had bought at Scott's just before she got sick. I had expected her to look all pale and waxy—like when I peeked through the crack in the bedroom door before the men from the funeral home came to take her body away—but her face was flushed and healthy, almost sunburned.

When they stepped onto the front stoop, I could see that she was wearing a lot of makeup. Mother never wore makeup. The two men also had pink cheeks. All three of them had the same smile.

When they came into the house, I think we all took a step back—except for Father. He put his hands on Mother's arms, looked at her a long time, and kissed her on the cheek. I don't think she kissed him back. Her smile did not change. Tears were running down Father's face. I felt embarrassed.

The Resurrectionists were saying something. Father and Aunt Helen nodded. Mother just stood there, still smiling slightly, and looked politely at the yellow-shirted man as he spoke and joked and patted Father on the back. Then it was our turn to hug Mother. Aunt Helen moved Simon forward, and I was still hanging onto Simon's hand. He kissed her on the cheek and quickly moved back to Father's side. I threw my arms around her neck and kissed her on the lips. I had *missed* her.

Her skin wasn't cold. It was just *different*.

She was looking right at me. Baxter, our German shepherd, began to whine and scratch at the back door.

Father took the Resurrectionists into the study. We heard snatches of conversation down the hall.

". . . if you think of it as a stroke . . ."

"How long will she . . ."

"You understand the tithing is necessary because of the expenses of monthly care and . . ."

The women relatives stood in a circle around Mother. There was an awkward moment until they realized that

Mother did not speak. Aunt Helen reached her hand out and touched her sister's cheek. Mother smiled and smiled.

Then Father was back and his voice was loud and hearty. He explained how similar it was to a light stroke— did we remember Uncle Richard? Meanwhile, Father kissed people repeatedly and thanked everyone.

The Resurrectionists left with smiles and signed papers. The remaining relatives began to leave soon after that. Father saw them down the walk, smiling and shaking their hands.

"Think of it as though she's been ill but has recovered," said Father. "Think of her as home from the hospital."

Aunt Helen was the last to leave. She sat next to Mother for a long time, speaking softly and searching Mother's face for a response. After a while Aunt Helen began to cry.

"Think of it as if she's recovered from an illness," said Father as he walked her to her car. "Think of her as home from the hospital."

Aunt Helen nodded, still crying, and left. I think she knew what Simon and I knew. Mother was not home from the hospital. She was home from the grave.

The night was long. Several times I thought I heard the soft slap of Mother's slippers on the hallway floor and my breathing stopped, waiting for the door to open. But it didn't. The moonlight lay across my legs and exposed a patch of wallpaper next to the dresser. The flower pattern looked like the face of a great, sad beast. Just before dawn, Simon leaned across from his bed and whispered, "Go to sleep, stupid." And so I did.

For the first week, Father slept with Mother in the same room where they had always slept. In the morning his face would sag and he would snap at us while we ate our cereal. Then he moved to his study and slept on the old divan in there.

•   •   •

The summer was very hot. No one would play with us, so Simon and I played together. Father had only morning classes at the University. Mother moved around the house and watered the plants a lot. Once Simon and I saw her watering a plant that had died and been removed while she was at the hospital in April. The water ran across the top of the cabinet and dripped on the floor. Mother did not notice.

When Mother did go outside, the forest preserve behind our house seemed to draw her in. Perhaps it was the darkness. Simon and I used to enjoy playing at the edge of it after twilight, catching fireflies in a jar or building blanket tents, but after Mother began walking there Simon spent the evenings inside or on the front lawn. I stayed back there because sometimes Mother wandered and I would take her by the arm and lead her back to the house.

Mother wore whatever Father told her to wear. Sometimes he was rushed to get to class and would say, "Wear the red dress," and Mother would spend a sweltering July day in heavy wool. She didn't sweat. Sometimes he would not tell her to come downstairs in the morning, and she would remain in the bedroom until he returned. On those days I tried to get Simon at least to go upstairs and look in on her with me; but he just stared at me and shook his head. Father was drinking more, like Uncle Will used to, and he would yell at us for nothing at all. I always cried when Father shouted; but Simon never cried anymore.

Mother never blinked. At first I didn't notice; but then I began to feel uncomfortable when I saw that she never blinked. But it didn't make me love her any less.

Neither Simon nor I could fall asleep at night. Mother used to tuck us in and tell us long stories about a magician named Yandy who took our dog, Baxter, on great adventures when we weren't playing with him. Father didn't make up stories, but he used to read to us from a big book he called Pound's *Cantos*. I didn't understand most of what he read, but the words felt good and I loved the sounds of words he said were Greek. Now nobody checked in on us after our baths. I tried telling stories to Simon for a few nights, but they were no good and Simon asked me to stop.

On the Fourth of July, Tommy Wiedermeyer, who had been in my class the year before, drowned in the swimming pool they had just put in.

That night we all sat out back and watched the fireworks above the fairgrounds half a mile away. You couldn't see the ground displays because of the forest preserve, but the skyrockets were bright and clear. First you would see the explosion of color and then, four or five seconds later it seemed, the sound would catch up. I turned to say something to Aunt Helen and saw Mother looking out from the second-story window. Her face was very white against the dark room, and the colors seemed to flow down over her like fluids.

It was not long after the Fourth that I found the dead squirrel. Simon and I had been playing Cavalry and Indians in the forest preserve. We took turns finding each other . . . shooting and dying repeatedly in the weeds until it was time to start over. Only this time I was having trouble finding him. Instead, I found the clearing.

It was a hidden place, surrounded by bushes as thick as our hedge. I was still on my hands and knees from crawling under the branches when I saw the squirrel. It was large and reddish and had been dead for some time. The head had been wrenched around almost backwards on the body. Blood had dried near one ear. Its left paw was clenched, but the other lay open on a twig as if it were resting there. Something had taken one eye, but the other stared blackly at the canopy of branches. Its mouth was open slightly, showing surprisingly large teeth gone yellow at the roots. As I watched, an ant came out of the mouth, crossed the dark muzzle, and walked out onto the staring eye.

This is what dead is, I thought.

The bushes vibrated to some unfelt breeze. I was scared to be there and I left, crawling straight ahead and bashing through thick branches that grabbed at my shirt.

In the autumn I went back to Longfellow School, but soon transferred to a private school. The Resurrectionist families were discriminated against in those days. The kids made fun of us or called us names and no one played with us. No one played with us at the new school either, but they didn't call us names.

Our bedroom had no wall switch but an old-fashioned hanging lightbulb with a cord. To turn on the light I had to cross half the dark room and feel around until I found the cord. Once when Simon was staying up late to do his homework, I went upstairs by myself. I was swinging my arm around in the darkness to find the string when my hand fell on Mother's face. Her teeth felt cool and slick. I pulled my hand back and stood there a minute in the dark before I found the cord and turned on the light.

"Hello, Mother," I said. I sat on the edge of the bed and looked up at her. She was staring at Simon's empty bed. I reached out and took her hand. "I miss you," I said. I said some other things, but the words got all mixed up and sounded stupid, so I just sat there, holding her hand, waiting for some returning pressure. My arm got tired, but I remained sitting there and holding her fingers in mine until Simon came up. He stopped in the doorway and stared at us. I looked down and dropped her hand. After a few minutes she went away.

Father put Baxter to sleep just before Thanksgiving. He was not an old dog, but he acted like one. He was always growling and barking, even at us, and he would never come inside anymore. After he ran away for the third time, the pound called us. Father just said, "Put him to sleep," and hung up the phone. They sent us a bill.

• • •

Father's classes had fewer and fewer students and finally he took a sabbatical to write his book on Ezra Pound. He was home all that year, but he didn't write much. Sometimes he would spend the morning down at the library, but he would be home by one o'clock and would watch TV. He would start drinking before dinner and stay in front of the television until really late. Simon and I would stay up with him sometimes; but we didn't like most of the shows.

Simon's dream started about then. He told me about it on the way to school one morning. He said the dream was always the same. When he fell asleep, he would dream that he was still awake, reading a comic book. Then he would start to set the comic on the nightstand, and it would fall on the floor. When he reached down to pick it up, Mother's arm would come out from under the bed and she would grasp his wrist with her white hand. He said her grip was very strong, and somehow · he knew that she wanted him under the bed with her. He would hang onto the blankets as hard as he could, but he knew that in a few seconds the bedclothes would slip and he would fall.

He said that last night's dream had finally been a little different. This time Mother had stuck her head out from under the bed. Simon said that it was like when a garage mechanic slides out from under a car. He said she was grinning at him, not smiling but grinning real wide. Simon said that her teeth had been filed down to points.

"Do you ever have dreams like that?" he asked. I knew he was sorry he'd told me.

"No," I said. I loved Mother.

That April the Farley twins from the next block accidentally locked themselves in an abandoned freezer and suffocated. Mrs. Hargill, our cleaning lady, found them, out behind their garage. Thomas Farley had been the only kid who still invited Simon over to his yard. Now Simon only had me.

It was just before Labor Day and the start of school that Simon made plans for us to run away. I didn't want to run away, but I loved Simon. He was my brother.

"Where are we gonna go?"

"We got to get out of here," he said. Which wasn't much of an answer.

But Simon had set aside a bunch of stuff and even picked up a city map. He'd sketched out our path through the forest preserve, across Sherman River at the Laurel Street viaduct, all the way to Uncle Will's house without ever crossing any major streets.

"We can camp out," said Simon. He showed me a length of clothesline he had cut. "Uncle Will will let us be farmhands. When he goes out to his ranch next spring, we can go with him."

We left at twilight. I didn't like leaving right before it got dark, but Simon said that Father wouldn't notice we were gone until late the next morning when he woke up. I carried a small backpack filled with food Simon had sneaked out of the refrigerator. He had some stuff rolled up in a blanket and tied over his back with the piece of clothesline. It was pretty light out until we got deeper into the forest preserve. The stream made a gurgling sound like the one that came from Mother's room the night she died. The roots and branches were so thick that Simon had to keep his flashlight on all the time, and that made it seem even darker. We stopped before too long, and Simon strung his rope between two trees. I threw the blanket over it and we both scrabbled around on our hands and knees to find stones.

We ate our bologna sandwiches in the dark while the creek made swallowing noises in the night. We talked a few minutes, but our voices seemed too tiny, and after a while we both fell asleep, on the cold ground with our jackets pulled over us and our heads on the nylon pack and all the forest sounds going on around us.

I woke up in the middle of the night. It was very still. Both of us had huddled down under the jackets, and Simon was snoring. The leaves had stopped stirring, the insects were gone, and even the stream had stopped making noise. The openings of the tent made two brighter triangles in the field of darkness.

I sat up with my heart pounding.

There was nothing to see when I moved my head near the opening. But I knew exactly what was out there. I put my head under my jacket and moved away from the side of the tent.

I waited for something to touch me through the blanket. At first I thought of Mother coming after us, of Mother walking through the forest after us with sharp twigs brushing at her eyes. But it wasn't Mother.

The night was cold and heavy around our little tent. It was as black as the eye of that dead squirrel, and it wanted in. For the first time in my life I understood that the darkness did not end with the morning light. My teeth were chattering. I curled up against Simon and stole a little of his heat. His breath came soft and slow against my cheek. After a while I shook him awake and told him we were going home when the sun rose, that I wasn't going with him. He started to argue, but then he heard something in my voice, something he didn't understand, and he only shook his head tiredly and went back to sleep.

In the morning the blanket was wet with dew and our skins felt clammy. We folded things up, left the rocks lying in their rough pattern, and walked home. We did not speak.

Father was sleeping when we got home. Simon threw our stuff in the bedroom and then he went out into the sunlight. I went to the basement.

It was very dark down there, but I sat on the wooden stairs without turning on a light. There was no sound from the shadowed corners, but I knew that Mother was there.

"We ran away, but we came back," I said at last. "It was my idea to come back."

Through the narrow window slats I saw green grass. A sprinkler started up with a loud sigh. Somewhere in the neighborhood, kids were shouting. I paid attention only to the shadows.

"Simon wanted to keep going," I said, "but I made us come back. It was *my* idea to come home."

I sat a few more minutes but couldn't think of anything else to say. Finally I got up, brushed off my pants, and went upstairs to take a nap.

A week after Labor Day, Father insisted we go to the shore for the weekend. We left on Friday afternoon and drove straight through to Ocean City. Mother sat alone in the rear seat. Father and Aunt Helen rode up front. Simon and I were crowded into the back of the station wagon, but he refused to count cows with me or talk to me or even play with the toy planes I'd brought along.

We stayed at an ancient hotel right on the boardwalk. The other Resurrectionists in Father's Tuesday group recommended the place, but it smelled of age and rot and rats in the walls. The corridors were a faded green, the doors a darker green, and only every third light worked. The halls were a dim maze, and you had to make two turns just to find the elevator. Everyone but Simon stayed inside all day Saturday, sitting in front of the laboring air conditioner and watching television. There were many more of the resurrected around now, and you could hear them shuffling through the dark halls. After sunset they went out to the beach, and we joined them.

I tried to make Mother comfortable. I set the beach towel down for her and turned her to face the sea. By this time the moon had risen and a cool breeze was blowing in. I put Mother's sweater across her shoulders. Behind us the midway splashed lights out over the boardwalk and the roller coaster rumbled and growled.

I would not have left if Father's voice hadn't irritated me so. He talked too loudly, laughed at nothing, and took deep drinks from a bottle in a brown bag. Aunt Helen said very little but watched Father sadly and tried to smile when he laughed. Mother was sitting peacefully, so I excused myself and walked up to the midway to hunt for Simon. I was lonely without him. The place was empty of families and children, but the rides were still running. Every few minutes there would be a roar and screams from the few riders as the roller coaster took its steepest plunge. I ate a hot dog and looked around, but Simon was nowhere to be found.

While walking back along the beach, I saw Father lean over and give Aunt Helen a quick kiss on the cheek. Mother had wandered away, and I quickly offered to go find her just to hide the tears of rage in my eyes. I walked up the beach past the place where the two teenagers had drowned the previous weekend. There were a few of the resurrected around. They were sitting near the water with their families; but no sight of Mother. I was thinking of heading back when I thought I noticed some movement under the boardwalk.

It was incredibly dark under there. Narrow strips of light, broken into weird sorts of patterns by the wooden posts and cross-braces, dropped down from cracks in the walkway overhead. Footsteps and rumbles from the midway sounded like fists pounding against a coffin lid. I stopped then. I had a sudden image of dozens of them being there in the darkness. Dozens, Mother among them, with thin patterns of light crossing them so that you could make out a hand or shirt or staring eye. But they were not there. Mother was not there. Something else was.

I don't know what made me look up. Footsteps from above. A slight turning, turning; something turning in the shadows. I could see where he had climbed the cross-braces, wedged a sneaker here, lifted himself there to the wide timber. It would not have been hard. We'd climbed like that a thousand times. I stared right into his face, but it was the clothesline I recognized first.

Father quit teaching after Simon's death. He never went back after the sabbatical, and his notes for the Pound book sat stacked in the basement with last year's newspapers. The Resurrectionists helped him find a job as a custodian in a nearby shopping mall, and he usually didn't get home before two in the morning.

After Christmas I went away to a boarding school that was two states away. The Resurrectionists had opened the Institute by this time, and more and more families were turning to them. I was later able to go to the University on a full scholarship. Despite the covenant, I rarely came home during those years. Father was drunk during my few visits. Once I drank with him and we sat in the kitchen and cried together. His hair was almost gone except for a few white strands on the sides, and his eyes were sunken in a lined face. The alcohol had left innumerable broken blood vessels in his cheeks, and he looked as though he was wearing more makeup than Mother.

Mrs. Hargill called three days before graduation. Father had filled the bath with warm water and then drawn the razor blade up the vein rather than across it. He had read his Plutarch. It had been two days before the housekeeper found him, and when I arrived home the next evening the bathtub was still caked with congealed rings. After the funeral I went through all of his old papers and found a journal he had been keeping for several years. I burned it along with the stacks of notes for his unfinished book.

Our policy with the Institute was honored despite the circumstances, and that helped me through the next few years. My career is more than a job to me—I believe in what I do and I'm good at it. It was my idea to lease some of the empty school buildings for our new neighborhood centers.

Last week I was caught in a traffic jam, and when I inched the car up to the accident site and saw the small figure covered by a blanket and the broken glass everywhere, I also noticed that a crowd of *them* had gathered on the curb. There are so many of them these days.

I used to have shares in a condominium in one of the last lighted sections of the city, but when our old house came up for sale I jumped at the chance to buy it. I've kept many of the old furnishings and replaced others so that it's almost the way it used to be. Keeping up an old house like that is expensive, but I don't spend my money foolishly. After work a lot of guys from the Institute go out to bars, but I don't. After I've put away my equipment and scrubbed down the steel tables, I go straight home. My family is there. They're waiting for me.

Introduction to
"Eyes I Dare Not Meet in Dreams"

The summer of 1969 was very hot. It was especially hot where I spend it—living in the "ghetto" section of Germantown, Pennsylvania. Germantown, a pleasant little village in pre-Revolutionary War days, was an inner-city enclave of Philadelphia by 1969. The streets were hot. Tempers—racial and otherwise—were even hotter.

I rented the attic of a neighborhood Settlement House/ birth control clinic/community medical center for $35 a month. It was a small attic. On evenings when the tiny second-floor wasn't busy serving as a waiting room, I could put it to use as a living room and use the tiny kitchen off of it. Most evenings it was busy. From my attic dormer windows, I watched several gang battles and one full-fledged riot that summer.

But it is the evenings seen from the front stoop I most remember: a brick canyon rich with human noise, the long sweep of Bringhurst Street's rowhouses illuminated in the sodium-yellow glow of "crime lights" while children jumped Double Dutch and played the dozens in the street, the endless parade of people strolling and laughing and chatting and making room on the step for visitors. To this day, confronted with the privacy-fenced sterility of suburban back-yard patios, I wonder what lunacy made us turn away from the front porch and the front step, the communal ownership of the street, to flee to these claustrophobic plots of isolation.

During the day in that long-ago summer of 1969, I

worked as a teacher's aide in the Upsal Day School for the Blind. The children often were not merely blind—some were also deaf and severely mentally retarded. Many of them had been this way since birth.

The wonderful thing about working in such an environment is that one learns quickly that human beings—even human beings with such terrible and relentless disadvantages—maintain not only the essence of humanity and the full panoply of human desires and strengths, but also somehow retain the capacity to struggle, to achieve . . . to *triumph*.

On the day after human beings first set foot on the moon in that hot summer of 1969, I celebrated the event with my class. They were very excited. Thomas, one of the young adolescents who had been blind and retarded since birth but who could hear, had taught himself to play the piano. Another hearing student—a young lady who had been brain-damaged as a result of extreme abuse as an infant—suggested that we end the celebration of the lunar landing by having Thomas play our national anthem.

He did.

He played "We Shall Overcome."

Eyes I Dare
Not Meet in Dreams

Bremen left the hospital and his dying wife and drove east to the sea. The roads were thick with Philadelphians fleeing the city for the weekend, and Bremen had to concentrate on traffic, leaving only the most tenuous of touches in his wife's mind. Gail was sleeping. Her dreams were fitful and drug-induced. She was seeking her mother through endlessly interlinked rooms filled with Victorian furniture.

As Bremen crossed the pine barrens, the images of the dreams slid between the evening shadows of reality. Gail awoke just as Bremen was leaving the parkway. For a few seconds after she awoke the pain was not with her. She opened her eyes, and the evening sunlight falling across the blue blanket made her think—for only a moment—that it was morning on the farm. Her thoughts reached out for her husband just as the pain and dizziness struck behind her left eye. Bremen grimaced and dropped the coin he was handing to the toll-booth attendant.

"What's the matter, buddy?"

Bremen shook his head, fumbled out a dollar, and thrust it blindly at the man. Throwing his change in the Triumph's cluttered console, he concentrated on pushing the car's speed to its limit. Gail's pain faded, but her confusion washed over him in a wave of nausea.

She quickly gained control despite the shifting curtains of fear that fluttered at the tightly held mindshield. She subvocalized, concentrating on narrowing the spectrum to a simulacrum of her voice.

"Hi, Jerry."

"Hi, yourself, kiddo." He sent the thought as he turned onto the exit for Long Beach Island. He shared the visual—the starting green of grass and pine trees overlaid with the gold of August light, the sports car's shadow leaping along the curve of asphalt. Suddenly the unmistakable salt freshness of the Atlantic came to him, and he shared that with her also.

The entrance to the seaside community was disappointing: dilapidated seafood restaurants, overpriced cinderblock motels, endless marinas. But it was reassuring in its familiarity to both of them, and Bremen concentrated on seeing all of it. Gail began to relax and appreciate the ride. Her presence was so real that Bremen caught himself turning to speak aloud to her. The pang of regret and embarrassment was sent before he could stifle it.

The island was cluttered with families unpacking station wagons and carrying late dinners to the beach. Bremen drove north to Barnegat Light. He glanced to his right and caught a glimpse of some fishermen standing along the surf, their shadows intersecting the white lines of breakers.

Monet, thought Gail, and Bremen nodded, although he had actually been thinking of Euclid.

Always the mathematician, thought Gail, and then her voice faded as the pain rose. Half-formed sentences shredded like clouds in a gale.

Bremen left the Triumph parked near the lighthouse and walked through the low dunes to the beach. He threw down the tattered blanket that they had carried so many times to just this spot. There was a group of children running along the surf. A girl of about nine, all long white legs in a suit two years too small, pranced on the wet sand in an intricate, unconscious choreography with the sea.

The light was fading between the Venetian blinds. A

nurse smelling of cigarettes and stale talcum powder came in to change the IV bottle and take a pulse. The intercom in the hall continued to make loud, imperative announcements, but it was difficult to understand them through the growing haze of pain. The new doctor arrived about ten o'clock, but Gail's attention was riveted on the nurse who carried the blessed needle. The cotton swab on her arm was a delightful preliminary to the promised surcease of pain behind her eye. The doctor was saying something.

". . . your husband? I thought he would be staying the night."

"Right here, doctor," said Gail. She patted the blanket and the sand.

Bremen pulled on his nylon windbreaker against the chill of the night. The stars were occluded by a high cloud layer that allowed only a few to show through. Far out to sea, an improbably long oil tanker, its lights blazing, moved along the horizon. The windows of the beach homes behind Bremen cast yellow rectangles on the dunes.

The smell of steak being grilled came to him on the breeze. Bremen tried to remember whether he had eaten that day or not. He considered going back to the convenience store near the lighthouse to get a sandwich but remembered an old Payday candy bar in his jacket pocket and contented himself with chewing on the rock-hard wedge of peanuts.

Footsteps continued to echo in the hall. It sounded as if entire armies were on the march. The rush of footsteps, clatter of trays, and vague chatter of voices reminded Gail of lying in bed as a child and listening to her parents' parties downstairs.

Remember the party where we met? thought Bremen.

Chuck Gilpen had insisted that Bremen go along. Bremen had never had much use for parties. He was lousy at small talk, and the psychic tension and neurobabble always left him with a headache from maintaining his mindshield tightly for hours. Besides, it was his first week teaching graduate tensor calculus and he knew that he should be home boning up on basic principles. But he had gone. Gilpen's nagging and the fear of being labeled a social misfit in his new academic community had brought

Bremen to the Drexel Hill townhouse. The music was palpable half a block away, and had he driven there by himself, he would have gone home then. He was just inside the door—someone had pressed a drink in his hand—when suddenly he sensed another mindshield quite near him. He had put out a gentle probe, and immediately the force of Gail's thoughts swept across him like a searchlight.

Both were stunned. Their first reaction had been to raise their mindshields and roll up like frightened armadillos. Each soon found that useless against the unconscious probes of the other. Neither had ever encountered another telepath of more than primitive, untapped ability. Each had assumed that he or she was a freak—unique and unassailable. Now they stood naked before each other in an empty place. Suddenly, almost without volition, they flooded each other's mind with a torrent of images, self-images, half-memories, secrets, sensations, preferences, perceptions, hidden fears, echoes, and feelings. Nothing was held back. Every petty cruelty committed, sexual shame experienced, and prejudice harbored poured out along with thoughts of past birthday parties, ex-lovers, parents, and an endless stream of trivia. Rarely had two people known each other as well after fifty years of marriage. A few minutes later they met for the first time.

The beacon from Barnegat Light passed over Bremen's head every twenty-four seconds. There were more lights burning out at sea now along the dark line of beach. The wind came up after midnight, and Bremen wrapped the blanket around himself tightly. Gail had refused the needle when the nurse had last made her rounds, but her mindtouch was still clouded. Bremen forced the contact through sheer strength of will. Gail had always been afraid of the dark. Many had been the times during their six years of marriage that he reached out in the night with his mind or arm to reassure her. Now she was the frightened little girl again, left alone upstairs in the big old house on Burlingame Avenue. There were things in the darkness beneath her bed.

Bremen reached through her confusion and pain and shared the sound of the sea with her. He told her stories about the antics of Gernisavien, their calico cat. He lay in the hollow of the sand to match his body with hers. Slowly she began to relax, to surrender her thoughts to his. She even managed to doze a few times, and her dreams were the movement of stars between clouds and the sharp smell of the Atlantic. Bremen described the week's work at the farm—the subtle beauty of his Fourier equations across the chalkboard in his study and the sunlit satisfaction of planting a peach tree by the front drive. He shared memories of their ski trip to Aspen and the sudden shock of a searchlight reaching in to the beach from an unseen ship out at sea. He shared what little poetry he had memorized, but the words kept sliding into images and feelings.

The night drew on, and Bremen shared the cold clarity of it with his wife, adding to each image the warm overlay of his love. He shared trivia and hopes for the future. From seventy-five miles away he reached out and touched her hand with his. When he drifted off to sleep for only a few minutes, he sent her his dreams.

Gail died just before the false light of dawn touched the sky.

The head of the mathematics department at Haverford urged Bremen to take a leave or a full sabbatical if he needed it. Bremen thanked him and resigned.

Dorothy Parks in the psychology department spent a long evening explaining the mechanics of grief to Bremen. "You have to understand, Jeremy," she said, "that moving is a common mistake made by people who have just suffered a serious loss. You may think that a new environment will help you forget, but it just postpones the inevitable confrontation with grief."

Bremen listed attentively and eventually nodded his agreement. The next day he put the farm up for sale, sold the Triumph to his mechanic on Conestoga Road, and took the bus to the airport. Once there, he went to the United Airlines counter and bought a ticket for the next departing flight.

For a year Bremen worked in central Florida, loading produce at a shipping center near Tampa. The next year Bremen did not work at all. He fished his way north from the Everglades to the Chattooga River in northern Georgia. In March he was arrested as a vagrant in Charleston, South Carolina. In May he spent two weeks in Washington, during which he left his room only to go to liquor stores and the Congressional Library. He was robbed and badly beaten outside of the Baltimore bus station at 2 A.M. on a June night. Leaving the hospital the next day, he returned to the bus station and headed north to visit his sister in New York. His sister and her husband insisted that he stay several weeks, but he left early on the third morning, propping a note up against the salt shaker on the kitchen table. In Philadelphia he sat in Penn Station and read the help-wanted ads. His progress was as predictable as the elegant, ellipsoid mathematics of a yo-yo's path.

Robby was sixteen, weighed one hundred seventy-five pounds, and had been blind, deaf, and retarded since birth. His mother's drug addiction during pregnancy and a placental malfunction had shut off Robby's senses as surely as a sinking ship condemns compartment after compartment to the sea by the shutting of watertight doors.

Robby's eyes were the sunken, darkened caverns of the irrevocably blind. The pupils, barely visible under drooping, mismatched lids, tracked separately in random movements. The boy's lips were loose and blubbery, his teeth gapped and carious. At sixteen, he already had the dark down of a mustache on his upper lip. His black hair stood out in violent tufts, and his eyebrows met above the bridge of his broad nose.

The child's obese body was balanced precariously on grub-white, emaciated legs. Robby had learned how to walk at age eleven but still would stagger only a few paces before toppling over. He moved in a series of pigeon-toed lurches, pudgy arms pulled as tight as broken wings, wrists cocked at an improbable angle, fingers separate and extended. Like so many of the retarded blind, his favorite motion was a perpetual rocking with his hand fanning above his sunken eyes as if to cast shadows into the pit of darkness.

He did not speak. His only sounds were occasional,

meaningless giggles and a rare squeal of protest, which sounded like nothing so much as an operatic falsetto.

Robby had been coming to the Chelton Day School for the Blind for six years. His life before that was unknown. He had been discovered by a social worker visiting Robby's mother in connection with a court-ordered methadone-treatment program. The door to the apartment had been left open, and the social worker heard noises. The boy had been sealed into the bathroom by the nailing of a piece of plywood over the bottom half of the door. There were wet papers on the tile floor, but Robby was naked and smeared with his own excrement. A tap had been left on, and water filled the room to the depth of an inch or two. The boy was rolling fitfully in the mess and making mewling noises.

Robby was hospitalized for four months, spent five weeks in the county home, and was then returned to the custody of his mother. In accordance with further court orders, he was dutifully bussed to Chelton Day School for five hours of treatment a day, six days a week. He made the daily trip in darkness and silence.

Robby's future was as flat and featureless as a line extending nowhere, holding no hope of intersection.

"Shit, Jer, you're going to have to watch after the kid tomorrow."

"Why me?"

"Because he won't go into the goddamn pool, that's why. You saw him today. Smitty just lowered his legs into the water, and the kid started swinging and screaming. Sounded like a bunch of cats had started up. Dr. Whilden says he stays back tomorrow. She says that the van is too hot for him to stay in. Just keep him company in the room till Jan McLellan's regular aide gets back from vacation."

"Great," said Bremen. He pulled his sweat-plastered shirt away from his skin. He had been hired to drive the school van, and now he was helping to feed, dress, and babysit the poor bastards. "Great. That's just great, Bill. What am I supposed to do with him for an hour and a half while you guys are at the pool?"

"Watch him. Try to get him to work on the zipper book. You ever see that page in there with the bra stuff—the eyes and hooks? Let him work on that. I useta practice on that with my eyes shut."

"Great," said Bremen. He closed his eyes against the glare of the sun.

Bremen sat on the front stoop and poured the last of the scotch into his glass. It was long past midnight, but the narrow street teemed with children playing. Two black teenagers were playing the dozens while their friends urged them on. A group of little girls jumped double dutch under the streetlamp. Insects milled in the light and seemed to dance to the girls' singing. Adults sat on the steps of identical rowhouses and watched one another dully. No one moved much. It was very hot.

It's time to move on.

Bremen knew that he had stayed too long. Seven weeks working at the day school had been too much. He was getting curious. And he was beginning to ask questions about the kids.

Boston, perhaps. Farther north. Maine.

Asking questions and getting answers Jan McLellan had told him about Robby. She had told him about the bruises on Robby's body, about the broken arm two years before. She told him about the teddy bear that a candy striper had given the blind boy. It had been the first positive stimulus to evoke an emotion from Robby. He had kept the bear in his arms for weeks. Refused to go to X-ray without it. Then, a few days after his return home, Robby got into the van one morning, screaming and whining in his weird way. No teddy bear. Dr. Whilden called his mother only to be told that the God-damned toy was lost. "God-damned toy" were the mother's words, according to Jan McLellan. No other teddy bear would do. Robby carried on for three weeks.

So what? What can I do?

Bremen knew what he could do. He had known for weeks. He shook his head and took another drink, adding to the already-thickened mindshield that separated him from the senseless, pain-giving world.

Hell, it'd be better for Robby if I didn't try it.

A breeze came up. Bremen could hear the screams from a lot down the street where two allied gangs played a fierce game of pick-up ball. Curtains billowed out open windows. Somewhere a siren sounded, faded. The breeze lifted papers from the gutter and ruffled the dresses of the girls jumping rope.

Bremen tried to imagine a lifetime with no sight, no sound.

Fuck it! He picked up the empty bottle and went upstairs.

The van pulled up the circular drive of the day school, and Bremen helped unload the children with a slow care born of practice, affection, and a throbbing headache.

Scotty emerged, smiling, hands extended to the unseen adult he trusted to be waiting. Tommy Pierson lurched out with knees together and hands pulled up to his chest. Bremen had to catch him or the frail boy would have fallen face first into the pavement. Teresa jumped down with her usual gleeful cries, imparting inexact but slobberingly enthusiastic kisses on everyone who touched her.

Robby remained seated after the others had exited. It took both Bremen and Smitty to get the boy out of the van. Robby did not resist; he was simply a mass of pliable but unresponsive fat. The boy's head tilted back in a disturbing way. His tongue lolled first from one corner of the slack mouth and then from the other. The short, pigeon-toed steps had to be coaxed out of him one at a time. Only the familiarity of the short walk to the classroom kept Robby moving at all.

The morning seemed to last forever. It rained before lunch, and for a while it looked as if the swimming would be canceled. Then the sun came out and illuminated the flowerbeds on the front lawn. Bremen watched sunlight dance off the moistened petals of Turk's prize roses and listened to the roar of the lawnmower. He realized that it was going to happen.

After lunch he helped them prepare for departure. The boys needed help getting into their suits, and it saddened Bremen to see pubic hair and a man's penis on the body of someone with a seven-year-old's mind. Tommy would always start masturbating idly until Bremen touched his arm and helped him with the elastic of the suit.

Then they were gone, and the hall, which had been filled with squealing children and laughing adults, was silent. Bremen watched the blue-and-white van disappear slowly down the drive. Then he turned back to the classroom.

Robby showed no awareness that Bremen had entered the room. The boy looked absurd dressed in a striped, green top and orange shorts that were too tight to button. Bremen thought of a broken, bronze Buddha he had seen once near Osaka. What if this child harbored some deep wisdom born of his long seclusion from the world?

Robby stirred, farted loudly, and resumed his slumped position.

Bremen sighed and pulled up a chair. It was too small. His knees stuck into the air, and he felt ridiculous. He grinned to himself. He would leave that night. Take a bus north. Hitchhike. It would be cooler in the country.

This would not take long. He need not even establish full contact. A one-way mindtouch. It was possible. A few minutes. He could look out the window for Robby, look at a picture book, perhaps put a record on and share the music. What would the boy make of these new impressions? A gift before leaving. Anonymous. Share nothing else. Better not to send any images of Robby, either. All right.

Bremen lowered his mindshield. Immediately he flinched and raised it again. It had been a long time since he had allowed himself to be so vulnerable. The thick, woolly blanket of the mindshield, thickened even further by alcohol, had become natural to him. The sudden surge of background babble—he thought of it as white noise—was abrasive. It was like coming into a glaringly bright room after spending months in a cave. He directed his at-

tention to Robby and lowered his barriers again. He tuned
out the neurobabble and looked deeply into Robby's mind.

Nothing.

For a confused second Bremen thought that he had lost
the focus of his power. Then he concentrated and was able
to pick out the dull, sexual broodings of Turk out in the
garden and the preoccupied fragments of Dr. Whilden's
thoughts as she settled herself into her Mercedes and
checked her stockings for runs. The receptionist was reading a novel—*The Plague Dogs*. Bremen read a few lines
with her. It frustrated him that her eyes scanned so slowly.
His mouth filled with the syrupy taste of her cherry
coughdrop.

Bremen stared intensely at Robby. The boy was
breathing asthmatically. His tongue was visible and heavily coated. Stray bits of food remained on his lips and
cheeks. Bremen narrowed his probe, strengthened it, focused it like a beam of coherent light.

Nothing.

No. Wait. There was—what?—an *absence* of something. There was a hole in the field of mindbabble where
Robby's thoughts should have been. Bremen realized that
he was confronting the strongest mindshield he had ever
encountered. Even Gail had not been able to concentrate a
barrier of that incredible tightness. For a second Bremen
was deeply impressed, even shaken, and then he realized
the cause of it. Robby's mind was damaged. Entire segments were probably inactive. With so few senses to rely
on and such limited awareness, it was little wonder that
the boy's consciousness—what there was of it—had turned
inward. What at first seemed to Bremen to be a powerful
mindshield was nothing more than a tight ball of intro-
spection going beyond autism. Robby was truly alone.

Bremen was still shaken enough to pause a minute and
take a few deep breaths. When he resumed, it was with
even more care, feeling along the negative boundaries of
the mindshield like a man groping along a rough wall in
the dark. Somewhere there had to be an opening.

There was. Not an opening so much as a soft spot—a
resilience set amidst the stone. Bremen half-perceived the
flutter of underlying thoughts, much as a pedestrian senses

the movement of trains in a subway under the pavement. He concentrated on building the strength of the probe until he felt his shirt beginning to soak with sweat. His vision and hearing were beginning to dim in the singleminded exertion of his effort. No matter. Once initial contact was made, he would relax and slowly open the channels of sight and sound.

He felt the shield give a bit, still elastic but sinking slightly under his unrelenting pressure. He concentrated until the veins stood out in his temples. Unknown to himself, he was grimacing, neck muscles knotting with the strain. The shield bent. Bremen's probe was a solid ram battering a tight, gelatinous doorway. It bent further. He concentrated with enough force to move objects, to pulverize bricks, to halt birds in their flight.

The shield continued to bend. Bremen leaned forward as into a strong wind. There was only the concentrated force of his will. Suddenly there was a ripping, a rush of warmth, a falling forward. Bremen lost his balance, flailed his arms, opened his mouth to yell.

His mouth was gone.

He was falling. Tumbling. He had a distant, confused glimpse of his own body writhing in the grip of an epileptic seizure. Then he was falling again. Falling into silence. Falling into nothing.

Nothing.

Bremen was inside. Beyond. Was diving through layers of slow thermals. Colorless pinwheels tumbled in three dimensions. Spheres of black collapsed outward. Blinded him. There were waterfalls of touch, rivulets of scent, a thin line of balance blowing in a silent wind.

Supported by a thousand hands—touching, exploring, fingers in the mouth, palms along the chest, sliding along the belly, cupping the penis, moving on.

He was buried. He was underwater. Rising in the blackness. But he could not breathe. His arms began to move. Palms flailed against the viscous current. Up. He was buried in sand. He flailed and kicked. He moved upwards, pulled on by a vacuum that gripped his head in a vise. The substance shifted. Compacted, pressed in by a thousand unseen hands, he was propelled through the constricting aperture. His head broke the surface. He opened his mouth to scream, and the air rushed into his chest like water filling a drowning man. The scream went on and on.

ME!

Bremen awoke on a broad plain. There was no sky. Pale, peach-colored light diffused everything. The ground was hard and scaled into separate orange segments which receded to infinity. There was no horizon. The land was cracked and serrated like a floodplain during a drought. Above him were levels of peachlit crystal. Bremen felt that it was like being in the basement of a clear plastic skyscraper. An empty one. He lay on his back and looked up through endless stories of crystallized emptiness.

He sat up. His skin felt as if it had been toweled with sandpaper. He was naked. He rubbed his hand across his stomach, touched his pubic hair, found the scar on his knee from the motorcycle accident when he was seventeen. A wave of dizziness rolled through him when he stood upright.

He walked. His bare feet found the smooth plates warm. He had no direction and no destination. Once he had walked a mile on the Bonneville Salt Flats just before sunset. It was like that. Bremen walked. *Step on a crack, break your mother's back.*

When he finally stopped, it was in a place no different from any other. His head hurt. He lay back and imagined himself as a bottom-dwelling sea creature looking up through layers of shifting currents. The peach-colored light bathed him in warmth. His body was radiant. He shut his eyes against the light and slept.

He sat up suddenly, with nostrils flaring, ears actually twitching with the strain of trying to pinpoint a half-heard sound. Darkness was total.

Something was moving in the night.

Bremen crouched in the blackness and tried to filter out the sound of his own ragged breathing. His glandular system reverted to programming a million years old. His fists clenched, his eyes rolled uselessly in their sockets, and his heart raced.

Something was moving in the night.

He felt it nearby. He felt the power of it. It was huge, and it had no trouble finding its way in the darkness. The thing was near him, above him. Bremen felt the force of its blind gaze. He kneeled on the cold ground and hugged himself into a ball.

Something touched him.

Bremen fought down the impulse to scream. He was caught in a giant's hand—something rough and huge and not a hand at all. It lifted him. Bremen felt the power of it through the pressure, the pain in his ribs. The thing could crush him easily. Again he felt the sense of being viewed, inspected, weighed on some unseen balance. He had the naked, helpless, but somehow reassuring feeling one has while lying on the X-ray table, knowing that invisible beams are passing through you, searching for any malignancy, probing.

Something set him down.

Bremen heard no sound but sensed great footsteps receding. A weight lifted from him. He sobbed. Eventually he uncurled and stood up. He called into the blackness, but the sound of his voice was tiny and lost and he was not even sure whether he had heard it at all.

The sun rose. Bremen's eyes fluttered open, stared into the distant brilliance, and then closed again before the fact registered fully in his mind. *The sun rose.*

He was sitting on grass. A prairie of soft, knee-high grass went off to the horizon in all directions. Bremen pulled a strand, stripped it, and sucked on the sweet marrow. It reminded him of childhood afternoons. He began walking.

The breeze was warm. It stirred the grass and set up a soft sighing, which helped to ease the headache that still throbbed behind his eyes. The walking pleased him. He contented himself with the feel of grass bending under his bare feet and the play of sunlight and wind on his body.

By early afternoon he realized that he was walking toward a smudge on the horizon. By late afternoon the smudge had resolved itself into a line of trees. Shortly be-

fore sunset he entered the edge of the forest. The trees
were the stately elms and oaks of his Pennsylvania boy-
hood. Bremen's long shadow moved ahead of him as he
moved deeper into the forest.

For the first time he felt fatigue and thirst begin to
work on him. His tongue was heavy, swollen with dryness.
He moved leadenly through the lengthening shadows, occasionally checking the visible patches of sky for any sign
of clouds. It was while he was looking up that he almost
stumbled into the pond. Inside a protective ring of weeds
and reeds lay the circle of water. A heavily laden cherry
tree sent roots down the bank. Bremen took the last few
steps forward, expecting the water to disappear as he
threw himself into it.

It was waist-deep and cold as ice.

It was just after sunrise that she came. He spotted the
movement immediately upon awakening. Not believing, he
stood still, just another shadow in the shade of the trees.
She moved hesitantly with the tentative step of the meek
or the barefoot. The tasseled sawgrass brushed at her
thighs. Bremen watched with a clarity amplified by the
rich, horizontal sweeps of morning light. Her body seemed
to glow. Her breasts, the left ever so slightly fuller than the
right, bobbed gently with each high step. Her black hair
was cut short.

She paused in the light. Moved forward again. Bremen's eyes dropped to her strong thighs, and he watched
as her legs parted and closed with the heart-stopping intimacy of the unobserved. She was much closer now, and
Bremen could make out the delicate shadows along her
fine ribcage, the pale, pink circles of areolae, and the
spreading bruise along the inside of one arm.

Bremen stepped out into the light. She stopped, arms
rising across her upper body in a second's instinctive
movement, then moved toward him quickly. She opened
her arms to him. He was filled with the clean scent of her
hair. Skin slid across skin. Their hands moved across muscle, skin, the familiar terrain of vertebrae. Both were sobbing, speaking incoherently. Bremen dropped to one knee

and buried his face between her breasts. She bent slightly
and cradled his head with her fingers. Not for a second did
they relax the pressure binding them together.

"Why did you leave me?" he muttered against her
skin. "Why did you go away?"

Gail said nothing. Her tears fell into his hair and her
hands tightened against his back. Wordlessly she kneeled
with him in the high grass.

Together they passed out of the forest just as the morning mists were burning away. In the early light the grass-
covered hills gave the impression of being part of a
tanned, velvety human torso, which they could reach out
and touch.

They spoke softly, occasionally intertwining fingers.
Each had discovered that to attempt telepathic contact
meant inviting the blinding headaches that had plagued
both of them at first. So they talked. And they touched.
And twice before the day was over, they made love in the
high, soft grass with only the golden eye of the sun looking down on them.

Late in the afternoon they crossed a rise and looked
past a small orchard at a vertical glare of white.

"It's the farm!" cried Gail, with wonder in her voice.
"How can that be?"

Bremen felt no surprise. His equilibrium remained as
they approached the tall old building. The saggy barn they
had used as a garage was also there. The driveway still
needed new gravel, but now it went nowhere, for there
was no highway at the end of it. A hundred yards of rusted
wire fence that used to border the road now terminated in
the high grass.

Gail stepped up on the front porch and peered in the
window. Bremen felt like a trespasser or a weekend house
browser who had found a home that might or might not
still be lived in. Habit brought them around to the back
door. Gail gingerly opened the outer screen door and
jumped a bit as the hinge squeaked.

"Sorry," Bremen said. "I know I promised to oil that."

It was cool inside and dark. The rooms were as they

had left them. Bremen poked his head into his study long enough to see his papers still lying on the oak desk and a long-forgotten transform still chalked on the blackboard. Upstairs, afternoon sunlight was falling from the skylight he had wrestled to install that distant September. Gail went from room to room, making small noises of appreciation, more often just touching things gently. The bedroom was as orderly as ever, with the blue blanket pulled tight and tucked under the mattress and her grandmother's patchwork quilt folded across the foot of the bed.

They fell asleep on the cool sheets. Occasionally a wisp of breeze would billow the curtains. Gail mumbled in her sleep, reaching out to touch him frequently. When Bremen awoke, it was almost dark, that late, lingering twilight of early summer.

There was a sound downstairs.

He lay without moving for a long while. The air was thick and still, the silence tangible. Then came another sound.

Bremen left the bed without waking Gail. She was curled on her side with one hand lifted to her cheek, the pillow moist against her lips. Bremen walked barefoot down the wooden stairs. He slipped into his study and carefully opened the lower-right-hand drawer. It was there under the empty folders he had laid atop it. He removed the rags from the drawer.

The .38 Smith and Wesson smelled of oil and looked as new as it had the day his brother-in-law had given it to him. Bremen checked the chambers. The bullets lay fat and heavy, like eggs in a nest. The roughened grip was firm in his hand, the metal cool. Bremen smiled ruefully at the absurdity of what he was doing, but kept the weapon in his hand when the kitchen screen door slammed again.

He made no sound as he stepped from the hallway to the kitchen door. It was very dim, but his eyes had adapted. From where he stood he could make out the pale white phantom of the refrigerator. Its recycling pump chunked on while he stood there. Holding the revolver down at his side, Bremen stepped onto the cool tile of the kitchen floor.

The movement startled him, and the gun rose an inch

or so before he relaxed. Gernisavien, the tough-minded little calico, crossed the floor to brush against his legs, paced back to the refrigerator, looked up at him meaningfully, then crossed back to brush against him. Bremen kneeled to rub her neck absently. The pistol looked idiotic in his clenched hand. He loosened his grip.

The moon was rising by the time they had a late dinner. The steaks had come from the freezer in the basement, the ice-cold beers from the refrigerator, and there had been several bags of charcoal left in the garage. They sat out back near the old pump while the steaks sizzled on the grill. Gernisavien had been well fed earlier but crouched expectantly at the foot of one of the big, old wooden lawn chairs.

Both of them had slipped into clothes—Bremen into his favorite pair of cotton slacks and his light blue workshirt and Gail into the loose, white cotton dress she often wore on trips. The sounds were the same they had heard from this backyard so many times before: crickets, night birds from the orchard, the variations of frog sounds from the distant stream, an occasional flutter of sparrows in the outbuildings.

Bremen served the steaks on paper plates. Their knives made crisscross patterns on the white. They had just the steaks and a simple salad from the garden, fresh radishes and onions on the side.

Even with the three-quarter moon rising, the stars were incredibly clear. Bremen remembered the night they had lain out in the hammock and waited for *Skylab* to float across the sky like a windblown ember. He realized that the stars were even clearer tonight because there were no reflected lights from Philadelphia or the tollway to dim their glory.

Gail sat back before the meal was finished. *Where are we, Jerry?* The mindtouch was gentle. It did not bring on the blinding headaches.

Bremen took a sip of Budweiser. "What's wrong with just being home, kiddo?"

There's nothing wrong with being home. But where are we?

Bremen concentrated on turning a radish in his fingers. It had tasted salty, sharp, and cool.

What is this place? Gail looked toward the dark line of trees at the edge of the orchard. Fireflies winked against the blackness.

Gail, what is the last thing you can remember?

"I remember dying." The words hit Bremen squarely in the solar plexus. For a moment he could not speak or frame his thoughts.

Gail went on. "We've never believed in an afterlife, Jerry." *Hypocritical fundamentalist parents. Mother's drunken sessions of weeping over the Bible.* "I mean . . . I don't . . . How can we be . . ."

"No," said Bremen, putting his dish on the arm of the chair and leaning forward. "There may be an explanation."

Where to begin? The lost years, Florida, the hot streets of the city, the day school for retarded blind children. Gail's eyes widened as she looked directly at this period of his life. She sensed his mindshield, but did not press to see the things he withheld. *Robby. A moment's contact. Perhaps playing a record. Falling.*

He paused to take a long swallow of beer. Insects chorused. The house glowed pale in the moonlight.

Where are we, Jerry?

"What do you remember about awakening here, Gail?"

They had already shared images, but trying to put them into words sharpened the memories. "Darkness," she said. "Then a soft light. Rocking. *Being rocked. Holding and being held.* Walking. Finding you."

Bremen nodded. He lifted the last piece of steak and savored the burnt charcoal taste of it. *It's obvious we're with Robby.* He shared images for which there were no adequate words. Waterfalls of touch. Entire landscapes of scent. A movement of power in the dark.

With Robby, Gail's thought echoed. *?????????? In his mind.* "How?"

The cat had jumped into his lap. He stroked it idly and set it down. Gernisavien immediately raised her tail and turned her back on him. "You've read a lot of stories about telepaths. Have you ever read a completely satisfying explanation of how telepathy works? Why some people have it and others don't? Why some people's thoughts are loud as bullhorns and others' almost imperceptible?"

Gail paused to think. The cat allowed herself to be rubbed behind the ears. "Well, there was a really good book—no, that only came close to describing what it *felt* like. No. They usually describe it as some sort of radio or TV broadcast. *You* know that, Jerry. We've talked about it enough."

"Yeah," Bremen said. Despite himself, he was already trying to describe it to Gail. His mindtouch interfered with the words. Images cascaded like printouts from an overworked terminal. Endless Schrödinger curves, their plots speaking in a language purer than speech. The collapse of probability curves in binomial progression.

"Talk," Gail said. He marveled that after all the years of sharing his thoughts she still did not always see through his eyes.

"Do you remember my last grant project?" he asked.

"The wavefront stuff," she said.

"Yeah. Do you remember what it was about?"

"Holograms. You showed me Goldmann's work at the university," she said. She seemed a soft, white blur in the dim light. "I didn't understand most of it, and I got sick shortly after that."

"It was based on holographic research," Bremen interrupted quickly, "but Goldmann's research group was working up an analog of human consciousness . . . of thought."

"What does that have to do with . . . with *this*?" Gail asked. Her hand made a graceful movement that encompassed the yard, the night, and the bright bowl of stars above them.

"It might help," Bremen said. "The old theories of mental activity didn't explain things like stroke effects, generalized learning, and memory function, not to mention the act of thinking itself."

"And Goldmann's theory does?"

"It's not really a theory yet, Gail. It was a new approach, using both recent work with holograms and a line of analysis developed in the Thirties by a Russian mathematician. That's where I was called in. It was pretty simple, really. Goldmann's group was doing all sorts of complicated EEG studies and scans. I'd take their data, do a Fourier analysis of them, and then plug it all into various modifications of Schrödinger's wave equation to see whether it worked as a standing wave."

"Jerry, I don't see how this helps."

"Goddamn it, Gail, it *did* work. Human thought *can* be described as a standing wavefront. Sort of a superhologram. Or, maybe more precisely, a hologram containing a few million smaller holograms."

Gail was leaning forward. Even in the darkness Bremen could make out the frown lines of attention that appeared whenever he spoke to her of his work. Her voice came very softly. "Where does that leave the mind, Jerry . . . the brain?"

It was his turn to frown slightly. "I guess the best answer is that the Greeks and the religious nuts were right to separate the two," he said. "The brain could be viewed as kind of a . . . well, electrochemical generator and interferometer all in one. But the mind . . . ah, the *mind* is something a lot more beautiful than that lump of gray matter." He was thinking in terms of equations, sine waves dancing to Schrödinger's elegant tune.

"So there *is* a soul that can survive death?" Gail asked. Her voice had taken on the slightly defensive, slightly querulous tone that always entered in when she discussed religious ideas.

"Hell, no," said Bremen. He was a little irritated at having to think in words once again. "If Goldmann was right and the personality is a complex wavefront, sort of a series of low-energy holograms interpreting reality, then the personality certainly couldn't survive brain death. The template would be destroyed as well as the holographic generator."

"So where does that leave us?" Gail's voice was almost inaudible.

Bremen leaned forward and took her hand. It was cold. "Don't you see why I got interested in this whole line

of research? I thought it might offer a way of describing
our ... uh ... ability."

Gail moved over and sat next to him in the broad,
wooden chair. His arm went around her, and he could feel
the cool skin of her upper arm. Suddenly a meteorite
lanced from the zenith to the south, leaving the briefest of
retinal echoes.

"And?" Gail's voice was very soft.

"It's simple enough," said Bremen. "When you visual-
ize human thought as a series of standing wavefronts creating interference patterns that can be stored and
propagated in holographic analogs, it begins to make
sense."

"Uh-huh."

"It *does*. It means that for some reason our minds are
resonant not only to wave patterns that we initiate but to
transforms that others generate."

"Yes," said Gail, excited now, gripping his hand
tightly. "Remember when we shared impressions of the
talent just after we met? We both decided that it would be
impossible to explain mindtouch to anyone who hadn't experienced it. It would be like describing colors to a blind
person ..." She halted and looked around her.

"Okay," said Bremen. "Robby. When I contacted him,
I tapped into a closed system. The poor kid had almost no
data to use in constructing a model of the real world. What
little information he did have was mostly painful. So for
sixteen years he had happily gone about building his own
universe. My mistake was in underestimating, hell, never
even *thinking* about, the power he might have in that
world. He grabbed me, Gail. And with me, you."

The wind came up a bit and moved the leaves of the
orchard. The soft rustling had a sad, end-of-summer sound
to it.

"All right," she said after a while, "that explains how
you got here. How about me? Am I a figment of your
imagination, Jerry?"

Bremen felt her shiver. Her skin was like ice. He took
her hand and roughly rubbed some warmth back into it.
"Come on, Gail, *think*. You weren't just a memory to me.
For over six years we were essentially one person with

two bodies. That's why when . . . that's why I went a little crazy, tried to shut my mind down completely for a couple of years. You *were* in my mind. But my ego sense, or whatever the hell keeps us sane and separate from the babble of all those minds, kept telling me that it was only the *memory* of you. You were a figment of my imagination . . . the way we all are. Jesus, we were both dead until a blind, deaf, retarded kid, a goddamn vegetable, ripped us out of one world and offered us another one in its place."

They sat for a minute. It was Gail who broke the silence. "But how can it seem so real?"

Bremen stirred and accidentally knocked his paper plate off the arm of the chair. Gernisavien jumped to one side and stared reproachfully at them. Gail nudged the cat's fur with the toe of her sandal. Bremen squeezed his beer can until it dented in, popped back out.

"You remember Chuck Gilpen, the guy who dragged me to that party in Drexel Hill? The last I heard he was working with the Fundamental Physics Group out at the Lawrence Berkely Labs."

"So?"

"So for the past few years they've been hunting down all those smaller and smaller particles to get a hook on what's real. And when they get a glimpse of reality on its most basic and pervasive level, you know what they get?" Bremen took one last swig from the beer can. "They get a series of equations that show standing wavefronts, not too different from the squiggles and jiggles Goldmann used to send me."

Gail took a deep breath, let it out. Her question was almost lost as the wind rose again and stirred the tree branches. "Where is Robby? When do we see *his* world?"

"I don't know," Bremen replied. He was frowning without knowing it. "He seems to be allowing us to define what should be real. Don't ask me why. Maybe he's enjoying a peek at a new universe. Maybe he can't do anything about it."

They sat still for a few more minutes. Gernisavien brushed up against them, irritated that they insisted on sitting out in the cold and dark. Bremen kept his mindshield raised sufficiently to keep from sharing the information

that his sister had written a year ago to say that the little
calico had been run over and killed in New York. Or that
a family of Vietnamese had bought the farmhouse and had
already added new rooms. Or that he had carried the .38
police special around for two years, waiting to use it on
himself.

"What do we do now, Jerry?"

We go to bed. Bremen took her hand and led her into
their home.

Bremen dreamed of fingernails across velvet, cold tile
along one cheek, and wool blankets against sunburned
skin. He watched with growing curiosity as two people
made love on a golden hillside. He floated through a white
room where white figures moved in a silence broken only
by the heartbeat of a machine. He was swimming and
could feel the tug of inexorable planetary forces in the pull
of the riptide. He was just able to resist the deadly current
by using all of his energy, but he could feel himself tiring,
could feel the tide pulling him out to deeper water. Just as
the waves closed over him he vented a final shout of despair and loss.

He cried out his own name.

He awoke with the shout still echoing in his mind. The
details of the dream fractured and fled before he could
grasp them. He sat up quickly in bed. Gail was gone.

He had taken two steps toward the stairway before he
heard her voice calling to him from the side yard. He returned to the window.

She was dressed in a blue sundress and was waving
her arms at him. By the time he was downstairs she had
thrown half a dozen items into the picnic basket and was
boiling water to make iced tea.

"Come on, sleepyhead. I have a surprise for you!"

"I'm not sure we need any more surprises," Bremen
mumbled.

"*This* one we do," she said, and she was upstairs, humming and thrashing around in the closet.

She led them, Gernisavien following reluctantly, to a trail that led off in the same general direction as the highway that had once been in front of the house. It led up through pasture to the east and over the rise. They carried the picnic basket between them, Bremen repeatedly asking for clues, Gail repeatedly denying him any.

They crossed the rise and looked down to where the path ended. Bremen dropped the basket into the grass. In the valley where the Pennsylvania Turnpike once had been was an ocean.

"Holy shit!" Bremen exclaimed softly.

It was not the Atlantic. At least not the New Jersey Atlantic that Bremen knew. The seacoast looked more like the area near Mendocino where he had taken Gail on their honeymoon. Far to the north and south stretched broad beaches and high cliffs. Tall breakers broke against black rock and white sand. Far out to sea, the gulls wheeled and pivoted.

"Holy shit!" Bremen repeated.

They picnicked on the beach. Gernisavien stayed behind to hunt insects in the dune grass. The air smelled of salt and sea and summer breezes. It seemed they had a thousand miles of shoreline to themselves.

Gail stood and kicked off her dress. She was wearing a one-piece suit underneath. Bremen threw his head back and laughed. "Is that why you came back? To get a suit? Afraid the lifeguards would throw you out?"

She kicked sand at him and ran to the water. Three strides in and she was swimming. Bremen could see from the way her shoulders hunched that the water was freezing.

"Come on in!" she called, laughing. "The water's fine!"

He began walking toward her.

The blast came from the sky, the earth, the sea. It knocked Bremen down and thrust Gail's head underwater. She flailed and splashed to make the shallows, crawled gasping from the receding surf.

NO!!!

Wind roared around them and threw sand a hundred feet in the air. The sky twisted, wrinkled like a tangled sheet on the line, changed from blue to lemon-yellow to gray. The sea rolled out in a giant slack tide and left dry, dead land where it receded. The earth pitched and shifted around them. Lightning flashed along the horizon.

When the buckling stopped, Bremen ran to where Gail lay on the sand, lifted her with a few stern words.

The dunes were gone, the cliffs were gone, the sea had disappeared. Where it had been now stretched a dull expanse of salt flat. The sky continued to shift colors down through darker and darker grays. The sun seemed to be rising again in the eastern desert. No. The light was moving. Something was crossing the wasteland. Something was coming to them.

Gail started to break away, but Bremen held her tight. The light moved across the dead land. The radiance grew, shifted, sent out streamers that made both of them shield their eyes. The air smelled of ozone and the hair on their arms stood out.

Bremen found himself clutching tightly to Gail and leaning toward the apparition as toward a strong wind. Their shadows leaped out behind them. The light struck at their bodies like the shock wave of a bomb blast. Through their fingers, they watched while the radiant figure approached. A double form became visible through the blaze of corona. It was a human figure astride a huge beast. If a god had truly come to Earth, this then was the form he would have chosen. The beast he rode was featureless, but besides light it gave off a sense of . . . warmth? Softness?

Robby was before them, high on the back of his teddy bear.

TOO STRONG CANNOT KEEP

He was not used to language but was making the effort. The thoughts struck them like electrical surges to the brain. Gail dropped to her knees, but Bremen lifted her to her feet.

Bremen tried to reach out with his mind. It was no use. Once at Haverford he had gone with a promising student to the coliseum, where they were setting up for a rock concert. He had been standing in front of a scaffolded bank of speakers when the amplifiers were tested. It was a bit like that.

They were standing on a flat, reticulated plain. There were no horizons. White banks of curling fog were approaching from all directions. The only light came from the Apollo-like figure before them. Bremen turned his head to watch the fog advance. What it touched, it erased.

"Jerry, what . . ." Gail's voice was close to hysteria.

Robby's thoughts struck them again with physical force. He had given up any attempt at language, and the images cascaded over them. The visual images were vaguely distorted, miscolored, and tinged with an aura of wonder and newness. Bremen and his wife reeled from their impact.

> A WHITE ROOM   WHITE
> THE HEARTBEAT OF A MACHINE
> SUNLIGHT ON SHEETS
> THE STING OF A NEEDLE
> VOICES   WHITE SHAPES MOVING
> A GREAT WIND BLOWING
> A CURRENT PULLING, PULLING,
>   PULLING

With the images came the emotional overlay, almost unbearable in its knife-sharp intensity: discovery, loneliness, wonder, fatigue, love, sadness, sadness, sadness.

Both Bremen and Gail were on their knees. Both were sobbing without being aware of it. In the sudden stillness after the onslaught, Gail's thoughts came loudly. *Why is he doing this? Why won't he leave us alone?*

Bremen took her by the shoulders. Her face was so pale that her freckles stood out in bold relief.

Don't you understand, Gail? It's not him doing it.

Not??? Who . . .?????

Gail's thoughts rolled in confusion. Splintered images and fragmented questions leaped between them as she struggled to control herself.

It's me. Gail. Me. Bremen had meant to speak aloud, but there was no sound now, only the crystalline edges of their thoughts. *He's been fighting to keep us together all along. I'm the one. I don't belong. He's been hanging on for me, trying to help me to stay, but he can't resist the pull any longer.*

Gail looked around in terror. The fog boiled and reached for them in tendrils. It was closing around the god figure on his mount. Even as they watched, his radiance dimmed.

Touch him, thought Bremen.

Gail closed her eyes. Bremen could feel the wings of her thought brushing by him. He heard her gasp.

My God, Jerry. He's just a baby. A frightened child!

If I stay any longer, I'll destroy us all. With that thought Bremen conveyed a range of emotions too complex for words. Gail saw what was in his mind and began to protest, but before she could pattern her thoughts, he had pulled her close and hugged her fiercely. His mindtouch amplified the embrace, added to it all the shades of feeling that neither language nor touch could communicate in full. Then he pushed her away from him, turned, and ran toward the wall of fog. Robby was visible as only a faint glow in the white mist, clutching the neck of his teddy bear. Bremen touched him as he passed. Five paces into the cold mist and he could see nothing, not even his own body. Three more paces and the ground disappeared. Then he was falling.

The room was white, the bed was white, the windows were white. Tubes ran from the suspended bottles into his arm. His body was a vast ache. A green plastic bracelet on his wrist said BREMEN, JEREMY H. The doctors wore white. A cardiac monitor echoed his heartbeat.

"You gave us all quite a scare," said the woman in white.

"It's a miracle," said the man to her left. There was a faint note of belligerence in his voice. "The EEG scans were flat for five days, but you came out of it. A miracle."

"We've never seen a case of simultaneous seizures like this," said the woman. "Do you have a history of epilepsy?"

"The school had no family information," said the man. "Is there anyone we could contact for you?"

Bremen groaned and closed his eyes. There was distant conversation, the cool touch of a needle, and the noises of leavetaking. Bremen said something, cleared his throat as they turned, tried again.

"What room?"

They stared, glanced at each other.

"Robby," said Bremen in a hoarse whisper. "What room is Robby in?"

"Seven twenty-six," said the woman. "The intensive care ward."

Bremen nodded and closed his eyes.

He made his short voyage in the early hours of the morning when the halls were dark and silent except for the occasional swish of a nurse's skirt or the low, fitful groans of the patients. He moved slowly down the hallway, sometimes clutching the wall for support. Twice he stepped into darkened rooms as the soft, rubber tread of quickly moving nurses came his way. On the stairway he had to stop repeatedly, hanging over the hard, metal railing to catch his breath, his heart pounding.

Finally he entered the room. Robby was there in the far bed. A tiny light burned on the monitor panel above his head. The fat, faintly odorous body was curled up in a tight fetal position. Wrists and ankles were cocked at stiff angles. Fingers splayed out against the tousled sheets. Robby's head was turned to the side, and his eyes were open, staring blindly. His lips fluttered slightly as he breathed, and a small circle of drool had moistened the sheets.

He was dying.

Bremen sat on the edge of the bed. The thickness of the night was palpable around him. A distant chime sounded once and someone moaned. Bremen reached his hand out and laid a palm gently on Robby's cheek. He could feel the soft down there. The boy continued his labored, asthmatic snoring. Bremen touched the top of the misshapen head tenderly, almost reverently. The straight, black hair stuck up through his fingers.

Bremen stood and left the room.

The suspension on the borrowed Fiat rattled over the rough bricks as Bremen swerved to avoid the streetcars. It was quite early, and the eastbound lane on the Benjamin Franklin Bridge was almost empty. The double strip of highway across New Jersey was quiet. Bremen cautiously lowered his mindshield a bit and flinched as the surge of mindbabble pushed against his bruised mind. He quickly raised his shield. Not yet. The pain throbbed behind his eyes as he concentrated on driving. There had not been the slightest hint of a familiar voice.

Bremen glanced toward the glove compartment, thought of the rag-covered bundle there. Once, long ago, he had fantasized about the gun. He had half-convinced himself that it was some sort of magic wand—an instrument of release. Now he knew better. He recognized it for what it was—a killing instrument. It would never free him. It would not allow his consciousness to fly. It would only slam a projectile through his skull and end once and for all the mathematically perfect dance within.

Bremen thought of the weakening, quiet figure he had left in the hospital that morning. He drove on.

He parked near the lighthouse, packed the revolver in a brown bag, and locked the car. The sand was very hot when it lopped over the tops of his sandals. The beach was almost deserted as Bremen sat in the meager shade of a dune and looked out to sea. The morning glare made him squint.

He took off his shirt, set it carefully on the sand behind him, and removed the bundle from the bag. The metal felt cool, and it was lighter than he remembered. It smelled faintly of oil.

You'll have to help me. If there's another way, you'll have to help me find it.

Bremen dropped his mindshield. The pain of a million aimless thoughts stabbed at his brain like an icepick. His mindshield rose automatically to blunt the noise, but Bremen pushed down the barrier. For the first time in his life Bremen opened himself fully to the pain, to the world that inflicted it, to the million voices calling in their isolation and loneliness. He accepted it. He willed it. The great chorus struck at him like a giant wand. Bremen sought a single voice.

Bremen's hearing dimmed to nothing. The hot sand failed to register; the sunlight on his body became a distant, forgotten thing. He concentrated with enough force to move objects, to pulverize bricks, to halt birds in their flight. The gun fell unheeded to the sand.

From down the beach came a young girl in a dark suit two seasons too small. Her attention was on the sea as it teased the land with its sliding strokes and then withdrew. She danced on the dark strips of wet sand. Her sunburned legs carried her to the very edge of the world's ocean and then back again in a silent ballet. Suddenly she was distracted by the screaming of gulls. Startled, she halted her dance, and the waves broke over her ankles with a sound of triumph.

The gulls dived, rose again, wheeled away to the north. Bremen walked to the top of the dune. Salt spray blew in from the waves. Sunlight glared on water.

The girl resumed her waltz with the sea while behind her, squinting slightly in the clean, sharp light of morning, the three of them watched through Bremen's eyes.

Introduction to
"Vanni Fucci Is Alive and Well
and Living in Hell"

In America as we enter the "discount decade" of the Twentieth Century ($19.90–$19.95, etc.), one is so used to thinking that progress equals improvement that it is almost heresy to be confronted with the absolute refutation of that premise.

For instance, take current theology. *Please.*

One can view Dante Alighieri's *Inferno* section of his *Comedy* as a personal venting of spleen mixed with a liberal dose of S&M, but to do so would be to see it only from our current, somewhat obsessed point of view. Dante was also obsessed, but his objects of obsession—besides the lovely, lost Beatrice—centered around Virgil's *Aeneid* and Aquinas's *Summa Theologica*. Little wonder then that the *Inferno* is a staggeringly complex theology, at once an exploration of cosmic structure and of the all too personal fear of death—that fear "so bitter—death is hardly more severe" *(Inferno, 1,7).*

Dante saw that fear of death as the one sure source of poetic and creative energy. In that respect, little has changed since the early 14th Century.

But let's turn on the TV and see what passes for theology these six and a half centuries later. In lieu of the poetry of the *Aeneid*, we have the south-baked howl of the sweating televangelist. In the stead of the intellectual cathedrals of the *Summa Theologica*, we have the entire cathode-ray-tubed, satellite-relayed, hair-sprayed and cosmetic-troweled message boiled down to two words: *Send money.*

Agreed, televangelists aren't the theologians of this century, and they *are* excessively easy targets after the revelations of the last few years—the Jimmy Swaggart vulgarities, the Rex Humbolt absurdities, and the Jimmy Bakker adulteries and breakdowns. If it's any excuse, the following story was written *before* these sideshows.

But the revelations were to be expected. As long as we live in a world where "theology" has become a mixture of P.T. Barnum and Johnny Carson, where we invite these parasites into our home via cable TV and satellite dish and radio . . . well, as the kid said in the classic *New Yorker* cartoon, "I say it's spinach, and I say to hell with it."

Vanni Fucci Is
Alive and Well
and Living in Hell

On his last day on earth, Brother Freddy rose early, showered, shaved his chins, sprayed his hair, put on his television make-up, dressed in his trademark three-piece white suit with white shoes, pink shirt, and black string tie, and went down to his office to have his pre-Hallelujah Breakfast Club breakfast with Sister Donna Lou, Sister Betty Jo, Brother Billy Bob, and George.

The four munched on sweet rolls and sipped coffee as the slate-gray sky began to lighten beyond the thirty-foot wall of bulletproof, heavily tinted glass. Clusters of tall, brick buildings comprising the campus of Brother Freddy's Hallelujah Bible College and Graduate School of Christian Economics seemed to solidify out of the predawn Alabama gloom. Far to the east, just visible above the pecan groves, rose the artificial mountain of the Mount Sinai Mad Mouse Ride in the Bible Land section of Brother Freddy's Born Again Family Amusement Complex and Christian Convention Center. Much closer, the great dish of a Holy Beamer, one of six huge satellite dishes on the grounds of Brother Freddy's Bible Broadcast Center, sliced a black

arc from the cloud-laden sky. Brother Freddy glanced at
the rain-sullen weather and smiled. It did not matter what
the real world beyond his office window offered. The large
"bay window" on the homey set of the Hallelujah Breakfast Club was actually a $38,000 rear-projection television
screen which played the same fifty-two minute tape of a
glorious May sunrise each morning. On Brother Freddy's
Hallelujah Breakfast Club, it was always spring.

"What's the line-up like?" asked Brother Freddy as he
took a sip of his coffee, his little finger lifted delicately,
the pinky ring gleaming in the light of the overhead spots.
It was eight minutes until air time.

"First half hour you got the usual lead-in from Brother
Beau, your opening talk and Prayer Partner plea, six-and-
a-half minutes of the Hallelujah Breakfast Club Choir
doing "We're On the Brink of a Miracle" and a medley of
off-Broadway Christian hits, and then your Breakfast
Guests come on," said Brother Billy Bob Grimes, the floor
director.

"Who we got today?" asked Brother Freddy.

Brother Billy Bob read from his clipboard. "You've
got Matt, Mark, and Luke the Miracle Triplet Evangelists,
Bubba Deeters who says he wants to tell the story again
how the Lord told him to throw himself on a grenade in
'Nam, Brother Frank Flinsey who's pushing his new book
After the Final Days, and Dale Evans."

Brother Freddy frowned slightly. "I thought we were
going to have Pat Boone today," he said softly. "I like
Pat."

Brother Billy Bob blushed and made a notation on his
thick sheath of forms. "Yessir," he said. "Pat wanted to be
here today but he did Swaggart's show last night, he has
a personal appearance with Paul and Jan at the Bakersfield
Revival this afternoon, and he has to be up at tomorrow's
Senate hearing testifying about those Satanic messages
you can hear on CDs when you aim the laser between the
grooves."

Brother Freddy sighed. It was four minutes until air
time. "All right," he said. "But try to get him for next
Monday. I like Pat. Donna Lou? How're we doing with
the Lord's work these days, little lady?"

Sister Donna Lou Patterson adjusted her glasses. As comptroller of Brother Freddy's vast conglomerate of tax-exempt religious organizations, corporations, ministries, colleges, missions, amusement parks and the chain of Brother Freddy's Motels for the Born Again, Donna Lou was dressed appropriately in a beige business suit, the seriousness of which was lightened only by a rhinestone Hallelujah Breakfast Club pin which matched the rhinestones on her glasses. "Projected earnings for this fiscal year are just under $187 million, up three per cent from last year," she said. "Ministry assets stand at $214 million with outstanding debts of $63 million, give or take .3 million depending upon Brother Carlisle's decision on replacing the Gulfstream with a new Lear."

Brother Freddy nodded and turned toward Sister Betty Jo. There were three minutes left until air time. "How'd we do yesterday, Sister?"

"Twenty-seven broadcast share Arbitron, twenty-five point five Nielsen," said the thin woman dressed in white. "Three new cable outlets; two in Texas, one in Montana. Current cable reaches 3.37 million homes, up .6 per cent from last month. The mail room handled 17,385 pieces yesterday, making a total of 86,217 for the week. Ninety-six per cent of the envelopes yesterday included donations. Thirty-nine per cent requested your Intercession Prayer. Total envelope volume handled this year is 3,585,220, with an approximate 2.5 million additional pieces projected by the end of the fiscal year."

Brother Freddy smiled and turned his gaze on George Cohen, legal counsel for Brother Freddy's Born Again Ministries. "George?" Two minutes remained until air time.

The thin man in the dark suit unhurriedly cleared his throat. "The IRS continues to make threatening noises but they don't have a leg to stand on. Since all of the ministry affiliates are under the Born Again Ministries exemption, you don't have to file a thing. The Huntsville papers have reported that your daughter's house has been assessed at one million five and they know that it and your son's ranch were built with a three million dollar loan from the ministry, but they're just guessing when it comes to sala-

ries. Even if they found out . . . which they won't . . . your
official annual salary from the Board comes to only
$92,300, a third of which you tithe back to the ministry.
Of course, your wife, daughter, son-in-law, and seven
other family members receive considerably more liberal
incomes from the ministry but I don't think . . ."

"Thank you, George," interrupted Brother Freddy. He
stood, stretched, and walked to the color monitor attached
to the computer terminal on his desk. "Sister Betty Jo, you
said there were several thousand requests for the Personal
Intercession Prayer?"

"Yes, Brother," said the woman in white, laying her
small hand on the console next to her chair.

Brother Freddy smiled at George Cohen. "I told these
folks I'd personally pray over their letters if they'd send in
a love offering," he said. "Might as well do it now. I've
got thirty seconds before Brother Beau goes into his intro.
Betty Jo?"

The woman tapped a button and smiled as the list of
thousands of names flashed by on the color monitor. After
each name was a code relating to the category of problem
for which intercession was requested according to the
checklist provided on the Love Offering form: H-health,
MP-marital problems, $-money problems, SG-spiritual
guidance, FS-forgiveness of sins, and so on. There were
twenty-seven categories. Any one of Brother Freddy's two
hundred mail room operators could code more than four
hundred intercession requests a day while simultaneously
sorting the letter contents into stacks of cash and checks
while cueing computers to provide the appropriate reply
letter.

"Dear Lord," intoned Brother Freddy, "please hear our
prayers for the receipt of Thy mercy for these requests
which are made in Jesus's name . . ." The list of names
and codes flashed past in a blur until the suddenly blank
screen held only a flashing cursor. "Amen."

Brother Freddy turned on his heel and led the suddenly
scurrying-to-keep-up retinue on the thirty yard walk to the
Hallelujah Breakfast Club studio just as the program's
opening graphics and triumphant music filled the sixty-two

monitors in the Broadcast Headquarters' corridors, offices, and board rooms.

Brother Freddy knew there was a problem eighteen minutes into the program when he introduced Dale Evans only to watch a tall, dark-skinned man with long, black hair walk onto the set. Brother Freddy knew at once that the man was a foreigner; the stranger's long hair was curled in ringlets which fell to his shoulders, he wore an expensive three-piece suit which looked to be made of silk, his immaculately polished shoes were of soft Italian leather, his starched collar and cuffs dazzled with their whiteness, and gold cufflinks gleamed in the studio lights. Brother Freddy knew that some mistake had been made; his born again guests—despite their personal wealth— went in for polyester blends, pastel shirts, and South Carolina haircuts if for no other reason than to stay in touch with their video faithful.

Brother Freddy glanced down at his notes and then looked helplessly at the floor director. Brother Billy Bob shrugged with a depth of confusion that Brother Freddy felt but could not show while the red eye of the camera glowed.

The Hallelujah Breakfast Club prided itself on being live in three time zones. Brother Freddy smiled at the advancing intruder and wished they had gone with the tape-delayed programs his competitors preferred. Brother Freddy usually prided himself on the fact that he wore no earphone to hear the booth director's instructions and comments, trusting instead on Brother Billy Bob's hand signals and his own well-honed sense of media timing. Now, as Brother Freddy rose to his feet to shake hands with the swarthy stranger, he wished that he had an earphone to learn what was going on. He wished that they had a commercial to cut to. He wished that *somebody* would tell him what was happening.

"Good morning," Brother Freddy said affably, retrieving his hand from the foreigner's firm grip. "Welcome to the Hallelujah Breakfast Club." He glanced toward Brother Billy Bob, who was muttering urgently into his bead microphone. Camera Three dollied in for a close-up of the swarthy stranger. Camera Two remained fixed on the long divan crowded with the Miracle Triplets, Bubba Deeters, and Frank Flinsey grinning mechanically from beneath his military-trimmed mustache. The floor monitors showed the medium close-up of Brother Freddy's florid, politely smiling, and only slightly perspiring face.

"Thank you, I've been looking forward to this for some time," said the stranger as he sat in the velour guest chair next to Brother Freddy's desk. There was a hint of Italian accent in the man's deep voice even though the English was precisely correct.

Brother Freddy sat, smile still fixed, and glanced toward Billy Bob. The floor director shrugged and made the hand signal for "carry on."

"I'm sorry," said Brother Freddy, "I guess I've mixed up the introductions. I also guess you're not my dear friend, Dale Evans." Brother Freddy paused and looked into the stranger's brown eyes, surprised at the anger and intensity he saw there, praying that this was only a scheduling mix-up and not some political terrorist or Pentecostal crazy who had gotten past Security. Brother Freddy was acutely aware that the signal was being telecast live to more than three million homes.

"No, I am not Dale Evans," agreed the stranger. "My name is Vanni Fucci." Again the hint of an Italian accent. Brother Freddy noted that the name had been pronounced VAH-nee FOO-tchee. Brother Freddy had nothing against Italians; growing up in Greenville, Alabama, he had known very few of them. As an adult he had learned not to call them wops. He presumed most Italians were Catholic, therefore not Christians, and therefore of little interest to him or his ministry. But now this particular Italian was a bit of a problem.

"Mr. Fucci," smiled Brother Freddy, "why don't you tell our viewers where you're from?"

Vanni Fucci turned his intense gaze toward the camera. "I was born in Pistoia," he said, "but for the last seven hundred years I have lived in Hell."

Brother Freddy's smile froze but did not falter. He glanced left at Billy Bob. The floor director was frantically making the signal of a star over his left breast. At first Brother Freddy thought it was some obscure religious symbol but then he realized that the man meant that Security . . . or the real police . . . had been called. Behind the wall of lights and cameras a live studio audience of almost three hundred people had ceased their usual background murmur of whispers and shiftings and stifled sneezes. The auditorium was dead silent.

"Ah," said Brother Freddy and chuckled softly. "Ah. I see your point, Mr. Fucci. In a sense all of us who were sinners have spent our time in Hell. It's only through the mercy of Jesus that we can avoid that as our ultimate address. When did you finally accept Christ as your Saviour?"

Vanni Fucci smiled, showing very white teeth against dark skin. "I never did," he said. "In my day, one was not—as you Fundamentalists put it—'saved.' We were baptized into the Church as children. But I made a slight mistake as a young man and your so-called Saviour saw fit to condemn me to an eternity of inhuman punishment in the Seventh Bolgia of the Eighth Circle of Hell."

"Uh-huh," said Brother Freddy. He swiveled around and gestured toward Camera One to dolly in closer for an extreme close-up on him. He waited until he could see only his own face on the floor monitor and said, "Well, we're having an enjoyable conversation here with our guest, Mr. Vanni Fucci, but I'm afraid we're going to have to take a break for a minute while we show you that tape I promised you of Brother Beau and I dedicating the new Holy Beamer we installed last week in Amarillo. Beau?" Below the frame of the close-up, out of sight of the viewing audience, Brother Freddy drew his right hand repeatedly across his throat. On the floor, Billy Bob nodded, turned toward the booth, and spoke rapidly into his microphone.

"No," said Vanni Fucci, "let us go on with our conversation."

The floor monitors showed a long shot of the entire set. The Miracle Triplets sat staring, the bottoms of their little shoes looking like exclamation marks. The Reverend Bubba Deeters raised his right arm as if he was going to

scratch his head, glanced at the steel hook that was the re-
minder of the Lord's Will during his Viet Nam days, and
lowered his arm to the divan. Frank Flinsey, a media pro,
was staring in astonishment at the three cameras where no
lights glowed and then back at the monitors which definitely showed a picture. Brother Freddy was frozen with
his hand still raised to his throat. Only Vanni Fucci seemed
unruffled.

"Do you think," said the Italian guest, "that if Dale
had passed away before Trigger, Roy would have had *her*
stuffed and mounted in the living room?"

"Ah?" managed Brother Freddy. He had heard very
old men make similar sounds in their sleep.

"Just a thought," continued Vanni Fucci. "Would you
rather I go on about my own situation?"

Brother Freddy nodded. Out of the corner of his eye he
saw three uniformed Security men trying to get on stage.
Someone seemed to have lowered an invisible Plexiglas
wall around the edge of the set.

"It actually has not been seven hundred years that I
have been in Hell," said Vanni Fucci, "only six hundred
and ninety. But you know how slowly time passes in such
a situation. Like in a dentist's office."

"Yes," said Brother Freddy. The word was a little better than a squeak.

"And did you know that one condemned soul from
each Bolgia is allowed one visit back to the mortal world
during our eternity of punishment? Much like your American custom of one phone call allotted to the arrested
man."

"No," said Brother Freddy and cleared his throat.
"No."

"Yes," said Vanni Fucci. "I think the idea is that the
visit sharpens our torments by reminding us of the pleasures we once knew. Something like that. Actually, we are
only allowed to return for fifteen minutes, so the pleasures
sampled could not be too extensive, could they?"

"No," said Brother Freddy, pleased that his voice was
stronger. The single syllable sounded wise and slightly
amused, mildly patronizing. He was deciding which Bibli-

cal verse he would use when it was time to regain control
of the conversation.

"That's neither here nor there," said Vanni Fucci. "The
point is that all of the condemned souls in the Seventh
Bolgia of the Eighth Circle voted unanimously for me to
come here, on your show." Vanni Fucci leaned forward,
his cuffs shooting perfectly so that gold cufflinks caught
the light. "Do you know what a Bolgia is, Brother
Freddy?"

"Ah . . . no," said Brother Freddy, derailed slightly
from his line of thought. He had decided on a verse but it
seemed inappropriate at right this instant. "Or rather . . .
yes," he said. "A Bolgia is that duchess or countess or
whatever who used to poison people in the Middle Ages."

Vanni Fucci leaned back and sighed. "No," he said,
"you're thinking of the Borgias. A Bolgia is a word in my
native language which means both 'ditch' and 'pouch.'
The Eighth Circle of Hell has ten such Bolgias filled with
shit and sinners."

The silent audience was silent no longer. Even the
cameramen gasped. Brother Freddy glanced at the monitors and closed his eyes as he realized that his very own
Hallelujah Breakfast Club, the top-rated Christian program
in the world except for the occasional Billy Graham Crusade, would be the first program in TBN and CBN history
to allow the word "shit" to go out over the airwaves. He
imagined what the Ministry Board of Trustees would say.
The fact that seven of the eleven Board members were
also members of his own family did not make the image
any more pleasant.

"Now listen here . . ." Brother Freddy began sternly.

"Have you read the *Comedy*?" asked Vanni Fucci.

There was something more than anger and intensity in
the man's eyes. Brother Freddy decided he was dealing
with an escaped mental patient.

"Comedy?" said Brother Freddy, wondering if the man
were some sort of deranged standup comic and all of this
a publicity stunt. On the floor, the cameramen had swung
the heavy cameras around and were peering in the lenses.
The monitors showed a steady shot framing only Vanni
Fucci and Brother Freddy. Brother Billy Bob was running

from camera to camera, occasionally tripping over a cable
or coming to the end of his mike cord and jerking to a stop
like a crazed Dachshund on a short leash.

"He called it his *Comedy*," said Vanni Fucci. "Later
generations of sycophants added the *Divine*." He frowned
at Brother Freddy, an impatient teacher waiting for a slow
child to respond.

"I'm sorry . . . I don't . . ." began Brother Freddy. One
of the cameramen was disassembling his camera. None of
the remaining cameras was aimed at the set. The picture
held steady.

"Alighieri?" prompted Vanni Fucci. "A dirty little
Florentine who lusted after an eight-year-old girl? Wrote
one readable thing in his entire miserable life?" He turned
toward the guests on the divan. "Come on, come on, don't
any of you read?"

The five Christians on the couch seemed to shrink
back.

"Dante!" shouted the handsome foreigner. "Dante
Alighieri. What's the deal here, gentlemen? To join the
Fundamentalists Club you have to park your brains at the
door and stuff your skull with hominy and grits, is that it?
Dante!"

"Just one minute . . ." said Brother Freddy, rising.

"Who do you think you . . ." began Frank Flinsey,
standing.

"What do you think you're . . ." said Bubba Deeters,
getting to his feet and brandishing his hook.

"Hey! Hey! Hey!" cried the Miracle Triplets, struggling to get their feet to the floor.

"SIT DOWN." It was not a human voice. At least not
an unamplified human voice. Brother Freddy had made the
mistake once on an outdoor Crusade of standing in front of
a bank of thirty huge speakers when the soundman tested
them at full volume. This was a little like that. Only
worse. Brother Billy Bob and others with headphones on
ripped them off and fell to their knees. Several overhead
spots shattered. The audience leaned backward like a single three-hundred-headed organism, whimpered once, and
adopted a silence unbroken even by the sound of breathing. Brother Freddy and the guests on the divan sat down.

"Alighieri did it," said Vanni Fucci in soft, conversational tones. "The man was a mental midget with the imagination of a moth, but he did it *because no one before him did it.*"

"Did what?" asked Brother Freddy, staring in fascinated horror at the madman in the crushed velour chair next to his desk.

"Created Hell," said Vanni Fucci.

"Nonsense!" cried Reverend Frank Flinsey, author of fourteen books about the end of the world. "The Lord God Jehovah created Hell as He did everything else."

"Oh?" said Vanni Fucci. "Where does it say so in that grab-bag of tribal stories and jingoist posturings you call a Bible?"

Brother Freddy thought that it was quite possible that he was going to have a heart attack right there on the Brother Freddy's Hallelujah Breakfast Club hour going live into three million three hundred thousand American homes. But even while his heart fibrillated and his red face grew redder, his mind raced to come up with the appropriate Scriptural verse.

"Let me tell you about an experiment performed in 1982," said Vanni Fucci, "at the University of Paris-South. A group of quantum physicists headed by Alain Aspect tested the behavior of two photons flying in opposite directions from a light source. The test confirmed an underlying theory of quantum mechanics—namely, that a measurement made on one photon has an instantaneous effect on the nature of another photon. *Photons*, gentlemen, traveling at the speed of *light*. Obviously no information could be transmitted faster than the speed of light itself, but the *act* of defining the nature of one photon *instantaneously* changed the nature of the other photon. The conclusion drawn from this is obvious, is it not?"

"Ah?" said Brother Freddy.

"Ah?" said the five guests on the divan.

"Precisely," said Vanni Fucci. "It confirms in the physical world what we in Hell have known for some time. *Reality* is shaped by the first great mind which focuses on measuring it. New concepts create new laws and the universe abides. Newton *created* universal gravity and the cosmos rearranged itself accordingly. Einstein defined space/time and the universe retrofitted itself to agree. And Dante Alighieri—that neurotic little whimshit—created the first comprehensive map of hell and Hell came into existence to appease the public perception."

"That's ridiculous," managed Brother Freddy, forgetting the cameras, forgetting the audience, forgetting everything but the monstrous illogic—not to mention blasphemy—of what this crazy Italian had just said. "If that was . . . true," cried Brother Freddy, "then the world . . . things . . . everything would be changing all the time."

"Precisely," smiled Vanni Fucci. His teeth looked small and white and very sharp.

"Then . . . well . . . Hell wouldn't be the same either," said Brother Freddy. "Dante wrote a long time ago. Three or four hundred years, at least . . ."

"He died in 1321," said Vanni Fucci.

"Yeah . . . well . . . so . . ." concluded Brother Freddy.

Vanni Fucci shook his head. "You understand nothing. When an idea is strong enough, large enough, *comprehensive* enough to redefine the universe, it has tremendous staying power. It lasts until an equally powerful paradigm is formulated . . . and accepted by the popular imagination . . . to replace it. For instance, your Old Testament God lasted thousands of years before it . . . He . . . was actively redefined by a much more civilized if somewhat schizophrenic New Testament deity. Even the newer and weaker version has lasted fifteen hundred years or so before being on the verge of being sneezed out of existence by the allergy of modern science."

Brother Freddy was certain he was going to have a stroke.

"But who has bothered to redefine Hell?" Vanni Fucci asked rhetorically. "The Germans came close in this century, but their visionaries were snuffed out before the new concept could take root in the mass mind. So we remain. Hell persists. Our eternal torments drag on with no more reason for existence than could be offered for your little toe or vermiform appendix."

Brother Freddy realized that he might be dealing with a demon here. After almost forty years of preaching about

demons, teaching about demons, finding the spiritual foot-
prints of demons in everything from rock music to FCC
legislation, warning against demons being in the schools
and kids' games and in the symbols on breakfast cereal
boxes, and generally making a fair-sized fortune by being
one of the nation's foremost experts on demons, Brother
Freddy found it a bit disconcerting to be sitting three feet
from someone who might very well be possessed by a demon if not actually *be* one. The closest he could recall to
coming to one before this was when he was around the
Reverend Jim Bakker's wife Tammy Faye when her
"shoppin' demons were hoppin' " back before the couple's
unfortunate publicity.

Brother Freddy clutched the Bible in his left hand and
raised his right hand in a powerfully curved claw over
Vanni Fucci's head. "I abjure thee, Satan!" he cried. "And
all of the powers and dominions and servants of Satan . . .
BE GONE from this place of God! In the name of JE-SUS
I *command* thee! In the name of JE-SUS I *command* thee!"

"Oh, shut up," said Vanni Fucci. He glanced at his
gold wristwatch. "Look, let me get to the important part of
all this. I don't have too much time."

As the Italian began to speak, Brother Freddy kept his
pose with the raised hand and clutched Bible. After a
minute his arm got tired and he lowered his hand. He did
not release the Bible.

"My crime was political," said Vanni Fucci, "even
though that Short Eyes Florentine put me in the Bolgia reserved for thieves. Yes, yes, I *know* you don't know what
I'm talking about. In those days the political battles between we Blacks and the dogspittle Whites were of great
importance—a third of Dante's damned *Inferno* is filled
with it—but I realize that today no one even knows what
the parties were, any more than people seven hundred
years from now will remember the Republicans or Demo-
crats.

"In 1293 two friends and I stole the treasure of San
Jacopo in the Duomo of San Zeno to help our political
cause. The Duomo was a church. The treasure included a
chalice. But I didn't go to Dante's Hell just because of one
little robbery about as common then as knocking over a

convenience store today. *No.* I have prime billing in the
Seventh Bolgia of the Eighth Circle because I was a Black
and because Dante was a White and the unfairness of it all
pisses me off."

Brother Freddy closed his eyes.

Vanni Fucci said, "You'd think an eternity of wallowing in a trench of *merde* and hot embers would be enough
revenge for the sickest S-M deity, but that's not the half of
it." Vanni Fucci swiveled toward the Breakfast Club guests
on the divan. "I admit it. I have a temper. When I get mad
I give God the fig."

Frank Flinsey, Reverend Deeters, and the Miracle Triplets looked blankly at Vanni Fucci.

"The fig," repeated the Italian. He clenched his fist,
ran his thumb out between his first and index fingers, and
thrust it rapidly back and forth. Based on the mass intake
of breath from the crowd, the symbol must have been clear
enough. Vanni Fucci swiveled back toward Brother
Freddy. "And then, of course, when I do that, every thief
within a hundred yards—which is everyone *in* that goddamned Bolgia, of course—turns into reptiles . . ."

"Reptiles?" croaked Brother Freddy.

"*Chelidrids, jaculi, phareans, cenchriads,* and *two-
headed amphisbands,* that sort of thing," confirmed Vanni
Fucci. "Alighieri got *that* right. And then, of course, every
one of these damned snakes attacks *me.* Naturally I burst
into flame and scatter into a heap of smoking ashes and
charred bone . . ."

Brother Freddy nodded attentively. Out of the corner of
his eye he could see Sisters Donna Lou and Betty Jo helping the three Security men use a chair as a battering ram
against the invisible barrier that kept them off the set. The
barrier held.

"I mean," said Vanni Fucci, leaning closer, "it's not
pleasant . . ."

Brother Freddy decided that when all of this was over
he would take a little vacation at his religious retreat in the
Bahamas.

"And being *Hell,*" continued Vanni Fucci, "the pieces,
my pieces, don't die, they just reassemble—which is the
most painful part, let me tell you—and then, when I'm

back together, the *unfairness* of it all gets me so pissed off that . . . well, you can guess . . ."

"The fig?" guessed Brother Freddy and clapped a hand over his own mouth.

Vanni Fucci nodded dolorously, "Both hands," he said, "And off we go again." He looked directly into Camera One. "But that's not the worst part."

"No?" said Brother Freddy.

"No?" echoed the five Breakfast Club guests.

"Hell is a lot like a theme park," said Vanni Fucci. "The management is always trying to improve the attractions, add a more effective touch to the entertainment. And can you guess what the Big Warden in the Sky has provided the last ten years or so to add to our torment?" The Italian's voice had climbed the scale as his anger visibly grew.

Brother Freddy and the Breakfast guests vigorously shook their heads.

"BROTHER FREDDY'S HALLELUJAH BREAKFAST CLUB!" screamed Vanni Fucci, rising to his feet. "EIGHT TIMES A GODDAMNED DAY. 90-INCH SYLVANIA SUPERSCREENS EVERY TWENTY-FIVE FEET IN BOLGIA SEVEN!"

Brother Freddy pushed back in his chair as Vanni Fucci's saliva spattered his desk top.

"I MEAN . . ." bellowed Vanni Fucci, his wide, glaring eyes fixed on something above the catwalks, ". . . IT'S ONE THING TO SPEND ALL OF ETERNITY BURNING IN HELL AND BEING RENT LIMB FROM LIMB EVERY FEW MINUTES BUT THIS . . . *THIS* . . ." He raised both arms skyward.

"No!" screamed Brother Freddy.

"No!" cried the Breakfast guests.

"THIS REALLY PISSES ME OFF!" bellowed Vanni Fucci and gave God the fig. Twice.

Things happened very quickly after that. To get the full effect, one has to play back the videotape in Extreme Slow Motion and even then the sequence of events can be confusing.

Brother Freddy went first. He doubled over the desk as if an Invisible Force were vigorously practicing the Heimlich Maneuver on him, opened his mouth to scream only to find that three rows of long fangs there made that highly impractical, and then grew scales and a tail faster than one could say "born again." The metamorphosis was so fast and the movement afterward was so quick that no one can say for sure, but most observers agree that the Reverend Brother Freddy looked a lot like a cross between a giant bullfrog and an orange python in the brief second before he—it—leaped across the desk with one thrash of its powerful tail and lashed itself around Vanni Fucci from crotch to throat.

Frank Flinsey turned into something altogether different; in less than a second the middle-aged Armageddon expert evolved into something resembling a six-armed newt with a jagged tail-stinger straight out of *Aliens*. The thing used its tail to plow a path through the carpet, floor, divan, and crushed velour to the hapless Vanni Fucci, where it joined the Brother Freddy python-thing in a full-fanged attack. Experts agreed that Flinsey was probably the *pharean* to Brother Freddy's *chelidrid*.

There was no doubt about Bubba Deeters transmogrification: the street preacher who had found God in a foxhole deliquesced like day-old fungi, reformed as a green-striped *amphisband* with a head at each end, and slithered toward Vanni Fucci to get in on the action.

The Miracle Triplets instantly changed into slimy, dart-shaped things which shot through the air, leaving contrails of green mucus, and embedded themselves deep in Vanni Fucci's flesh. Scholars are certain that the Triplets had become what Dante and Lucan had described as *jaculi*, but most viewers of the videotape today merely refer to them as "the snot rockets."

While these creatures threw themselves on Vanni Fucci in a roiling, writhing, snake-biting mass, there was more action on the set and elsewhere.

Brother Billy Bob had put his earphones back on just in time to turn into what a nearby cameraman later described as ". . . a thirteen-foot-long garter snake with leprosy." A second cameraman, since relieved of his duties by the Born Again Ministries, was reported to have said, "I didn't see no change in Billy Bob. All them directors look the same to me."

Sisters Donna Lou and Betty Jo fell to the ground only to slither onto the set a second later as two immense pink worms. Much has been written about the phallic symbolism inherent in this particular set of metamorphoses, but the irony was lost on the three security guards who emptied their service revolvers into the giant worms and then ran like hell.

The audience was not untouched. Vanni Fucci had said that all thieves within a hundred yards of his blasphemy traditionally were transformed. Out of 319 audience members present that morning 226 were unaccounted for the next day. The auditorium was filled with screams as those who stayed human watched their husbands or wives or parents or in-laws or the stranger next to them transform in a flash into snakes, fanged newt-things, legless toads, giant iguanas, four-armed boa constrictors, and the usual assortment of *chelidrids, jaculi, phareans, cenchriads*, and *amphisbands*. A University of Alabama study done a month after the incident showed that most of the thieves-turned-reptiles in the audience had been in sales, but other occupations included—lawyers (8), politicians (3), visiting ministers (31), psychiatrists (1), advertising executives (2), judges (4), medical doctors (4), stock market brokers (12), absentee landlords (7), accountants (3), and a car thief (1) who had ducked into the auditorium to get away from the Alabama Highway Patrol (2).

In less than ten seconds, Vanni Fucci was the center of a mass of scales and fangs representing every reptile-thing in the Bible Broadcast Center auditorium. The Italian struggled to get his hands free to get off another fig.

Brother Freddy sank its bullfrog-python *chelidrid* fangs deep into Vanni Fucci's throat and the blasphemer burst into flame.

The studio filled with a stink of sulphur so strong that thousands of cable subscribers later swore that they could smell it at home.

The entire mass of reptiles exploded into flame along

with Vanni Fucci, disappearing with him in a napalmish, orange-green flash that left the vidicon tubes of the RCA computerized color cameras with a 40-second after-image.

The Hallelujah Breakfast Club set was suddenly empty except for the flaming wreckage of the divan, desk, and crushed velour chair. Overhead sprinklers came on and the "bay window" imploded with a shower of sparks and glass. The sunrise did not survive.

Later that night, the *Nightline* video replay drew a sixty-share. On the same show, Dr. Carl Sagan went on record with Ted Koppel as saying that the entire event could be attributed to natural causes.

That week Brother Freddy's Hallelujah Breakfast Club Prayer Partners sent in Love Offerings totalling $23,267,894.79.

Except for the occasional Billy Graham Crusade, it set a new weekly record.

Introduction to
"Vexed to Nightmare by a Rocking Cradle"

This is another story about televangelists.

Wait! Before you close the book or decide that my only form of recreation is harpooning this particular brand of helpless sea slug, let me explain.

Some time back, the award-winning writer Edward Bryant approached me about a project. It seems that a Colorado-based publication wanted four short-shorts for their Christmas edition. The publication was . . . you see it was a . . . well, it was a comic book catalogue. But a *good* comic book catalogue. Actually, it was much more than that, since it carried a book review column by Ed and a fine film-review section by the discerning critic Leanne C. Harper.

Anyway, four of us would do these Christmas short-shorts and Ed would write the framing tale. (A difficult task at the best of times.) There were no restrictions—except for length—and the fact that the story had to be about Christmas and had to include an "overlooked present." The other writers were all members of the Colorado Mafia—Steve Rasnic Tem, Connie Willis, and Cynthia Felice. Cynthia had already suggested that her tale would be "upbeat," so the rest of us were allowed to return to our crypts and release whatever demons waited there.

The results, as one would expect, included a typically brilliant, subtle, and haunting piece by Willis, a powerful and seriously disturbing story in Steve Tem's inimitable style, my own offering reprinted here, and a clever framing tale by Ed Bryant that somehow managed to tie these disparate efforts together. But Cynthia Felice had to bow out due to other pressing demands, and the result was a trio of tales so unrelievedly dark that the reader would probably ask Santa for a razor blade or cyanide capsule that year.

The distant publisher of this comic book catalogue was said to have suffered instant seizure upon reading the first fiction to grace his pages, began spinning and bouncing off walls like a Linda Blair doll, and reportedly didn't respond to Thorazine until well after New Year's.

The truth is, I'd indulged myself in the story to the point of including a few in-jokes, one at the expense of my book publisher and another gently poking an editor I actually thought very highly of. *What the heck,* I thought, *who's gonna read a comic catalogue?*

It seems everybody did. And if that wasn't enough, the trio of tales was soon sold to *Asimov's SF Magazine* where it served to darken the *next* Christmas for a host of people. And if *that* wasn't enough, Bryant had sent copies out as Christmas gifts to everyone he knew—which just happens to be everyone in the publishing industry and probably everyone in Known Space.

It wasn't long before I had the reputation as The Man Who Sacrificed Christmas with a Survival Knife. Compared to Simmons, the Grinch and Scrooge were Santa's helpful elves.

It doesn't help that I assure everyone who will listen that Christmas is my second-favorite holiday (after Halloween, of course), or that every Christmas Eve my wife Karen and I accompany our small daughter up to a nearby snow-covered hillside to watch for Santa's sleigh, or that I once played Billy the Orphan who was really the disguised Christ Child in our fifth-grade operetta, or that . . .

No, I didn't think it would help.

Meanwhile, ponder this: when the Big Mistake finally happens and some computer pushes its own button, uncorking the Ultimate Detergent and putting us all through the Rinse and Burn cycle, when the accumulated weaponry of forty years of stockpiling gets launched just to scratch someone's itch to see if it will work, when the mushroom clouds have withered and the nuclear winter has grayed to nuclear spring . . . well, ask yourself: Self, what institution in the U.S. of A. has the infrastructure to withstand such a boot in the anthill? Who has the relay satellites already warmed up and plugged into our homes and communities, just waiting to carry the Leader's voice whispering in the nuclear night? Who has the followers in the millions . . . followers who already show the precise blend of fanaticism, obedience, and joyous aggression necessary to carry on with the Program while the rest of us are digging Uncle Charlie out of the rubble?

Got the answer yet?

Move over, Walter F. Miller.

Oh, yes—one final footnote for future biographers and bibliographers: the more discerning among you may note that in this story and in *all* of my stories and novels that include money-grubbing, venial, dishonest and otherwise fake TV ministers, the center of their web is invariably Dothan, Alabama. Now some of you may ask, "What terrible trauma, what dark, unrecorded and possibly unprintable incident occurred in Dothan, Alabama, to cast such an indelible blot on the escutcheon of this fine southern community?"

Well, you'll never hear the answer from me.

Vexed to Nightmare
by a Rocking Cradle

Brother Jimmy-Joe Billy-Bob brought the Word to the New Yorkers on the eve of Christmas Eve, paddling his long dugout canoe east up the Forty-second Street Confluence and then north, against the tide, up Fifth Avenue, past the point where the roof of the Public Library glowed greenly under the surface of the darkening waters. It was a cold but peaceful evening. The sunset was red and beautiful—as all sunsets had been for the two-and-a-half decades since the Big Mistake of '98—and cooking fires had been lit on the many tiers and tops of shattered towers rising from the dark sea like the burned-out cypress stumps Brother remembered from the swamps of his childhood.

Brother paddled carefully, aware of the difficulty of handling the long canoe and even more aware of the precious cargo he had brought so far through so much. Behind him, nestled across the thwarts like some great cooking pot, lay the Sacred Dish, it's God's Ear raised to the burning sky as if already poised to catch the fist emanations from the Holy Beamer that Brother Jimmy-Joe Billy-Bob had left in Dothan, Alabama, fourteen months earlier. Set behind the Sacred Dish, crated and cradled, was the Holy Tube, and behind it, wrapped in clear plastic, sat the Lord's Bike. The Coleman generator was set near the bow, partially blocking Brother's vision but balancing the weight of the cargo of sacred relics astern.

Brother Jimmy-Joe Billy-Bob paddled north past the trellised remnants of Rockefeller Center and the ragged spire of St. Patricks. There were dozens of occupied towers in this section of Rimwall Bay, hundreds of fires twinkling on the vined and rusted ruins above him, but Brother ignored them and paddled purposefully northward to 666 Fifth Avenue.

The building still stood—at least thirty-five floors of it, twenty-eight still above the water line—and Brother let the long dugout drift near the base of it. He stood—balancing carefully and shifting the weight of the Heckler and Koch HK 91 Semi-Automatic Christian Survival Network Assault Rifle across his back—raising his arms high, hands empty. Shadowed figures looked down from gaps in dark glass. Somewhere a baby cried and was hushed.

"I bring you glad tidings of Christ's Resurrection!" shouted Brother Jimmy-Joe Billy-Bob. His voice echoed off water and steel. "Good News of your coming Salvation from tribulations and woe!"

There was a silence and then a voice called down. "Who do you seek?"

"I seek the eldest Clan. That with the strongest totem so that I may bring gifts and the Word of the Lord from the True Church of Christ Assuaged."

The echoes lasted several seconds and the silence longer. Then a woman's voice from higher up called, "That be our Red Bantam Clan. Be welcome, stranger, and know that we already have the word of God here. Join us. Share our fire and preparations for the Holy Day."

Brother Jimmy-Joe Billy-Bob nodded and moved the canoe in to tie up to a rusted girder. The Holy Spirit had not yet spoken to him. He did not know how the Way would be prepared. He did know that within forty-eight hours they would be ready to murder him or to worship him. He would allow neither.

•   •   •

All through the day of Christmas Eve they worked to raise the gift of the Sacred Dish to the rooftop. The stair-wells were too small and the elevator shafts too cluttered with rope ladders, pulleys, lift baskets, and vines. Brother supervised the arrangement of block and tackle to raise the Dish the two-hundred-fifty feet to the top of the building. The three flights of stairs above the occupied twenty-fifth floor were perilous even for the cliffdwellers of the Red Bantam Clan. Brother had insisted that they improve the way up the cluttered staircase. "We will be coming up here often once the Holy Beamer connects you with the Word," he said. "And so will be other Clans of the Rimwall Trading League. The way must be cleared so that the youngest and the eldest of these can easily make the climb."

Old McCarty, the wrinkled matriarch of the Red Ban-tam Clan, had shrugged and directed a group of women to carry out repairs in the stairwell while the men raised the Sacred Dish.

By the time the sunset streaked the heavens red, all was in place: the Sacred Dish was firmly affixed atop the highest section of rooftop, the God's Ear was aimed as carefully as Brother's skills and his rusty sextant would al-low, the Formica altar was set in place below the Dish, and cables ran down to the Clan's Common Room on the twenty-fifth floor. The generator was in place there and the strongest Clan Hunters had been appointed to take turns on the Lord's Bike for the sunrise services.

Tara, the elf-faced five-year-old, tugged at Brother's coat as he was setting away his plastic buckets. "It's al-most dark," she said. "Will you come with us to see the tree and open presents?"

"Yes," said Brother Jimmy-Joe Billy-Bob. He glanced at the red-dyed bantam tattoo on the back of the child's hand. "And I will give the sermon."

The room was very large, the walls were coated with soot from cooking fires, and the rotted carpets had been covered with rush mats. The seventeen members of the Red Bantam Clan gathered around the Holy Tube and the small aluminum Christmas tree near the hearth. Candles glowed. A child's paper star decorated the top of the tree. Brother looked at the small scattering of crudely wrapped presents under the tree and closed his eyes.

Old McCarty cleared her throat. The tiny bantam tattoo on her forehead glowed redly in the candlelight. "Beloved Clan," she said, "it is our custom to give thanks to God on this most sacred of nights, and then to open the presents that Santa has brought. But this year our Brother from the Dothan True Church has arrived . . ." She paused, swallowed as if tasting something bitter, and finished. "Who will now tell us of tomorrow's celebration and read from the Word of God."

Brother Jimmy-Joe Billy-Bob moved into the open area in front of the tree and set his HK 91 against the table, within easy reach. He took his worn CSN Bible from his pack and set it on top of the Holy Tube. "Brothers and Sisters in Christ," he said. "Tomorrow morning, when the sun rises and the Way is purified, the Holy Beamer will cast its light into darkness, and once again you will hear the Word and become part of the True Church of Jesus Christ Assuaged. My trip here has not been an easy one. The Enemy was active. Five of my Brothers in Christ died so that I might arrive here." Brother stopped and looked at the faces in front of him. Old McCarty was frowning, the men were staring with interest or indifference, and many of the women and children were looking at him with an awe bordering on reverence.

"The time of Tribulations has come upon us and been long and heavy," Brother said at last. "But from this chosen place, the True Word—as spoken by Our Savior through the Eight Evangelists—will be heard again and will spread throughout the land." He paused again and looked at the faces lit by candlelight. Some of the children's gazes were drifting to the presents.

"Listen to what is written," Brother said and opened the Bible. "Revelation 13: 16, 17—'And he causes all, small and great, rich and poor, free and bond, to receive a MARK in their right hand, or in their foreheads: and that no man might buy or sell, save that he has the MARK, or

the name of the beast, or the numbers of a man: and his
number is six hundred, threescore and six.' "

There was a slight stirring in the crowd. Brother turned
the page and read aloud again without once glancing down
at the text. " 'Revelation 14:9–11,' " he said. " 'If any man
worship the beast and his image, and receive his mark in
his forehead, or in his hand, the same shall drink the wine
of the wrath of God; and he shall be tormented with fire
and brimstone in the presence of the holy angels, and in
the presence of the Lamb: and the smoke of their torments
ascendeth up for ever and ever: and they rest no day or
night, who worship the beast and image, and whosoever
receiveth the mark of his name.' "

Brother Jimmy-Joe Billy-Bob closed his eyes and
smiled. "But I read to you also from John 3: 16, 17," he
said. "I find no pleasure in the death of the wicked. Believe in the Lord Jesus Christ and you shall be saved.' "
Brother opened his eyes and said, "Amen."

"Amen," said Old McCarty. "Let's see what Santa
brought us this year."

Conversation and laughter resumed. Tara cuddled next
to Brother as the Clan gathered around the tree. "I'm
afraid you won't have a present," said Tara. Tears filled
her eyes. "Santa brought the presents on the second Sunday of Advent. I guess he didn't know you were coming."

"It doesn't matter," said Brother. "The tree and
presents are pagan customs. There is no Santa Claus."

The girl blinked but her nine-year-old brother Sean
chimed in, "He's right, Tarie. Uncle Lou and the hunters
get this stuff when they make the November voyage to the
warehouse. They keep it hidden up on the twenty-seventh
floor. "I've *seen* it."

Tara blinked again and said in a small voice, "Santa
brought me this doll that I just got. Sometimes he comes
back on Christmas Eve to bring us canned fruit. Maybe
he'll bring you something if he does. You can share my
doll 'til then if you want."

Brother shook his head.

"Hey, look!" cried Sean. "There *is* an extra present."

He scrambled under the tree and came up with a blue-wrapped box. "I bet it's extra 'cause Uncle Henry died last month an' they forgot not to put it out."

Brother Jimmy-Joe Billy-Bob started to return the present to its place but the Holy Spirit spoke to him then and he began to tremble violently. A hush fell on the group and the Clan watched as Brother calmed himself, tore off the wrapping, lifted a leather sheath from the box, and exposed a long blade to the light.

"Wow!" breathed Sean. He grabbed a yellowed pamphlet from the box and read aloud. " 'Congratulations. You are now the proud owner of a Christian Survival Network LINAL M-20 Survival Knife. Each LINAL M-20 is a whopping twelve inches long and yet is so perfectly balanced that it cuts and thrusts like an ex . . . exten . . . *extension* of your own hand. The LINAL M-20 blade is crafted entirely of 420 mo . . . molecular stainless steel and is tough enough to split wood or shatter bone. In the pom . . . pommel . . . of your LINAL M-20 is a precision RX-360 Liquid Damped Compass. Unscrew the compass and you will find a complete Survival Network Kit including a packet of waterproof wrapped matches, half-a-dozen fishing hooks, sinkers, nylon test fishing line, a sewing needle kit, an 18-inch cable saw capable of cutting down a small tree, and, of course, a copy of the CSN Miniaturized Bible.' " The boy shook his head and exhaled. "Wow," he said again.

Old McCarty also shook her head and looked at Lou, the eldest of the hunters. "I don't remember that being in the Warehouse load," she said sharply. The hunter shrugged and said nothing.

Brother Jimmy-Joe Billy-Bob slipped the knife in its sheath and the sheath in his belt. He listened as the last whispers of the Holy Spirit faded away. He smiled at the group. "I will go now to the rooftop to prepare the Way," he said softly. "In the morning we will gather to hear the Word."

He had turned to go when he felt Tara's small hand tugging at his pantleg. "Will you come and tuck us in first?" she asked.

Brother glanced at Rita, the girl's mother. The young

woman took her children's hands and nodded shyly.
Brother Jimmy-Joe Billy-Bob followed them toward the
dark hallway.

The children's bedroom had been a book storage room
for the publishing company that had once had offices on
the floor. While the children slipped into their bedrolls,
Brother looked at the shelves of rotting books, each one
marked with the small red bantam emblem.

Rita kissed her children goodnight and stepped into the
hall.

"Will you be up on the roof all night?" Tara asked
Brother. The child was hugging her new cloth doll to her
in the tumble of rags that made up her bed.

"Yes," said Brother, stepping back into the room.

"Then you'll see Santa and his reindeer land when he
comes back," she said excitedly.

Brother started to speak and then stopped. He smiled.
"Yes," he said. "I imagine I will."

"But you said . . ." began Sean.

"Anyone up on the roof tonight would see Santa Claus
and his reindeer," Brother Jimmy-Joe Billy-Bob said
firmly.

"Now let's say our prayers," said the children's
mother.

Tara, with eyes still wide, nodded and looked down.
"God bless Mommy, and Old 'Em, and the ghosts of
Daddy and Uncle Henry," she said.

"Amen," said Sean.

"No," said Brother. "There is a new prayer."

"Tell us," said both children.

"Matthew, Mark, Luke, and John," he said, "Bless the
beds that we lay on." He waited while the two repeated the
rhyme and then he went on. "Jim and Tammy, Jan and
Paul," he said, "Find the demons, smite them all."

The children recited flawlessly and Tara said, "Will
you really see Santa?"

"Yes," said Brother Jimmy-Joe Billy-Bob. "And
goodnight."

●   ●   ●

Brother looked in on the Clan before going to the roof. A small group had been huddled near the tree, murmuring, listening to Old McCarty, but the hunters scattered under Brother's gaze and went to their bedrolls. The matriarch stood and returned Brother Jimmy-Joe Billy-Bob's stare for a long moment but then she too looked down and moved away, just an old woman shuffling off to bed.

On the rooftop, Brother kneeled at the Formica altar and prayed loudly for several minutes. Finally he stood and removed all of his clothing. It was very cold. Moonlight reflected off his pale flesh and the curve of the Sacred Dish. Brother took out the plastic buckets and set them beneath the four corners of the altar. Then he removed the long knife from its sheath, held it high in both hands until the steel caught the cold light, and clamped it between his teeth.

Brother moved silently across the rooftop until he blended into the shadows near the head of the stairwell. He knelt there, at first feeling the rooftop gravel against his bare knee and tasting the cold steel in his mouth; then feeling nothing but the rising exaltation.

It did not take long. First came the gentle noises from the stairwell, then the shadowy figure emerged from the darkness, and finally came the soft voice. "Brother Jimmy-Joe?"

So it was not to be the old woman, thought Brother. So be it.

"Brother Jimmy-Joe?" The small figure moved toward the altar. Moonlight touched the dark braid of the doll's hair. "Santa?"

Brother Jimmy-Joe Billy-Bob said a silent prayer, removed the blade from his teeth, and moved forward softly and swiftly to celebrate the coming day.

Introduction to
"Remembering Siri"

I'm interested in how few writers cross the osmotic boundaries between science fiction and horror, between genre and what those in genre call mainstream. Or, rather, I should say that I'm fascinated with how many cross and do not return.

Part of it, I think, is the vast difference in states of mind between dreaming the dark dreams of horror and constructing the rational structures of SF, or between tripping the literary light fantastic and being shackled by the gravity of "serious" fiction. It *is* hard to do both—painful to the psyche to allow one hemisphere to become dominant while bludgeoning the other into submission. Perhaps that's why readership of SF and horror, genre and New Yorker fiction overlap less than one would think.

Whatever the reason, it's a pity that more writers feel constrained—sometimes by limitations of talent or interest but more frequently by market considerations and the simple fact that they find *success* in one field—to stay in one genre.

Of course, the exceptions are always interesting. George R.R. Martin moves easily between genres and expectations, rarely repeating, always surprising. Dean Koontz left SF just as he was becoming a star there—possibly because he sensed his destiny lay in becoming a supernova elsewhere. Edward Bryant took a "sabbatical" from SF a few years ago and has been producing world-class horror ever since. Kurt Vonnegut and Ursula K.

LeGuin "graduated" from SF to mainstream acceptance. (To Vonnegut's credit for honesty if nothing else, he allows as to how he gets nostalgic every once in a while, opens the lowest desk drawer where he keeps his old pulp SF efforts, and then urinates into it.) Doris Lessing, Margaret Atwood and others write their most memorable fiction in SF, but they deny any association with the field. Neither lady mentions urinating into desk drawers, but one suspects that they would feel a certain pressure on their respective bladders if forced to accept a Hugo or Nebula.

Harlan Ellison simply refused ever to be nailed down to a genre—even while he revolutionized them. We all have heard the stories where Ellison suffers the ten-millionth reporter or critic or TV personality who is demanding to know what descriptive word comes before "writer" in this case. Sci-fi? Fantasy? Horror?

"What's wrong with just . . . *writer?*" Ellison says softly in his most cordial cobra hiss.

Well, what's wrong with it is that the semiliterate have feeble but tidy little minds filled with tidy little boxes, and no matter how much one struggles, the newspaper article (or review, or radio intro, or TV superimposed title) will read something akin to—"SCI-FI GUY SAYS HIS SCI-FI STUFF NOT SCI-FI."

And the next step is for someone to stand up at a convention (sorry, a Con), grab the microphone, and shout—"How come you're always saying in interviews and stuff that you're not just a science fiction writer? I'm proud to be associated with science fiction!" (Or horror. Or fantasy. Or . . . fill in the blank.)

The crowd roars, righteousness fills the air, hostility lies just under the surface as if you're a black at a Huey Newton rally who's been caught "passing"—revealed as an oreo, or a Jew in the Warsaw ghetto who's been caught helping the Nazis with the railroad timetables, or—worse yet, a Dead Head at a Grateful D. concert who's been found listening to Mozart on his Walkman.

I mean, you *are* at this guy's convention. (Sorry, "Con.")

How do you explain to the guy gripping the mike that there are a thousand pressures forcing a writer down narrower and narrower alleys—agents trying to make you marketable and pulling their hair out because you insist on staying a jump ahead of a readership, publishers trying to shape you into a commodity, editors trying to get you to Chrissakes be consistent for once, booksellers complaining because your new SF novel just came out and it looks silly racked with your World Fantasy Award winning novel (which is really about Calcutta and has no fantasy in it), which, in turn, is next to your Sci-Fi opus and your fat horror novel (it is horror, isn't it? There wasn't any blood or holograms or demon-eyed kids on the cover . . .) and now . . . NOW! . . . this new book has come out . . . this *thing* . . . and it looks, oh sweet Christ, it looks . . . MAIN-STREAM!

How do you explain that every modifier before writer becomes another nail in the coffin of your hopes of writing what you want? What you care about?

So you look at the guy with the mike and you stare down the irate booksellers and you put your editor on hold, and you think—*I can explain. I can tell them that the one wonderful thing about being a writer is the freedom to explore all venues, the luxury . . . no, the responsibility . . . to work with the dreams the Muse sends you, to shape them to the best of your ability and to send them along whether a guaranteed readership is waiting or not; I can explain the compulsion to write a good book whether the cover artist knows what to do with it or not, explain the honor involved in trying new things despite the fact that the manager at the local B. Dalton's has racked your most recent novel in* OCCULT NON-FICTION *and asked . . . no, ordered the distributor not to send any more books written by this obvious schizophrenic. I can explain all that. I can take every single reader, every defensive SF chauvinist and horror fan and snooty New York reviewer and sparrowfart reader of "serious fiction," and show them what being a writer means!*

And then you look out at the guy with the mike, and you think—*Nahhh.* And you say, "My next book'll be SF."

The next story is SF. I loved writing it. I loved returning to this universe when I finally used "Remembering Siri" as a starting point to write the 1,500 or so pages of *HYPERION* and *THE FALL OF HYPERION*.

Oh, and the seed crystal for this tale was the thought one night, while dozing off, *What if Romeo and Juliet had lived?*

You know—Romeo and Juliet? By that sci-fi/fantasy/horror hack who wrote sit-coms and historical soap operas in his spare time?

Watch for the allusions. And the illusions.

Remembering Siri

I climb the steep hill to Siri's tomb on the day the islands return to the shallow seas of the Equatorial Archipelago. The day is perfect and I hate it for being so. The sky is as tranquil as tales of Old Earth's seas, the shallows are dappled with ultramarine tints, and a warm breeze blows in from the sea to ripple the russet willowgrass on the hillside near me.

Better low clouds and gray gloom on such a day. Better mist or a shrouding fog which sets the masts in Firstsite Harbor dripping and raises the lighthouse horn from its slumbers. Better one of the great sea-simoons blowing up out of the cold belly of the south, lashing before it the motile isles and their dolphin herders until they seek refuge in lee of our atolls and stony peaks.

Anything would be better than this warm spring day when the sun moves through a vault of sky so blue that it makes me want to run, to jump in great loping arcs, and to roll in the soft grass as Siri and I have done at just this spot.

Just this spot. I pause to look around me. The willowgrass bends and ripples like the fur of some great beast as the salt-tinged breeze gusts up out of the south. I shield my eyes and search the horizon but nothing moves there. Out beyond the lava reef, the sea begins to chop and lift itself in nervous strokes.

"Siri," I whisper. I say her name without meaning to do so. A hundred meters down the slope, the crowd pauses to watch me and to catch its collective breath. The procession of mourners and celebrants stretches for more than a kilometer to where the white buildings of the city begin. I can make out the gray and balding head of my younger son in the vanguard. He is wearing the blue and gold robes of the Hegemony. I know that I should wait for him, walk with him, but he and the other aging council members can not keep up with my young, shiptrained muscles and steady stride. Decorum dictates that I should walk with him and my granddaughter Lira and the other ladies of the society.

To hell with it. And to hell with them.

I turn and jog up the steep hillside. Sweat begins to soak my loose cotton shirt before I reach the curving summit of the ridge and catch sight of the tomb.

Siri's tomb.

I stop. The wind chills me although the sunlight is warm enough as it glints off the flawless white stone of the silent mausoleum. The grass is high near the sealed entrance to the crypt. Rows of faded festival pennants on ebony staffs line the narrow gravel path.

Hesitating, I circle the tomb and approach the steep cliff edge a few meters beyond. The willowgrass is bent and trampled here where irreverent picnickers have laid their blankets. There are several fire rings formed from the perfectly round, perfectly white stones purloined from the border of the gravel path.

I cannot stop a smile. I know the view from here; the great curve of the outer harbor with its natural seawall, the low, white buildings of Firstsite, and the colorful hulls and masts of the catamarans bobbing at anchorage. Near the pebble beach beyond Common Hall, a young woman in a white skirt moves toward the water. For a second I think that it is Siri and my heart pounds. I half prepare to throw up my arms in response to her wave but she does not wave. I watch in silence as the distant figure turns away and is lost in the shadows of the old boat building.

Above me, far out from the cliff, a wide-winged Thomas Hawk circles above the lagoon on rising thermals and scans the shifting bluekelp beds with its infrared vision, seeking out harpseals or torpids. *Nature is stupid,* I think and sit in the soft grass. Nature sets the stage all wrong for such a day and then it is insensitive enough to throw in a bird searching for prey which have long since fled the polluted waters near the growing city.

I remember another Thomas Hawk on that first night when Siri and I came to this hilltop. I remember the moonlight on its wings and the strange, haunting cry which echoed off the cliff and seemed to pierce the dark air above the gaslights of the village below.

Siri was sixteen . . . no, not quite sixteen . . . and the moonlight that touched the hawk's wings above us also painted her bare skin with milky light and cast shadows beneath the soft circles of her breasts. We looked up guiltily when the bird's cry cut the night and Siri said, "It was the nightingale and not the lark,/That pierc'd the fearful hollow of thine ear."

"Huh?" I said. Siri was almost sixteen. I was nineteen. But Siri knew the slow pace of books and the cadences of theater under the stars. I knew only the stars.

"Relax, young Shipman," she whispered and pulled me down beside her then. "It's only an old Tom's Hawk hunting. Stupid bird. Come back, Shipman. Come back, Merin."

The *Los Angeles* had chosen that moment to rise above the horizon and to float like a wind-blown ember west across the strange constellations of Maui-Covenant, Siri's world. I lay next to her and described the workings of the great C-plus spinship which was catching the high sunlight against the drop of night above us, and all the while my hand was sliding lower along her smooth side, her skin seemed all velvet and electricity, and her breath came more quickly against my shoulder. I lowered my face to the hollow of her neck, to the sweat-and-perfume essence of her tousled hair.

"Siri," I say and this time her name is not unbidden. Below me, below the crest of the hill and the shadow of the white tomb, the crowd stands and shuffles. They are impatient with me. They want me to unseal the tomb, to enter, and to have my private moment in the cool silent emptiness that has replaced the warm presence that was Siri. They want me to say my farewells so they can get on with their rites and rituals, open the waiting farcaster doors, and join the waiting worldweb of the Hegemony.

To hell with that. And to hell with them.

I pull up a tendril of the thickly woven willowgrass, chew on the sweet stem, and watch the horizon for the first sign of the migrating islands. The shadows are still long in the morning light. The day is young. I will sit here for awhile and remember.

I will remember Siri.

Siri was a . . . what? . . . a bird, I think, the first time I saw her. She was wearing some sort of mask with bright feathers. When she removed it to join in the raceme quadrille, the torchlight caught the deep auburn tints of her hair. She was flushed, cheeks aflame, and even from across the crowded Common I could see the startling green of her eyes contrasting with the summer heat of her face and hair. It was Festival Night, of course. The torches danced and sparked to the stiff breeze coming in off the harbor and the sound of the flutists on the breakwall playing for the passing isles was almost drowned out by surf sounds and the crack of pennants snapping in the wind. Siri was almost sixteen and her beauty burned more brightly than any of the torches set round the throng-filled square. I pushed through the dancing crowd and went to her.

It was five years ago for me. It was more than sixty-five years ago for us. It seems only yesterday.

This is not going well.

Where to start?

"What say we go find a little nooky, kid?" Mike Osho was speaking. Short, squat, his pudgy face a clever caricature of a Buddha, Mike was a god to me then. We were all gods: long-lived if not immortal, well-paid if not quite divine. The Hegemony had chosen us to help crew one of its precious quantum leap C-plus spinships, so how could we be less than gods? It was just that Mike, brilliant, mercurial, irreverent Mike, was a little older and a little higher in the Shipboard pantheon than young Merin Aspic.

"Hah. Zero probability of that," I said. We were scrubbing up after a twelve-hour shift with the farcaster construction crew. Shuttling the workers around their chosen singularity-point some 163,000 kilometers out from Maui-Covenant was a lot less glamorous for us than the four month leap from Hegemony-space. During the C-plus portion of the trip we had been master specialists; forty-nine starship experts shepherding some two hundred nervous passengers. Now the passengers had their hardsuits on and we Shipmen had been reduced to serving as glorified truck drivers as the construction crew wrestled the bulky singularity containment-sphere into place.

"Zero probability," I repeated. "Unless the groundlings have added a whorehouse to that quarantine island they leased us."

"Nope. They haven't," grinned Mike. He and I had our three days of planetary R-and-R coming up, but we knew from Shipmaster Singh's briefings and the moans of our Shipmates that the only groundtime we had to look forward to would be spent on a 7 by 4-mile island administered by the Hegemony. It wasn't even one of the motile isles we had heard about, just another volcanic peak near the equator. Once there, we could count on real gravity underfoot, unfiltered air to breathe, and the chance to taste unsynthesized food. But we could also count on the fact that the only intercourse we would have with the Maui-Covenant colonists would be through buying local artifacts at the duty-free store. Even those were sold by Hegemony trade specialists. Many of our Shipmates had chosen to spend their R-and-R on the *Los Angeles*.

"So how do we find a little nooky, Mike? The colonies are off limits until the farcaster's working. That's about 60 years away, local time. Or are you talking about Meg in Spincomp?"

"Stick with me, kid," said Mike. "Where there's a will, there's a way."

I stuck with Mike. There were only five of us in the dropship. It was always a thrill to me to fall out of high orbit into the atmosphere of a real world. Especially a world that looked as much like Old Earth as Maui-Covenant did. I stared at the blue and white limb of the planet until the seas were *down* and we were in atmosphere, approaching the twilight terminator in a gentle glide at three times the speed of our own sound.

We were gods then. But even gods must descend from their high thrones upon occasion.

Siri's body never ceased to amaze me. That time on the Archipelago. Three weeks in that huge, swaying treehouse under the billowing treesails with the dolphin herders keeping pace like outriders, tropical sunsets filling the evening with wonder, the canopy of stars at night, and our own wake marked by a thousand phosphorescent swirls that mirrored the constellations above. And still it is Siri's body I remember. For some reason—shyness, the years of separation—she wore two strips of swimsuit for the first few days of our Archipelago stay and the soft white of her breasts and lower belly had not darkened to match the rest of her tan before I had to leave again.

I remember her that first time. Triangles in the moonlight as we lay in the soft grass above Firstsite Harbor. Her silk pants catching on a weave of willowgrass. There was a child's modesty then; the slight hesitation of something given prematurely. But also pride. The same pride that later allowed her to face down the angry mob of Separatists on the steps of the Hegemony Consulate in South Tern and send them to their homes in shame.

I remember my fifth planetfall, our Fourth Reunion. It was one of the few times I ever saw her cry. She was almost regal in her fame and wisdom by then. She had been elected four times to the All Thing and the Hegemony Council turned to her for advice and guidance. She wore her independence like a royal cloak and her fierce pride had never burned more brightly. But when we were alone in the stone villa south of Fevarone, it was she who turned away. I was nervous, frightened by this powerful stranger, but it was Siri—Siri of the straight back and proud eyes, who turned her face to the wall and said through tears, "Go away. Go away, Merin. I don't want you to see me. I'm a crone, all slack and sagging. *Go away.*"

I confess that I was rough with her then. I pinned her wrists with my left hand—using a strength which surprised even me—and tore her silken robe down the front in one move. I kissed her shoulders, her neck, the faded shadows of stretchmarks on her taut belly, and the scar on her upper leg from the skimmer crash some forty of her years earlier. I kissed her greying hair and the lines etched in the once-smooth cheeks. I kissed her tears.

"Jesus, Mike, this can't be legal," I'd said when my friend unrolled the hawking mat from his backpack. We were on Island 241, as the Hegemony traders had so romantically named the desolate volcanic blemish which they had chosen for our R-and-R site. Island 241 was less than 50 kilometers from the oldest of the colonial settlements, but it might as well have been 50 light years away. No native ships were to put in at the island while *Los Angeles* crewmen or farcaster workmen were present. The Maui-Covenant colonists had a few ancient skimmers still in working order, but by mutual agreement there would be no overflights. Except for the dormitories, swimming beach, and the duty-free store, there was little on the island to interest us Shipmen. Some day, when the last components had been brought in-system by the *Los Angeles* and the farcaster finished, Hegemony officials would make Island 241 into a center for trade and tourism. Until then it was a primitive place with a dropship grid, newly finished buildings of the local white stone, and a few bored maintenance people. Mike checked the two of us out for three days of backpacking on the steepest and most inaccessible end of the little island.

"I don't want to go backpacking, for Chrissake," I'd said. "I'd rather stay on the *L.A.* and plug into a stimsim."

"Shut up and follow me," said Mike, and like a lesser member of the pantheon following an older and wiser deity, I had shut up and followed. Two hours of heavy

tramping up the slopes through sharp-branched scrub-trees
brought us to a lip of lava several hundred meters above
the crashing surf. We were near the equator on a mostly
tropical world, but on this exposed ledge the wind was
howling and my teeth were chattering. The sunset was a
red smear between dark cumulus to the west and I had no
wish to be out in the open when full night descended.

"Come on," I said. "Let's get out of the wind and
build a fire. I don't know how the hell we're going to set
up a tent on all of this rock."

Mike sat down and lit a cannabis stick. "Take a look
in your pack, kid."

I hesitated. His voice had been neutral but it was the
flat neutrality of the practical joker's voice just before the
bucket of water descends. I crouched down and began
pawing through the nylon sack. The pack was empty except for old flowfoam packing cubes to fill it out. Those
and a harlequin's costume complete with mask and bells
on the toes.

"Are you . . . is this . . . are you goddamn *crazy?*" I
spluttered. It was getting dark quickly now. The storm
might or might not pass to the south of us. The surf was
rasping below like a hungry beast. If I had known how to
find my own way back to the trade compound in the dark,
I might have considered leaving Mike Osho's remains to
feed the fishes far below.

"Now look at what's in my pack," he said. Mike
dumped out some flowfoam cubes and then removed some
jewelry of the type I'd seen hand-crafted on Renaissance,
an inertial compass, a laser pen which might or might not
be labelled a concealed weapon by Ship Security, another
harlequin costume—this one tailored to his more rotund
form—and a hawking mat.

"Jesus, Mike," I said while running my hand over the
exquisite design of the old carpet, "this can't be legal."

"I didn't notice any customs agents back there,"
grinned Mike. "And I seriously doubt that the locals have
any traffic control ordinances."

"Yes, but . . ." I trailed off and unrolled the rest of the
mat. It was a little more than a meter wide and about two
meters long. The rich fabric had faded with age but the

flight threads were still as bright as new copper. "Where did you get it?" I asked. "Does it still work?"

"On Garden," said Mike and stuffed my costume and his other gear into his backpack. "Yes, it does."

It had been more than a century since old Vladimir Sholokov, Old Earth emigrant, master lepidopterist, and E-M systems engineer, had hand-crafted the first hawking mat for his beautiful young niece on Nova Terra. Legend had it that the niece had scorned the gift but over the decades the toys had become almost absurdly popular—more with rich adults than with children—until they were outlawed on most Hegemony worlds. Dangerous to handle, a waste of shielded monofilaments, almost impossible to deal with in controlled airspace, hawking mats had become curiosities reserved for bedtime stories, museums, and a few colony worlds.

"It must have cost you a fortune," I said.

"Thirty marks," said Mike and settled himself on the center of the carpet. "The old dealer in Carvnal Marketplace thought it was worthless. It was . . . for him. I brought it back to the ship, charged it up, reprogrammed the inertia chips, and *viola!*" Mike palmed the intricate design and the mat stiffened and rose fifteen centimeters above the rock ledge.

I stared doubtfully. "All right," I said, "but what if it . . ."

"It won't," said Mike and impatiently patted the carpet behind him. "It's fully charged. I know how to handle it. Come on, climb on or stand back. I want to get going before that storm gets any closer."

"But I don't think . . ."

"Come *on*, Merin. Make up your mind. I'm in a hurry."

I hesitated for another second or two. If we were caught leaving the island, we would both be kicked off the ship. Shipwork was my life now. I had made that decision when I accepted the eight-mission Maui-Covenant contract. More than that, I was two hundred light years and five and a half leap years from civilization. Even if they brought us back to Hegemony-space, the round trip would have cost us eleven years worth of friends and family. The time-debt was irrevocable.

I crawled on the hovering hawking mat behind Mike. He stuffed the backpack between us, told me to hang on, and tapped at the flight designs. The mat rose five meters above the ledge, banked quickly to the left, and shot out over the alien ocean. Three hundred meters below us, the surf crashed whitely in the deepening gloom. We rose higher above the rough water and headed north into the night.

In such seconds of decision entire futures are made.

I remember talking to Siri during our Second Reunion, shortly after we first visited the villa along the coast near Fevarone. We were walking along the beach. Alón had been allowed to stay in the city under Magritte's supervision. It was just as well. I was not truly comfortable with the boy. Only the undeniable green solemnity of his eyes and the disturbing mirror-familiarity of his short, dark curls and snub of a nose served to tie him to me . . . to us . . . in my mind. That and the quick, almost sardonic smile I would catch him hiding from Siri when she reprimanded him. It was a smile too cynically amused and self-observant to be so practiced in a ten-year-old. I knew it well. I would have thought such things were learned, not inherited.

"You know very little," Siri said to me. She was wading, shoeless, in a shallow tidepool. From time to time she would lift the delicate shell of a frenchhorn-conch, inspect it for flaws, and drop it back into the silty water.

"I've been well-trained," I replied.

"Yes, I'm sure you've been well-trained," agreed Siri. "I know you are quite skillful, Merin. But you *know* very little."

Irritated, unsure of how to respond, I walked along with my head lowered. I dug a white lavastone out of the sand and tossed it far out into the bay. Rainclouds were piling along the eastern horizon. I found myself wishing that I was back aboard the ship. I had been reluctant to return this time and now I knew that it had been a mistake.

It was my third visit to Maui-Covenant, our Second Reunion as the poets and her people were calling it. I was five months away from being 21 standard years old. Siri had just celebrated her thirty-seventh birthday three weeks earlier.

"I've been to a lot of places you've never seen," I said at last. It sounded petulant and childish even to me.

"Oh, yes," said Siri and clapped her hands together. For a second, in her enthusiasm, I glimpsed my other Siri—the young girl I had dreamed about during the long nine months of turn-around. Then the image slid back to harsh reality and I was all too aware of her short hair, the loosening neck muscles, and the cords appearing on the backs of those once beloved hands. "You've been to places I'll *never* see," said Siri in a rush. Her voice was the same. Almost the same. "Merin, my love, you've already seen things I cannot even imagine. You probably know more facts about the universe than I would guess exist. But you *know* very little, my darling."

"What the hell are you talking about, Siri?" I sat down on a half-submerged log near the strip of wet sand and drew my knees up like a fence between us.

Siri strode out of the tidepool and came to kneel in front of me. She took my hands in hers and although mine were bigger, heavier, blunter of finger and bone, I could feel the *strength* in hers. I imagined it as the strength of years I had not shared. "You have to live to really know things, my love. Having Alón has helped me to understand that. There is something about raising a child that helps to sharpen one's sense of what is real."

"How do you mean?"

Siri squinted away from me for a few seconds and absently brushed back a strand of hair. Her left hand stayed firmly around both of mine. "I'm not sure," she said softly. "I think one begins to feel when things aren't *important*. I'm not sure how to put it. When you've spent thirty years entering rooms filled with strangers you feel less pressure than when you've had only half that number of years of experience. You know what the room and the people in it probably hold for you and you go looking for it. If it's not there, you sense it earlier and leave to go

about your business. You just *know* more about what is,
what isn't, and how little time there is to learn the difference. Do you understand, Merin? Do you follow me even
a little bit?"

"No," I said.

Siri nodded and bit her lower lip. But she did not
speak again for a while. Instead, she leaned over and
kissed me. Her lips were dry and a little questioning. I
held back for a second, seeing the sky beyond her, wanting
time to think. But then I felt the warm intrusion of her
tongue and closed my eyes. The tide was coming in behind us. I felt a sympathetic warmth and rising as Siri un-
buttoned my shirt and ran sharp fingernails across my
chest. There was a second of emptiness between us and I
opened my eyes in time to see her unfastening the last buttons on the front of her white dress. Her breasts were
larger than I remembered, heavier, the nipples broader and
darker. The chill air nipped at both of us until I pulled the
fabric down her shoulders and brought our upper bodies
together. We slid down along the log to the warm sand. I
pressed her closer, all the while wondering how I possibly
could have thought her the stronger one. Her skin tasted of
salt.

Siri's hands helped me. Her short hair pressed back
against bleached wood, white cotton, and sand. My pulse
outraced the surf.

"Do you understand, Merin?" she whispered to me
seconds later as her warmth connected us.

"Yes," I whispered back. But I did not.

Mike brought the hawking mat in from the east toward
Firstsite. The flight had taken over an hour in the dark and
I had spent most of the time huddling from the wind and
waiting for the carpet to fold up and tumble us both into
the sea. We were still half an hour out when we saw the
first of the motile isles. Racing before the storm, treesails
billowing, the islands sailed up from their southern feeding
grounds in seemingly endless procession. Many were lit
brilliantly, festooned with colored lanterns and shifting
veils of gossamer light.

"You sure this is the way?" I shouted.

"Yes," shouted Mike. He did not turn his head. The wind whipped his long, black hair back against my face. From time to time he would check his compass and make small corrections to our course. It might have been easier to follow the isles. We passed one—a large one almost half a kilometer in length—and I strained to make out details, but the isle was dark except for the glow of its phosphorescent wake. Dark shapes cut through the milky waves. I tapped Mike on the shoulder and pointed.

"Dolphins!" he shouted. "That's what this colony was all about, remember? A bunch of do-gooders during the Hegira wanted to save all the mammals in Old Earth's oceans. Didn't succeed."

I would have shouted another question but at that moment the headland and Firstsite Harbor came into view.

I had thought the stars were bright above Maui-Covenant. I had thought the migrating islands were memorable in their colorful display. But the city of Firstsite, wrapped about with harbor and hills, was a blazing beacon in the night. Its brilliance reminded me of a torchship I once had watched while it created its own plasma nova against the dark limb of a sullen gas giant. The city was a five-tiered honeycomb of white buildings, all illuminated by warmly glowing lanterns from within and by countless torches from without. The white lavastone of the volcanic island itself seemed to glow from the city light. Beyond the town were tents, pavilions, campfires, cooking fires, and great flaming pyres, too large for function, too large for anything except to serve as a welcome to the returning isles.

The harbor was filled with boats: bobbing catamarans with cowbells clanking from their masts; large-hulled, flat-bottomed houseboats built for creeping from port to port in the calm, equatorial shallows but proudly ablaze with strings of lights this night; and then the occasional ocean-going yacht, sleek and functional as a shark. A lighthouse set out on the pincer's end of the harbor reef threw its beam far out to sea, illuminated wave and isle alike, and then swept its light back in to catch the colorful bobbing of ships and men.

Even from two kilometers out we could hear the noise. Sounds of celebration were clearly audible. Above the shouts and constant susurration of the surf rose the unmistakable notes of a Bach flute sonata. I learned later that this welcoming chorus was transmitted through hydrophones to the Passage Channels where dolphins leapt and cavorted to the music.

"My God, Mike, how did you know all of this was going on?"

"I asked the main ship computer," said Mike. The hawking mat banked right to keep us far out from the ships and lighthouse beam. Then we curved back in north of Firstsite toward a dark spit of land. I could hear the soft booming of waves on the shallows ahead. "They have this festival every year," Mike went on, "but this is their sesquicentennial. The party's been going on for three weeks now and is scheduled to continue another two. There are only about 100,000 colonists on this whole world, Merin, and I bet half of them are here partying."

We slowed, came in carefully, and touched down on a rocky outcropping not far from the beach. The storm had missed us to the south but intermittent flashes of lightning and the distant lights of advancing isles still marked the horizon. Overhead, the stars were not dimmed by the glow from Firstsite just over the rise from us. The air was warmer here and I caught the scent of orchards on the breeze. We folded up the hawking mat and hurried to get into our harlequin costumes. Mike slipped his laser pen and jewelry into loose pockets.

"What are those for?" I asked as we secured the backpack and hawking mat under a large boulder.

"These?" asked Mike as he dangled a Renaissance necklace from his fingers. "These are currency in case we have to negotiate for favors."

"Favors?"

"Favors," repeated Mike. "A lady's *largesse.* Comfort to a weary space-farer. Nooky to you, kid."

"Oh," I said and adjusted my mask and fool's cap. The bells made a soft sound in the dark.

"Come on," said Mike. "We'll miss the party." I nod-

ded and followed him, bells jangling, as we picked our
way over stone and scrub toward the waiting light.

I sit here in the sunlight and wait. I am not totally certain what I am waiting for. I can feel a growing warmth on
my back as the morning sunlight is reflected from the
white stone of Siri's tomb.

Siri's tomb?

There are no clouds in the sky. I raise my head and
squint skyward as if I might be able to see the *L.A.* and
the newly finished farcaster array through the glare of atmosphere. I cannot. Part of me knows that they have not
risen yet. Part of me knows to the second the time remaining before ship and farcaster complete their transit to the
zenith. Part of me does not want to think about it.

Siri, am I doing the right thing?

There is the sudden sound of pennants stirring on their
staffs as the wind comes up. I sense rather than see the
restlessness of the waiting crowd. For the first time since
my planetfall for this, our Sixth Reunion, I am filled with
sorrow. No, not sorrow, not yet, but a sharptoothed sadness
which soon will open into grief. For years I have carried
on silent conversations with Siri, framing questions to myself for future discussion with her, and it suddenly strikes
me with cold clarity that we will never again sit together
and talk. An emptiness begins to grow inside me.

Should I let it happen, Siri?

There is no response except for the growing murmurs
of the crowd. In a few minutes they will send Donel, my
younger and surviving son, or his daughter Lira up the hill
to urge me on. I toss away the sprig of willowgrass I've
been chewing on. There is a hint of shadow on the horizon. It could be a cloud. Or it could be the first of the
isles, driven by instinct and the spring northerlies to mi-
grate back to the great band of the equatorial shallows
from whence they came. It does not matter.

Siri, am I doing the right thing?

There is no answer and the time grows shorter.

•   •   •

Sometimes Siri seemed so ignorant it made me sick.

She knew nothing of my life away from her. She would ask questions but I sometimes wondered if she was interested in the answers. I spent many hours explaining the beautiful physics behind our C-plus spinships but she never did seem to understand. Once, after I had taken great care to detail the differences between their ancient seedship and the *Los Angeles*, Siri astounded me by asking, "But why did it take my ancestors 80 years of shiptime to reach Maui-Covenant when you can make the trip in 130 *days*?" She had understood nothing.

Siri's sense of history was, at best, pitiful. She viewed the Hegemony and the worldweb the way a child would view the fantasy world of a pleasant but rather silly myth; there was an indifference there that almost drove me mad at times.

Siri knew all about the early days of the Hegira—at least insofar as they pertained to the Maui-Covenant and the colonists—and she occasionally would come up with delightful bits of archaic trivia or phraseology, but she knew nothing of post-Hegira realities. Names like Garden and Ouster, Renaissance and Lusus meant little to her. I could mention Salmen Brey or General Horace Glennon-Hight and she would have no associations or reactions at all. None.

The last time I saw Siri she was 70 standard years old. She was *70 years old* and still she had never: traveled offworld, used a comlog, tasted any alcoholic drink except wine; interfaced with an empathy surgeon, stepped through a farcaster door, smoked a cannabis stick, received any gene tailoring, plugged into a stimsim, received any formal schooling, taken any RNA medication, heard of Zen Christianity, or flown any vehicle except an ancient Vikken skimmer belonging to her family.

Siri had never made love to anyone except me. Or so she said. And so I believed.

It was during our First Reunion, that time on the Archipelago, when Siri took me to talk with the dolphins. We had risen to watch the dawn. The highest levels of the treehouse were a perfect place from which to watch the eastern sky pale and fade to morning. Ripples of high cirrus turned to rose and then the sea itself grew molten as the sun lifted above the flat horizon.

"Let's go swimming," said Siri. The rich, horizontal light bathed her skin and threw her shadow four meters across the boards of the platform.

"I'm too tired," I said. "Later." We had lain awake most of the night talking, making love, talking, and making love again. In the glare of morning I felt empty and vaguely nauseated. I sensed the slight movement of the isle under me as a tinge of vertigo, a drunkard's disconnection from gravity.

"No. Let's go now," said Siri and grasped my hand to pull me along. I was irritated but did not argue. Siri was 26, seven years older than me during that First Reunion, but her impulsive behavior often reminded me of the teenaged Siri I had carried away from the Festival only ten of my months earlier. Her deep, unselfconscious laugh was the same. Her green eyes cut as sharply when she was impatient. The long mane of auburn hair had not changed. But her body had ripened, filled out with a promise which had been only hinted at before. Her breasts were still high and full, almost girlish, bordered above by freckles that gave way to a whiteness so translucent that a gentle blue tracery of veins could be seen. But they were *different* somehow. She was different.

"Are you going to join me or just sit there staring?" asked Siri. She had slipped off her caftan as we came out onto the lowest deck. Our small ship was still tied to the dock. Above us, the island's treesails were beginning to open to the morning breeze. For the past several days, Siri had insisted on wearing swimstrips when we went into the water. She wore none now. Her nipples rose in the cool air.

"Won't we be left behind?" I asked, squinting up at the flapping treesails. On previous days we had waited for the doldrums in the middle of the day when the isle was still in the water, the sea a glazed mirror. Now the jibvines were beginning to pull taut as the thick leaves filled with wind.

"Don't be silly," said Siri. "We could always catch a

keelroot and follow it back. That or a feeding tendril.
Come on." She tossed an osmosis mask at me and donned
her own. The transparent film made her face look slick
with oil. From the pocket of her caftan she lifted a thick
medallion and set it in place around her neck. The metal
looked dark and ominous against her skin.

"What's that?" I asked.

Siri did not lift the osmosis mask to answer. She set
the comthreads in place against her neck and handed me
the hearplugs. Her voice was tinny. "Translation disk," she
said. "Thought you knew all about gadgets, Merin. Last
one in's a seaslug." She held the disk in place between her
breasts with one hand and stepped off the isle. I could see
the pale globes of her buttocks as she pirouetted and
kicked for depth. In seconds she was only a white blur
deep in the water. I slipped my own mask on, pressed the
comthreads tight, and stepped into the sea.

The bottom of the isle was a dark stain on a ceiling of
crystalline light. I was wary of the thick feeding tendrils
even though Siri had amply demonstrated that they were
interested in devouring nothing larger than the tiny zoo-
plankton that even now caught the sunlight like dust in an
abandoned ballroom. Keelroots descended like gnarled
stalactites for hundreds of meters into the purple depths.

The isle was moving. I could see the faint fibrilation of
the tendrils as they trailed along. A wake caught the light
ten meters above me. For a second I was choking, the gel
of the mask smothering me as surely as the surrounding
water would, and then I relaxed and the air flowed freely
into my lungs.

"Deeper, Merin," came Siri's voice. I blinked—a slow
motion blink as the mask readjusted itself over my eyes—
and caught sight of Siri twenty meters lower, grasping a
keelroot and trailing effortlessly above the colder, deeper
currents where the light did not reach. I thought of the
thousands of meters of water under me, of the things
which might lurk there, unknown, unsought-out by the human colonists. I thought of the dark and the depths and my
scrotum tightened involuntarily.

"Come on down." Siri's voice was an insect buzz in
my ears. I rotated and kicked. The buoyancy here was not

so great as in Old Earth's seas, but it still took energy to
dive so deep. The mask compensated for depth and nitrogen but I could feel the pressure against my skin and ears.
Finally I quit kicking, grabbed a keelroot, and roughly
hauled myself down to Siri's level.

We floated side by side in the dim light. Siri was a
spectral figure here, her long hair swirling in a wine-dark
nimbus, the pale strips of her body glowing in the blue-
green light. The surface seemed impossibly distant. The
widening V of the wake and the drift of the scores of tendrils showed that the isle was moving more quickly now,
moving mindlessly to other feeding grounds, distant waters.

"Where are the . . ." I began to subvocalize.

"Shhh," said Siri. She fiddled with the medallion. I
could hear them then; the shrieks and trills and whistles
and cat purrs and echoing cries. The depths were suddenly
filled with strange music.

"Jesus," I said and because Siri had tuned our
comthreads to the translator, the word was broadcast as a
senseless whistle and toot.

"Hello!" she called and the translated greeting echoed
from the transmitter; a high-speed bird's call sliding into
the ultrasonic. "Hello!" she called again.

Minutes passed before the dolphins came to investi-
gate. They rolled past us, surprisingly large, alarmingly
large, their skin looking slick and muscled in the uncertain
light. A large one swam within a meter of us, turning at
the last moment so that the white of his belly curved past
us like a wall. I could see the dark eye rotate to follow me
as he passed. One stroke of his wide fluke kicked up a tur-
bulence strong enough to convince me of the animal's
power.

"Hello," called Siri but the swift form faded into distant haze and there was a sudden silence. Siri clicked off
the translator. "Do you want to talk to them?" she asked.

"Sure." I was dubious. More than three centuries of effort had not raised much of a dialogue between man and
sea-mammal. Mike had once told me that the thought
structures of Old Earth's two groups of orphans were too
different, the referents too few. One pre-Hegira expert had

written that speaking to a dolphin or porpoise was about as rewarding as speaking to a one-year-old human infant. Both sides usually enjoyed the exchange and there was a simulacrum of conversation, but neither party would come away the more knowledgeable. Siri switched the translator disk back on. "Hello," I said.

There was a final minute of silence and then our earphones were buzzing while the sea echoed shrill ululations.

distance/no-fluke/hello-tone?/current pulse/circle me/ funny?

"What the hell?" I asked Siri and the translator trilled out my question. Siri was grinning under her osmosis mask.

I tried again. "Hello! Greetings from ... uh ... the surface. How are you?"

The large male ... I assumed it to be a male ... curved in toward us like a torpedo. He arch-kicked his way through the water ten times faster than I could have swum even if I had remembered to don flippers that morning. For a second I thought he was going to ram us and I raised my knees and clung tightly to the keelroot. Then he was past us, climbing for air, while Siri and I reeled from his turbulent wake and the high tones of his shout.

no-fluke/no-feed/no-swim/no-play/no-fun.

Siri switched off the translator and floated closer. She lightly grasped my shoulders while I held onto the keelroot with my right hand. Our legs touched as we drifted through the warm water. A school of tiny, crimson warriorfish flickered above us while the dark shapes of the dolphins circled further out.

"Had enough?" she asked. Her hand was flat on my chest.

"One more try," I said. Siri nodded and twisted the disk to life. The current pushed us together again. She slid her arm around me.

"Why do you herd the islands?" I asked the bottle-nosed shapes circling in the dappled light. "How does it benefit you to stay with the isles?"

sounding now/old songs/deep water/no-Great Voices/ no-Shark/old songs/new songs.

Siri's body lay along the length of me now. Her left arm tightened around me. "Great Voices were the whales," she whispered. Her hair fanned out in streamers. Her right hand moved down and seemed surprised at what it found.

"Do you miss the Great Voices?" I asked the shadows. There was no response. Siri slid her legs around my hips. The surface was a churning bowl of light forty meters above us.

"What do you miss most of Old Earth's oceans?" I asked. With my left arm I pulled Siri closer, slid my hand down along the curve of her back to where her buttocks rose to meet my palm, and held her tight. To the circling dolphins we must have appeared a single creature. Siri lifted herself against me and we became a single creature.

The translator disk had twisted around so it trailed over Siri's shoulder. I reached to shut it off but paused as the answer to my question buzzed urgently in our ears.

miss Shark/miss Shark/miss Shark/miss Shark/Shark/ Shark/Shark

I turned off the disk and shook my head. I did not understand. There was so much I did not understand. I closed my eyes as Siri and I moved gently to the rhythms of the current and ourselves while the dolphins swam nearby and the cadence of their calls took on the sad, slow trilling of an old lament.

I sit here in the sunlight and wait. Now that I have made my decision, I wonder if it is what Siri wanted all along.

The tomb is a white glare behind me. The sunlight touches my skin. I can hear a low murmur from the restless crowd on the hillside. Several of the council members are conferring with Donel. Soon he will climb the slope to urge me on. The farcaster ceremonies cannot wait for me.

Is this what you wanted, Siri?"

I desperately want to talk to her now. I want to ask her who it was who so deftly crafted and shaped the legend that was our love.

Was it you, Siri? Could a not-quite sixteen-year-old have planned so far ahead?

Surf breaks against the lavastone seawall. I can hear

the bells ringing as the small boats bob at anchorage. I sit
in the sunlight and wait.

Where were you when I awoke that first time, Siri?

Somewhere to the south a Thomas Hawk screams.
There is no other answer.

Siri and I came down out of the hills and returned to
the Festival just before sunrise of the second day. For a
night and a day we had roamed the hills, eaten with
strangers in pavilions of orange silk, bathed together in the
icy waters of the Shree, and danced to the music which
never ceased going out to the endless file of passing isles.
We were hungry. I had awakened at sunset to find Siri
gone. She returned before the moon of Maui-Covenant
rose. She told me that her parents had gone off with
friends for several days on a slow-moving houseboat.
They had left the family skimmer in Firstsite. Now we
worked our way from dance to dance, bonfire to bonfire,
back to the center of the city. We planned to fly west to
her family estate near Fevarone.

It was very late but Firstsite Common still had its
share of revelers. I was very happy. I was nineteen and I
was in love and the .93 gravity of Maui-Covenant seemed
much less to me. I could have flown had I wished. I could
have done anything.

We had stopped at a booth and bought fried dough and
mugs of black coffee. Suddenly a thought struck me. I
asked, "How did you know I was a Shipman?"

"Hush, friend Merin. Eat your poor breakfast. When
we get to the villa, I will fix a true meal to break our fast."

"No, I'm serious," I said and wiped grease off my chin
with the sleeve of my less-than-clean harlequin's costume.
"This morning you said that you knew right away last
night that I was from the ship. Why was that? Was it my
accent? My costume? Mike and I saw other fellows
dressed like this."

Siri laughed and brushed back her hair. "Just be glad
it was I who spied you out, Merin my love. Had it been
my Uncle Gresham or his friends it would have meant
trouble."

"Oh? Why is that?" I picked up one more fried ring and Siri paid for it. I followed her through the thinning crowd. Despite the motion and the music all about, I felt weariness beginning to work on me.

"They are Separatists," said Siri. "Uncle Gresham recently gave a speech before the All Thing urging that we fight rather than agree to be swallowed into your Hegemony. He said that we should destroy your farcaster device before it destroys us."

"Oh?" I said. "Did he say how he was going to do that? The last I heard you folks had no craft to get offworld in."

"Nay, nor for the past fifty years have we," said Siri. "But it shows how irrational the Separatists can be."

I nodded. Shipmaster Singh and Councillor Halmyn had briefed us on the so-called Separatists of Maui-Covenant. "The usual coalition of colonial jingoists and throwbacks," Singh had said. "Another reason we go slowly and develop the world's trade potential before finishing the farcaster. The worldweb doesn't need these ya-hoos coming in prematurely. And groups like the Separatists are another reason to keep you crew and construction workers the hell away from the groundlings."

"Where is your skimmer?" I asked. The Common was emptying quickly. Most of the bands had packed up their instruments for the night. Gaily costumed heaps lay snoring on the grass or cobblestones amid the litter and unlit lanterns. Only a few enclaves of merriment remained, groups dancing slowly to a lone guitar or singing drunkenly to themselves. I saw Mike Osho at once, a patchworked fool, his mask long gone, a girl on either arm. He was trying to teach the hora to a rapt but inept circle of admirers. One of the troupe would stumble and they would all fall down. Mike would flog them to their feet among general laughter and they would start again, hopping clumsily to his basso-profundo chant.

"There it is," said Siri and pointed to a short line of skimmers parked behind the Common Hall. I nodded and waved to Mike but he was too busy hanging on to his two ladies to notice me. Siri and I had crossed the square and were in the shadows of the old building when the shout went up.

"Shipman! Turn around, you Hegemony son-of-a-bitch."

I froze and then wheeled around with fists clenched but no one was near me. Six young men had descended the steps from the grandstand and were standing in a semicircle behind Mike. The man in front was tall, slim, and strikingly handsome. He was twenty-five or twenty-six years old and his long blonde curls spilled down on a crimson silk suit that emphasized his physique. In his right hand he carried a meter-long sword that looked to be of tempered steel.

Mike turned slowly. Even from a distance I could see his eyes sobering as he surveyed the situation. The women at his side and a couple of the young men in his group tittered as if something humorous had been said. Mike allowed the inebriated grin to stay on his face. "You address me, sir?" he asked.

"I address you, you Hegemony whore's son," hissed the leader of the group. His handsome face was twisted into a sneer.

"Bertol," whispered Siri. "My cousin. Gresham's younger son." I nodded and stepped out of the shadows. Siri caught my arm.

"That is twice you have referred unkindly to my mother, sir," slurred Mike. "Have she or I offended you in some way? If so, a thousand pardons." Mike bowed so deeply that the bells on his cap almost brushed the ground. Members of his group applauded.

"Your presence offends me, you Hegemony bastard. You stink up our air with your fat carcass."

Mike's eyebrows rose comically. A young man near him in a fish costume waved his hand. "Oh, come on, Bertol. He's just . . ."

"Shut up, Ferick. It is this fat shithead I am speaking to."

"Shithead?" repeated Mike, eyebrows still raised. "I've traveled two hundred light years to be called a fat shithead? It hardly seems worth it." He pivoted gracefully, untangling himself from the women as he did so. I would have joined Mike then but Siri clung tightly to my arm, whispering unheard entreaties. When I was free I saw that Mike was still smiling, still playing the fool. But his left hand was in his baggy shirt pocket.

"Give him your blade, Creg," snapped Bertol. One of the younger men tossed a sword hilt-first to Mike. Mike watched it arc by and clang loudly on the cobblestones.

"You can't be serious," said Mike in a soft voice that was suddenly quite sober. "You cretinous cowturd. Do you really think I'm going to play duel with you just because you get a hard-on acting the hero for these yokels?"

"Pick up the sword," screamed Bertol, "or by God I'll carve you where you stand." He took a quick step forward. The youth's face contorted with fury as he advanced.

"Fuck off," said Mike. In his left hand was the laser pen.

"No!" I yelled and ran into the light. That pen was used by construction workers to scrawl marks on girders of whiskered alloy.

Things happened very quickly then. Bertol took another step and Mike flicked the green beam across him almost casually. The colonist let out a cry and leaped back; a smoking line of black was slashed diagonally across his silk shirtfront. I hesitated. Mike had the setting as low as it could go. Two of Bertol's friends started forward and Mike swung the light across their shins. One dropped to his knees cursing and the other hopped away holding his leg and hooting.

A crowd had gathered. They laughed as Mike swept off his fool's cap in another bow. "I thank you," said Mike. "My mother thanks you."

Siri's cousin strained against his rage. Froths of spittle spilled on his lips and chin. I pushed through the crowd and stepped between Mike and the tall colonist.

"Hey, it's all right," I said. "We're leaving. We're going now."

"Goddamn it, Merin, get out of the way," said Mike.

"It's all right," I said as I turned to him. "I'm with a girl named Siri who has a . . ." Bertol stepped forward and lunged past me with his blade. I wrapped my left arm around his shoulder and flung him back. He tumbled heavily onto the grass.

"Oh, shit," said Mike as he backed up several paces. He looked tired and a little disgusted as he sat down on a stone step. "Aw, *damn*," he said softly. There was a short line of crimson in one of the black patches on the left side of his harlequin costume. As I watched, the narrow slit spilled over and blood ran down across Mike Osho's broad belly.

"Oh, Jesus, Mike." I tore a strip of fabric from my shirt and tried to staunch the flow. I could remember none of the first-aid we'd been taught as midShipmen. I pawed at my wrist but my comlog was not there. We had left them on the *Los Angeles*.

"It's not so bad, Mike," I gasped. "It's just a little cut." The blood flowed down over my hand and wrist.

"It will serve," said Mike. His voice was held taut by a cord of pain. "Damn. A fucking sword. Do you believe it, Merin? Cut down in the prime of my prime by a piece of fucking cutlery out of a fucking one-penny opera. Oh, *damn* that smarts."

"Three-penny opera," I said and changed hands. The rag was soaked.

"You know what your fucking problem is, Merin? You're always sticking your fucking two cents in. Awwwww." Mike's face went white and then gray. He lowered his chin to his chest and breathed deeply. "To *hell* with this, kid. Let's go home, huh?"

I looked over my shoulder. Bertol was slowly moving away with his friends. The rest of the crowd milled around in shock. "Call a doctor!" I screamed. "Get some medics up here!" Two men ran down the street. There was no sign of Siri.

"Wait a minute! Wait a minute!" said Mike in a stronger voice, as if he had forgotten something important. "Just a minute," he said and died.

Died. A real death. Brain death. His mouth opened obscenely, his eyes rolled back so only the whites showed, and a minute later the blood ceased pumping from the wound.

For a few mad seconds I cursed the sky. I could see the

L.A. moving across the fading starfield and I knew that I could bring Mike back if I could get him there in a few minutes. The crowd backed away as I screamed and ranted at the stars.

Eventually I turned to Bertol. "You," I said.

The young man had stopped at the far end of the Common. His face was ashen. He stared wordlessly.

"You," I said again. I picked up the laser pen from where it had rolled, clicked the power to maximum, and walked to where Bertol and his friends stood waiting.

Later, through the haze of screams and scorched flesh, I was dimly aware of Siri's skimmer setting down in the crowded square, of dust flying up all around, and of her voice commanding me to join her. We lifted away from the light and madness. The cool wind blew my sweat-soaked hair away from my neck.

"We will go to Fevarone," said Siri. "Bertol was drunk. The Separatists are a small, violent group. There will be no reprisals. You will stay with me until the All Thing holds the inquest."

"No," I said. "There. Land there." I pointed to a spit of land not far from the city.

Siri landed despite her protests. I glanced at the boulder to make sure the backpack was still there and then climbed out of the skimmer. Siri slid across the seat and pulled my head down to hers. "Merin, my love." Her lips were warm and open but I felt nothing. My body felt anaesthetized. I stepped back and waved her away. She brushed her hair back and stared at me from green eyes filled with tears. Then the skimmer lifted, turned, and sped to the south in the early morning light.

Just a minute, I felt like calling. I sat on a rock and gripped my knees as several ragged sobs were torn up out of me. Then I stood and threw the laser pen into the surf below. I tugged out the backpack and dumped the contents on the ground.

The hawking mat was gone.

I sat back down, too drained to laugh or cry or walk away. The sun rose as I sat there. I was still sitting there three hours later when the large, black skimmer from Ship Security set down silently beside me.

• • •

"Father? Father, it is getting late."

I turn to see my son Donel standing behind me. He is
wearing the blue and gold robe of the Hegemony Council.
His bald scalp is flushed and beaded with sweat. Donel is
only 43 but he seems much older to me.

"Please, Father," he says. I nod and rise, brushing off
the grass and dirt. We walk together to the front of the
tomb. The crowd has pressed closer now. Gravel crunches
under their feet as they shift restlessly. "Shall I enter with
you, Father?" Donel asks.

I pause to look at this aging stranger who is my child.
There is a little of Siri or me reflected in him. His face is
friendly, florid, and tense with the excitement of the day.
I can sense in him the open honesty which often takes the
place of intelligence in some people. I cannot help but
compare this balding puppy of a man to Alón—Alón of
the dark curls and silences and sardonic smile. But Alón is
33 years dead, cut down in a stupid battle which had nothing to do with him.

"No," I say. "I'll go in by myself. Thank you, Donel."

He nods and steps back. The pennants snap above the
heads of the straining crowd. I turn my attention to the
tomb.

The entrance is sealed with a palmlock. I have only to
touch it.

During the past few minutes I have developed a fantasy which will save me from both the growing sadness
within and the external series of events which I have initiated. Siri is not dead. In the last stages of her illness she
had called together the doctors and the few technicians left
in the colony and they rebuilt for her one of the ancient hibernation chambers used in their seedship two centuries
earlier. Siri is only sleeping. What is more, the year-long
sleep has somehow restored her youth. When I wake her
she will be the Siri I remember from our early days. We
will walk out into the sunlight together and when the
farcaster doors open we shall be the first through.

"Father?"

"Yes." I step forward and set my hand to the door of

the crypt. There is a whisper of electric motors and the white slab of stone slides back. I bow my head and enter Siri's tomb.

"Damn it, Merin, secure that line before it knocks you overboard. Hurry!" I hurried. The wet rope was hard to coil, harder to tie off. Siri shook her head in disgust and leaned over to tie a bowline knot with one hand.

It was our Fifth Reunion. I had been three months too late for her birthday but more than five thousand other people had made it to the celebration. The President of the All Thing had wished her well in a forty-minute speech. A poet read his most recent verses to the Love Cycle Sonnets. The Hegemony Ambassador had presented her with a scroll and a new ship, a small submersible powered by the first fusion-cells to be allowed on Maui-Covenant.

Siri had eighteen other ships. Twelve belonged to her fleet of swift catamarans that plied their trade between the wandering Archipelago and the Home Islands. Two were beautiful racing yachts that were used only twice a year to win the Founder's Regatta and the Covenant Criterium. The other four craft were ancient fishing boats, homely and awkward, well-maintained but little more than scows.

Siri had nineteen ships but we were on a fishing boat—the *Ginnie Paul*. For the past eight days we had fished the shelf of the Equatorial Shallows; a crew of two, casting and pulling nets, wading knee-deep through stinking fish and crunching trilobites, wallowing over every wave, casting and pulling nets, keeping watch, and sleeping like exhausted children during our brief rest periods. I was not quite 23. I thought I was used to heavy labor aboard the *L.A.* and it was my custom to put in an hour of exercise in the 1.3-gee pod every second shift, but now my arms and back ached from the strain and my hands were blistered between the callouses. Siri had just turned 70.

"Merin, go forward and reef the foresail. Do the same for the jib and then go below to see to the sandwiches. Plenty of mustard."

I nodded and went forward. For a day and a half we had been playing hide and seek with a storm; sailing be-

fore it when we could, turning about and accepting its
punishment when we had to. At first it had been exciting,
a welcome respite from the endless casting and pulling and
mending. But after the first few hours the adrenaline rush
faded to be replaced by constant nausea, fatigue, and a terrible tiredness. The seas did not relent. The waves grew to
six meters and higher. The *Ginnie Paul* wallowed like the
broad-beamed matron she was. Everything was wet. My
skin was soaked under three layers of rain gear. For Siri it
was a long-awaited vacation.

"This is nothing," she had said during the darkest hour
of the night as waves washed over the deck and smashed
against the scarred plastic of the cockpit. "You should see
it during simoon season."

The clouds still hung low and blended into gray waves
in the distance but the sea was down to a gentle five-foot
chop. I spread mustard across the roast beef sandwiches
and poured steaming coffee into thick, white mugs. It
would have been easier to transport the coffee in zero-gee
without spilling it than to get it up the pitching shaft of the
companionway. Siri accepted her depleted cup without
commenting. We sat in silence for a bit, appreciating the
food and the tongue-scalding warmth of the coffee. I took
the wheel when Siri went below to refill our mugs. The
gray day was dimming almost imperceptibly into night.

"Merin," she said after handing me my mug and taking
a seat on the long, cushioned bench which encircled the
cockpit, "what will happen after they open the farcaster?"

I was surprised by the question. We rarely talked about
the time when Maui-Covenant would join the Hegemony. I
glanced over at Siri and was shocked by the countenance revealed by the harsh, upward glare of the instrument lights.
Siri's face showed a hidden mosaic of seams and shadows
which would soon replace the pale, translucent complexion
of the woman I had known. Her beautiful, green eyes were
hidden in wells of darkness and the cruel light turned her
cheekbones into knife-edges against brittle parchment. Siri's
gray hair was cut short and now it stuck out in damp spikes.
I could see the tendoned cords under the loose skin of her
neck and wrists. Age was laying claim to Siri.

"What do you mean?" I asked.

"What will happen after they open the farcaster?"

"You know what the Council says." I spoke loudly, as if she were hard of hearing. "It will open a new era of trade and technology for Maui-Covenant. You won't be restricted to one little world any longer. When you become citizens, everyone will be entitled to use the farcaster doors."

"Yes," said Siri. Her voice was weary. "I have heard all of that, Merin. But what will *happen*? Who will be the first through to us?"

I shrugged. "More diplomats, I suppose. Cultural contact specialists. Anthropologists. Ethnologists. Marine biologists."

"And then?"

I paused. It was dark out. The sea was almost gentle. Our running lights glowed red and green against the night. I felt the same anxiety I had known two days earlier when the wall of storm appeared on the horizon. I said, "And then will come the missionaries. The petroleum geologists. The sea farmers. The developers."

Siri sipped at her coffee. "I would have thought your Hegemony was far beyond a petroleum economy."

I laughed and locked the wheel in. "Nobody gets beyond a petroleum economy. Not while the petroleum's there. We don't burn it, if that's what you mean. But it's still essential for the production of plastics, synthetics, food base, and keroids. Two hundred billion people use a lot of plastic."

"And Maui-Covenant has oil?"

"Oh, yes," I said. There was no more laughter in me. "There are billions of barrels reservoired under the Equatorial Shallows alone."

"How will they get it, Merin? Platforms?"

"Yeah. Platforms. Submersibles. Sub-sea colonies with tailored workers brought in from Ouster or the Tau Ceti Cities."

"And the motile isles?" asked Siri. "They must return each year to the shallows to feed on the bluekelp there and to reproduce. What will become of the isles?"

I shrugged again. I had drunk too much coffee and it left a bitter taste in my mouth. "I don't know," I said.

"They haven't told the crew much. But back on our first trip out, Mike heard that they planned to develop as many of the isles as they can, so some will be protected."

"Developed?" Siri's voice showed surprise for the first time. "How can they develop the isles? Even the Founder's Families must ask permission of the Sea Folk to build our treehouse retreats there."

I smiled at Siri's use of the local term for the dolphins. The Maui-Covenant colonists were such children when it came to their damned dolphins. "The plans are all set," I said. "There are 128,573 motile isles big enough to build a dwelling on. Leases to those have long since been sold. The smaller isles will be broken up, I suppose. The Home Islands will be developed for recreation purposes."

"Recreation purposes," echoed Siri. "How many people from the Hegemony will use the farcaster to come here . . . for recreation purposes?"

"At first, you mean?" I asked. "Just a few thousand the first year. As long as the only door is on Island 241 . . . the Trade Center . . . it will be limited. Perhaps 50,000 the second year when Firstsite gets its door. It'll be quite the luxury tour. Always is after a seed colony is first opened to the web."

"And later?"

"After the five-year probation? There will be thousands of doors, of course. I would imagine that there will be twenty or thirty million new residents coming through during the first year of full citizenship."

"Twenty or thirty million," said Siri. The light from the compass stand illuminated her lined face from below. There was still a beauty there. But there was no anger or shock. I had expected both.

"But you'll be citizens then yourself," I said. "Free to step anywhere in the worldweb. There will be sixteen new worlds to choose from. Probably more by then."

"Yes," said Siri and set aside her empty mug. A fine rain streaked the glass around us. The crude radar screen set in its hand-carved frame showed the seas empty, the storm past. "Is it true, Merin, that people in the Hegemony have their homes on a dozen worlds? One house, I mean, with windows facing out on a dozen skies?"

"Sure," I said. "But not many people. Only the rich can afford multi-world residences like that."

Siri smiled and set her hand on my knee. The back of her hand was mottled and blue-veined. "But you are very rich, are you not, Shipman?"

I looked away. "Not yet I'm not."

"Ah, but soon, Merin, soon. How long for you, my love? Less than two weeks here and then the voyage back to your Hegemony. Five months more of your time to bring the last components back, a few weeks to finish, and then you step home a rich man. *Step* two hundred empty light years home. What a strange thought . . . but where was I? That is how long? Less than a standard year."

"Ten months," I said. "Three hundred and six standard days. Three hundred fourteen of yours. Nine hundred eighteen shifts."

"And then your exile will be over."

"Yes."

"And you will be twenty-four years old and very rich."

"Yes."

"I'm tired, Merin. I want to sleep now."

We programmed the tiller, set the collision alarm, and went below. The wind had risen some and the old vessel wallowed from wavecrest to trough with every swell. We undressed in the dim light of the swinging lamp. I was first in the bunk and under the covers. It was the first time Siri and I had shared a sleep period. Remembering our last Reunion and her shyness at the villa, I expected her to douse the light. Instead she stood a minute, nude in the chill air, thin arms calmly at her sides.

Time had claimed Siri but had not ravaged her. Gravity had done its inevitable work on her breasts and buttocks and she was much thinner. I stared at the gaunt outlines of ribs and breastbone and remembered the sixteen-year-old girl with baby fat and skin like warm velvet. In the cold light of the swinging lamp I stared at Siri's sagging flesh and remembered moonlight on budding breasts. Yet somehow, strangely, inexplicably, it was the *same* Siri who stood before me now.

"Move over, Merin." She slipped into the bunk beside me. The sheets were cool against our skin, the rough blanket welcome. I turned off the light. The little ship swayed to the regular rhythm of the sea's breathing. I could hear the sympathetic creak of masts and rigging. In the morning we would be casting and pulling and mending but now there was time to sleep. I began to doze to the sound of waves against wood.

"Merin?"

"Yes?"

"What would happen if the Separatists attacked the Hegemony tourists or the new residents?"

"I thought the Separatists had all been carted off to the isles."

"They have been. But what if they resisted?"

"The Hegemony would send in troops who could kick the shit out of the Separatists."

"What if the farcaster itself were attacked . . . destroyed before it was operational?"

"Impossible."

"Yes, I know, but what if it were?"

"Then the *Los Angeles* would return nine months later with Hegemony troops who would proceed to kick the shit out of the Separatists . . . and anyone else on Maui-Covenant who got in their way."

"Nine months shiptime," said Siri. "Eleven years of our time."

"But inevitable either way," I said. "Let's talk about something else."

"All right," said Siri but we did not speak. I listened to the creak and sigh of the ship. Siri had nestled in the hollow of my arm. Her head was on my shoulder and her breathing was so deep and regular that I thought her to be asleep. I was almost asleep myself when her warm hand slid up my leg and lightly cupped me. I startled even as I began to stir and stiffen. Siri whispered an answer to my unasked question. "No, Merin, one is never really too old. At least not too old to want the warmth and closeness. You decide, my love. I will be content either way."

I decided. Towards the dawn we slept.

· · ·

The tomb is empty.

"Donel, come in here!"

He bustled in, robes rustling in the hollow emptiness. The tomb *is* empty. There is no hibernation chamber—I did not truly expect there to be one—but neither is there sarcophagus nor coffin. A bright bulb illuminates the white interior. "What the hell is this, Donel? I thought this was Siri's tomb."

"It is, Father."

"Where is she interred? Under the floor for Chrissake?"

Donel mops at his brow. I remember that it is his mother I am speaking of. I also remember that he has had almost two years to accustom himself to the idea of her death.

"No one told you?" he asks.

"Told me what?" The anger and confusion is already ebbing. "I was rushed here from the dropship station and told that I was to visit Siri's tomb before the farcaster opening. What?"

"Mother was cremated as per her instructions. Her ashes were spread on the Great South Sea from the highest platform of the family isle."

"Then why this . . . *crypt*?" I watch what I say. Donel is sensitive.

He mops his brow again and glances toward the door. We are shielded from the view of the crowd but we are far behind schedule. Already the other members of the Council have had to hurry down the hill to join the other dignitaries on the bandstand. My slow grief this day has been worse than bad timing—it has turned into bad theater.

"Mother left instructions. They were carried out." He touches a panel on the inner wall and it slides up to reveal a small niche containing a metal box. My name is on it.

"What is that?"

Donel shakes his head. "Personal items Mother left for you. Only Magritte knew the details and she died last winter without telling anyone."

"All right," I say. "Thank you. I'll be out in a moment."

Donel glances at his chronometer. "The ceremony

begins in eight minutes. They will activate the farcaster in twenty minutes."

"I know," I say. I *do* know. Part of me knows precisely how much time is left. "I'll be out in a moment."

Donel hesitates and then departs. I close the door behind him with a touch of my palm. The metal box is surprisingly heavy. I set it on the stone floor and crouch beside it. A smaller palmlock gives me access. The lid clicks open and I peer into the container.

"Well, I'll be damned," I say softly. I do not know what I expected—artifacts perhaps, nostalgic mementos of our hundred and three days together—perhaps a pressed flower from some forgotten offering or the frenchhorn conch we dove for off Fevarone. But there are no mementos—not as such.

The box holds a small Steiner-Ginn handlaser, one of the most powerful projection weapons ever made. The accumulator is attached by a powerlead to a small fusion-cell that Siri must have cannibalized from her new submersible. Also attached to the fusion-cell is an ancient comlog, an antique with a solid state interior and a liquid crystal diskey. The charge indicator glows green.

There are two other objects in the box. One is the translator medallion we had used so long ago. The final object makes me smile ruefully.

"Why you little bitch," I say softly. I know now where Siri had been when I awoke alone that first time in the hills above Firstsite. I shake my head and smile again. "You dear, conniving, little bitch." There, rolled carefully, powerleads correctly attached, lies the hawking mat which Mike Osho had purchased for thirty marks in Carvnal Market.

I leave the hawking mat there, disconnect the comlog, and lift it out. The device is ancient, possibly dating back to pre-Hegira times. I can imagine it being handed down in Siri's family from the seedship generation. I sit cross-legged on the cold stone and thumb the diskey. The light in the crypt fades and suddenly Siri is there before me.

•   •   •

They did not throw me off the ship when Mike died.
They could have but they did not. They did not leave me
to the mercy of provincial justice on Maui-Covenant. They
could have but they chose not to. For two days I was held
in Security and questioned, once by Shipmaster Singh
himself. Then they let me return to duty. For the four
months of the long leap back I tortured myself with the
memory of Mike's murder. I knew that in my clumsy way
I had helped to murder him. I put in my shifts, dreamed
my sweaty nightmares, and wondered if they would dismiss me when we reached the web. They could have told
me but they chose not to.

They did not dismiss me. I was to have my normal
leave in the web but could take no off-Ship R-and-R while
in the Maui-Covenant system. In addition, there was a
written reprimand and temporary reduction in rank. That
was what Mike's life had been worth—a reprimand and reduction in rank.

I took my three-week leave with the rest of the crew
but unlike the others I did not plan to return. I farcast to
Esperance and made the classic Shipman's mistake of trying to visit family. Two days in the crowded residential
hive was enough and I stepped to Lusus and took my pleasure in three days of whoring on the *Rue des Chats*. When
my mood turned darker I 'cast to Ouster and lost most of
my ready marks betting on the bloody Shrike fights there.

Finally I found myself farcasting to Homesystem Station and taking the two-day pilgrim shuttle down to Hellas
Basin. I had never been to Homesystem or Mars before
and I never plan to return, but the ten days I spent there,
alone and wandering the dusty, haunted corridors of the
Monastery, served to send me back to the Ship. Back to
Siri.

Occasionally I would leave the red-stoned maze of the
megalith and, clad only in skinsuit and mask, stand on one
of the uncounted thousands of stone balconies and stare
skyward at the pale gray star which had once been Old
Earth. Sometimes then I thought of the brave and stupid
idealists heading out into the great dark in their slow and
leaking ships, carrying embryos and ideologies with equal
faith and care. But most times I did not try to think. Most

times I simply stood in the purple night and let Siri come
to me. There in the Master's Rock, where perfect satori
had eluded so many much more worthy pilgrims, I
achieved it through the memory of a not-quite sixteen-
year-old womanchild's body lying next to mine while
moonlight spilled from a Thomas Hawk's wings.

When the *Los Angeles* spun back up to a quantum
state, I went with her. Four months later I was content to
pull my shift with the construction crew, plug into my
usual stims, and sleep my R-and-R away. Then Singh
came to me. "You're going down," he said. I did not understand. "In the past eleven years the groundlings have
turned your screw-up with Osho into a goddamned legend," said Singh. "There's an entire cultural mythos built
around your little roll in the hay with that colonial girl."

"What are you talking about?" I asked. I was irritated
and frightened. "Are you throwing me off the Ship?"

Singh grunted and brushed idly at his right eyebrow.
The gold bracelet on his wrist caught the light. "Did you
know that your groundside girlfriend was a member of
their original Shipmaster's family?" he asked. "Sort of the
local equivalent of royalty."

"Siri?" I said stupidly.

"She told the story of your . . . what shall we call it . . .
your love affair to everyone she could. Poems have been
written about it. There was a play performed every year on
one of those floating islands of theirs. Evidently there's an
entire cult that's sprung up. You seem to be at the center
of a romantic legend that's caught the imagination of most
of the yokels on the planet."

"Are you throwing me off the Ship?"

"Don't be stupid, Aspic," growled Singh. "You'll
spend your three weeks of leave groundside. The Hegemony needs this planet. The Ambassador says that we
need the cooperation of the groundlings until the
farcaster's operational and we get some occupation troops
through. If this half-assed, star-crossed-lovers myth can
smooth things for us during the next few trips, fine. The
experts say you'll do the Hegemony more good down
there than up here. We'll see."

"Siri?" I said again.

"Get your gear," ordered Singh. "You're going down."

The world was waiting. Crowds were cheering. Siri was waving. We left the harbor in a yellow catamaran and sailed south-southeast, bound for the Archipelago and her family isle.

"Hello, Merin." Siri floats in the darkness of her tomb. The holo is not perfect; a haziness mars the edges. But it is Siri—Siri as I last saw her, gray hair shorn rather than cut, head high, face sharpened with shadows. "Hello, Merin my love."

"Hello, Siri," I say. The tomb door is closed.

"I am sorry I cannot share our Sixth Reunion, Merin. I looked forward to it." Siri pauses and looks down at her hands. The image flickers slightly as dust motes float through her form. "I had carefully planned what to say here," she goes on. "How to say it. Arguments to be pled. Instructions to be given. But I know now how useless that would have been. Either I have said it already and you have heard or there is nothing left to say and silence would best suit the moment."

Siri's voice had grown even more beautiful with age. There is a fullness and calmness there which can come only from knowing pain. Siri moves her hands and they disappear beyond the border of the projection. "Merin my love, how strange our days apart and together have been. How beautifully absurd the myth that bound us. My days were but heartbeats to you. I hated you for that. You were the mirror that would not lie. If you could have seen your face at the beginning of each Reunion! The least you could have done was to hide your shock . . . that, at least, you could have done for me.

"But through your clumsy naïveté there has always been . . . what? . . . something, Merin. There is something there that belies the callowness and thoughtless egotism which you wear so well. A caring, perhaps. A *respect* for caring, if nothing else.

"Therein lay the slim basis for so much hope through these long years, Merin. Even through your Hive-born and Ship-bred shallowness there was that sense of caring. I believe ... no, I *know* that you sometimes cared for me. If you could care for me, you could care for our world. In our brief hours of sharing, you might find an understanding. Therein lay our hope. Therein lay the only possible source of our salvation.

"I confess that I did not plan this when I stole your silly flying carpet. I don't know now *what* I was thinking and planning when I let you lead me from the Festival that first time. Of kidnapping you, perhaps. Of delaying and seducing you until Uncle Gresham could use any information you might have. Perhaps I dreamed even then of your joining us, of both of us swimming free with the Sea Folk and protecting the Covenant together. Then Bertol ruined everything ...

"I miss you, Merin. Tonight I will go down to the harbor and watch the stars awhile and think of you. It will not be the first time I have done that.

"I'm sorry that I will not be waiting for you this time, Merin. But our world will be waiting. The seas that I listen to tonight will greet you with the same song. Preserving that song is not such an impossible idea, my love. They can't have this world without controlling the isles and the Sea Folk control the isles.

"I've kept this diary since I was thirteen. It has hundreds of entries. By the time you see this, they will all have been erased except the few that follow. Our love was not all myth and machination. We were good friends and some of our times together were sweet, were they not?

"Stay well, Merin. Stay well."

I shut off the comlog and sit in silence for a minute. The crowd sounds are barely audible through the thick walls of the tomb. I take a breath and thumb the diskey.

Siri appears. She is in her late forties. I know immediately the day and place she recorded this image. I remember the cloak she wears, the eelstone pendant at her neck, and the strand of hair which has escaped her barrette and even now falls across her cheek. I remember everything about that day. It was the last day of our Third Reunion and we were with friends on the heights above South Tern.

Donel was ten and we were trying to convince him to slide on the snowfield with us. He was crying. Siri turned away from us even before the skimmer settled. When Magritte stepped out we knew from Siri's face that something had happened.

The same face stares at me now. She brushes absently at the unruly strand of hair. Her eyes are red but her voice is controlled. "Merin, they killed our son today. Alón was twenty-one and they killed him. You were so confused today, Merin. 'How could such a mistake have happened?' you kept repeating. You did not really know our son but I could see the loss in your face when we heard. Merin, it was not an accident. If nothing else survives, no other record, if you never understand why I allowed a sentimental myth to rule my life, let this be known—*it was not an accident that killed Alón.* He was with the Separatists when the Council police arrived. Even then he could have escaped. We had prepared an alibi together. The police would have believed his story. He chose to stay.

"Today, Merin, you were impressed with what I said to the crowd . . . the mob . . . at the embassy. Know this, Shipman—when I said, 'Now is not the time to show your anger and your hatred,' that is precisely what I meant. No more, no less. Today is not the time. But the day will come. It will surely come. The Covenant was not taken lightly in those final days, Merin. It is not taken lightly now. Those who have forgotten will be surprised when the day comes but it will surely come.

The image fades to another and in the split second of overlap the face of a 26-year-old Siri appears superimposed on the older woman's features. "Merin, I am pregnant. I'm so glad. You've been gone five weeks now and I *miss* you. Ten *years* you'll be gone. More than that. Merin, why didn't you think to invite me to go with you? I could not have gone, but I would have loved it if you had just *invited* me. But I'm pregnant, Merin. The doctors say that it will be a boy. I will tell him about you, my love. Perhaps someday you and he will sail in the Archipelago and listen to the songs of the Sea Folk as you and

I have done these past few weeks. Perhaps you'll understand them by then. Merin, I *miss* you. Please hurry back."

The holographic image shimmers and shifts. The
16-year-old girl is red-faced. Her long hair cascades over
bare shoulders and a white nightgown. She speaks in a
rush, racing tears. "Shipman Merin Aspic, I'm sorry about
your friend—I really am—but you left without even saying *good-bye*. I had such plans about how you would help
us . . . how you and I . . . you didn't even say good-bye.
I don't care *what* happens to you. I hope you go back to
your stinking, crowded Hegemony hives and rot for all I
care. In fact, Merin Aspic, I wouldn't want to see you
again even if they paid me. *Good-bye*."

She turns her back before the projection fades. It is
dark in the tomb now but the audio continues for a second.
There is a soft chuckle and Siri's voice—I cannot tell the
age—comes one last time. "Adieu, Merin, Adieu."

"Adieu," I say and thumb the diskey off.

The crowd parts as I emerge blinking from the tomb.
My poor timing has ruined the drama of the event and
now the smile on my face incites angry whispers. Loud-
speakers carry the rhetoric of the official ceremony even to
our hilltop. ". . . beginning a new era of cooperation,"
echoes the rich voice of the Ambassador.

I set the box on the grass and remove the hawking mat.
The crowd presses forward to see as I unroll the carpet.
The tapestry is faded but the flight threads gleam like new
copper. I sit in the center of the mat and slide the heavy
box on behind me.

". . . and more will follow until space and time will
cease to be obstacles."

The crowd moves back as I tap the flight design and
the hawking mat rises four meters into the air. Now I can
see beyond the roof of the tomb. The islands are returning
to form the Equatorial Archipelago. I can see them, hundreds of them, borne up out of the hungry south by gentle
winds.

"So it is with great pleasure that I close this circuit and

welcome you, the colony of Maui-Covenant, into the community of the Hegemony of Man."

The thin thread of the ceremonial com-laser pulses to the zenith. There is a spattering of applause and the band begins playing. I squint skyward just in time to see a new star being born. Part of me knows to the microsecond what has just occurred.

For a few microseconds the farcaster had been functional. For a few microseconds time and space *had* ceased to be obstacles. Then the massive tidal pull of the artificial singularity triggered the thermite charge I had placed on the outer containment sphere. That tiny explosion had not been visible but a second later the expanding Schwarzschild radius is eating its shell, swallowing thirty-six thousand tons of fragile dodecahedron, and growing quickly to gobble several thousand kilometers of space around it. And *that* is visible—magnificently visible—as a miniature nova flares whitely in the clear blue sky.

The band stops playing. People scream and run for cover. There is no reason to. There is a burst of X-rays tunneling out as the farcaster continues to collapse into itself, but not enough to cause harm through Maui-Covenant's generous atmosphere. A second streak of plasma becomes visible as the *Los Angeles* puts more distance between itself and the rapidly decaying little black hole. The winds rise and the seas are choppier. There will be strange tides tonight.

I want to say something profound but I can think of nothing. Besides, the crowd is in no mood to listen. I tell myself that I can hear some cheers mixed in with the screams and shouts.

I tap at the flight designs and the hawking mat speeds out over the cliff and above the harbor. A Thomas Hawk lazing on mid-day thermals flaps in panic at my approach.

"Let them come!" I shout at the fleeing hawk. "Let them come! I'll be thirty-five and not alone and let them come if they dare!" I drop my fist and laugh. The wind is blowing my hair and cooling the sweat on my chest and arms.

Cooler now, I take a sighting and set my course for the most distant of the isles. I look forward to meeting the others. Even more, I look forward to talking to the Sea Folk and telling them that it is time for the Shark to come at last to the seas of Maui-Covenant.

Later, when the battles are won and the world is theirs, I will tell them about her. I will sing to them of Siri.

Introduction to "Metastasis"

It's odd to think that within the walls of concentration camps such as Auschwitz and even in camps such as Treblinka and Sobibor where extermination of human beings was the *only* official activity, wives of the commandants kept gardens, children of the high-ranking German officers attended classes and competed at sports, musicians played Mozart and Bach and Mahler at dinner parties, wives worried about their figures while their husbands checked for receding hairlines . . . all the banal preoccupations which constitute the human condition that we share today.

While all around them, humans were being starved and beaten and gassed and fed to the ovens. The ash that had been human flesh an hour before now lightly dusted the roses in the gardens. Barbed wire separated the boys' soccer fields from the killing fields. The music of Mozart carried to the barracks where former musicians and composers and conductors lay shivering with the other human skeletons there.

In the commandant's comfortable home, the administrator checked his hairline in the mirror and the administrator's wife looked in her mirror, pirouetted, pouted, and decided that she would have one less torte for dessert that night.

Did the mirrors reflect human beings?

Of course they did. People can adapt to almost anything.

During the days of the Black Death in the 13th Century, when entire villages were wiped out, when the death carts rumbled through the streets at night with the cry "Bring out your dead!" until there was no one left to bury them, there was much preoccupation with the macabre, many flirtations with death—skull-masked revelers danced nightly in the burial catacombs of Paris—but overall, the small wheel of daily life creaked along as usual.

Are we doing the same today?

I always flinch when I hear someone use the word *decimate* to mean "wipe out," as in, "The Sioux decimated Custer's men."

The word actually comes from the Latin and the action it implies from the Romans. When someone in an occupied province defied the Roman governor or killed a Roman soldier, the Romans would hold a lottery and kill every tenth person. *(Decimate* as in *Decimat(us)* past participle of *decimare.)*

The Jews weren't decimated in Poland and Europe; they were almost wiped out.

The people of 13th Century Europe weren't decimated; a fourth to half of the entire population was wiped out. And the plague returned—again and again. The people could not see the plague bacillus so in a sense it did not exist for them. They saw only the results piled high in the death carts each night, staring eyes and exposed teeth illuminated by the light of torches.

We're not being decimated by cancer in the latter part of the 20th Century—the odds are worse than that. The lottery calls one in six. Or perhaps it's already one in five. (It's been getting worse for a long time.)

Meanwhile, we grow our gardens, play our games, listen to our music, and look in our mirrors.

We just try not to see too much.

Metastasis

On the day Louis Steig received a call from his sister saying that their mother had collapsed and been admitted to a Denver hospital with a diagnosis of cancer, he promptly jumped into his Camaro, headed for Denver at high speed, hit a patch of black ice on the Boulder Turnpike, flipped his car seven times, and ended up in a coma from a fractured skull and a severe concussion. He was unconscious for nine days. When he awoke he was told that a minute sliver of bone had actually penetrated the left frontal lobe of his brain. He remained hospitalized for eighteen more days—not even in the same hospital as his mother—and when he left it was with a headache worse than anything he had ever imagined, blurred vision, word from the doctors that there was a serious chance that some brain damage had been suffered, and news from his sister that their mother's cancer was terminal and in its final stages.

The worst had not yet begun.

It was three more days before Louis was able to visit his mother. His headaches remained and his vision retained a slightly blurred quality—as with a television channel poorly tuned—but the bouts of blinding pain and uncontrolled vomiting had passed. His sister Lee drove

and his fiancée Debbie accompanied him on the twenty
mile ride from Boulder to Denver General Hospital.

"She sleeps most of the time but it's mostly the drugs,"
said Lee. "They keep her heavily sedated. She probably
won't recognize you even if she is awake."

"I understand," said Louis.

"The doctors say that she must have felt the lump . . .
understood what the pain meant . . . for at least a year. If
she had only . . . It would have meant losing her breast
even then, probably both of them, but they might have
been able to . . ." Lee took a deep breath. "I was with her
all morning. I just can't . . . can't go back up there again
today, Louis. I hope you understand."

"Yes," said Louis.

"Do you want me to go in with you?" asked Debbie.

"No," said Louis.

Louis sat holding his mother's hand for almost an
hour. It seemed to him that the sleeping woman on the bed
was a stranger. Even through the slight blurring of his
sight, he knew that she looked twenty years older than the
person he had known; her skin was gray and sallow, her
hands were heavily veined and bruised from IVs, her arms
lacked any muscle tone, and her body under the hospital
gown looked shrunken and concave. A bad smell surrounded her. Louis stayed thirty minutes beyond the end of
visiting hours and left only when his headaches threatened
to return in full force. His mother remained asleep. Louis
squeezed the rough hand, kissed her on the forehead, and
rose to go.

He was almost out of the room when he glanced at the
mirror and saw movement. His mother continued to sleep
but someone was sitting in the chair Louis had just vacated. He wheeled around.

The chair was empty.

Louis's headache flared like the thrust of a heated wire
behind his left eye. He turned back to the mirror, moving
his head slowly so as not to exacerbate the pain and vertigo. The image in the mirror was more clear than his vision had been for days.

Something was sitting in the chair he had just vacated.

Louis blinked and moved closer to the wall mirror, squinting slightly to resolve the image. The figure on the chair was somewhat misty, slightly diffuse against a more focused background, but there was no denying the reality and solidity of it. At first Louis thought it was a child—the form was small and frail, the size of an emaciated ten-year-old—but then he leaned closer to the mirror, squinted through the haze of his headache, and all thoughts of children fled.

The small figure leaning over his mother had a large, shaven head perched on a thin neck and even thinner body. Its skin was white—not flesh white but paper white, fish-belly white—and the arms were skin and tendon wrapped tightly around long bone. The hands were pale and enormous, fingers at least six inches long, and as Louis watched they unfolded and hovered over his mother's bed-clothes. As Louis squinted he realized that the figure's head was not shaven but simply hairless—he could see veins through the translucent flesh—and the skull was disturbingly broad, brachycephalic, and so out of proportion with the body that the sight of it made him think of photographs of embryos and fetuses. As if in response to this thought, the thing's head began to oscillate slowly as if the long, thin neck could no longer support its weight. Louis thought of a snake closing on its prey.

Louis could do nothing but stare at the image of pale flesh, sharp bone and bruise-colored shadows. He thought fleetingly of concentration camp inmates shuffling to the wire, of week-dead corpses floating to the surface like inflatable things made of rotted white rubber. This was worse.

It had no ears. A rimmed, ragged hole with reddened flanges of flesh opened directly into the misshapen skull. The eyes were bruised holes, sunken blue-black sockets in which someone had set two yellowed marbles as a joke. There were no eyelids. The eyes were obviously blind, clouded with yellow cataracts so thick that Louis could see layers of striated mucus. Yet they darted to and fro purposefully, a predator's darting, lurking glare, as the great head moved closer to his mother's sleeping form. In its own way, Louis realized, the thing could see.

Louis whirled around, opened his mouth to shout, took two steps toward the bed and the suddenly empty chair, stopped with fists clenched, mouth still straining with his silent scream, and turned back to the mirror.

The thing had no mouth as such, no lips, but under the long, thin nose the bones of cheeks and jaw seemed to flow forward under white flesh to form a funnel, a long tapered snout of muscle and cartilage which ended in a perfectly round opening that pulsed slightly as pale-pink sphincter muscles around the inner rim expanded and contracted with the creature's breath or pulse. Louis staggered and grasped the back of an empty chair, closing his eyes, weak with waves of headache pain and sudden nausea. He was sure that nothing could be more obscene than what he had just seen.

Louis opened his eyes and realized that he was wrong.

The thing had slowly, almost lovingly, pulled down the thin blanket and topsheet which covered Louis's mother. Now it lowered its misshapen head over his mother's chest until the opening of that obscene proboscis was scant inches away from the faded blue-flower print of her hospital gown. Something appeared in the flesh-rimmed opening, something gray-green, segmented, and moist. Small, fleshy antennae tested the air. The great, white head bent lower, cartilage and muscle contracted, and a five-inch slug was slowly extruded, wiggling slightly as it hung above Louis's mother.

Louis threw his head back in a scream that finally could be heard, tried to turn, tried to remove his hands from their deathgrip on the back of the empty chair, tried to look away from the mirror. And could not.

Under the slug's polyps of antennae was a face that was all mouth, the feeding orifice of some deep-sea parasite. It pulsed as the moist slug fell softly onto his mother's chest, coiled, writhed, and burrowed quickly away from the light. Into his mother. The thing left no mark, no trail, not even a hole in the hospital gown. Louis could see the slightest ripple of flesh as the slug disappeared under the pale flesh of his mother's chest.

The white head of the child-thing pulled back, the yellow eyes stared directly at Louis through the mirror, and then the face lowered to his mother's flesh again. A second slug appeared, dropped, burrowed. A third.

Louis screamed again, found freedom from paralysis, turned, ran to the bed and the apparently empty chair, thrashed the air, kicked the chair into a distant corner, and ripped the sheet and blanket and gown away from his mother.

Two nurses and an attendant came running as they heard Louis's screams. They burst into the room to find him crouched over his mother's naked form, his nails clawing at her scarred and shrunken chest where the surgeons had recently removed both breasts. After a moment of shocked immobility, one nurse and the attendant seized and held Louis while the other nurse filled a syringe with a strong tranquilizer. But before she could administer it, Louis looked in the mirror, pointed to a space near the opposite side of the bed, screamed a final time, and fainted.

"It's perfectly natural," said Lee the next day after their second trip to the Boulder Clinic. "A perfectly understandable reaction."

"Yes," said Louis. He stood in his pajamas and watched her fold back the top sheet on his bed.

"Dr. Kirby says that injuries to that part of the brain can cause strange emotional reactions," said Debbie from her place by the window. "Sort of like whatshisname . . . Reagan's press secretary who was shot years ago, only temporary, of course."

"Yeah," said Louis, lying back, settling his head into the tall stack of pillows. There was a mirror on the wall opposite. His gaze never left it.

"Mom was awake for a while this morning," said Lee. "*Really* awake. I told her you'd been in to see her. She doesn't . . . doesn't remember your visit, of course. She wants to see you."

"Maybe tomorrow," said Louis. The mirror showed the reversed images of the three of them. Just the three of them. Sunlight fell in a yellow band across Debbie's red hair and Lee's arm. The pillowcases behind Louis's head were very white.

"Tomorrow," agreed Lee. "Or maybe the day after. Right now you need to take some of the medication Dr. Kirby gave you and get some sleep. We can go visit Mom together when you feel better."

"Tomorrow," said Louis, and he closed his eyes.

He stayed in bed for six days, rising only to go to the bathroom or to change channels on his portable TV. The headaches were constant but manageable. He saw nothing unusual in the mirror. On the seventh day he rose about ten A.M., showered slowly, dressed in his camel slacks, white shirt, and blue blazer, and was prepared to tell Lee that he was ready to visit the hospital when his sister came into the room red-eyed.

"They just called," she said. "Mother died about twenty minutes ago."

The funeral home was about two blocks from where his mother had lived, where Louis had grown up after they had moved from Des Moines when he was ten, just east of the Capitol Hill area where old brick homes were becoming rundown rentals and where Hispanic street gangs had claimed the night.

According to his mother's wishes there would be a "visitation" this night where Denver friends could pay their respects before the casket was flown back to Des Moines the next day for the funeral Mass at St. Mary's and final interment at the small city cemetery where Louis's father was buried. Louis thought that the open casket was an archaic act of barbarism. He stayed as far away from it as he could, greeting people at the door, catching glimpses only of his mother's nose, folded hands, or rouged cheeks.

About sixty people showed up during the two-hour ordeal, most of them in their early seventies—his mother's age—people from the block whom he hadn't seen in fifteen years or new friends she had met through Bingo or the Senior Citizens Center. Several of Louis's Boulder friends showed up, including two members of his Colorado Mountain Club hiking group and two colleagues from the physics labs at C.U. Debbie stayed by his side the entire time, watching his pale, sweaty face and occasionally squeezing his hand when she saw the pain from the headache wash across him.

The visitation period was almost over when suddenly he could no longer stand it. "Do you have a compact?" he asked Debbie.

"A what?"

"A compact," he said. "You know, one of those little make-up things with a mirror."

Debbie shook her head. "Louis, have you *ever* seen me with something like that?" She rummaged in her purse. "Wait a minute. I have this little hand mirror that I use to check my . . ."

"Give it here," said Louis. He raised the small plastic-backed rectangle, turning toward the doorway to get a better view behind him.

About a dozen mourners remained, talking softly in the dim light and flower-scented stillness. Someone in the hallway beyond the doorway laughed and then lowered his voice. Lee stood near the casket, her black dress swallowing light, speaking quietly to old Mrs. Narmoth from across the alley.

There were twenty or thirty other small figures in the room, moving like pale shadows between rows of folding chairs and dark-suited mourners. They moved slowly, carefully, seeming to balance their oversized heads in a delicate dance. Each of the child-sized forms awaited its turn to approach the casket and then moved forward, its pale body and bald head emitting its own soft penumbra of greenish-grayish glow. Each thing paused by the casket briefly and then lowered its head slowly, almost reverently.

Gasping in air, his hand shaking so badly the mirror image blurred and vibrated, Louis was reminded of lines of celebrants at his First Communion . . . and of animals at a trough.

"Louis, what is it?" asked Debbie.

He shook off her hand, turned and ran toward the casket, shouldering past mourners, feeling cold churnings in his belly as he wondered if he was passing *through* the white things.

"What?" asked Lee, her face a mask of concern as she took his arm.

Louis shook her away and looked into the casket. Only the top half of the lid was raised. His mother lay there in her best blue dress, the make-up seeming to return some fullness to her ravaged face, her old rosary laced through her folded fingers. The cushioned lining under her was silk and beige and looked very soft. Louis raised the mirror. His only reaction then was slowly to lift his left hand and to grasp the rim of the casket very tightly, as if it were the railing of a ship in rough seas and he were in imminent danger of plunging overboard.

There were several hundred of the slug-things in the coffin, flowing over everything inside it, filling it to the brim. They were more white than green or gray now and much, much larger, some as thick through the body as Louis's forearm. Many were more than a foot long. The antennae tendrils had contracted and widened into tiny yellow eyes and the lamprey mouths were recognizably tapered now.

As Louis watched, one of the pale, child-sized figures to his right approached the casket, laid long white fingers not six inches from Louis's hands, and lowered its face as if to drink.

Louis watched as the thing ingested four of the long, pale slugs, the creature's entire face contracting and expanding almost erotically to absorb the soft mass of its meal. The yellow eyes did not blink. Others approached the casket and joined in the communion. Louis lowered the angle of the mirror and watched two more slugs flow effortlessly out of his mother, sliding through blue material into the churning mass of their fellows. Louis moved the mirror, looked behind him, seeing the half-dozen pale forms standing there, waiting patiently for him to move. Their bodies were pale and sexless blurs. Their fingers were very long and very sharp. Their eyes were hungry.

Louis did not scream. He did not run. Very carefully he palmed the mirror, released his death grip on the edge of the casket, and walked slowly, carefully, away from there. Away from the casket. Away from Lee and Debbie's distantly heard cries and questions. Away from the funeral home.

He was hours and miles away, in a strange section of dark warehouses and factories, when he stopped in the mercury-arc circle of a streetlight, held the mirror high, swiveled 360 degrees to ascertain that nothing and no one was in sight, and then huddled at the base of the streetlight to hug his knees, rock, and croon.

"I think they're cancer vampires," Louis told the psychiatrist. Between the wooden shutters on the doctor's windows, Louis caught a glimpse of the rocky slabs that were the Flatirons. "They lay these tumor-slugs that hatch and change inside people. What we call tumors are really eggs. Then the cancer vampires take them back into themselves."

The psychiatrist nodded, tamped down his pipe, and lighted another match. "Do you wish to tell me more . . . ah . . . details . . . about these images you have?" He puffed his pipe alight.

Louis started to shake his head and then stopped suddenly as headache pain rippled through him. "I've thought it all out in the last few weeks," he said. "I mean, go back more than a hundred years and give me the name of one famous person who died of cancer. Go ahead."

The doctor drew on his pipe. His desk was in front of the shuttered windows and his face was in shadow, only occasionally illuminated when he turned as he relit his pipe. "I can't think of one right now," the doctor said, "but there must be many."

"Exactly," said Louis in a more excited tone than he had meant to use. "I mean, today we *expect* people to die of cancer. One in six. Or maybe it's one in four. I mean, I didn't know *anyone* who died in Viet Nam, but *everybody* knows somebody—usually somebody in our family—who's died of cancer. Just think of all the movie stars and politicians. I mean, it's everywhere. It's the plague of the Twentieth Century."

The doctor nodded and kept any patronizing tones out of his voice. "I see your point," he said. "But just because modern diagnostic methods did not exist before this does not mean people did not die of cancer in previous centuries. Besides, research has shown that modern technology, pollutants, food additives and so forth have increased the risk of encountering carcinogens which . . ."

"Yeah," laughed Louis, "carcinogens. That's what I used to believe in. But, Jesus, Doc, have you ever read over the AMA's and American Cancer Society's official lists of carcinogens? I mean it's everything you eat, breathe, wear, touch, and do to have fun. I mean it's *everything*. That's the same as just saying that they don't know. Believe me, I've been reading all of that crap, they don't even know what makes a tumor start growing."

The doctor steepled his fingers. "But you believe that you do, Mr. Steig?"

Louis took one of his mirrors from his shirt pocket and moved his head in quick half-circles. The room seemed empty. "Cancer vampires," he said. "I don't know how long they've been around. Maybe something we did this century allowed them to come through some . . . some gate or something. I don't know."

"From another dimension?" the doctor asked in conversational tones. His pipe tobacco smelled vaguely of pine woods on a summer day.

"Maybe," shrugged Louis. "I don't know. But they're here and they're busy feeding . . . and multiplying . . ."

"Why do you think that you are the only one who has been allowed to see them?" asked the doctor brightly.

Louis felt himself growing angry. "Goddammit, I don't *know* that I'm the only one who can see them. I just know that something happened after my accident . . ."

"Would it not be . . . equally probable," suggested the doctor, "that the injury to your skull has caused some *very* realistic hallucinations? You admit that your sight has been somewhat affected." He removed his pipe, frowned at it, and fumbled for his matches.

Louis gripped the arms of his chair, feeling the anger in him rise and fall on the waves of his headache. "I've been back to the Clinic," he said. "They can't find any sign of permanent damage. My vision's a little funny—but that's just because I can see *more* now. I mean, more colors and things. It's like I can see radio waves almost."

"Let us assume that you do have the power to see these ... cancer vampires," said the doctor. The tobacco glowed on his third inhalation. The room smelled of sunwarmed pine needles. "Does this mean that you also have the power to *control* them?"

Louis ran his hand across his brow, trying to rub away the pain. "I don't know."

"I'm sorry, Mr. Steig. I couldn't hear ..."

"I don't know!" shouted Louis. "I haven't tried to *touch* one. I mean, I don't know if ... I'm afraid that it might ... Look, so far the things ... the cancer vampires—they've ignored me, but ..."

"If you can see them," said the doctor, "doesn't it follow that they can see you?"

Louis rose and went to the window, tugging open the shutters so the room was filled with late afternoon light. "I think they see what they want to see," said Louis, staring at the foothills beyond the city, playing with his hand mirror. "Maybe we're just blurs to them. They find us easily enough when it's time to lay their eggs."

The doctor squinted in the sudden brightness but removed his pipe and smiled. "You talk about eggs," he said, "but what you described sounded more like feeding behavior. Does this discrepancy and the fact that the ... vision ... first occurred when your mother was dying suggest any deeper meanings to you? We all search for ways to control things we have no power over—things we find too difficult to accept. Especially when one's mother is involved."

"Look," sighed Louis, "I don't need this Freudian crap. I agreed to come here today because Deb's been on my case for weeks but ..." Louis stopped and raised his mirror, and stared.

The doctor glanced up as he scraped at his pipe bowl. His mouth was slightly open, showing white teeth, healthy gums, and a hint of tongue slightly curled in concentration. From beneath that tongue came first the fleshy antennae and then the green-gray body of a tumor slug, this one no more than a few centimeters long. It moved higher along the psychiatrist's jaw, sliding in and out of the muscles and skin of the man's cheek as effortlessly as a maggot moving in a compost heap. Deeper in the shadows of the doctor's mouth, something larger stirred.

"It can't hurt to talk about it," said the doctor. "After all, that's what I'm here for."

Louis nodded, pocketed his mirror, and walked straight to the door without looking back.

Louis found that it was easy to buy mirrors cheaply. They were available, framed and unframed, at used furniture outlets, junkshops, discount antique dealers, hardware stores, glass shops and even in people's stacks of junk sitting on the curb awaiting pickup. It took Louis less than a week to fill his small apartment with mirrors.

His bedroom was the best protected. Besides the twenty-three mirrors of various sizes on the walls, the ceiling had been completely covered with mirrors. He had put them up himself, pressing them firmly into the glue, feeling slightly more secure with each reflective square he set in place.

Louis was lying on his bed on a Saturday afternoon in May, staring at the reflections of himself, thinking about a conversation he had just had with his sister Lee, when Debbie called. She wanted to come over. He suggested that they meet on the Pearl Street Mall instead.

There were three passengers and two of *them* on the bus. One had been in the rear seat when Louis boarded, another came through the closed doors when the bus stopped for a red light. The first time he had seen one of the cancer vampires pass through a solid object, Louis had been faintly relieved, as if something so insubstantial could not be a serious threat. He no longer felt that way. They did not float through walls in the delicate, effortless glide of a ghost; Louis watched while the hairless head and sharp shoulders of this thing struggled to penetrate the closed doors of the bus, wiggling like someone passing through a thick sheet of cellophane. Or like some vicious newborn predator chewing its way through its own amniotic sac.

Louis pulled down another of the small mirrors attached by wires to the brim of his Panama hat and watched while the second cancer vampire joined the first and the two closed on the old lady sitting with her shopping bags two rows behind him. She sat stiffly upright, hands on her lap, staring straight ahead, not even blinking, as one of the cancer vampires raised its ridged funnel of a mouth to her throat, the motion as intimate and gentle as a lover's opening kiss. For the first time Louis noticed that the rim of the thing's proboscis was lined with a circle of blue cartilage which looked as sharp as razor blades. He caught a glimpse of gray-green flowing into the folds of the old lady's neck. The second cancer vampire lowered its ponderous head to her belly like a tired child preparing to rest on its mother's lap.

Louis stood, pulled the cord, and got off five blocks before his stop.

Few places in America, Louis thought, showed off health and wealth better than the three outdoor blocks of Boulder's Pearl Street Mall. A pine-scented breeze blew down from the foothills less than a quarter of a mile to the west as shoppers browsed, tourists strolled, and the locals lounged. The average person in sight was under thirty-five, tanned and fit, and wealthy enough to dress in the most casual pre-washed, pre-faded, pre-wrinkled clothes. Young men dressed only in brief trunks and sweat jogged down the mall, occasionally glancing down at their watches or their own bodies. The young women in sight were almost unanimously thin and braless, laughing with beautifully capped teeth, sitting on grassy knolls or benches with their legs spread manfully in poses out of *Vogue*. Healthy looking teenagers with spikes of hair dyed unhealthy colors licked at their two-dollar Dove bars and three-dollar Häagen-Dazs cones. The spring sunlight on the brick walkways and flower beds promised an endless summer.

"Look," said Louis as he and Debbie sat near Freddy's hot dog stand and watched the crowds flow past, "my view of things right now is just too goddamn ugly to ac-

cept. Maybe *everybody* could see this shit if they wanted
to, but they just refuse to." He lowered two of his mirrors
and swiveled. He had tried mirrored sunglasses but that
had not worked; only the full mirror-reversal allowed him
to see. There were six mirrors clipped to his hat, more in
his pockets.

"Oh, Louis," said Debbie. "I just don't understand . . ."

"I'm serious," snapped Louis. "We're like the people
who lived in the villages of Dachau or Auschwitz. We see
the fences, watch the trainloads of loaded cattle cars go by
everyday, smell the smoke of the ovens . . . and *pretend it
isn't happening.* We let these things take everybody, as
long as it isn't us. *There*! See that heavyset man near the
bookstore?"

"Yes?" Debbie was near tears.

"Wait," said Louis. He brought out his larger pocket
mirror and turned at an angle. The man was wearing tan
slacks and a loose Hawaiian shirt that did not hide his fat.
He sipped at a drink in a red styrofoam cup and stood
reading a folded copy of the *Boulder Daily Camera.* Four
child-sized blurs clustered around him. One closed long
fingers around the man's throat and pulled himself up
across the man's arm and belly.

"Wait," repeated Louis and moved away from Debbie,
scuttling sideways to keep the group framed in the mirror.
The three cancer vampires did not look up as Louis came
within arm's length; the fourth slid its long cone of a
mouth toward the man's face.

"Wait!" screamed Louis and struck out, head averted,
seeing his fist pass through the pale back of the clinging
thing. There was the faintest of gelatinous givings and a
chill numbed the bones of his fist and arm. Louis stared at
his mirror.

All four of the cancer vampires' heads snapped
around, blind yellow eyes fixed on Louis. He sobbed and
struck again, feeling his fist pass through the thing with no
effect and bounce weakly off the fat man's chest. Two of
the white blurs swiveled slowly toward Louis.

"Hey, goddammit!" shouted the fat man and struck at
Louis's arm.

The mirror flew out of Louis's left hand and shattered

on the brick pavement. "Oh, Jesus," whispered Louis, backing away. "Oh Jesus." He turned and ran, snapping down a mirror on his hat as he did so, seeing nothing but the dancing, vibrating frame. He grabbed Debbie by the wrist and tugged her to her feet. "Run!"

They ran.

Louis awoke sometime after two A.M., feeling disoriented and drugged. He felt for Debbie, remembered that he had gone back to his own apartment after they had made love. He lay in the dark, wondering what had awakened him.

His nightlight had burned out.

Louis felt a flush of cold fear, cursed, and rolled over to turn on the table lamp next to his bed. He blinked in the sudden glare, seeing blurred reflections of himself blink back from the ceiling, walls, and door.

Other things also moved in the room.

A pale face with yellow eyes pushed its way through the door and mirror. Fingers followed, finding a hold on the doorframe, pulling the body through like a climber mastering an overhang. Another face rose to the right of Louis's bed with the violent suddenness of someone stepping out of one's closet in the middle of the night, extracted its arm, and reached for the blanket bunched at the foot of Louis's bed.

"Ah," panted Louis and rolled off the bed. Except for the closet there was only the single door, closed and locked. He glanced up at the ceiling mirrors in time to see the first white shape release itself from the wood and glass and stand between the door and him. As he stared upward at his own reflection, at himself dressed in pajamas and lying on his back on the tan carpet, he watched wide-eyed as something white rippled and rose through the carpet not three feet from where he lay: a broad curve of dead grub flesh followed by a second white oval, the back and head of the thing floating up through the floor like a swimmer rising to his knees in three feet of water. The eye sockets were close enough for Louis to touch; all he had to do was extend his arm. The scent of old carrion came to him from the thing's sharp circle of a mouth.

Louis rolled sideways and back, scrambled to his feet, used a heavy chair by his bed to smash the window glass and threw the chair behind him. The rope ladder tied to the base of his bed had been left behind by a paranoid ex-roommate of Louis's who had refused to live on a third floor without a fire escape.

Louis looked up, saw white hands converging, threw the knotted rope out the window and followed it, bruising knuckles and knees against the brick wall as he clambered down.

He looked up repeatedly but there were no mirrors in the cold spring darkness and he had no idea if anything was following.

They used Debbie's car to leave, driving west up the canyon into the mountains. Louis was wearing an old pair of jeans, green sweatshirt, and paint-spattered sneakers he had left at Debbie's after helping to paint her new apartment in January. She owned only a single portable mirror—an eighteen by twenty-four inch glass set into an antique frame above the fireplace—and Louis had ripped it off the wall and brought it along, checking every inch of the car before allowing her to enter it.

"Where are we going?" she asked as they turned south out of Nederland on the Peak to Peak Highway. The Continental Divide glowed in weak moonlight to their right. Their headlights picked out black walls of pine and stretches of snow as the narrow road wound up and around.

"Lee's cabin," said Louis. "West on the old Rollins Pass road."

"I know the cabin," said Debbie. "Will Lee be there?"

"She's still in Des Moines," he said. He blinked rapidly. "She called just before you did this afternoon. She found a . . . lump. She saw a doctor there but is going to fly back to get the biopsy."

"Louis, I . . ." began Debbie.

"Turn here," said Louis.
They drove the last two miles in silence.

The cabin had a small generator to power lights and
the refrigerator but Louis preferred not to spend time filling it and priming it in the darkness out back. He asked
Debbie to stay in the car while he took the mirror inside,
lit two of the large candles Lee kept on the mantel, and
walked through the three small rooms of the cabin with
the mirror reflecting the flickering candle flame and his
own pale face and staring eyes. By the time he waved
Debbie inside, he had a fire going in the fireplace and the
sleeper sofa in the main room was pulled out.

In the dancing light from the fireplace and candles,
Debbie's hair looked impossibly red. Her eyes were tired.

"It's only a few hours until morning," said Louis. "I'll
go into Nederland when we wake up and get some sup-
plies."

Debbie touched his arm. "Louis, can you tell me
what's going on?"

"Wait, wait," he said, staring into the dark corners.
"There's one more thing. Undress.

"Louis . . ."

"Undress!" Louis was already tugging off his shirt and
pants. When they were both out of their clothes, Louis
propped the mirror on a chair and had them stand in front
of it, turning slowly. Finally satisfied, he dropped to his
knees and looked up at Debbie. She stood very still, the
firelight rising and falling on her white breasts and the soft
V of red pubic hair. The freckles on her shoulders and upper chest seemed to glow.

"Oh, God," said Louis and buried his face in his
hands. "God, Deb, you must think I'm absolutely crazy."

She crouched next to him and ran her fingers down his
back. "I don't know what's going on, Louis," she whispered, "but I know that I love you."

"I'll tell you . . ." began Louis, feeling the terrible
pressure in his chest threaten to expand into sobs.

"In the morning," whispered Debbie and kissed him
softly.

They made love slowly, seriously, time and their senses slowed and oddly amplified by the late hour, strange place, and fading sense of danger. Just when both of them felt the urgency quickening, Louis whispered, "Wait a second," and lay on one side, running his hand and then his mouth under the folds of her breasts, up, licking the nipples back into hardness, then kissing the curve of her belly and opening her thighs with his hand, sliding his face and body lower.

Louis closed his eyes and imagined a kitten lapping milk. He tasted the salt sweetness of the sea while Debbie softened and opened herself further to him. His palms stroked the tensed smoothness of her inner thighs while her breathing came more quickly, punctuated by soft, sharp gasps of pleasure.

There was a sudden hissing behind them. The light flared and wavered.

Louis turned, sliding off the foot of the bed onto one knee, aware of the pounding of his heart and the extra vulnerability his nakedness and excitement forced on him. He looked and gasped a laugh.

"What?" whispered Debbie, not moving.

"It's just the candle I set on the floor," he whispered back. "It's drowning in its own melted wax. I'll blow it out."

He leaned over and did so, pausing as he moved back to the foot of the bed to take in a single, voyeuristic glance in the mirror propped on the chair.

Firelight played across the two lovers framed there, Louis's flushed face and Debbie's white thighs, both glistening slightly from perspiration and the moisture of their lovemaking. Seen from this angle the dancing light illuminated the copper tangle of her pubic hair and roseate ovals of moist labia with a soft clarity too purely sensuous to be pornographic. Louis felt the tides of love and sexual excitement swell in him.

He caught the movement in the mirror out of the corner of his eye a second before he would have lowered his head again. A glimmer of slick gray-green between pale pink lips. No more than a few centimeters long. Undeterred by the dim light, the twin polyps of antennae emerged slowly, twisting and turning slightly as if to taste the air.

"I didn't know you had an interest in oncology," said Dr. Phil Collins. He grinned at Louis across his cluttered desk. "I thought you rarely came out of the physics lab up at the University."

Louis stared at his old classmate. He was much too tired for banter. He had not slept for 52 hours and his eyes felt like they were lined with sand and broken glass. "I need to see the radiation treatment part of chemotherapy," he said.

Collins tapped manicured nails against the edge of his desk. "Louis, we can't just give guided tours of our therapy sessions every time someone gets an interest in the process."

Louis forced his voice to stay even. "Look, Phil, my mother died of cancer a few weeks ago. My sister just underwent a biopsy that showed malignancy. My fiancée checked into Boulder Community a few hours ago with a case of cervical cancer that they're pretty sure also involves her uterus. Now will you let me watch the procedure or not?"

"Jesus," said Collins. He glanced at his watch. "Come on, Louis, you can make the rounds with me. Mr. Taylor is scheduled to receive his treatment in about twenty minutes."

The man was forty-seven but looked thirty years older. His eyes were sunken and bruised. His skin had a yellowish cast under the fluorescent lights. His hair had fallen out and Louis could make out small pools of blood under the skin.

They stood behind a lead-lined shield and watched through thick ports. "The medication is a very important part of it," said Collins. "It both augments and complements the radiation treatment."

"And the radiation kills the cancer?" asked Louis.

"Sometimes," said Collins. "Unfortunately it kills healthy cells as well as the ones which have run amok."

Louis nodded and raised his hand mirror. When the device was activated he made a small, involuntary sound. A brilliant burst of violet light filled the room, centering on the tip of the X-ray machine. Louis realized that the glow was similar to that of the bug-zapper devices he had seen in yards at night, the light sliding beyond visible frequencies in a maddening way. But this was a thousand times brighter.

The tumor slugs came out. They slid out of Mr. Taylor's skull, antennae thrashing madly, attracted by the brilliant light. They leaped the ten inches to the lens of the device, sliding on slick metal, some falling to the floor and then moving back up onto the table and through the man's body again to reemerge from the skull seconds later only to leap again.

Those that reached the source of the X-rays fell dead to the floor. The others retreated into the darkness of flesh when the X-ray light died.

". . . hope that helps give you some idea of the therapy involved," Collins was saying. "It's a frustrating field because we're not quite sure of why everything works the way it does, but we're making strides all of the time."

Louis blinked. Mr. Taylor was gone. The violet glow of the X-rays was gone. "Yes," he said. "I think that helps a lot."

Two nights later, Louis sat next to his sleeping sister in the semi-darkness of her hospital room. The other bed was empty. Louis had sneaked in during the middle of the night and the only sound was the hiss of the ventilation system and the occasional squeak of a rubber-soled shoe in the corridor. Louis reached out a gloved hand and touched Lee's wrist just below the green hospital identity bracelet. "I thought it'd be easy, kiddo," he whispered. "Remember the movies we watched when we were little? James Arness in *The Thing*? Figure out what kills it and rig it up." Louis felt the nausea sweep over him again and he lowered his head, breathing in harsh gulps. A minute later he straightened again, moving to wipe the cold sweat off his brow but frowning when the leather of the thick glove contacted his skin. He held Lee's wrist again. "Life ain't so easy, kiddo. I worked nights in Mac's high energy lab at the University. It was easy to irradiate things with that X-ray laser toy Mac cobbled together to show the sophomores the effects of ionizing radiation."

Lee stirred, moaned slightly in her sleep. Somewhere a soft chime sounded three times and was silenced. Louis heard two of the floor nurses chatting softly as they walked to the staff lounge for their two A.M. break. Louis left his gloved hand just next to her wrist, not quite touching.

"Jesus, Lee," he whispered. "I can see the whole damn spectrum below 100 angstroms. So can *they*. I banked on the cancer vampires being drawn to the stuff I'd irradiated just like the tumor slugs were. I came here last night—to the wards—to check on it. They *do* come, kiddo, but it doesn't kill them. They flock around the irradiated stuff like moths to a flame, but it doesn't kill them. Even the tumor slugs need high dosages if you're going to get them all. I mean, I started in the millirem dosages—like the radiation therapy they use here—and found that it just didn't get enough of them. To be sure, I had to get in the region of 300 to *400* roentgens. I mean, we're talking Chernobyl here, kiddo."

Louis quit talking and walked quickly to the bathroom, lowering his head to the toilet to vomit as quietly as possible. Afterward he washed his face as best he could with the thick gloves on and returned to Lee's bedside. She was frowning slightly in her drugged sleep. Louis remembered the times he had crept into her bedroom as a child to frighten her awake with garter snakes or squirt guns or spiders. "Fuck it," he said and removed his gloves.

His hands glowed like five-fingered, blue-white suns. As Louis watched in the mirrors snapped down on his hat brim, the light filled the room like cold fire. "It won't hurt, kiddo," he whispered as he unsnapped the first two buttons on Lee's pajama tops. Her breasts were small, hardly larger than when he had peeked in on her emerging from the shower when she was fifteen. He smiled as he remembered the whipping he had received for that, and then he laid his right hand on her left breast.

For a second nothing happened. Then the tumor slugs

came out, antennae rising like pulpy periscopes from Lee's flesh, their gray-green color bleached by the brilliance of Louis's glowing hand.

They slid into him through his palm, his wrist, the back of his hand. Louis gasped as he felt them slither through his flesh, the sensation faint but nauseating, like having a wire inserted in one's veins while under a local anaesthetic.

Louis counted six ... eight of the things sliding from Lee's breast into the blue-white flaring of his hand and arm. He held his palm flat for a full minute after the last slug entered, resisting the temptation to scream or pull his hand away as he saw the muscles of his forearm writhe as one of the things flowed upward, swimming through his flesh.

As an extra precaution, Louis moved his palm across Lee's chest, throat, and belly, feeling her stir in her sleep, fighting the sedatives in an unsuccessful battle to awaken. There was one more slug—hardly more than a centimeter long—which rose from the taut skin just below her sternum, but it flared and withered before coming in contact with his blue-white flesh, curling like a dried leaf too close to a hot fire.

Louis rose and removed his thick layers of clothes, watching in the wide mirror opposite Lee's bed. His entire body fluoresced, the brilliance fading from white to blue-white to violet and then sliding away into frequencies even he could not see. Again he thought of the bug lights one saw near patios and the blind-spot sense of frustration the eye conveyed as it strained at the fringes of perception. The mirrors hanging from the brim of his hat caught and scattered the light.

Louis folded his clothes neatly, laid them on the chair near Lee, kissed her softly on the cheek, and walked from room to room, the brilliance from his body leaping ahead of him, filling the corridors with blue-white shadows and pinwheels of impossible colors.

There was no one at the nurse's station. The tile floor felt cool beneath Louis's bare feet as he went from room to room, laying on his hands. Some of the patients slept on. Some watched him with wide eyes but neither moved nor cried out. Louis wondered at this but glanced down without his mirrors and realized that for the first time he could see the brilliance of his heavily irradiated flesh and bone with his own eyes. His body was a pulsing star in human form. Louis could easily hear the radio waves as a buzzing, crackling sound, like a great forest fire still some miles away.

The tumor slugs flowed from their victims and into Louis. Not everyone on this floor had cancer, but in most rooms he had only to enter to see the frenzied response of green-gray or grub-white worms straining to get at him. Louis took them all. He felt his body swallow the things, sensed the maddened turmoil within. Only once more did he have to stop to vomit. His bowels shifted and roiled, but there was so much motion in him now that Louis ignored it.

In Debbie's room, Louis pulled the sheet off her sleeping form, pulled up the short gown, and laid his cheek to the soft bulge of her belly. The tumor slugs flowed into his face and throat; he drank them in willingly.

Louis rose, left his sleeping lover, and walked to the long, open ward where the majority of cancer patients lay waiting for death.

The cancer vampires followed him. They flowed through walls and floors to follow him. He led them to the main ward, a blazing blue-white pied piper leading a chorus of dead children.

There were at least a score of them by the time he stopped in the center of the ward, but he did not let them approach until he had gone from bed to bed, accepting the last of the tumor slugs into himself, seeing with his surreal vision as the eggs inside these victims hatched prematurely to give up their writhing treasure. Louis made sure the tumor slugs were with him before he moved to the center of the room, raised his arms, and let the cancer vampires come closer.

Louis felt heavy, twice his normal weight, pregnant with death. He glanced at his blazing limbs and belly and saw the very surface of himself alive with the motion of maggots feeding on his light.

Louis raised his arms wider, pulled his head far back, closed his eyes, and let the cancer vampires feed.

The things were voracious, drawn by the X-ray beacon of Louis's flesh and the silent beckoning of their larval offspring. They shouldered and shoved each other aside in their eagerness to feed. Louis grimaced as he felt a dozen sharp piercings, felt himself almost lifted off the floor by nightmare energies suddenly made tangible. He looked once, saw the terrible curve of the top of a dead-child's head as the thing buried its face to the temples in Louis's chest, and then he closed his eyes until they were done.

Louis staggered, gripped the metal footboard of a bed to keep from falling. The score of cancer vampires in the room had finished feeding but Louis could feel his own body still weighted with slugs. He watched.

The child-thing nearest to him seemed bloated, its body as distended as a white spider bursting with eggs. Through its translucent flesh, Louis could see glowing tumor slugs shifting frantically like electric silverfish.

Even through his nausea and pain, Louis smiled. Whatever the reproductive-feeding cycle of these things had been, Louis now felt sure that he had disrupted it with the irradiated meal he had offered the tumor slugs.

The cancer vampire in front of him staggered, leaned far forward, and looked even more spiderish as its impossibly long fingers stretched to keep it from falling.

A blue-white gash appeared along the thing's side and belly. Two bloated, thrashing slugs appeared in a rush of violent energy. The cancer vampire arched its back and raised its feeding mouth in a scream that was audible to Louis as someone scraping their teeth down ten feet of blackboard.

The slugs ripped free of the vampire's shredded belly, dumping themselves on the floor and writhing in a bath of ultraviolet blood, steaming and shriveling there like true slugs Louis had once seen sprinkled with salt. The cancer vampire spasmed, clutched at its gaping, eviscerated belly, and then thrashed several times and died, its bony limbs and long fingers slowly closing up like the legs of a crushed spider.

There were screams, human and otherwise, but Louis

paid no attention as he watched the death throes of the two dozen spectral forms in the room. His vision had altered permanently now and the beds and their human occupants were mere shadows in a great space blazing in ultraviolet and infrared but dominated by the blue-white corona which was his own body. He vomited once more, doubling over to retch up blood and two dying, glowing slugs, but this was a minor inconvenience as long as his strength held out and at that second he felt that it would last forever.

Louis looked down, through the floor, through *five* floors, seeing the hospital as levels of clear plastic interlaced with webs of energy from electrical wiring, lights, machines, and organisms. Many organisms. The healthy ones glowed a soft orange but he could see the pale yellow infections, the grayish corruptions, and the throbbing black pools of incipient death.

Rising, Louis stepped over the dying corpses of cancer vampires and the acid-pools which had been thrashing slugs seconds before. Although he already could see beyond, he opened wide doors and stepped out onto the terrace. The night air was cool.

Drawn by the extraordinary light, they waited. Hundreds of yellow eyes turned upwards to stare from blue-black pits set in dead faces. Mouths pulsed. Hundreds more of the things converged as Louis watched.

Louis raised his own eyes, seeing more stars than anyone had ever seen as the night sky throbbed with uncountable X-ray sources and infinite tendrils of unnamed colors. He looked down to where they continued to gather, by the thousands now, their pale faces glowing like candles in a procession. Louis prayed for a single miracle. He prayed that he could feed them all. "Tonight, Death," he whispered, the sound too soft for even him to hear, "you shall die."

Louis stepped to the railing, raised his arms, and went down to join those who waited.

Introduction to "The Offering"

Just recently, as I write this in the early autumn of 1989, I optioned my novel *Carrion Comfort* to a film and TV production group. As is the case with many would-be Ben Hechts, I wanted first crack at the screenplay.

All right, said the production group, but first let's see what you can do with a half-hour TV script.

I've never written a teleplay or screenplay before, but being a child of the second half of the Twentieth Century, I feel like I've *lived* in the movies for most of my life. As a writer, I've heard all of the horror stories about doing work-for-hire in this particular collaborative medium: the senseless rewrite demands, the producer's girlfriend suggesting a "great idea" that guts your script, the contempt so much of the industry has for writers ("Didja hear the one about the Polish starlet visiting Hollywood? To get ahead she slept with all the *writers*!"), the endless compromises of quality in the face of budget or perceived market demands or whim or . . . you name it. The list of aggravations seems infinite.

That's why it was interesting to me that my first attempt at script writing was a lot of fun. The rewrite suggestions not only were minimal but definitely improved the product. The people I dealt with were professionals, and I always enjoy working with people who know their business—whether it's in carpentry or filmmaking. Of course, my agent says that it was a fluke . . . *that* studio was OK but the next will drive me to drink and beyond. My agent is a gentleman and a friend . . . he humors me

. . . but I know that in his heart he thinks that I should quit while I'm ahead.

Well, maybe. Maybe after one more TV show. Then perhaps a movie. Just a little movie . . . and then, just maybe, a twenty-hour mini-series. And then . . .

Meanwhile, I thought you might be interested in how I decided to adapt "Metastasis" to teleplay form. Reading scripts is not the easiest or most enjoyable literary pursuit, so if you skip over this entry it's understandable.

But if you *do* bear on, it might interest you to know some of the demands and restrictions a low-budget syndicated TV series makes on the writer who's adapting a story.

First, the thing has to run about 22 or 23 pages to fit its half-hour format, averaging about a minute per page, since the rest of the time is taken up by the fershtugginer commercials that keep so many of us from *watching* these syndicated shows.

Second, as I'm sure you know, the "exciting parts" come right before the commercial cluster breaks. (They don't really give a damn what happens the last few minutes of the show . . . they don't need to get you back after *that* break.)

Third, budget restrictions on this show allowed only three or four characters, or at least only that many characters who could *speak*. No exterior shots (but the director wanted the "windshield" shots in the opening). Only two interior sets and those easy to construct. Limited special effects—one or two optical processes, a few seconds of simple animation, and a guy in a monster suit and/or mask.

Fourth, they wanted a new title. "Metastasis" was out. They were afraid the audience would flip channels rather than watch something with such an ominous, disease-ridden sound to it.

Fifth, one of the top people thought I should also throw out the idea of "cancer vampires"—but, hey, I had to draw the line somewhere. I pointed out that this was the concept for which they had bought the story. I reasoned with them. I used logic. Then I held my breath until I turned blue, pounded my heels on the linoleum, and threatened to fax them six bales of junk mail if they didn't let me keep my cancer vampire. They relented.

There's more, but I think you get the idea. The question I faced was—could I adapt "Metastasis" so that the essence of the short story survived even while I tossed out major plot elements, characters, settings, and structure for the reasons listed above?

I found the challenge rather enjoyable. As I write this, the studio is just finishing the filming (actually taping) of "The Offering" and I have no idea when I'll see it. I don't know which actors were chosen. I can only guess what changes were made in the script during the actual production. (For those of you interested, the program will be aired on a syndicated series called MONSTERS, scheduled somewhere between 11:00 P.M. and 4:00 A.M. in most local markets. God knows where and when it will be by the time you read this.)

I'd be curious to know what you think of this adaptation.

The Offering

ACT I

FADE IN:

1. EXT. A CAR. NIGHT.

We open with a montage of images: E.C.U. of rain on a windshield, the blur of a windshield wiper; we close on LOUIS—a handsome young man but agitated now, unshaven, intense, blinking in the glare of oncoming lights and obviously upset about something—a sudden flash of light too bright to be a passing car, brakes squealing, metal tearing . . . from Louis's P.O.V. we see everything spinning and the glare expanding, the sound of impact, filling the universe with rising noise and moving light . . .

DISSOLVE TO:

2. INT. HOSPITAL ROOM. DAY.

The moving light blurs, comes into focus, and we see that it is a penlight held by DR. HUBBARD, an avuncular, older man wearing a white hospital coat over his suit.

DR. HUBBARD
Louis? Louis, can you hear me? Louis?

Louis tries to lift his head but is restrained by the doctor.

DR. HUBBARD
Easy, Louis. Easy. Just lie still for a moment. Do
you know where you are?

Louis's head is heavily bandaged. He groans again, tries to
lift both hands to his head, but stops—staring at his hospital ID bracelet, the IV in his left arm, his hospital gown—
looking around in surprise. He moves his head slowly,
obviously in great pain, and squints up at the doctor.

LOUIS
Dr. Hubbard? Yeah, I know where I am . . . the
hospital . . . but why? What happened?

The doctor smiles, plays with his unlit pipe.

DR. HUBBARD
We've been worried about you, Louis. You had
quite a serious concussion. You've been unconscious for almost seventy-two hours. Do you remember the accident?

LOUIS
Accident? Uh-uh, I don't remember any . . . Wait,
I remember *you* calling me . . . telling me that
Mom had been admitted to Mt. Sinai . . . that you
had to operate . . . Oh, God, I remember . . . can-
cer! She has cancer! Like Dad.

Louis starts to sit up but the pain is so intense that he almost passes out. Dr. Hubbard takes him firmly by the
shoulders, sets him gently back on the pillows.

DR. HUBBARD
(attempting to make his voice light)
Louis, I told you to *come* to the hospital, not put

yourself *in* it. Do you remember anything about
the accident?

Louis's eyes are still closed as he fights the pain, concentrates. Finally he shakes his head ... he can't quite remember.

> DR. HUBBARD
> After I told you about your mother's illness, you
> drove across town like a madman. Evidently your
> car hit some black ice on the Youngman Express-
> way ... rolled four or five times, the patrolman
> said ... Well, you've always been a bit reckless,
> Louis. Or at least since ...

Dr. Hubbard removes the pipe, frowns at it as if just discovering it is unlit, and shakes his head.

> LOUIS
> (voice thick)
> Was anyone else hurt?

> DR. HUBBARD
> No ... no one else. And you were lucky, my boy.
> The pressure on the left frontal lobe of your brain
> was ... well, it could have been very serious. As
> it is, you'll have quite a headache for a week or
> two ... possibly some double vision ...

Louis opens his eyes and it is obvious by the intensity of
his gaze that he is not worried about his own well-being.

> LOUIS
> Dr. Hubbard, how's Mom? You said on the phone
> that she had to go into surgery right away. Did
> you operate? Did you get all the cancer? Or is it
> ... like Dad's cancer when I was a kid. Is it too
> late?

Dr. Hubbard removes his pipe again, turns it over and over
in his hands and stares at it.

DR. HUBBARD
This is a filthy habit, Louis. I gave it up a year
ago, but still carry the pipe around ... can't get
used to not having the thing with me ...

Louis sits up in spite of the pain, grips the doctor's white
coat and pulls him closer.

LOUIS
Tell me, damn it. How is she? How serious is the
cancer? Is Mom going to be all right?

DR. HUBBARD
Louis, I've known your family for years ... I was
your father's doctor when you were just a child,
all during his long struggle ...

Dr. Hubbard looks straight at Louis, all business now, his
voice brisk.

DR. HUBBARD
When I spoke to you before your mother's operation ... before your accident ... I had some
hope that the surgery alone might eradicate her
cancer. But the metastasis was more rapid than
we thought and now ... well, we'll have to take
it one day at a time now. There's always something else to try ...

Louis is stunned, speechless. Dr. Hubbard grips the younger man's shoulder.

DR. HUBBARD
We're going ahead with radiation treatment,
Louis. We have new drugs now, medication to
help diminish the pain of the ... of the coming

weeks. We can hope for a remission. New proce-
dures are being perfected all the time . . .

                            LOUIS
Where is she, Dr. Hubbard? Is Mom nearby?

                        DR. HUBBARD
She's right down the hall, Louis. Room 2119. You
can visit her in a couple of days . . . when we're
sure you're better. The kind of head injury you
sustained can have all sorts of nasty side effects . . .

Louis struggles to get his legs off the bed, to stand up.

                            LOUIS
Mom!

Dr. Hubbard restrains him, forces him back onto the pillows.

                        DR. HUBBARD
                  (shouting over his shoulder)
Nurse!

A syringe is brought to the doctor. He checks the contents,
administers it via Louis's IV.

                        DR. HUBBARD
You can see your mother tomorrow. Right now
you have to rest. This will help you sleep.

Again in Louis's P.O.V., we see the doctor go out of focus
and the overhead light glow brighter, brighter . . .

                        DR. HUBBARD
                  (as if from a great distance)
There's nothing you can do tonight, Louis. Just
rest now. Rest. Rest . . .

CUT TO:

3.   NIGHT. HOSPITAL ROOM.

Louis awakens to see the hospital room transformed by
night. The curtain is drawn around the bed next to him.
Rain taps against the windows and tall shadows are thrown
on the opposite wall by the single nightlight in the monitor
panel on the wall above his bed. Louis sits up, groans, removes his IV drip, and swings his legs over the edge of
the bed. He is still groggy, half out of it.

> LOUIS
> I'm sorry I wasn't here, Mom . . . They wouldn't
> let me in to see Dad . . . I was too little . . .

Louis gets to his feet, sways, and staggers to the far wall,
using it to brace himself as he moves toward the door.

> LOUIS
> I'm coming, Mom.

CUT TO:

4.   INT. ANOTHER HOSPITAL ROOM. NIGHT.

The door to a hospital room slowly opens and we see
Louis in his hospital gown. He is hanging on to the doorframe and obviously exhausted and in much pain. He
moves into the room, weaves, and leans against the wall to
keep from falling. There is a single bed in this room. It is
dark and a curtain is drawn most of the way around the
bed, but Louis can see his mother's head and shoulders
through the opening. She is asleep, obviously sedated, and
Louis is shocked at her appearance.

> LOUIS
> Mom! Mom it's me!

Louis steps forward and throws back the curtain.

LOUIS

Oh, my God . . .

There is a figure leaning over his mother. It is the size of
a child, but this is no child. The body is thin and white . . .
fish-belly white . . . and the arms are skin and tendon
wrapped around long bone. The hands are pale and enormous, fingers three times the length of those on a human
hand. The head is huge and misshapen, brachycephalic,
reminiscent of photographs of fetuses. The eyes are
bruised holes from which two yellowed marbles, striated
with mucus and yellow cataracts, stare out blindly . . . but
even though the thing must be blind, the yellow eyes dart
back and forth purposely. The thing has no mouth, but the
bones of its cheek and jaw seem to flow forward under
white flesh to form a funnel, a long tapered snout of muscle and cartilage which ends in a perfectly round opening.
This opening pulses as Louis watches, pale-pink sphincter
muscles around the inner rim expanding and contracting as
the thing breathes. It is a CANCER VAMPIRE.

LOUIS

Oh, dear God . . .

Louis staggers toward the thing, grasps the back of a chair
to keep from falling. His expression changes from revulsion to total horror as he watches the cancer vampire
slowly, almost lovingly, pull back the thin blanket and
topsheet above Louis's mother. The cancer vampire lowers
its head until the opening of its obscene proboscis is
inches above Louis's mother's chest. A SLIDING, RASP-
ING is audible. Something appears in the flesh-rimmed
opening of its snout . . . something gray-green, segmented,
and moist. Cartilage and muscle contract and a five-inch
TUMOR SLUG is slowly extruded from the cancer vampire's proboscis and hangs wiggling above his sleeping
mother.

FADE OUT
END ACT I

FADE IN on: ACT II

5.   INT. HOSPITAL ROOM. NIGHT.

The moist slug falls softly onto his mother's bare skin. It coils, writhes, slides across his mother's chest, and burrows quickly away from the light. Into flesh. Into his mother.

>   LOUIS
>   Stop! . . . Aw, no . . . no

Louis staggers to the tray table, throws a glass at the cancer vampire. The creature lifts its head as if sensing Louis's presence, stands, extends its impossibly long fingers, and drops out of sight behind the bed . . . it remains stiffly upright as it disappears, as if a hydraulic lift were lowering it through the floor.

>   LOUIS
>   (sobbing)
>   No . . . no . . . no . . . no . . .

Louis lunges toward his mother's bed, falls against the side of it, wraps his fingers in the bedclothes, and slides to the floor, still sobbing, slipping into unconsciousness.

>   DISSOLVE TO:

6.   NIGHT. HOSPITAL ROOM.

Louis awakens in his own room. He looks around, disoriented. It is still dark, rain still sends streaks down the window and shadows onto the wall, but he is lying in his own bed, his IV attached. He moans and touches his head.

LOUIS
God, did I dream that . . . that *thing?*

Louis suddenly becomes aware of a wet, swallowing,
SLURPING sound. This is what awakened him and has
been in the background all the while. Now the slurping
rises in volume. Louis realizes that it is coming from behind the drawn curtain pulled around the bed next to his.
The bed that had been empty when the doctor had been
there.

LOUIS
(whispering)
Hello?

The SLURPING continues.

LOUIS
(louder)
Hello? Is someone there?

The noise continues, growing even louder. Louis leans out
of bed, reaches the end of his IV tether, raises his free
hand to the curtain, and flings it back.

LOUIS
Ah . . .

An old man, JACK WINTERS, looks up from SLURPING
whiskey in a glass through a bent hospital straw. A bottle
of cheap booze, almost empty, is on his tray table. In the
glow of the nightlight and the occasional lightning flashes,
the old man is a sight—pale and obviously ravaged by illness, hairless except for the gray stubble on his wrinkled
cheeks. He is toothless but grins up at Louis even as he
continues slurping.

LOUIS
Jeez . . . I'm sorry . . . I didn't know anyone else
was in here.

JACK

That's all right, young fella. My name's Jack
Winters. Been your roommate all along but you
slept for three straight days after they brought you
in an' I guess I was downstairs for my radiation
treatment when you woke up yesterday.

Louis collapses back in his pillows, holding his head.

LOUIS

God, I had the worst dream.

Jack gives another toothless grin and pours out more of his
whiskey.

JACK

That's what Ol' Nurse Haversmith . . . she's the
night nurse and mean as a junkyard dog . . . that's
what she said when they brought you back in a
couple of hours ago after you'd gone
sleepwalkin'. She said you was screaming and
carrying on somethin' fierce while you was in
your mommy's room. I had me a cousin once
who was a sleepwalker . . . they useta have to tie
him to his bed with a clothesline . . .

Louis had been on the verge of drifting off again despite
the old man's monologue, but suddenly he realizes what is
being said and snaps awake, sitting up and leaning over to
grasp Jack's arm.

LOUIS

What's that? What did you say about me being in
my mother's room?

Jack shields his whiskey bottle as if Louis is trying to steal
it.

JACK

I just said what Nurse Haversmith said when she
an' the others brung you back, Boy. Said you got

to your mommy's room and passed out or
somethin' ...

Louis releases Jack's arm and collapses back into the pillows.

> LOUIS
> (to himself)
> It wasn't a dream. I saw it ...

Jack resumes slurping up the whiskey, edging to the far
side of his own bed to stay away from Louis. The drink re-
vives his spirits.

> JACK
> Hellfire, Boy, consider yourself lucky if you just
> got a bump on the head that makes you a mite
> crazy. Most of us on this floor are in for the Big
> C ...

> LOUIS
> The Big C? You mean cancer?

> JACK
> Damn right I mean cancer. Look at me, Boy, three
> months here and they took out 'bout everythin' I
> had two of ... and some things I only had one of
> ... cut so many things off me and outta me that
> there ain't nothin' left to remove that I can get
> along without. So now they just zap me with ra-
> diation and fill me up with drugs that make me
> puke.
> (grins toothlessly)
> So now I prescribe me my own medicine. My
> daughter Esther Mae sneaks it in ...
> (Jack hesitates and then offers Louis the bottle)
> Care for a little late night pick-me-up?

> LOUIS
> (shakes his head and grimaces from the motion)
> No ... thanks. Mr. ... uh ... Winters ...

JACK

Jack.

LOUIS

Jack. You say this is a cancer ward?

Jack chuckles but the laughter soon turns to thick coughing. He sets aside the straw and gulps the last of the whiskey. The coughs subside.

JACK

Ain't *supposed* to be a cancer ward ... but that's
what it amounts to. It upsets the regular patients
to bunk with us terminal cases ... that's what
Nurse Haversmith calls us when she don't think
we're listenin' ... so Doc Hubbard and the other
cancer docs just sorta dump us in this ward.
(then, mumbling to himself)
Makes it easier for the damn night critters to find
us, too ...

Jack fumbles behind his pillow and finds another bottle.
He busies himself with filling his glass and replacing the
straw.

LOUIS

What? What did you say about night critters?

Jack freezes in mid-slurp. He glares suspiciously at Louis.

JACK

I didn't say nothin'.

LOUIS

Yes you did. About night critters.

JACK

Just things I seen while in my DT's, Boy. Nothin'
real.

                          LOUIS
Yes it is. You've *seen* something ... got a
glimpse of something that shouldn't be here.
Something that shouldn't *exist* ...

Jack looks as if he is about to speak, to talk about something that he *has* seen late at night there in the cancer
ward, but instead he glares at Louis, makes a motion with
his hand as if warding off evil spirits, leans forward, and
draws the curtain back between them. The room seems to
darken further. From behind the curtain we hear resumed
SLURPING.

                                              CUT TO:

7. INTERIOR. DAY. HOSPITAL ROOM.

Sunlight fills the room. Fresh flowers overflow from a
vase on a tray table pushed against the wall. Jack Winters
is out of the room for one of his tests and his bed is neatly
made. Dr. Hubbard sits on a chair by Louis's bed, fiddling
with his pipe and listening intently as Louis paces back
and forth. Louis has been removed from the IV and is
wearing a robe over pajamas rather than his hospital gown,
but his head is still bandaged and his eyes look feverish.
He gestures as he talks and his voice is rapid, almost
manic.

                          LOUIS
Let's just say that I *did* see something last night.
Is that all right? Can we just suppose ... for argument's sake ... that I *saw* something rather
than *hallucinated* that I saw something? Can we
just work under that assumption for a moment?

                       DR. HUBBARD
All right, let's work with that assumption, Louis.
What did you see?

Louis stops pacing for a moment and holds his arms as if
chilled by the memory of what he saw.

LOUIS
Well, it wasn't human, but . . .

DR. HUBBARD
Yes, yes, . . . you've told me several times *what*
this thing looked like. But what *is* it? Assuming
you saw it, what *was* it? A ghost?
(he allows himself a single, reassuring smile)
Perhaps it was an extraterrestrial . . . an alien
M.D. interested in our medical facilities?

Louis pays no attention to the sarcasm. Lost in thought, he
walks over to the window and stares out . . . seeing nothing . . . letting the light warm his face. After a moment he
speaks.

LOUIS
I'm not sure what it is. Some . . . some *thing* that
brings those slugs I told you about. Maybe it's
from another dimension or something. Maybe
these things are around us all the time . . . coex-
isting . . . but we can't *see* them . . .
(he touches his bandages ruefully)
. . . unless we have a certain type of concussion
with certain types of pressure on certain parts of
the left frontal lobe . . .

Dr. Hubbard continues smiling but he is sufficiently
shaken by the absurdity of Louis's explanation that he tries
to inhale smoke from his pipe . . . forgetting that it is
empty.

DR. HUBBARD
All right, Louis . . . assuming this thing you saw
was . . . was not human. Assuming that only *you*
could see it because of your injury. Was it at-
tacking your mother?

LOUIS
Yes . . . no . . . Look, somehow it was *using*
Mom . . .

                          DR. HUBBARD
But you said it was *leaving* this ... this slug
thing. It put something *into* your mother's body
you said. Now why would it ...

                            LOUIS
          (interrupting, agitated, pacing again,
                  voice high and rapid)
Look, I don't *know!* Maybe it has to do with
Mom's cancer. Maybe they lay these slugs in people and they grow or change inside our bodies.
Maybe what we call tumors are really the eggs of
these ... these things ... and we're only incuba-
tors to them. Or maybe ... maybe they sow those
slugs, let them multiply in us ... isn't that what
cancer does, Doctor? ... and then these creatures
come back and harvest the slugs for food. Like
vampires ...
          (Louis stops, struck by a revelation)
My God, that's what they are ... *cancer vampires!*

Dr. Hubbard nods, appearing to listen, anything to calm
Louis down. Louis stops suddenly, makes a motion with
both hands as if starting a final appeal to a jury.

                            LOUIS
                         (excitedly)
Look, Dr. Hubbard, that makes sense! I mean, tell
me the name of a famous person who died of cancer a hundred years ago. Go ahead ...

                          DR. HUBBARD
I don't understand ...

                            LOUIS
I mean, this cancer scourge is like an *invasion.*
An invasion of cancer vampires. And a recent
one. Tell me someone who died of cancer a century ago.

DR. HUBBARD
I can't think of a name right now, Louis. But
there must have been many . . .

LOUIS
Exactly! I mean, today we *expect* people to get
cancer. One in six. Or maybe it's one in four.
These things must be everywhere, using us . . .
Planting their slugs in us. I mean, *everybody*
knows somebody who's died of cancer. Look at
my family . . . first my dad years ago, now Mom.
Those creatures must be all around us . . . feeding
on us . . . we just can't *see* them!

DR. HUBBARD
All right . . . all right. But we don't need your . . .
ah . . . cancer vampires . . . to explain this recent
so-called scourge of cancer. In the modern world
we're exposed to more carcinogens . . .

LOUIS
(laughing almost hysterically)
Oh, yeah . . . *carcinogens!* That's what I used to
believe in. And we read the official list of carcinogens and they're in everything we eat, breathe,
wear, . . . I mean, *come on!* You medical experts
want us to believe in "carcinogens" . . . and you
don't even know where tumors come from.

DR. HUBBARD
(angry but trying to hide the fact)
But you do?

LOUIS
Yes. Cancer vampires!

Triumphant but exhausted, Louis sits on the edge of his
bed. Dr. Hubbard removes his pipe and leans forward to
grab the young man by his upper arms.

DR. HUBBARD

All right, Louis, I've listened to your fantasies
and allowed your assumptions. Now will you listen to my theory?

Louis nods, totally drained of energy.

DR. HUBBARD

My theory is that you're *very* concerned about
your mother and very upset that she has cancer. In
addition, you have a serious subdural hematoma
that is creating low grade hallucinations. Your
concern about your mother is dictating the form
of these hallucinations.
    (pauses, decides to be blunt)
Louis, be honest . . . your father's death from cancer when you were a boy *changed* you . . . I remember a happy boy . . . outgoing . . . generous
. . . in recent years you've been withdrawn,
moody, your behavior alternating between danger-
ously reckless and near-paranoid.
    (beat)
I know you'd love to see . . . a *thing* . . . something solid . . . something you could fight rather
than the intangible assassin of cells running
amok. But it's an hallucination, Louis . . . a visual
malfunction . . . and the sooner you admit it, the
sooner you can get well so you can help your
mother get well.

Louis is staring at the doctor. He manages to nod.

DR. HUBBARD

(flushed, chewing on his pipe to calm down)
Good. Now Mr. Winters is having his radiation
treatment about now. The same sort of treatment
your mother will be receiving in a few days.
Would you care to see it?

Still staring, Louis nods again.

                    DR. HUBBARD
Fine. Now you have to try to be sensible. No
more nonsense about cancer vampires.
                    (he smiles)
It could upset Mr. Winters and the other patients
on the floor.

Louis nods again.

                    DR. HUBBARD
Excellent. Then I'll go see if we're ready to start
his treatment. We'll send an orderly up for you.
                    (he realizes that the pipe is in his mouth,
                       removes it, and smiles)
Now, don't you feel better, Louis?

Louis nods a final time. Then, in a very tight shot, from
Louis's P.O.V., we are in E.C.U. of Dr. Hubbard's face: his
mouth is slightly open, showing white teeth, healthy gums,
and a hint of tongue. From beneath that tongue comes first
the fleshy antennae and then the green-gray body of a tumor slug. It moves farther out and then withdraws, as if
burrowing from the light.

FADE OUT

FADE IN on: ACT III

8.   INTERIOR. RADIOLOGY TREATMENT
     AND CONTROL ROOM. DAY.

Louis has been wheeled into the Radiology Control Room
in a wheelchair but now he stands to peer through a thick
window into the Treatment Room where Jack Winters lies
on the treatment couch under the overhanging eye of a
massive supervoltage cobalt 60 machine. Jack Winters
looks small and frail and terribly vulnerable as he lies on
the treatment couch—parts of his body shielded by lead
"molds", his upper torso bare with a target outline drawn
on his upper chest in bright dye, an unsubtle + centered

where the powerful X-rays will penetrate. We can see Jack
breathing rapidly, shallowly, his emaciated chest rising and
falling, his skin offering almost the only color in a vast
Treatment Room which is mostly white machinery and
black and white tile fading into black shadows. Dr. Hubbard is in the Control Room with Louis and a RADIA-
TION THERAPIST who stands next to the complicated
controls.

> DR. HUBBARD
> This will be Mr. Winters' next-to-last session. We
> believe that the tumors are responding very nicely
> to treatment.
> (glances at Louis)
> Radiation treatment and chemotherapy have come
> a long way since the days of your father's illness.

The therapist taps controls while watching his monitors
and the massive machine above Jack Winters hums,
moves, and lowers its ominous "eye" to a firing position
just above the + on the old man's upper chest. A light
from the machine snaps on and illuminates the target area.

> LOUIS
> (clearing his throat, obviously impressed
> and a bit frightened)
> How much radiation does Jack have to receive to
> beat the cancer?

> DR. HUBBARD
> We estimate that seven thousand rads should be
> sufficient to sterilize this tumor.

> LOUIS
> (turning away from the window)
> Seven thousand rads? That sounds like a lot. How
> much is a rad?

> DR. HUBBARD
> Well, to give you an idea ... a regular chest
> X-ray ... such as you received when you were

brought in after your accident the other day ...
would expose you to about five millirem ...
that's a total of about five *thousandths* of a single
rad.

LOUIS

My God ... and Jack has to receive *seven thousand rads* ... a million times as much.
      (he looks back through the window
          at the waiting man)
How can he take it?

DR. HUBBARD

In small doses. A single dose of seven *hundred*
rads would be fatal to about half the people who
received it. So we parcel it out ... a bit at a time
... and still there are side effects.
      (quickly, to avoid Louis dwelling
          on the negative)
But the principle of radiation treatment is well-
proven, Louis. The benefits are well-documented.

LOUIS
      (lost in thought as he stares at Jack
          alone in the other room)
And my mother will be receiving these treat-
ments?

DR. HUBBARD

Depending upon post-surgical recovery and results of other biopsies ... yes.
      (he nods to the radiation therapist)
We're ready ...

The radiation therapist throws the switch. Louis is startled
as violet radiation fills the window, bathes his face in
light.

LOUIS

I *see* it!

DR. HUBBARD
The actual radiation is invisible, of course.

The radiation *is* visible. Visible to Louis, at least. We share
his altered vision as the Treatment Room is filled with a
brilliant violet radiation, centering on the cobalt 60 machine's lens but arcing and pulsing in wild geometries as
the radiation leaps from the machine to Jack. The others
see none of this but we CLOSE ON Louis's startled face,
painted violet in reflected light, and see the sudden shock
and revulsion as the TUMOR SLUGS begin to slide out of
Jack's chest.

LOUIS
Look! The . . .
(he bites off his exclamation
before tipping off Dr. Hubbard)

DR. HUBBARD
What, Louis?

LOUIS
(attempting a smile)
Nothing. Nothing at all.

The tumor slugs emerge, attracted by the bright light from
the cobalt 60 machine. First one, then a second, then a
third . . . They emerge from Jack's chest—some completely, some only partially—as if they are drawn irresist-
ibly to the glow. The radiation therapist throws a switch.
The hum disappears and the explosion of violet light fades
and dies. The tumor slugs that emerged completely have
shriveled and died . . . the survivors burrow back into flesh
once again.

LOUIS
(unable to contain himself)
There wasn't enough time . . . not enough radiation!

DR. HUBBARD
(checks a dial)
Twenty-eight point six seconds. Precisely enough
for this treatment.

Louis begins to explain but sees Dr. Hubbard watching
him carefully. Louis shuts up. He is thinking quickly.

LOUIS
What ... what is the source of the radiation?

RADIATION THERAPIST
In this case, radioisotopes of Cobalt 60.

LOUIS
Can I see them?

The radiation therapist glances at Dr. Hubbard and the
oncologist nods, still humoring his young patient. The
therapist goes to a wall safe, casually runs through a brief
combination—we see Louis watching carefully and we
also catch the numbers, 17-right, 43-left, 11-right—and
then the therapist dons ridiculously thick gloves, opens the
thick vault door, and removes one of several heavy lead
storage cylinders emblazoned with the international warning symbol for radiation hazard.

LOUIS
Are those the isotopes?

DR. HUBBARD
These are their shielded lead storage units. The
actual isotopes are tiny ... but dangerous. One
isotope would power the cobalt 60 machine for
many hours. Each ... unshielded ... would deliver several thousand rads *at once*.

LOUIS
How are the isotopes loaded into the machine?

> DR. HUBBARD
> Very, very carefully. Remote mechanical handlers.
> Lead aprons. Lead shielding . . . it's quite compli-
> cated. Have you seen enough?
>> (he nods for the therapist to return
>> the isotope to safe keeping)

Louis looks through the window at Jack. The old man is
shivering slightly from the cold. He turns his head toward
the window and smiles. The dead and blackened tumor
slugs are still visible on his bare chest.

> LOUIS
>> (to himself)
> Yes . . . I've seen enough.

>>>>>>>>>> CUT TO:

9.   INT. NIGHT. LOUIS'S HOSPITAL ROOM

Louis comes awake with a start. It is dark. From somewhere down the hall comes a soft chime and the squeak of
rubber-soled shoes on tile. But it is a closer sound which
has awakened Louis. The SLURPING is coming from behind Jack's curtain . . . an even louder, ruder noise than
that of the night before.

> LOUIS
>> (groggily, still half asleep)
> Jack?

Louis slides back the curtains. Jack is dead, mouth agape,
fingers curled into rigid claws, eyes wide and staring. The
SLURPING, SLIDING noise comes from tumor slugs
sliding on and around his body . . . his pajamas writhe and
ripple from their movement and some are spilling from the
gaps in his pajama tops. A cancer vampire squats over the
corpse, head lowered, proboscis deep *inside* Jack's chest
like some nightmarish mosquito drinking its fill. The
SLURPING is very loud.

> LOUIS

Ahhh ...

The cancer vampire lifts its face. Tumor slugs drip from its long snout ... one slides up the opening with a RASP-ING sound. The cancer vampire *looks* directly at Louis, its caked, yellow eyes peering myopically.

> LOUIS

Uh-uh ... *uh-uh* ...

Louis fumbles on his littered dinner tray, finds a knife, and throws it with all of his strength. It strikes the chest of the cancer vampire with a soft, rotten sound, but instead of sticking it sinks into the pulpy flesh like a dropped utensil floating in a pool of mucus. The cancer vampire idly extracts the knife with long fingers and casts it aside. It has not been hurt. It raises a hand toward Louis.

> LOUIS

No ... uh-uh ...

Louis stumbles out of the bed backward, knocking over the IV stand, crashing into the tray table and sending the vase of flowers flying as he edges along the wall, staying as far away from the cancer vampire as possible while heading for the door. We MOVE IN on the cancer vampire's yellow, blind eyes, its head turning, as we hear Louis's footfalls receding down the empty corridor.

> CUT TO:

10. INT. NIGHT. RADIOLOGY CONTROL ROOM.

Louis staggers into the dark room, remains panting at the doorway for a moment. There is no pursuit. Looking around, he snaps on a single low-wattage lamp above the control board. The adjoining Treatment Room is in total darkness. He looks around wildly, sees the safe with the radiation symbol, and takes deep breaths to calm down.

He knows what he has to do. He fiddles with the dial. In
E.C.U. we see 17-right, 43-left, 11-right. The safe door
swings open and Louis steps back, shocked at how easy it
was. Inside the safe, the lead storage cylinders sit like
small bombs. Louis glances over his shoulder, then looks
around until he finds the heavy gloves. Donning them, he
removes the cylinders and sets them carefully on a table.

DISSOLVE TO:

11.   INT. NIGHT. RADIOLOGY CONTROL ROOM.

Louis is crouching by the table so that only his head and
shoulders are visible. The storage cylinders rise in front of
him. The rest is darkness. Still wearing the heavy gloves,
he fumbles with the complicated latch and lid on the first
cylinder.

                        LOUIS
    Damn.

He tugs off his gloves, easily breaks the seal, flips the
latch, and removes the lid. A fierce violet light illuminates
his face. The glow becomes even brighter as he shakes the
radioisotope into his bare hand. The pellet is small but incredibly brilliant—a point source of blazing light. He lifts
it with both hands.

                        LOUIS
                    (whispering)
    There's got to be another way.
                    (beat)
    But I don't know what it is . . .

Louis takes a breath and lifts the isotope higher with shaking hands. There is an element of the sacramental to his
motions—a radioactive Communion service. He swallows
the cobalt 60 pellet, struggles to keep from gagging, and
keeps it down.

                              LOUIS
Ah, God . . .

He opens another storage cylinder, lifts the isotope. The
light in the room begins to fade . . .

                                        DISSOLVE TO:

12. INT. NIGHT. LOUIS'S MOTHER'S ROOM.

We see a close shot of Louis's mother—her head on the
pillow—as she moans in her sleep, turning fitfully, perhaps
on the verge of coming out of the sedative-induced sleep.
We move down her shoulder to her arm, her hand. Suddenly a huge, misshapen form comes into the frame and
clumsily enfolds her hand. It is Louis's hand, again in the
heavy radiation glove. We PULL BACK and see Louis as
he sits by her bedside, holding her hand in the dark room.
Lightning ripples soundlessly outside the window.

                              LOUIS
                          (very softly)
    I remember once when I was a kid . . . it must
    have been just after Dad died . . . I woke up on a
    stormy night like this and found you sitting on the
    edge of my bed . . . like you were protecting me
    from the storm.

The lightning illuminates the room again. Louis quickly
looks around. There is no sign of the cancer vampire.

                              LOUIS
    I pretended I was asleep, but I wanted to tell you
    that *nobody* could protect *anybody*. Not from the
    storm . . . not from what killed Dad . . .
                            (beat)
    I wanted to tell you then that all a person could
    do was *run* . . . run from the people you loved the
    most . . . run so that it didn't hurt so much when
    you couldn't protect them.

Louis squeezes her hand.

> LOUIS
> Well, Mom, maybe I'm through running for a while.

He looks around again.

> LOUIS
> I could see those ... *things* ... the cancer vampires ... in almost every room I passed on this floor.
> (shivers)
> White blurs in the dark rooms. Waiting. Waiting to feed on the people there ...

He takes a deep breath.

> LOUIS
> It's time, Mom. Time to see if it'll do any good.

Louis removes one of the heavy gloves. His hand blazes with violet light. He removes the other glove and the glare from his two hands throws wild shadows around the room. He raises his hands, staring at them.

> LOUIS
> This won't hurt, Mom.

He lays the palm of one glowing hand an inch from flesh just below her throat. We wait a second and then see the ripple as a tumor slug slides up toward the light. Louis grimaces but does not remove his hand as the slug emerges from her skin, tests the air with its moist antennae, and then slides *into* Louis's palm. A second one follows, enters Louis's hand. A third. Louis holds his hand there a moment longer but no more emerge.

> LOUIS
> (gasping, close to fainting)
> I think that's all.

He lifts his hand and we can see the turmoil under the violet-hued flesh of his bare forearm as the slugs curl and writhe in their new home. Louis shifts sideways in the chair and lowers his head almost to his knees, hugging his arm to his chest.

LOUIS
OK, Mom ... now ... now we ... wait.

The lightning flashes soundlessly. Behind and above Louis, high on the wall, the head and shoulders of a cancer vampire emerge from the solid wall like a predator pressing its way through its own amniotic sac. Louis can not see it behind him. The thing makes no noise as it pulls its arms through, finds purchase on the wall with its impossibly long fingers, and pulls itself out like a swimmer emerging from a pool. The cancer vampire slides down the wall, as silent as a lizard, and disappears behind the hunched-over Louis. Louis's mother moans in her sleep and Louis stands, whirls, and knocks the chair aside.

LOUIS
(to the thing, his voice tremulous)
Hey! Here ... here I am ... damn you.

The cancer vampire was crouching over Louis's mother but now it rises, lifts long fingers and its funneled face toward the glow that is Louis.

LOUIS
Here ... that's right ... food.

Louis extends his hands in the motion that is, once again, vaguely sacramental. The cancer vampire flows toward him, lowers its terrible face toward the outstretched, glowing hands.

LOUIS
That's right ... take ... *eat.*

The thing's proboscis seems to extend right into the flesh

of Louis's open palms. Louis's forearms writhe with the
motion of tumor slugs. We hear the SLURPING, SLID-
ING. Finished, the thing suddenly pulls its head back and
begins jerking, spasming.

> LOUIS
> (triumphantly but in a whisper)
> Tonight, Death, . . . *you* die.

The cancer vampire spasms and convulses. The violet
glow increases as the radiation spreads. There is a HISS-
ING, BURNING sound as of acid burning through thick
paper. The cancer vampire collapses, curls into itself, and
seems to shrivel while the HISSING continues. Its long
fingers close slowly . . . like the legs of a dying spider.
Louis staggers to his mother's bed, collapses on the edge
of it, and pulls on the heavy gloves.

> LOUIS
> I'd like to stay, Mom. See if Dr. Hubbard can
> help me . . . be around when he tells you that
> your tumors are gone . . .

We see a close-up of his mother's face—she is resting
more comfortably. He again takes her hand, pats it clumsily through his heavy gloves.

> LOUIS
> I'd like to stay . . . but I can't . . . I can feel the
> burning inside me. So *hot* . . .
> > (he clutches his stomach,
> > bends over, then straightens)
> There are all those other people in the ward,
> Mom . . . all those other *things* . . . waiting.
> > (glancing toward the door)
> I'm scared. But at least now I know what I should
> do . . .

In E.C.U. we see her hand twitch, possibly a random
movement, possibly squeezing his in affirmation. Louis
stands, looks toward the dark hall.

LOUIS
(whispering)
I only hope that I can feed them all.

Louis touches his mother's hand a final time and walks to
the door, pausing before stepping into the darkness there.

LOUIS
I love you, Mom.

Louis steps out and is gone. We watch and listen from a
low angle near his mother's sleeping form as his footsteps
recede ... for a moment there is silence ... and then the
SLURPING, SLIDING, RASPING begins, grows in volume, builds to a chorus. But with the noises comes a
promising violet glow, growing brighter down the corridor,
filling the doorway, filling the entire room with its
warmth, as we ...

FADE OUT

Introduction to
"E-Ticket to 'Namland"

I was born in 1948. By the time Kennedy was elected in 1960, World War II seemed like ancient history. Not just to *me* . . . everything is ancient history to a twelve-year-old . . . but, I believe, to most people in America then. The countless veterans had come home, and while many individuals had to deal with the traumas of war, the vast majority of them put the war behind them in various ways: went on to school on the GI Bill or got on with starting families, bought homes, and renewed their lives. Many of the men and women in my parents' generation had changed during the war, but most for the better. Travel and combat had brought some half-sensed maturity to the men; work and participation in the war effort had brought some inexpressable confidence and widening of horizons to the women. *America* had changed forever—gone forever was the isolationist, essentially rural nation recovering from the trauma of the Depression. I was born into the world's greatest superpower. We had the Bomb, economic prosperity, an unlimited future, and a young president who promised a New Frontier.

World War II was ancient history. Fifteen years had passed since our victory over the dictatorships, and even the brutal dress rehearsal of Korea hadn't changed our optimism. The *real* war was long ago and far away.

As I write this, fifteen years have passed since the last Americans fled Vietnam. Seventeen years have gone by since we withdrew our fighting forces. Two *decades*—a fifth of our century—have elapsed since the height of our involvement there. Yet, I feel, we're just beginning to find some collective peace of mind about Vietnam.

I suppose someone has suggested the parallel (it may be a cliché by now, for all I know), but it occurs to me that the stages of our national response to the trauma of Vietnam closely reflect the classic stages of response to the death of a loved one or the reaction to learning one has a terminal illness. Just look at our movies about Vietnam over the past twenty years.

First, denial: No major films. *Nada*.

Then anger: The cathartic "Coming Home" mental rewrites where the veterans were either anti-war martyrs or nutcases, followed by the revisionist fantasies of Rambo and his clones.

Then depression: The one brilliant depiction of the war was "Apocalypse Now," but Coppola jumped a stage in our recovery cycle so his effort was shunned. If he had waited until *after* we'd sickened of our Rambo fantasies, the film would have been received quite differently.

Finally, acceptance: "Platoon" and "Full Metal Jacket" and "Casualties of War" and the other post-trauma films have—despite the ballyhoo to the contrary—little content, less philosophy. What they *do* have is a shockingly correct texture—something quite close to the real smell of sweat and crotch rot, something surprisingly near to the actual language and true fatigue and terrible claustrophobia of a patrol in the boonies, something almost *right* about the fear that rises from the actors on the screen and spreads to the audience like the stench from a day-old corpse.

And so, after two decades and with an entire new generation which has grown up bored with the whole topic, after more changes in the texture of daily life than we can imagine or accept, I think we're finally beginning to *feel*—if not really understand—the true dimensions of the terrible national traffic accident that was Vietnam.

But for some people, that's just the beginning of the process.

E-Ticket to 'Namland

The twenty-eight Huey gunships moved out in single file, each hovering a precise three meters above the tarmac, the sound of their rotors filling the world with a roar that could be felt in teeth and bones and testicles. Once above the treeline and gaining altitude, the helicopters separated into four staggered V-formations and the noise diminished to the point where shouts could be heard.

"First time out?" cried the guide.

"What?" Justin Jeffries turned away from the open door where he had been watching the shadow of their helicopter slide across the surface of the mirrored rice paddies below. He leaned toward the guide until their combat helmets were almost touching.

"First time out?" repeated the guide. The man was small even for a Vietnamese. He wore a wide grin and the uniform and shoulder patch of the old First Air Cav Division.

Jeffries was big even for an American. He was dressed in green shorts, a flowered Hawaiian shirt, Nike running sandals, an expensive Rolex comlog, and a U.S. Army helmet that had become obsolete the year he was born. Jeffries was draped about with cameras; a compact Yashika SLR, a Polaroid Holistic-360, and a new Nikon imager. He returned the guide's grin. "First time for us. We're here with my wife's father."

Heather leaned over to join the conversation. "Daddy was here during . . . you know . . . the war. They thought it might be good for him to take the Vet Tour." She nodded in the direction of a short, solid, gray-haired man leaning against the M-60 machine-gun mount near the door's safety webbing. He was the only person in the cabin not wearing a helmet. The back of his blue shirt was soaked with sweat.

"Yes, yes," smiled the guide and stepped back to plug his microphone jack into a bulkhead socket. His voice echoed tinnily in every helmet and from hidden speakers. "Ladies and gentlemen, please notice the treeline to your right."

There was a lurch as the passengers shifted their positions and craned for a view. Ten-year-old Sammee Jeffries and his eight-year-old sister Elizabeth shoved their way through the crowded space to stand next to where their grandfather sat by the open door. The barrel of Elizabeth's plastic M-16 accidentally struck the older man on his sunburned neck but he did not turn or speak.

Suddenly a series of flashes erupted from the treeline along one rice paddy. The passengers gasped audibly as a line of magnesium-bright tracer bullets rose up and lashed toward their ship, missing the rotors by only a few meters. Immediately one of the gunships at the rear of their V-formation dove, curved back the way they had come in a centrifugally perfect arc, and raked the treeline with rocket and minigun fire. Meanwhile, at the guide's urging, Sammee stood on a low box, grasped the two-handed grip of the heavy M-60, swung it awkwardly to bear in the general direction of the now-distant treeline, and depressed the firing studs. The passengers instinctively clutched at their helmets to block their ears. Heavy cartridges, warm but not hot enough to burn anyone, clattered onto the metal deck.

An explosion split the treeline, sending phosphorous streamers fifty meters into the air and setting several tall palms ablaze. Bits of flaming debris splashed into the quiet rice paddy. The passengers laughed and applauded. Sammee grinned back at them and flexed his muscles.

Elizabeth leaned against her grandfather and spoke loudly into his ear. "Isn't this *fun*, Grandpa?"

He turned to say something but at that second the guide announced that their destination would be coming up on the left side of the ship and Elizabeth was away, shoving her brother aside to get a better view, eager to see the village appear below out of the heat-haze and smoke.

Later that evening five men sat around a table on the fifth-floor terrace of the Saigon Oberoi Sheraton. The air was warm and humid. Occasional gusts of laughter and splashing sounds came up from the pool on the fourth-floor terrace. It was well past nine, but the tropical twilight lingered.

"You were on the village mission-tour this morning, weren't you?" asked Justin Jeffries of the young Oriental next to him.

"Yes, I was. Most interesting." The man sat in a relaxed manner, but something about his bearing, the precisely creased safari suit, the intensity of his gaze, suggested a military background.

"You're Nipponese, aren't you?" asked Justin. At the man's smile and nod, Justin went on. "Thought so. Here with the military mission?"

"No, merely on leave. 'R and R' I believe your people used to call it."

"Christ," said the overweight American who sat next to Justin's father-in-law. "You've been up north in the PRC fighting Chen's warlords, haven't you?"

"Just so," said the Nipponese and extended his hand to Justin. "Lieutenant Keigo Naguchi."

"Justin Jeffries, Kansas City." Justin's huge hand enclosed the lieutenant's and pumped twice. "This here is my father-in-law, Ralph Disantis."

"A pleasure," said the lieutenant with a quick nod.

"Pleased to meet you," said Disantis.

"I believe I saw you with your grandchildren at the village today," said Naguchi. "A boy and a girl?"

Disantis nodded and sipped his beer. Justin gestured to the heavy-set man next to his father-in-law. "And this is Mr. . . . ah . . . Sears, right?"

"Sayers," said the man. "Roger Sayers. Nice to make your acquaintance, Lieutenant. So how's is going up there? Your guys finally getting those little bastards out of the hillcaves?"

"Most satisfactory," said Lieutenant Naguchi. "The situation should be stabilized before the next rainy season."

"Japanese brains and Vietnamese blood, huh?" laughed Sayers. He turned to the fifth man at the table, a silent Vietnamese in a white shirt and dark glasses, and added quickly, "No offense meant. Everybody knows that your basic Viet peasant makes the best foot soldier in the world. Showed us that forty years ago, eh, Mr. . . . ah . . .?"

"Minh," said the little man and shook hands around the table. "Nguyen van Minh." Minh's hair was black, his face unlined, but his eyes and hands revealed that he was at least in his sixties, closer to Disantis's age than that of the others.

"I saw you on the plane from Denver," said Justin. "Visiting family here?"

"No," said Minh. "I have been an American citizen since 1976. This is my first trip back to Vietnam. I have no family here now." He turned toward Naguchi. "Lieutenant, I am surprised that you chose to spend your leave on an American's Veterans' Tour."

Naguchi shrugged and sipped at his gin and tonic. "I find it a sharp contrast to modern methods. Up north I am more technician than warrior. Also, of course, learning more about the first of the helicopter wars is valuable to anyone who is interested in military history. You were a veteran of that war, Mr. Disantis?"

Justin's father-in-law nodded and took a long swallow of beer.

"I just missed it," said Sayers with real regret in his voice. "Too young for Vietnam. Too goddamn old for the Banana Wars."

Justin grunted. "You didn't miss much there."

"Ah, you were involved in that period?" asked Naguchi.

"Sure," said Justin. "Everybody who came of age in the discount decade got in on the Banana Wars. The tour today could have been Tegucicalpa or Estanzuelas, just substitute in coffee plantations for the rice paddies."

"I want to hear about that," said Sayers and waved a waiter over to the table. "Another round for everyone," he said. From somewhere near the pool a steel drum band started up, unsuccessfully trying to mix American pop tunes, a Caribbean beat, and local musicians. The sound seemed sluggish in the wet, thick air. Tropical night had fallen and even the stars appeared dimmed by the thickness of atmosphere. Naguchi looked up at a band of brighter stars moving toward the zenith and then glanced down at his comlog.

"Checking azimuth for your spottersat, right?" asked Justin. "It's a hard habit to break. I still do it."

Disantis rose. "Sorry I can't stay for the next round, gentlemen. Going to sleep off some of this jet lag." He moved into the air-conditioned brightness of the hotel.

Before going to his own room, Disantis looked in on Heather and the children. His daughter was in bed already, but Sammee and Elizabeth were busy feeding data from their father's Nikon through the terminal and onto the wallscreen. Disantis leaned against the door molding and watched.

"This is the LZ," Sammee said excitedly.

"What's an LZ?" asked Elizabeth.

"Landing Zone," snapped Sammee. "Don't you remember *anything*?"

The wall showed image after image of dust, rotors, the predatory shadows of Hueys coming in above Justin's camera position, the thin line of passengers in combat garb, men and women instinctively bent low despite obvious clearance from the rotors, tourists clutching at their helmets with one hand and hugging cameras, purses, and plastic M-16s to their chests with the other, groups moving quickly away from the raised landing platform along rice paddy dikes.

"There's Grandpa!" cried Elizabeth. Disantis saw himself, aging, overweight, puffing heavily as he heaved himself down from the helicopter, disdaining the guide's outstretched hand. Sammee tapped at the terminal keys. The picture zoomed and enlarged until only Disantis's grainy face filled the screen. Sammee shifted through colors and widened his grandfather's face until it became a purple balloon ready to pop.

"Stop it," whined Elizabeth.

"Crybaby," said Sammee, but some sixth sense made him glance over his shoulder to where Disantis stood. Sammee made no acknowledgment of his grandfather's presence but advanced the picture through a montage of new images.

Disantis blinked and watched the jerky newsreel proceed. The abandoned village of rough huts. The lines of tourist-troops along each side of the narrow road. Closeups of huts being searched. Heather emerging from a low doorway, blinking in the sunlight, awkwardly lifting her toy M-16 and waving at the camera.

"This is the good part," breathed Sammee.

They had been returning to the LZ when figures along a distant dike had opened fire. At first the tourists milled around in confusion, but at the guides' urging they finally, laughingly, had taken cover on the grassy side of the dike. Justin remained standing to take pictures. Disantis watched as those images built themselves on the wallscreen at a rate just slower than normal video. Data columns flashed by to the right. He saw himself drop to one knee on the dike and hold Elizabeth's hand. He remembered noting that the grass was artificial.

The tourists returned fire. Their M-16s flashed and recoiled, but no bullets were expended. The din was tremendous. On the screen a two-year-old near Justin had begun to cry.

Eventually the guides helped a young tourist couple use a field radio to call in an airstrike. The jets were there in less than a minute—three A-4D Skyhawks with antiquated U.S. naval markings bright and clear on the white wings. They screamed in under five hundred feet high. Justin's camera shook as the explosions sent long shadows across the dikes and made the tourists cringe and hug the earth from their vantage point six hundred meters away. Justin had managed to steady the camera even as the napalm continued to blossom upward.

"Watch," said Sammee. He froze the frame and then zoomed in. The image expanded. Tiny human forms, black silhouettes, became visible against the orange explosions. Sammee enlarged the image even further. Disantis could make out the silhouette of an outflung arm, a shirttail gusting, a conical peasant's hat flying off.

"How'd they do that, Grandpa?" asked Sammee without turning around.

Disantis shrugged. "Holos, maybe."

"Naw, not holos," said Sammee. He did not try to hide his condescension. "Too bright out there. Besides, you can see the pieces fly. Betcha they were animates."

Elizabeth rolled over from where she was sprawled. Her pajamas carried a picture of Wonder Duck on the front. "What'd Mr. Sayers mean on the way back, Grandpa?"

"When?"

"In the helicopter when he said, 'Well, I guess we really showed Charlie today.'" Elizabeth took a breath. "Who's Charlie, Grandpa?"

"Stupid," said Sammee. "Charlie was the VC. The bad guys."

"How come you called him Charlie, Grandpa?" persisted Elizabeth. The frozen explosion on the wallscreen cast an orange glow on her features.

"I don't remember," said Disantis. He paused with his hand on the door. "You two had better get to bed before your father comes up. Tomorrow's going to be a busy day."

Later, alone in his room, sitting in silence broken only by the hum of the air-conditioner, Disantis realized that he could *not* remember why the Vietcong had been called Charlie. He wondered if he had ever known. He turned out the light and opened the sliding doors to the balcony. The humid air settled on him like a blanket as he stepped out. Three floors below, Justin, Sayers, and the others still sat drinking. Their laughter floated up to Disantis and mixed with the rumble of thunder from a storm on the distant and darkened horizon.

On their way to a picnic the next day, Mr. Sayers tripped a claymore mine.

The guide had put them on a simulated patrol down a narrow jungle trail. Sayers was in the lead, paying little attention to the trail, talking to Reverend Dewitt, an airwaves minister from Dothan, Alabama. Justin and Heather were walking with the Newtons, a young couple from Hartford. Disantis was further back in line, walking between Sammee and Elizabeth to keep them from quarreling.

Sayers stepped into a thin tripwire stretched across the trail, a section of dirt erupted a meter in front of him, and the claymore jumped three meters into the air before exploding in a white puff.

"Shit," said Sayers. "Excuse me, Reverend." The Vietnamese guide came forward with an apologetic smile and put a red KIA armband on Sayers. The Reverend Dewitt and Tom Newton each received a yellow WIA armband.

"Does this mean I don't get to go to the picnic?" asked Sayers.

The guide smiled and directed the others on how to prepare a medevac LZ in a nearby clearing. Lieutenant Naguchi and Minh cleared underbrush with machetes while Heather and Sue Newton helped spread marker panels of iridescent orange plastic. Sammee was allowed to pop the tab on a green smoke marker.

The dust-off bird came in with a blast of downdraft that flattened the tall grass and blew Disantis's white tennis hat off. Sayers, Dewitt, and Newton sat propped on their elbows and waved as their stretchers were loaded. The patrol resumed when the dust-off 'copter was just a distant throbbing in the sky.

Justin took point. He moved carefully, frequently holding his hand up to halt the line behind him. There were two more tripwires and a stretch of trail salted with antipersonnel mines. The guide showed them all how to probe ahead with bayonets. For the last half-kilometer, they stayed in the grass on either side of the trail.

The picnic ground was on a hill overlooking the sea. Under a thatched pavilion sat three tables covered with sandwich makings, salads, assorted fruits, and coolers of beer. Sayers, Newton, and Dewitt were already there, helping two guides cook hamburgers and hot dogs over charcoal fires. "What kept you?" called Sayers with a deep laugh.

After a long lunch, several of the tourists went down to the beach to swim or sunbathe or take a nap. Sammee found a network of tunnels in the jungle near the picnic pavilion and several of the children gathered around as the guide showed them how to drop in CS gas and fragmentation and concussion grenades before actually searching the tunnels. Then the children and a few of the younger adults wiggled in on their bellies to explore the complex. Disantis could hear their excited shouts as he sat alone at one of the picnic tables, drinking his beer and looking out to sea. He could also hear the conversation of his daughter and Sue Newton as they sat on beach towels a few meters away.

"We wanted to bring my daddy but he just refused to come," said the Newton woman. "So Tommy says, 'Well, shoot, so long as the government's paying part of it, let's go ourselves.' So we did."

"We thought it'd be good for my father," said Heather. "I wasn't even born then, but when he got back from the war, way back in the Seventies, he didn't even come home to Mother. He went and lived in the woods in Oregon or Washington or somewhere for a couple of years."

"Really!" said Sue Newton. "My daddy never did anything crazy like that."

"Oh, he got better after a while," said Heather. "He's been fine the last ten years or so. But his therapy program said that it'd be good for him to come on the Vet's Tour, and Justin was able to get time off 'cause the dealership is doing so good."

The talk turned to children. Shortly after that it began to rain heavily and three Hueys and a lumbering Chinook picked them up to return them to the Sheraton. The dozen or so people in Disantis's group sang "Ninety-nine Bottles of Beer on the Wall" during the short flight back.

There was nothing scheduled for the afternoon and after the storm passed several people decided to go shopping at one of the large malls between the hotel complex and the Park. Disantis caught an electric bus into downtown Saigon where he walked the streets until nightfall.

The change of names to Ho Chi Minh City had never really taken and the metropolis had officially been renamed Saigon in the early Nineties. The city bore little resemblance to the excited jumble of pedestrians, motorbikes, strip joints, bars, restaurants, and cheap hotels Disantis remembered from forty years earlier. The foreign money had all gone into the tourist enclaves near the Park and the city itself reflected the gray era of the New Socialist Reality more than it did the feverish pulse of old Saigon. Efficient, faceless structures and steel and glass high-rises sat on either side of busy boulevards. Occasionally Disantis would see a decaying sidestreet which reminded him of the cluttered stylishness of Tu-Do Street in the late Sixties.

Nguyen van Minh joined him as Disantis waited for a light to change on Thong Njut Boulevard.

"Mr. Disantis."

"Mr. Minh."

The short Vietnamese adjusted his glasses as they strolled past the park where the Independence Palace had once stood. "You are enjoying the sights?" he asked. "Do you see much that is familiar?"

"No," said Disantis. "Do you?"

Minh paused and looked around him as if the idea had not pertained to him. "Not really, Mr. Disantis," he said at last. "Of course, I rarely visited Saigon. My village was in a different province. My unit was based near Da Nang."

"ARVN?" asked Disantis.

"Hac Bao," said Minh. "The Black Panthers of the First Division. You remember them, perhaps?"

Disantis shook his head.

"We were . . . I say without pride . . . the most feared

fighting unit in all of South Vietnam ... including the Americans. The Hac Bao had put fear into the hearts of the communist insurgents for ten years before the fall."

Disantis stopped to buy a lemon ice from a street vendor. The lights were coming on all along the boulevard.

"You see the embassy there?" asked Minh, pointing to an antiquated six-story structure set back behind an ornate fence.

"That's the old U.S. Embassy?" asked Disantis without much interest in his voice. "I would have thought that the building would've been torn down by now."

"Oh, no," said Minh, "it is a museum. It has been restored very much to its original appearance."

Disantis nodded and glanced at his comlog.

"I stood here," continued Minh, "right here ... in April of 1975, and watched the helicopters take the last of the Americans off the roof of the embassy. It was only my third time in Saigon. I had just been released from four days in prison."

"Prison?" Disantis turned to look at Minh.

"Yes. I had been arrested by the government after members of my unit commandeered the last Boeing 727 out of Da Nang to Saigon. We fought civilians—women and children—to get aboard that plane. I was a lieutenant. I was twenty-three years old."

"So you got out of Vietnam during the panic?"

"They released us from jail when the North Vietnamese were in the suburbs," said Minh. "I was not able to leave the country until several months later."

"Boat?" asked Disantis. The lemon ice was melting quickly in the warm air.

Minh nodded. "And you, Mr. Disantis, when did you leave Vietnam?"

Disantis tossed the paper wrapper into a trashcan and licked his fingers. "I came here early in '69," he said.

"And when did you leave?" Minh asked again.

Disantis lifted his head as if to sniff the night air. The evening was thick with the scent of tropical vegetation, mimosa blossoms, stagnant water, decay. When he looked at Minh there was a dark gleam in his blue eyes. He shook his head. "I never left," he said.

•   •   •

Justin, Sayers, and Tom Newton came up to the guide as he sat alone at a table near the back of the hotel bar. The three Americans hesitated and looked at each other. Finally Justin stepped forward. "Howdy," he said.

"Good afternoon, Mr. Jeffries," said the guide.

"We . . . uh . . . we'd all, I mean the three of us and a couple of other guys, we wanted to see you about something."

"Ahhh, there is some problem with the tour?" asked the guide.

"No, no, everything's great," said Justin and glanced back at the other two. He sat down and leaned toward the Vietnamese. His voice was a hoarse whisper. "We . . . ah . . . we wanted a little more than the regular tour."

"Oh?" The guide blinked. His mouth was not quite curled in a smile.

"Yeah," said Justin, "you know. Something *extra*."

"Extra?" said the guide.

Roger Sayers stepped forward. "We want some special action," he said.

"Ahhh," said the guide and finished his drink.

Justin leaned forward again. "Nat Pendrake told us it was OK," he whispered loudly. "He said he . . . uh . . . arranged it through Mr. Tho."

"Mr. Tho?" the guide said blankly. But the smile was there now.

"Yeah. Nat said that . . . uh . . . a special action would be about a thousand."

"Two thousand," the guide said softly. "Each."

"Hey," interjected Sayers, "Nat was here just a few months ago and . . ."

"Quiet," said Justin. "All right. That's fine. Here." He slid his universal card across the table.

The Vietnamese smiled and pushed Jeffries's card back. "Cash, please. Each of you will have it tonight. American dollars."

"I don't know about . . ." began Sayers.

"Where?" asked Justin.

"The frontage road beyond the hotel maintenance buildings," said the guide. "Twenty-three hundred hours."

"Right," said Justin as the guide stood up. "See you then."

"Have a nice day," said the guide and was gone.

The trucks transported them to a point in the jungle where the road ended and a trail began. The five men jumped down and followed the guide through the darkness. The trail was muddy from the evening rains and wet fronds brushed at their cork-smudged faces. Justin Jeffries and Tom Newton kept close to the guide. Behind them, stumbling occasionally in the dark, came Sayers and Reverend Dewitt. Lieutenant Naguchi brought up the rear. Each man was in uniform. Each carried an M-16.

"Shit," hissed Sayers as a branch caught him in the face.

"Shut up," whispered Justin. The guide motioned them to a stop and the Americans pressed close to peer at a clearing visible through a gap in the dense foliage. A few kerosene lanterns threw light from the doorways of a dozen huts of the village.

"Vietcong sympathizers," whispered the guide. "They can tell you where the cadre headquarters is. Everyone in the village knows the VC."

"Huh," said Sayers. "So our job is to get the information, right?"

"Yes."

"And they're VC sympathizers?" whispered Tom Newton.

"Yes."

"How many?" asked Lieutenant Naguchi. His voice was barely audible above the drip of water from palm leaves.

"Maybe thirty," said the guide. "No more than thirty-five."

"Weapons?" asked Naguchi.

"There may be some hidden in the huts," said the guide. "Be careful of the young men and women. VC. Well-trained."

There was a long silence as they stared at the quiet village. Finally Justin stood and clicked the safety off on his rifle. "Let's do it," he said. Together they moved into the clearing.

Ralph Disantis and Nguyen van Minh sat together in a dark booth in an old bar not far from what had once been Tu-Do Street. It was late. Minh was quite drunk and Disantis let himself appear to be in the same condition. An ancient juke box in the corner played recent Japanese hits and oldies-but-goodies dating back to the eighties.

"For many years after the fall of my country, I thought that America had no honor," said Minh. The only sign of the little man's drunkenness was the great care with which he enunciated each word. "Even as I lived in America, worked in America, became a citizen of America, I was convinced that America had no honor. My American friends told me that during the Vietnam War there was news from my country on the televisions and radios every day, every evening. After Saigon fell . . . there was nothing. Nothing. It was as if my nation had never existed."

"Hmmm," said Disantis. He finished his drink and beckoned for more.

"But you, Mr. Disantis, you are a man of honor," said Minh. "I know this. I sense this. You are a man of honor."

Disantis nodded at the retreating waiter, removed the swizzle stick from his fresh drink, and placed the plastic saber in a row with seven others. Mr. Minh blinked and did the same with his.

"As a man of honor you will understand why I have returned to avenge my family," Minh said carefully.

"Avenge?" said Disantis.

"Avenge my brother who died fighting the North Vietnamese," said Minh. "Avenge my father—a teacher—who spent eight years in a reeducation camp only to die soon after his release. Avenge my sister who was deported by this regime for . . ." Minh paused. "For alleged crimes against morality. She drowned when their overcrowded boat went down somewhere between here and Hong Kong."

"Avenge," repeated Disantis. "How? With what?"

Minh sat up straight and looked over his shoulder. No one was near. "I will avenge my family's honor by striking against the maggots who have corrupted my nation," he said.

"Yeah," said Disantis. "With what? Do you have a weapon?"

Minh hesitated, licked his lips, and looked for a second like he was sobering. Then he leaned over and grasped Disantis's forearm. "I have a weapon," he whispered. "Two of them. I smuggled them in. A rifle and my service automatic from the Hac Bao." He hesitated again. "I can tell you this, Mr. Disantis. You are a man of honor." This time it was a question.

"Yes," said Disantis. "Tell me."

Two of the huts were on fire. Justin and the other four had come in shouting and firing. There had been no opposition. The thirty-two villagers, mostly children and old people, knelt in the dust at the center of the village. Sayers had knocked over a lantern in one of the huts and the thatch and bamboo had blazed like an incendiary flare. The fat American had beat uselessly at the flames until Justin called, "Forget the fucking hootch and get back here."

Tom Newton swung his rifle to cover the cringing villagers. "Where are the VC?" he shouted.

"VC!" shouted Sayers. "Where are their tunnels? Tell us, goddammit!" A kneeling woman holding a baby bowed her forehead to the dust. Flames cast bizarre shadows on the dirt and the smell of smoke made the men's nostrils flare.

"They don't understand," said Reverend Dewitt.

"The hell they don't," snapped Justin. "They're just not talking."

Lieutenant Naguchi stepped forward. He was relaxed but he kept his M-16 trained on the cowering villagers. "Mr. Jeffries, I will stand guard here if you wish to conduct an interrogation."

"Interrogation?" said Justin.

"There is an empty hut there, away from the fire," said the lieutenant. "It is best to isolate them during questioning."

"Yeah," said Justin. "I remember. Tom, cut a couple of them out of the herd. Hurry!"

Newton lifted a young man and an old woman by the arm and began moving them toward the hut.

"Not her," said Justin. "Too old. Get that one." He pointed to a wide-eyed girl of fifteen or sixteen. "She's probably got a brother or boyfriend fighting with the VC."

Newton pushed the old woman back to her knees and roughly lifted the girl to her feet. Justin felt his mouth go dry. Behind him the flames had set a third hut on fire and sparks drifted up to mix with the stars.

Disantis set the ninth plastic saber carefully in a row with the others. "How about ammunition?" he asked.

Minh blinked slowly and smiled. "Three thousand rounds for the rifle," he said. He lifted his glass in slow motion, drank, swallowed. "Thirty clips for the .45 caliber service automatic. Enough . . ." He paused, swayed a second, and straightened his back. "Enough to do the job, yes?"

Disantis dropped the colored money on the table to pay the tab. He helped Minh to his feet and guided the smaller man toward the door. Minh stopped, grasped Disantis's arm in both hands, and brought his face close. "Enough, yes?" he asked.

Disantis nodded. "Enough," he said.

"Shit," said Tom Newton, "he's not going to tell us anything." The young man from the village knelt before them. His black shirt had been pulled back to pin his arms. Blood was smeared from the corners of his mouth and nostrils. There were cigarette burn marks dotted across his chest.

"Bring the girl here," said Justin. Sayers pushed her to her knees, took a fistful of hair, and jerked her head back sharply.

"Where are the VC?" asked Justin. Smoke came through the open door of the hootch. "Tunnels? VC?"

The girl said nothing. Her eyes were very dark and dilated with fear. Small, white teeth showed between her slightly parted lips.

"Hold her arms," Justin said to Newton and Sayers. He took a long knife out of its sheath on his web belt, slipped the point under her buttoned shirtfront, and slashed upward. Cloth ripped and parted. The girl gasped and writhed but the two Americans held her tightly. Her breasts were small, conical, and lightly filmed with moisture.

"Jesus," said Newton and giggled.

Justin tugged her black pants halfway down, slapped her knee aside when she kicked, and used the knife to tear the cloth away from her ankles.

"Hey!" yelled Sayers. The young Vietnamese had lurched to his feet and was struggling to free his arms. Justin turned quickly, dropped the knife, lifted the M-16, and fired three times in rapid succession. Flesh exploded from the boy's chest, throat, and cheek. He kicked backward, spasmed once, and lay still in a growing red pool.

"Oh, Jesus," Newton said again. "Jesus Christ, this is something."

"Shut up," said Justin. He placed the butt of his rifle against the dazed girl's collarbone and pushed her onto her back in the dirt. "Hold her legs," he said. "You'll get your turns."

After seeing Minh to his hotel room and putting him to bed, Disantis went back to his own room and sat out on the balcony. Some time after three a.m., his son-in-law and four other men materialized out of the darkness and sat down around one of the round tables on the abandoned terrace below. Disantis could hear the sounds of beer cans being tossed into trash bins, the pop of more tabs, and bits of conversation.

"How the hell did all the firing start out there anyway?" asked Justin in the darkness. Several of the others giggled drunkenly.

A firm voice with a Japanese accent answered. "One of them ran. The Reverend opened fire. I joined him in stopping them from escaping."

". . . damn brains all over the place." Disantis recognized Sayers's voice. "I'd like to know how they did that."

"Bloodbags and charges every six centimeters or so under the synflesh," came the slurred voice of the young man named Newton. "Used to work for Disney. Know all about that animate stuff."

"If they *were* animates," said the Sayers shadow and someone giggled.

"You damn well know they were," came Justin's voice. "We never got out of the damned Park. Ten thousand goddamn bucks."

"It was so . . . *real*," said a voice that Disantis recognized as belonging to the airwaves minister. "But surely there were no . . . bullets."

"Hell, no," said Newton. "'Scuse me, Reverend. But they couldn't use real slugs. Customers'd kill each other by mistake."

"Then how . . ."

"Lasered UV pulses," said Justin.

"Triggered the charges under the skin," said Newton. "Easy to reset."

"But the blood," said Reverend Dewitt in the darkness. "The . . . the brain matter. The bone fragments . . ."

"All right, already!" shouted Sayers so loudly that several of the other men shushed him. "Come on, let's just say we got our money's worth, okay? They can buy a lot of spare parts for that much, right?"

"You can buy a lot of spare gooks for that much," said Newton and there was a ripple of laughter. "Jesus," he went on, "did you see that gook girl wiggle when Jeffries slipped it to her the first time . . ."

Disantis listened for a few minutes more and then went into his room and carefully closed the sliding door.

The morning was beautiful with tall, white clouds piling up above the sea to the east while the family had a leisurely breakfast on the restaurant terrace. Sammee and

Elizabeth had eggs, toast, and cereal. Heather ordered an omelette. Disantis had coffee. Justin joined them late, cradled his head in his hands, and ordered a Bloody Mary.

"You came in late last night, dear," said Heather.

Justin massaged his temples. "Yeah. Tom and some of us went to the gaming rooms and played poker 'til late."

"You missed the excitement this morning, Dad," said Sammee.

"Yeah, what?" Justin sipped at his drink and grimaced.

"They arrested Mr. Minh this mornin'," Sammee said happily.

"Oh?" Justin looked at his wife.

"It's true, dear," said Heather. "He was arrested this morning. Something to do with illegal contraband in his luggage."

"Yeah," said Sammee, "I heard the guy downstairs tellin' somebody that he had a rifle. You know, like ours, only *real*."

"Well, I'll be damned," said Justin. "Is he going to stand trial or what?"

"No," said Disantis. "They just asked him to leave. They shipped him out on the morning shuttle to Tokyo."

"There're a lot of nuts around," muttered Justin. He opened the menu. "I think I will have breakfast. Do we have time before the morning tour?"

"Oh, yes," said Heather. "The helicopters don't leave until ten-thirty this morning. We're going up the river somewhere. Dad says that it should be very interesting."

"I think all this junk is *boring*," whined Elizabeth.

"That's 'cause you think *every*thing's boring, stupid," said Sammee.

"Be quiet, both of you," said Heather. "We're here for your grandfather's benefit. Eat your cereal."

The twenty-eight Huey slicks moved out in single file, climbed above the line of trees, and sorted themselves into formation as they leveled off at three thousand feet. The panorama of highways and housing developments beneath them changed to rice paddies and jungle as they entered the Park. Then they were over the river and heading west.

Peasants poling small craft upstream looked up and waved as shadows of the gunships passed over them.

Disantis sat in the open door, hands hooked in the safety webbing, and let his legs dangle. On his back was Sammee's blue backpack. Justin dozed on a cushioned bench. Elizabeth sat on Heather's lap and complained of the heat. Sammee swung the heavy M-60 to the left and right and made machine-gun noises.

The guide plugged his microphone into the bulkhead. "Ladies and gentlemen, today we are on a mission up the Mekong River. Our goal is twofold—to intercept illicit river traffic and to inspect any area of jungle near Highway 1 where movement of NVA regulars has been reported. Following completion of the mission, we will tour an eight-hundred-year-old Buddhist temple. Lunch will be served after the temple tour."

The helicopter throbbed north and westward. Elizabeth complained that she was hungry. Reverend Dewitt tried to get everyone to sing camp songs but few people were interested. Tom Newton pointed out historical landmarks to his wife. Justin awoke briefly, shot a series of images with his Nikon, and went back to sleep.

Sometime later the guide broke the silence. "Please watch the river as we turn south. We will be searching for any small boats which look suspicious or attempt to flee at our approach. We should see the river in the next few minutes."

"No, we won't," said Disantis. He reached under his flowered shirt and removed the heavy .45 from his waistband. He aimed it at the guide's face and held it steady. "Please ask the pilot to turn north."

The cabin resounded with babble and then fell silent as the guide smiled. "A joke, Mr. Disantis, but not a funny one, I am afraid. Please let me see the . . ."

Disantis fired. The slug ripped through the bulkhead padding three centimeters from the guide's face. People screamed, the guide flinched and raised his hands instinctively, and Disantis swung his legs into the cabin. "North, please," he said. "Immediately."

The guide spoke quickly into his microphone, snapped two monosyllabic answers to unheard questions from the pilot, and the Huey swung out of formation and headed north.

"Daddy," said Heather.

"What the fuck do you think you're doing, Ralph?" said Justin. "Now give me that goddamn relic before someone gets . . ."

"Shut up," said Disantis.

"Mr. Disantis," said Reverend Dewitt, "there are women and children aboard this aircraft. If we could just talk about whatever . . ."

"Put the damn gun down, Ralph," growled Justin and began to rise from the bench.

"Be quiet." Disantis swung the pistol in Justin's direction and the big man froze in mid-movement. "The next person to speak will be shot."

Sammee opened his mouth, looked at his grandfather's face, and remained silent. For several minutes the only sound was the throb of the rotors and Heather's soft weeping.

"Take it down here," Disantis said at last. He had been watching the jungle, making sure they were well out of the Park. "Here."

The guide paused and then spoke rapid-fire Vietnamese into his mike. The Huey began to descend, circling in toward the clearing Disantis had pointed to. He could see two black Saigon Security hovercraft coming quickly from the east, the downblast of their fans rippling the leaf canopy of the jungle as they roared ten meters above it.

The Huey's skids touched down and the high grass rippled and bent from the blast of the rotors. "Come on, kids," said Disantis. He moved quickly, helping Elizabeth out and tugging Sammee from his perch before Heather could grab him. Disantis jumped down beside them.

"The *hell* you say," bellowed Justin and vaulted down.

Disantis and the children had moved a few feet and were crouching in the whipping grass. Disantis half-turned and shot Justin in the left leg. The force of the blow swung the big man around. He fell back toward the open doorway as people screamed and reached for him.

"This is real," Disantis said softly. "Goodbye." He fired twice past the cockpit windshield. Then he took Elizabeth by the hand and pulled her toward the jungle as the helicopter lifted off. A multitude of hands pulled Justin in the open door as the Huey swung away over the trees. Sammee hesitated, looked at the empty sky, and then stumbled after his sister and grandfather. The boy was sobbing uncontrollably.

"Hush," said Disantis and pulled Sammee inside the wall of vegetation. There was a narrow trail extending into the jungle darkness. Disantis removed the light backpack and took out a new clip for the automatic. He ejected the old magazine and clicked the new one in with a slap of his palm. Then he grabbed both children and moved as quickly as he could in a counter-clockwise jog around the perimeter of the clearing, always remaining concealed just within the jungle. When they stopped he pushed the children down behind a fallen tree. Elizabeth began to wail. "Hush," Disantis said softly.

The Huey gunship came in quickly, the guide leaped to the ground, and then the helicopter was spiralling upward again, clawing for altitude. A second later the first of the Saigon Security hovercrafts roared in over the treetops and settled next to the guide. The two men who jumped out wore black armorcloth and carried Uzi miniguns. The guide pointed to the spot on the opposite side of the clearing where Disantis had first entered the jungle.

They lifted their weapons and took a step in that direction. Disantis walked out behind them, dropped to one knee when he got to within five meters, braced the pistol with both hands, and fired as they turned. He shot the first policeman in the face. The second man had time to raise his gun before he was struck twice in the chest. The bullets did not penetrate the armorcloth but the impact knocked him onto his back. Disantis stepped forward, straightened his arm, and shot the man in the left eye.

The guide turned and ran into the jungle. Disantis fired once and then crouched next to the dead policeman as a wash of hot air struck him. The hovercraft was ten meters high and turning toward the trees when Disantis lifted the policeman's Uzi and fired. He did not bother to aim. The minigun kicked and flared, sending two thousand fléchettes a second skyward. Disantis had a brief glimpse of the pilot's face before the entire canopy starred and burst into white powder. The hovercraft listed heavily to the left and plowed into the forest wall. There was the heavy sound of machinery and trees breaking but no explosion.

Disantis ran back to the jungle just as the second hovercraft appeared. It circled once and then shot straight up until it was lost in the sun. Disantis grabbed the children and urged them on, circling the edge of the clearing again until they reached the spot where the guide had entered the forest. The narrow trail led away from the light into the jungle.

Disantis crouched for a second and then touched the high grass at the side of the trail. Drops of fresh blood were visible in the dappled light. Disantis sniffed at his fingers and looked up at the white faces of Sammee and Elizabeth. They had stopped crying.

"It's all right," he said, and his voice was soft and soothing. Behind them and above them there were the sounds of rotors and engines. Gently, ever so gently, he turned the children and began leading them, unresisting, along the path into the jungle. It was darker there, quiet and cool. The way was marked with crimson. The children moved quickly to keep up with their grandfather.

"It's all right," he whispered and touched their shoulders lightly to guide them down the narrowing path. "Everything's all right. I know the way."

Introduction to "Iverson's Pits"

We Americans have a knack for turning our most beloved national shrines into something tacky and vulgar. Perhaps it's because we're too young to have a real sense of history; perhaps it's because our nation—not counting the Confederacy—has never been bombed or occupied or even invaded by a foreign power (no, I don't count the British when they burned Washington City . . . few Americans noticed and fewer cared), and there is little real sense of sacrifice to our shrines.

There are, of course, a few shrines that defy our efforts to tackify them. It's hard to stand in front of the Lincoln Memorial at night without beginning to feel like Mr. Smith just come to Washington. I had a Jimmy Stewart stammer for three days after my first midnight visit there.

But if you stand there long enough, you can almost hear the bureaucrats conferring with the Disney Imagineers behind the marble walls; come back six months later and Old Abe will probably stand, recite his Second Inaugural in Hal Holbrook's voice, wade the Reflecting Pool, and tapdance down Constitution Avenue.

All in good taste, of course.

But then there are the Civil War battlefields.

You've probably visited Gettysburg. Despite the best efforts of sincere people to preserve it, the place has been littered with statues and dusted with memorials. The Park Service erected a phallic monstrosity of a tower at the highest point so that there is no escaping the intrusion of 20th Century ugliness. Computerized dioramas blink lights in the museum and you can buy souvenir t-shirts in the local shops.

It doesn't matter. It just doesn't matter.

As with a score of less famous Civil War battlefields, Gettysburg has an almost overpowering sense of *rightness* about it: an almost physical effect on the visitor and a psychic impact that must be felt to be believed. It is a haunting place in every sense of the word. No castle in Scotland, no druidic circle of stones, no crypt beneath a Pharaoh's pyramid could be eerier or could channel more voices of the dead to the ears of the living.

And few places could be more moving or peaceful.

For what it's worth, this tale grew—literally—from a footnote, but every supporting detail in "Iverson's Pits" is as accurate as I could make it. The burial pits were real. One account in Glenn Tucker's classic *High Tide at Gettysburg* records:

> The unhappy spirits of the slaughtered North Carolina soldiers were reputed to abide in this section of the battlefield. Lieutenant Montgomery returned in 1898, thirty-five years after the battle, and learned from John S. Forney that a superstitious terror had long hung over the area. Farm laborers would not work there after night began to settle.

My Colonel Iverson is a fictional construct, of course. The real Colonel Alfred Iverson, Jr., *did* send his regiment to slaughter and *was* relieved after his men—his few surviving men—refused to follow him, but there is no evidence that the real Iverson was anything other than a politically appointed military incompetent. Also, a fellow named Jessup Sheads *did* build a house on the site where the 97th New York had faced the 12th North Carolina. Local historians confirm that Sheads offered wine to visitors— wine from the arbors which grew so luxuriantly above Iverson's Pits.

Iverson's Pits

As a young boy, I was not afraid of the dark. As an old man, I am wiser. But it was as a boy of ten in that distant summer of 1913 that I was forced to partake of communion with that darkness which now looms so close. I remember the taste of it. Even now, three-quarters of a century later, I am unable to turn over black soil in the garden or to stand alone in the grassy silence of my grandson's backyard after the sun has set without a hint of cold fingers on the back of my neck.

The past is, as they say, dead and buried. But even the most buried things have their connections to the present, gnarled old roots rising to the surface, and I am one of these. Yet there is no one to connect to, no one to tell. My daughter is grown and gone, dead of cancer in 1953. My middle-aged grandson is a product of those Eisenhower years, that period of endless gestation when all the world seemed fat and confident and looking to the future. Paul has taught science at the local high school for twenty-three years and were I to tell him now about the events of that hot first day and night of July, 1913, he would think me mad. Or senile.

My great-grandchildren, a boy and a girl in an age that finds little reason to pay attention to such petty distinctions as gender, could not conceive of a past as ancient and irretrievable as my own childhood before the Great War, much less the blood-and-leather reality of the Civil War era from which I carry my dark message. My great-grandchildren are as colorful and mindless as the guppies Paul keeps in his expensive aquarium, free from the terrors and tides of the ocean of history, smug in their almost total ignorance of everything that came before themselves, Big Macs, and MTV.

So I sit alone on the patio in Paul's backyard (why was it, I try to recall, that we turned our focus away from the front porch attention to the communal streets and sidewalks into the fenced isolation of our own backyards?) and I study the old photograph of a serious ten-year-old in his Boy Scout uniform.

The boy is dressed far too warmly for such a hot summer day—his small form is almost lost under the heavy, woolen Boy Scout tunic, broad-brimmed campaign hat, baggy wool trousers, and awkward puttees laced almost to the knees. He is not smiling—a solemn, miniature doughboy four years before the term doughboy had passed into the common vocabulary. The boy is me, of course, standing in front of Mr. Everett's ice wagon on that day in June when I was about to leave on a trip much longer in time and to places much more unimaginably distant than any of us might have dreamed.

I look at the photograph knowing that ice wagons exist now only as fading memories in aging skulls, that the house in the background has long since been torn down to be replaced by an apartment building which in turn was replaced by a shopping mall, that the wool and leather and cotton of the Boy Scout uniform have rotted away, leaving only the brass buttons and the boy himself to be lost somewhere, and that—as Paul would explain—every cell in that unsmiling ten-year-old's body has been replaced several times. For the worse, I suspect. Paul would say that the DNA is the same, and then give an explanation which makes it sound as if the only continuity between me *now* and me *then* is some little parasite-architect, blindly sitting and smirking in each otherwise unrelated cell of the then-me and the now-me.

Cow manure.

I look at that thin face, those thin lips, the eyes narrowed and squinting in the light of a sun seventy-five years younger (and hotter, I *know*, despite the assurances of reason and the verities of Paul's high school science) and I feel the thread of sameness which unites that unsuspecting boy of ten—so confident for one so young, so unafraid—with the old man who has learned to be afraid of the dark.

I wish I could warn him.

The past is dead and buried. But I know now that buried things have a way of rising to the surface when one least expects them to.

In the summer of 1913 the Commonwealth of Pennsylvania made ready for the largest invasion of military veterans the nation had ever seen. Invitations had been sent out from the War Department for a Great Reunion of Civil War veterans to commemorate the fiftieth anniversary of the three-day battle at Gettysburg.

All that spring our Philadelphia newspapers were filled with details of the anticipated event. Up to 40,000 veterans were expected. By mid-May, the figure had risen to 54,000 and the General Assembly had to vote additional monies to supplement the Army's budget. My mother's cousin Celia wrote from Atlanta to say that the Daughters of the Confederacy and other groups affiliated with the United Confederate Veterans were doing everything in their power to send their old men North for a final invasion.

My father was not a veteran. Before I was born, he had called the trouble with Spain "Mr. Hearst's War" and five years after the Gettysburg Reunion he would call the trouble in Europe "Mr. Wilson's War." By then I would be in high school, with my classmates chafing to enlist and show the Hun a thing or two, but by then I shared my father's sentiments; I had seen enough of war's legacy.

But in the late spring and early summer of 1913 I would have given anything to join those veterans in Gettysburg, to hear the speeches and see the battle flags and crouch in the Devil's Den and watch those old men reenact Pickett's Charge one last time.

And then the opportunity arrived.

Since my birthday in February I had been a Boy Scout. The Scouts were a relatively new idea then—the first groups in the United States had been formed only three years earlier—but in the spring of 1913 every boy I knew was either a Boy Scout or waiting to become one.

The Reverend Hodges had formed the first Troop in Chestnut Hill, our little town outside of Philadelphia, now a suburb. The Reverend allowed only boys of good character and strong moral fiber to join: Presbyterian boys. I had sung in the Fourth Avenue Presbyterian Boys' Choir for three years and, in spite of my frailness and total inability to tie a knot, I was allowed to become a Boy Scout three days after my tenth birthday.

My father was not totally pleased. Our Scout uniforms might have been castoffs from the returning Roughriders' army. From hobnailed boots to puttees to campaign hats we were little troopers, drowning in yards of khaki and great draughts of military virtue. The Reverend Hodges had us on the high school football field each Tuesday and Thursday afternoon from four to six and every Saturday morning from seven until ten, practicing close-order drill and applying field dressings to one another until our Troop resembled nothing so much as a band of mummies with swatches of khaki showing through our bandages. On Wednesday evening we met in the church basement to learn Morse Code—what the Reverend called General Service Code—and to practice our semaphore signals.

My father asked me if we were training to fight the Boer War over again. I ignored his irony, sweated into my khaki woolens through those warming weeks of May, and loved every minute of it.

When the Reverend Hodges came by our house in early June to inform my parents that the Commonwealth had requested all Boy Scout Troops in Pennsylvania to send representatives to Gettysburg to help with the Great Reunion, I knew that it had been Divine Intervention which would allow me to join the Reverend, thirteen-year-old Billy Stargill (who would later die in the Argonne), and a pimply-faced overweight boy whose name I cannot recall on the five-day visit to Gettysburg.

My father was noncommittal but my mother agreed at once that it was a unique honor, so on the morning of June 30 I posed in front of Mr. Everett's ice wagon for a photograph taken by Dr. Lowell, Chestnut Hill's undertaker and official photographer, and at a little after two p.m. on that same day I joined the Reverend and my two comrades-in-arms for the three-hour train ride to Gettysburg.

As a part of the official celebration, we paid the veterans' travel rate of one cent a mile. The train ride cost me $1.21. I had never been to Gettysburg. I had never been away from home overnight.

We arrived late in the afternoon; I was tired, hot, thirsty, and desperately needing to relieve myself since I had been too shy to use the lavatory aboard the train. The small town of Gettysburg was a mass of crowds, confusion, noise, horses, automobiles, and old men whose heavy uniforms smelled of camphor. We stumbled after Reverend Hodges through muddy lanes between buildings draped in flags and bunting. Men outnumbered women ten to one and most of the main streets were a sea of straw boaters and khaki caps. As the Reverend checked in the lobby of the Eagle Hotel for word from his Scouting superiors, I slipped down a side hall and found a public restroom.

Half an hour later we dragged our duffel bags into the back of a small motor carriage for the ride out southwest of town to the Reunion tent city. A dozen boys and their Scoutmasters were crowded into the three benches as the vehicle labored its way through heavy traffic down Franklin Street, past a temporary Red Cross Hospital on the east side of the street and a score of Ambulance Corps wagons parked on the west side, and then right onto a road marked Long Lane and into a sea of tents which seemed to stretch on forever.

It was past seven o'clock and the rich evening light illuminated thousands of canvas pyramids covering hundreds of acres of open farmland. I craned to make out which of the distant hills was Cemetery Ridge, which heap of rocks the Little Round Top. We passed State Policemen on horseback, Army wagons pulled by Army mules, huge heaps of firewood, and clusters of portable field bakeries where the aroma of fresh-baked bread still lingered.

Reverend Hodges turned in his seat. "Afraid we missed the evening chow lines, boys," he said. "But we weren't hungry, were we?"

I shook my head despite the fact my stomach was cramping with hunger. My mother had packed me a dinner of fried chicken and biscuits for the train, but the Reverend had eaten the drumstick and the fat boy had begged the rest. I had been too excited to eat.

We turned right onto East Avenue, a broad dirt road between neat rows of tents. I looked in vain for the Great Tent I had read about—a huge bigtop with room for 13,000 chairs where President Wilson was scheduled to speak in four days, on Friday, the Fourth of July. Now the sun was low and red in the haze to the west, the air thick with dust and the scent of trampled grass and sun-warmed canvas. I was starving and I had dirt in my hair and grit between my teeth. I do not remember ever being happier.

Our Boy Scout Station was at the west end of East Avenue, a hundred yards past a row of portable kitchens set in the middle of the Pennsylvania veterans' tent area. Reverend Hodges showed us to our tents and commanded us to hurry back to the station for our next day's assignments.

I set my duffel on a cot in a tent not far from the latrines. I was slow setting out my bedroll and belongings and when I looked up the fat boy was asleep on another cot and Billy was gone. A train roared by on the Gettysburg and Harrisburg tracks not fifty feet away. Suddenly breathless with the panic of being left behind, I ran back to the Scoutmasters' tent to receive my orders.

Reverend Hodges and Billy were nowhere to be seen but a fat man with a blond mustache, thick spectacles, and an ill-fitting Scoutmaster's uniform snapped, "You there, Scout!"

"Yessir?"

"Have you received your assignment?"

"No, sir."

The fat man grunted and pawed through a stack of yellow cardboard tags lying on a board he was using as a desk. He pulled one from the stack, glanced at it, and tied it to the brass button on my left breast pocket. I craned my neck to read it. Faint blue, typewritten letters said: MONT-GOMERY, P.D., Capt., 20th N.C. Reg., SECT. 27, SITE 3424, North Carolina Veterans.

"Well, *go*, boy!" snapped the Scoutmaster.

"Yessir," I said and ran toward the tent entrance. I paused. "Sir?"

"What is it?" The Scoutmaster was already tying another ticket on another Scout's blouse.

"Where am I to go, sir?"

The fat man flicked his fingers as if brushing an insect away. "To find the veteran you are assigned to, of course."

I squinted at the ticket. "Captain Montgomery?"

"Yes, yes. If that is what it says."

I took a breath. "Where do I find him, sir?"

The fat man scowled, took four angry steps toward me, and glared at the ticket through his thick glasses. "20th North Carolina . . . Section 27 . . . up *there*." He swept his arm in a gesture that took in the railroad tracks, a distant stream lined with trees, the setting sun, and another tent city on a hill where hundreds of pyramid tents glowed redly in the twilight.

"Pardon me, sir, but what do I do when I find Captain Montgomery?" I asked the Scoutmaster's retreating back.

The man stopped and glowered at me over his shoulder with a thinly veiled disgust that I had never guessed an adult would show toward someone my age. "You do whatever he *wants*, you young fool," snapped the man. "Now *go*."

I turned and ran toward the distant camp of the Confederates.

Lanterns were being lighted as I made my way through long rows of tents. Old men by the hundreds, many in heavy gray uniforms and long whiskers, sat on campstools and cots, benches and wooden stumps, smoking and talking and spitting into the early evening gloom. Twice I lost my way and twice I was given directions in slow, Southern drawls that might as well have been German for all I understood them.

Finally I found the North Carolina contingent sandwiched in between the Alabama and Missouri camps, just a short walk from the West Virginians. In the years since, I have found myself wondering why they put the Union-loyal West Virginian veterans in the midst of the rebel encampment.

Section 27 was the last row on the east side of the North Carolina camp and Site 3424 was the last tent in the row. The tent was dark.

"Captain Montgomery?" My voice was little more than a whisper. Hearing no answer from the darkened tent, I ducked my head inside to confirm that the veteran was not home. It was not my fault, I reasoned, that the old gentleman was not here when I called. I would find him in the morning, escort him to the breakfast tent, run the necessary errands for him, help him to find the latrine or his old comrades-in-arms, or whatever. *In the morning.* Right now I thought I would run all the way back to the Boy Scout Station, find Billy and Reverend Hodges, and see if anyone had any cookies in their duffel bags.

"I been waitin' for you, Boy."

I froze. The voice had come from the darkness in the depths of the tent. It was a voice from the South but sharp as cinders and brittle with age. It was a voice that I imagined the Dead might use to command those still beyond the grave.

"Come in here, Johnny. Step lively!"

I moved into the hot, canvas-scented interior and blinked. For a second my breath would not come.

The old man who lay on the cot was propped on his elbows so that his shoulders looked like sharp wings in the dim light, predatory pinions rising above an otherwise indistinct bundle of gray cloth, gray skin, staring eyes, and faded braid. He was wearing a shapeless hat which had once boasted a brim and crown but which now served only to cast his face into deeper shadow. A beak of a nose jutted into the dim light above wisps of white beard, thin purplish lips, and a few sharp teeth gleaming in a black hole of a mouth. For the first time in my life I realized that a human mouth was really an opening into a skull. The old man's eye sockets were darker pits of shadow beneath brows still black, the cheeks hollowed and knife-edged. Huge, liver-spotted hands, misshapen with age and arthritis, glowed with a preternatural whiteness in the gloom and I saw that while one leg ended in the black gleam of a high boot, the other terminated abruptly below the knee. I could see the rolled trouser leg pulled above pale, scarred skin wrapped tautly around the bone of the stump.

"Goddamnit, boy, did you bring the wagon?"

"Pardon me, sir?" My voice was a cicada's frightened chirp.

"The wagon, goddamnit, Johnny. We need a wagon. You should be knowin' that, boy." The old man sat up, swung his leg and his stump over the edge of the cot, and began fumbling in his loose coat.

"I'm sorry, Captain Montgomery ... uh ... you *are* Captain Montgomery, aren't you, sir?"

The old man grunted.

"Well, Captain Montgomery, sir, my name's not Johnny, it's ..."

"*Goddamnit*, boy!" bellowed the old man. "Would you quit makin' noise and go get the goddamned wagon! We need to get up there to the Pits before that bastard Iverson beats us to it."

I started to reply and then found myself with no wind with which to speak as Captain Montgomery removed a pistol from the folds of his coat. The gun was huge and gray and smelled of oil and I was certain that the crazy old man was going to kill me with it in that instant. I stood there with the wind knocked out of me as certainly as if the old Confederate had struck me in the solar plexus with the barrel of that formidable weapon.

The old man laid the revolver on the cot and reached into the shadows beneath it, pulling out an awkward arrangement of straps, buckles, and mahogany which I recognized as a crude wooden leg. "Come on now, Johnny," he mumbled, bending over to strap the cruel thing in place, "I've waited long enough for you. Go get the wagon, that's a good lad. I'll be ready and waitin' when you get back."

"Yessir," I managed, and turned, and escaped.

I have no rational explanation for my next actions. All I had to do was the natural thing, the thing that every fiber of my frightened body urged me to do—run back to the Boy Scout Station, find Reverend Hodges, inform him that my veteran was a raving madman armed with a pistol, and get a good night's sleep while the grownups sorted things out. But I was not a totally rational creature at this point. (How many ten-year-old boys are, I wonder?) I was tired, hungry, and already homesick after less than seven hours away from home, disoriented in space and time, and— perhaps most pertinent—not used to disobeying orders. And yet I am sure to this day that I would have run the entire way back to the Boy Scout Station and not thought twice about it if my parting glance of the old man had not been of him painfully strapping on that terrible wooden leg. The thought of him standing in the deepening twilight on that awful pegleg, trustingly awaiting a wagon which would never arrive was more than I could bear.

As fate arranged it, there was a wagon and untended team less than a hundred yards from Captain Montgomery's tent. The back of the slat-sided thing was half-filled with blankets, but the driver and deliverers were nowhere in sight. The team was a matched set of grays, aged and sway-backed but docile enough as I grabbed their bridles and clumsily turned them around and tugged them back up the hill with me.

I had never ridden a horse or driven a team. Even in 1913, I was used to riding in automobiles. Chestnut Hill still saw buggies and wagons on the street occasionally, but already they were considered quaint. Mr. Everett, our iceman, did not allow boys to ride on his wagon and his horse had the habit of biting any child who came in range.

Gingerly, trying to keep my knuckles away from the grays' teeth, I led the team up the hill. The thought that I was stealing the wagon never crossed my mind. Captain Montgomery needed a wagon. It was my job to deliver it.

"Good boy, Johnny. Well done." Outside, in the light, the old man was only slightly less formidable. The long gray coat hung in folds and wrinkles and although there was no sight of the pistol, I was sure that it was tucked somewhere close to hand. A heavy canvas bag hung from a strap over his right shoulder. For the first time I noticed a faded insignia on the front of his hat and three small medals on his coat. The ribbons were so faded that I could not make out their colors. The Captain's bare neck reminded me of the thick tangle of ropes dangling into the dark maw of the old well behind our house.

"Come on, Boy. We have to move smartly if we're to beat that son-of-a-bitch Iverson." The old man heaved himself up to the seat with a wide swing of his wooden leg and seized the reins in fists that looked like clusters of gnarled roots. With no hesitation I ran to the left side of the wagon and jumped to the seat beside him.

Gettysburg was filled with lights and activity that last, late evening in June, but the night seemed especially dark and empty as we passed through town on our way north. The house and hotel lights felt so distant to our purpose— whatever that purpose was—that the lights appeared pale and cold to me, the fading glow of fireflies dying in a jar.

In a few minutes we were beyond the last buildings on the north end of town and turning northwest on what I later learned was Mummasburg Road. Just before we passed behind a dark curtain of trees, I swiveled in my seat and caught a last glimpse of Gettysburg and the Great Reunion Camp beyond it. Where the lights of the city seemed pale and paltry, the flames of the hundreds of campfires and bonfires in the Tent City blazed in the night. I looked at the constellations of fires and realized that there were more old veterans huddling around them that night than there were young men in many nations' armies. I wondered if this is what Cemetery Ridge and Culp's Hill had looked like to the arriving Confederate armies fifty years earlier.

Suddenly I had the chilling thought that fifty years ago Death had given a grand party and 140,000 revelers had

arrived in their burial clothes. My father had told me that
the soldiers going into battle had often pinned small scraps
of paper to their uniforms so that their bodies could be
identified after the killing was finished. I glanced to my
right as if half-expecting to see a yellowed scrap of paper
pinned to the old man's chest, his name, rank, and home
town scrawled on it. Then I realized with a start that *I* was
wearing the tag.

I looked back at the lights and marveled that fifty years
after Death's dark festival, 50,000 of the survivors had returned for a second celebration.

We passed deeper into the forest and I could see no
more of the fires of the Reunion Camp. The only light
came from the fading glow of the summer sky through
limbs above us and the sporadic winking of fireflies along
the road.

"You don't remember Iverson, do you, Boy?"

"No, sir."

"Here." He thrust something into my hands. Leaning
closer, squinting, I understood that it was an old tintype,
cracked at the edges. I was able to make out a pale square
of face, shadows which might have been mustaches. Captain Montgomery grabbed it back. "He's not registered at
the goddamn reunion," he muttered. "Spent the goddamn
day lookin'. Never arrived. Didn't expect him to. Newspaper in Atlanta two years ago said he died. Goddamn lie."

"Oh," I said. The horses' hooves made soft sounds in
the dirt of the road. The fields we were passing were as
empty as my mind.

"Goddamn lie," said the Captain. "He's goin' be back
here. No doubt about it, is there, Johnny?"

"No, sir." We came over the brow of a low hill and the
old man slowed the wagon. His pegleg had been making
a rhythmic sound as it rattled against the wooden slat
where it was braced and as we slowed the tempo changed.
We had passed out of the thickest part of the forest but
dark farmfields opened out to the left and right between
stands of trees and low stone walls. "Damn," he said. "Did
you see Forney's house back there, boy?"

"I . . . no, sir. I don't think so." I had no idea if we had
passed Forney's house. I had no idea who Forney was. I

had no idea what I was doing wandering around the countryside at night with this strange old man. I was amazed to find myself suddenly on the verge of tears.

Captain Montgomery pulled the team to a stop under some trees set back off the right side of the road. He panted and wheezed, struggling to dismount from the driver's seat. "Help me down, Boy. It's time we bivouacked."

I ran around to offer my hand but he used my shoulder as a brace and dropped heavily to the ground. A strange, sour scent came from him and I was reminded of an old, urine-soaked mattress in a shed near the tracks behind our school where Billy said hobos slept. It was fully dark now. I could make out the Big Dipper above a field across the road. All around us, crickets and tree toads were tuning up for their nightly symphony.

"Bring some of them blankets along, Boy." He had picked up a fallen limb to use as a walking stick as he moved clumsily into the trees. I grabbed some Army blankets from the back of the wagon and followed him.

We crossed a wheat field, passed a thin line of trees, and climbed through a meadow before stopping under a tree where broad leaves stirred to the night breeze. The Captain directed me to lay the blankets out into rough bedrolls and then he lowered himself until he was lying with his back propped against the tree and his wooden leg resting on his remaining ankle. "You hungry, Boy?"

I nodded in the dark. The old man rummaged in the canvas bag and handed me several strips of something I thought was meat but which tasted like heavily salted leather. I chewed on the first piece for almost five minutes before it was soft enough to swallow. Just as my lips and tongue were beginning to throb with thirst, Captain Montgomery handed me a wineskin of water and showed me how to squirt it into my open mouth.

"Good jerky, ain't it, Boy?" he asked.

"Delicious," I answered honestly and worked to bite off another chunk.

"That Iverson was a useless son-of-a-bitch," the Captain said around his own jawful of jerky. It was as if he were picking up the sentence he had begun half an hour earlier back at the wagon. "He would've been a harmless son-of-a-bitch if those dumb bastards in my own 20th North Carolina hadn't elected him camp commander back before the war begun. That made Iverson a colonel sort of automatic like, and by the time we'd fought our way up North, the stupid little bastard was in charge of one of Rodes's whole damn brigades."

The old man paused to work at the jerky with his few remaining teeth and I reflected on the fact that the only other person I had ever heard curse anything like the Captain was Mr. Bolton, the old fire chief who used to sit out in front of the firehouse on Third Street and tell stories to the new recruits, apparently oblivious to the uninvited presence of us younger members of the audience. Perhaps, I thought, it has something to do with wearing a uniform.

"His first name was Alfred," said the Captain. The old man's voice was soft, preoccupied, and his southern accent was so thick that the meaning of each word reached me some seconds after the sound of it. It was a bit like lying in bed, already dreaming, and hearing the soft voices of my mother and father coming upstairs through a curtain of sleep. Or like magically understanding a foreign language. I closed my eyes to hear better. "Alfred," said the Captain, "just like his daddy. His daddy'd been a Senator from Georgia, good friend of the President." I could feel the old man's gaze on me. "President Davis. It was Davis, back when he was a senator too, who give young Iverson his first commission. That was back durin' the trouble with Mexico. Then when the real war come up, Iverson and his daddy got 'em up a regiment. Them days, when a rich goddamn family like the Iversons wanted to play soldiers, they just bought themselves a regiment. Bought the goddamn uniforms and horses and such. Then they got to be officers. Goddamn grown men playin' at toy soldiers, Boy. Only once't the real war begun, *we* was the toy soldiers, Johnny."

I opened my eyes. I could not recall ever having seen so many stars. Above the slope of the meadow, constellations came all the way down to the horizon; others were visible between the dark masses of trees. The Milky Way crossed the sky like a bridge. Or like the pale tracks of an army long since passed by.

"Just goddamned bad luck we got Iverson," said the Captain, "because the brigade was good 'un and the 20th North Carolina was the best goddamn regiment in Ewell's corps." The old man shifted to look at me again. "You wasn't with us yet at Sharpsburg, was you, Johnny?"

I shook my head, feeling a chill go up my back as he again called me by some other boy's name. I wondered where that boy was now.

"No, of course not," said Captain Montgomery. "That was in '62. You was still in school. The regiment was still at Fredericksburg after the campaign. Somebody'd ordered up a dress parade and Nate's band played 'Dixie.' All of the sudden, from acrost the Rappahannock, the Yankee band starts playin' Dixie back at us. Goddamnest thing, Boy. You could hear that music so clear acrost the water it was like two parts of the same band playin'. So our band—all boys from the 20th—they commence to playin' 'Yankee Doodle.' All of us standin' there at parade rest in that cold sunlight, feelin' mighty queer by then, I don't mind tellin' you. Then, when our boys is done with 'Yankee Doodle,' just like they all rehearsed it together, both bands commence playin' 'Home Sweet Home.' Without even thinkin' about it, Perry and ol' Thomas and Jeffrey an' me and the whole line starts singin' along. So did Lieutenant Williams—young Mr. Oliver hisself—and before long the whole brigade's singin'—the damn Yankees too—their voices comin' acrost the Rappahannock and joinin' ours like we'd been one big choir that'd gotten busted up by mistake or accident or somethin'. I tell you, Boy, it was sorta like singin' with ghosts. And sorta like we was ghosts our own selves."

I closed my eyes to hear the deep voices singing that sad, sweet song, and I realized suddenly that even grownups—soldiers even—could feel as lonely and homesick as I had felt earlier that evening. Realizing that, I found that all of my own homesickness had fled. I felt that I was where I should be, part of the Captain's army, part of all armies, camping far from home and uncertain what the next day would bring but content to be with my friends. My comrades. The voices were as real and as sad as the soughing of wind through the mid-summer leaves.

The Captain cleared his throat and spat. "And then that bastard Iverson kilt us," he said. I heard the sound of buckles as the old man unstrapped his false leg.

I opened my eyes as he pulled his blanket over his shoulders and turned his face away. "Get some sleep, Boy," came his muffled voice. "We step off at first light come mornin'."

I pulled my own blanket up to my neck and laid my cheek against the dark soil. I listened for the singing but the voices were gone. I went to sleep to the sound of the wind in the leaves sounding like angry whispers in the night.

I awoke once before sunrise when there was just enough false light to allow me to see Captain Montgomery's face a few inches from my own. The old man's hat had slipped off in the night and the top of his head was a relief map of reddened scalp scarred by liver spots, sores, and a few forlorn wisps of white hair. His brow was furrowed as if in fierce concentration, eyebrows two dark eruptions of hair, eyelids lowered but showing a line of white at the bottom. Soft snores whistled out of his broken gourd of a mouth and a thin line of drool moistened his whiskers. His breath was as dry and dead as a draft of air from a cave unsealed after centuries of being forgotten.

I stared at the time-scoured flesh of the old face inches from mine, at the swollen and distorted fingers clutching, childlike, at his blanket, and I realized, with a precise and prescient glimpse at the terrible fate of my own longevity, that age was a curse, a disease, and that all of us unlucky to survive our childhoods were doomed to suffer and perish from it. Perhaps, I thought, it is why young men go willingly to die in wars.

I pulled the blanket across my face.

When I awoke again, just after sunrise, the old man was standing ten paces from the tree and staring toward Gettysburg. Only a white cupola was visible above the trees, its dome and sides painted in gold from the sun. I disentangled myself from the blankets and rose to my feet, marveling at how stiff and clammy and strange I felt. I had never slept out of doors before. Reverend Hodges had promised us a camp-out but the Troop had been too busy learning close order drill and semaphore. I decided that I might skip the camp-out part of the agenda. Staggering upright on legs still half asleep, I wondered how Captain Montgomery had strapped on his wooden leg without awakening me.

"Mornin', Boy," he called as I returned from the edge of the woods where I had relieved myself. His gaze never left the cupola visible to the southeast.

We had breakfast while standing there under the tree—more beef jerky and water. I wondered what Billy, the Reverend, and the other Scouts were having down in the tents near the field kitchens. Pancakes, probably. Perhaps with bacon. Certainly with tall glasses of cold milk.

"I was there with Mr. Oliver when muster was called on the mornin' of the first," rasped the old man. "1,470 present for duty. 114 was officers. I wasn't among 'em. Still had my sergeant stripes then. Wasn't 'til the second Wilderness that they gave me the bar. Anyway, word had come the night before from A.P. Hill that the Federals was massin' to the south. Probably figurin' to cut us off. Our brigade was the first to turn south to Hill's call.

"We heard firin' as we come down the Heidlersburg Pike, so General Rodes took us through the woods 'til we got to Oak Hill." He turned east, smoothly pivoting on his wooden leg, shielding his eyes from the sun. "'Bout there, I reckon, Johnny. Come on." The old man spun around and I rolled the blankets and scurried to follow him back down the hill toward the southeast. Toward the distant cupola.

"We come right down the west side of this ridge then, too, didn't we, Boy? Not so many trees then. Been marchin' since before sunup. Got here sometime after what should've been dinner time. One o'clock, maybe one-thirty. Had hardtack on the hoof. Seems to me that we stopped a while up the hill there so's Rodes could set out some guns. Perry an' me was glad to sit. He wanted to start another letter to our Ma, but I told him there wasn't goin' to be time. There wasn't, either, but I wish to hell I'd let him write the damned thing.

"From where we was, you could see the Yanks comin'
up the road from Gettysburg and we knew there'd be a
fight that day. Goddamnit, Boy, you can put them blankets
down. We ain't goin' to need 'em today."

Startled, I dropped the blankets in the weeds. We had
reached the lower end of the meadow and only a low, split
rail fence separated us from what I guessed to be the road
we had come up the night before. The Captain swung his
pegleg over the fence and after we crossed we both paused
a minute. I felt the growing heat of the day as a thickness
in the air and a slight pounding in my temples. Suddenly
there came the sound of band music and cheering from the
south, dwindled by distance.

The Captain removed a stained red kerchief from his
pocket and mopped at his neck and forehead. "Goddamn
idiots," he said. "Celebratin' like it's a county fair.
Damned nonsense."

"Yessir," I said automatically, but at that moment I was
thrilled with the idea of the Reunion and with the reality
of being with a veteran—*my* veteran—walking on the actual ground he had fought on. I realized that someone seeing us from a distance might have mistaken us for *two*
soldiers. At that moment I would have traded my Boy
Scout khaki for butternut brown or Confederate gray and
would have joined the Captain in any cause. At that moment I would have marched against the Eskimoes if it
meant being part of an army, setting off at sunrise with
one's comrades, preparing for battle, and generally feeling
as *alive* as I felt at that instant.

The Captain had heard my "yessir" but he must have
noticed something else in my eyes because he leaned forward, rested his weight on the fence, and brought his face
close to mine. "Goddamnit, Johnny, don't you fall for such
nonsense twice. You think these dumb sons-of-bitches
would've come back all this way if they was honest
enough to admit they was celebratin' a slaughterhouse?"

I blinked.

The old man grabbed my tunic with his swollen fist.
"That's all it is, Boy, don't you see? A goddamn *abattoir*
that was built here to grind up *men* and now they're
reminiscin' about it and tellin' funny stories about it and

weepin' old man tears about what good times we had when we was fed to it." With his free hand he stabbed a finger in the direction of the cupola. "Can't you see it, Boy? The holdin' pens and the delivery chutes and the killin' rooms—only not everybody was so lucky as to have their skull busted open on the first pop, some of us got part of us fed to the grinder and got to lay around and watch the others swell up and bloat in the heat. Goddamn slaughterhouse, Boy, where they kill you and gut you down the middle ... dump your insides out on the goddamn floor and kick 'em aside to get at the next fool ... hack the meat off your bones, grind up the bones for fertilizer, then grind up everythin' else you got that ain't prime meat and wrap it in your own guts to sell it to the goddamn public as sausage. Parades. War stories. Reunions. *Sausage*, Boy." Panting slightly, he released me, spat, wiped his whiskers and stared a long minute at the sky. "And we was led into that slaughterhouse by a Judas goat named Iverson, Johnny," he said at last, his voice empty of all emotion. "Never forget that."

The hill continued to slope gently downward as we crossed the empty road and entered a field just to the east of an abandoned farmhouse. Fire had gutted the upper stories years ago and the windows on the first floor were boarded up, but irises still grew tall around the foundation and along the overgrown lane leading to sagging outbuildings. "John Forney's old place," said Captain Montgomery. "He was still here when I come back in '98. Told me then that none of his farmhands'd stay around here after night begun to settle. Because of the Pits."

"Because of what, sir?" I was blinking in the early heat and glare of a day in which the temperatures certainly would reach the mid-nineties. Grasshoppers hopped mindlessly in the dusty grass.

The old man did not seem to hear my question. The cupola was no longer visible because we were too close to the trees, but the Captain's attention was centered on the field which ran downhill less than a quarter of a mile to a thicker line of trees to the southeast. He withdrew the pistol from his coat and my heart pounded as he drew back the hammer until it clicked. "This is a double-action, Boy," he said. "Don't forget that."

We forced our way through a short hedge and began crossing the field at a slow walk. The old man's wooden leg made soft sounds in the soil. Grass and thistles brushed at our legs. "That son-of-a-bitch Iverson never got this far," said the Captain. "Ollie Williams said he heard him give the order up the hill there near where Rodes put his guns out. 'Give 'em hell,' Iverson says, then goes back up to his tree there to sit in the shade an' eat his lunch. Had him some wine too. Had wine every meal when the rest of us was drinkin' water out of the ditch. Nope, Iverson never come down here 'til it was all over and then it was just to say we'd tried to surrender and order a bunch of dead men to stand up and salute the general. Come on, Boy."

We moved slowly across the field. I could make out a stone fence near the treeline now, half-hidden in the dapple of leaf shadow. There seemed to be a jumble of tall grass or vines just this side of the wall.

"They put Daniels' brigade on our right." The Captain's pistol gestured toward the south, the barrel just missing the brim of my hat. "But they didn't come down 'til we was shot all to pieces. Then Daniels' boys run right into the fire of Stone's 149th Pennsylvania . . . them damn sharpshooters what were called the Bogus Bucktails for some damn reason I don't recall now. But we was all alone when we come down this way before Daniels and Ramseur and O'Neil and the rest come along. Iverson sent us off too soon. Ramseur wasn't ready for another half hour and O'Neal's brigade turned back even before they got to the Mummasburg Road back there."

We were half way across the field by then. A thin screen of trees to our left blocked most of the road from sight. The stone wall was less than three hundred yards ahead. I glanced nervously at the cocked pistol. The Captain seemed to have forgotten he was carrying it.

"We come down like this at an angle," he said. "Brigade stretched about halfway acrost the field, sorta slantin' northeast to southwest. The 5th North Carolina was on our left. The 20th was right about here, couple of hundred of us in the first line, and the 23rd and 12th was off to our right there and sorta trailin' back, the right flank of the 12th about halfway to that damned railroad cut down there."

I looked toward the south but could see no railroad tracks. There was only the hot, wide expanse of field which may have once borne crops but which had now gone back to brambles and sawgrass.

The Captain stopped, panting slightly, and rested his weight on his good leg. "What we didn't know, Johnny, was that the Yanks was all set behind that wall there. Thousands of them. Not showin' a goddamn cap or battle flag or rifle barrel. Just hunkerin' down there and waitin'. Waitin' for the animals to come in the door so the slaughter could begin. And Colonel Iverson never even ordered skirmishers out in front of us. I never even *seen* an advance without skirmishers, and there we was walkin' across this field while Iverson sat up on Oak Hill eatin' lunch and havin' another glass of wine."

The Captain raised his pistol and pointed at the treeline. I stepped back, expecting him to fire, but the only noise was the rasp of his voice. "Remember? We got to that point . . . 'bout there where them damn vines is growing . . . and the Yanks rise up along that whole quarter mile of wall there and fire right into us. Like they're comin' up out of the ground. No noise at all except the swish of our feet 'n legs in the wheat and grass and then they let loose a volley like to sound like the end of the world. Whole goddamn world disappears in smoke and fire. Even a Yank couldn't miss at that range. More of 'em come out of the trees back up there . . ." The Captain gestured toward our left where the wall angled northwest to meet the road. "That puts us in an enfilade fire that just sweeps through the 5th North Carolina. Like a scythe, Boy. There was wheat in these fields then. But it was just stubble. No place to go. No place to hide. We could've run back the way we come but us North Carolina boys wasn't goin' to start learning' ourselves how to run this late in the day. So the scythe just come sweepin' into us. Couldn't move forward. That goddamn wall was just a wall of

smoke with fire comin' through it there fifty yards away.
I seen Lieutenant Colonel Davis of the 5th—Old Bill his
boys called him—get his regiment down into that low area
there to the south. See about where that line of scrub brush
is? Not nearly so big as a ditch, but it give 'em some
cover, not much. But us in the 20th and Cap'n Turner's
boys in the 23rd didn't have no choice but to lie down
here in the open and take it."

The old man advanced slowly for a dozen yards and
stopped where the grass grew thicker and greener, joining
with tangles of what I realized were grapevines to create
a low, green thicket between us and the wall. Suddenly he
sat down heavily, thrusting his wooden leg out in front of
him and cradling the pistol in his lap. I dropped to my
knees in the grass near him, removed my hat, and unbut-
toned my tunic. The yellow tag hung loosely from my
breast pocket button. It was very hot.

"The Yank's kept pourin' the fire into us," he said. His
voice was a hoarse whisper. Sweat ran down his cheeks
and neck. "More Federals come out of the woods down
there . . . by the railroad gradin' . . . and started enfiladin'
Old Bill's boys and our right flank. We couldn't fire back
worth horseshit. Lift your head outta the dirt to aim and
you caught a Minié ball in the brain. My brother Perry
was layin' next to me and I heard the ball that took him
in the left eye. Made a sound like someone hammerin' a
side of beef with a four-pound hammer. He sort of rose up
and flopped back next to me. I was yellin' and cryin', my
face all covered with snot and dirt and tears, when all of
a sudden I feel Perry tryin' to rise up again. Sort of jerkin', like somebody was pullin' him up with strings. Then
again. And again. I'd got a glimpse of the hole in his face
where his eye'd been and his brains and bits of the back
of his head was still smeared on my right leg, but I could
fell him jerkin' and pullin', like he was tuggin' at me to go
with him somewhere. Later, I seen why. More bullets had
been hittin' him in the head and each time it'd snap him
back some. When we come back to bury him later, his
head looked like a mushmelon someone'd kicked apart. It
wasn't unusual, neither. Lot of the boys layin' on the field

that day got just torn apart by that Yankee fire. Like a scythe, Boy. Or a meatgrinder."

I sat back in the grass and breathed through my mouth. The vines and black soil gave off a thick, sweet smell that made me feel lightheaded and a little ill. The heat pressed down like thick, wet blankets.

"Some of the boys stood up to run then," said Captain Montgomery, his voice still a hoarse monotone, his eyes focused on nothing. He was holding the cocked pistol in both hands with the barrel pointed in my direction, but I was sure that he had forgotten I was there. "Everybody who stood up got hit. The sound was . . . you could hear the balls hittin' home even over the firin'. The wind was blowin' the smoke back into the woods so there wasn't even any cover you usually got once't the smoke got heavy. I seen Lieutenant Ollie Williams stand up to yell at the boys of the 20th to stay low and he was hit twice while I watched.

"The rest of us was tryin' to form a firin' line in the grass and wheat, but we hadn't got off a full volley before the Yanks come runnin' out, some still firin', some usin' their bayonets. And that's when I seen you and the other two little drummers get kilt, Johnny. When they used them bayonets . . ." The old man paused and looked at me for the first time in several minutes. A cloud of confusion seemed to pass over him. He slowly lowered the pistol, gently released the cocked hammer, and raised a shaking hand to his brow.

Still feeling dizzy and a little sick myself, I asked, "Is that when you lost your . . . uh . . . when you hurt your leg, sir?"

The Captain removed his hat. His few white hairs were stringy with sweat. "What? My leg?" He stared at the wooden peg below his knee as if he had never noticed it before. "My leg. No, Boy, that was later. The Battle of the Crater. The Yankees tunneled under us and blowed us up while we was sleepin'. When I didn't die right away, they shipped me home to Raleigh and made me an honorary Cap'n three days before the war ended. No, that day . . . *here* . . . I got hit at least three times but nothin' serious. A ball took the heel of my right boot off. Another'n

knocked my rifle stock all to hell and gave me some splinters in my cheek. A third'n took off a chunk of my left ear,
but hell, I could still hear all right. It wasn't 'til I sat down
to try to go to sleep that night that I come to find out that
another ball'd hit me in the back of the leg, right below
the ass, but it'd been goin' so slow it just give me a big
bruise there."

We sat there for several minutes in silence. I could
hear insects rustling in the grass. Finally the Captain said,
"And that son-of-a-bitch Iverson never even come down
here until Ramseur's boys finally got around to clearin'
the Yankees out. That was later. I was layin' right around
here somewhere, squeezed in between Perry and Nate's
corpses, covered with so much of their blood an' brains
that the goddamn Yanks just stepped over all three of us
when they ran out to stick bayonets in our people or drive
'em back to their line as prisoners. I opened my eyes long
enough to see ol' Cade Tarleton bein' clubbed along by a
bunch of laughin' Yankees. They had our regimental flag,
too, goddamnit. There was no one left alive around it to
put up a fight.

"Ramseur, him who the Richmond papers was always
callin' the Chevalier Bayard, whatever the hell that meant,
was comin' down the hill into the same ambush when
Lieutenant Crowder and Lieutenant Dugger run up and
warned him. Ramseur was an officer but he wasn't nobody's fool. He crossed the road further east and turned
the Yankee's right flank, just swept down the backside of
that wall, drivin' 'em back toward the seminary.

"Meanwhile, while the few of us who'd stayed alive
was busy crawlin' back towards Forney's house or layin'
there bleedin' from our wounds, that son-of-a-bitch
Iverson was tellin' General Rodes that he'd seen our regiment put up a white flag and go over to the Yanks. Goddamn lie, Boy. Them who got captured was mostly
wounded who got drove off at the point of a bayonet.
There wasn't any white flags to be seen that day. Least-
ways not here. Just bits of white skull and other stuff
layin' around.

"Later, while I was still on the field lookin' for a rifle
that'd work, Rodes brings Iverson down here to show him

where the men had surrendered, and while their horses is pickin' their way over the corpses that used to be the 20th North Carolina, that bastard Iverson . . ." Here the old man's voice broke. He paused a long minute, hawked, spat, and continued. "That *bastard* Iverson sees our rows of dead up here, 700 men from the finest brigade the South ever fielded, layin' shot dead in lines as straight as a dress parade, and Iverson thinks they're still duckin' from fire even though Ramseur had driven the Yanks off, and he stands up in his stirrups, his goddamn sorrel horse almost steppin' on Perry, and he screams, 'Stand up and salute when the general passes, you men! Stand up this instant!' It was Rodes who realized that they was lookin' at dead men."

Captain Montgomery was panting, barely able to get the words out between wracking gasps for breath. I was having trouble breathing myself. The sickeningly sweet stench from the weeds and vines and dark soil seemed to use up all of the air. I found myself staring at a cluster of grapes on a nearby vine; the swollen fruit looked like bruised flesh streaked with ruptured veins.

"If I'd had my rifle," said the Captain, "I would have shot the bastard right then." He let out a ragged breath. "Him and Rodes went back up the hill together and I never seen Iverson again. Captain Halsey took command of what was left of the regiment. When the brigade reassembled the next mornin', 362 men stood muster where 1,470 had answered the call the day before. They called Iverson back to Georgia and put him in charge of a home guard unit or somethin'. Word was, President Davis saved him from bein' court-martialed or reprimanded. It was clear none of us would've served under the miserable son-of-a-bitch again. You know how the last page of our 20th North Carolina regimental record reads, Boy?"

"No, sir," I said softly.

The old man closed his eyes. "Initiated at Seven Pines, sacrificed at Gettysburg, and surrendered at Appomattox. Help me get to my feet, Boy. We got to find a place to hide."

"To hide, sir?"

"Goddamn right," said the Captain as I acted as a

crutch for him. "We've got to be ready when Iverson
comes here today." He raised the heavy pistol as if it explained everything. "We've got to be ready when he
comes."

It was mid-morning before we found an adequate place
to hide. I trailed along behind the limping old man and
while part of my mind was desperate with panic to find a
way out of such an insane situation, another part—a larger
part—had no trouble accepting the logic of everything.
Colonel Alfred Iverson, Jr., would have to return to his
field of dishonor this day and we had to hide in order to
kill him.

"See where the ground's lower here, Boy? Right about
where these damn vines is growin'?"

"Yessir."

"Them's Iverson's Pits. That's what the locals call 'em
according to John Forney when I come to visit in '98. You
know what they are?"

"No, sir," I lied. Part of me knew very well what they
were.

"Night after the battle . . . battle, hell, *slaughter* . . . the
few of us left from the regiment and some of Lee's Pio-
neers come up and dug big shallow pits and just rolled our
boys in where they lay. Laid 'em in together, still in their
battle lines. Nate 'n Perry's shoulders was touchin'. Right
where I'd been layin'. You can see where the Pits start
here. The ground's lower an' the grass is higher, ain't it?"

"Yessir."

"Forney said the grass was always higher here, crops
too, when they growed them. Forney didn't farm this field
much. Said the hands didn't like to work here. He told his
niggers that there weren't nothing to worry about, that the
U.C.V.'d come up and dug up everythin' after the war to
take our boys back to Richmond, but that ain't really
true."

"Why not, sir?" We were wading slowly through the
tangle of undergrowth. Vines wrapped around my ankle
and I had to tug to free myself.

"They didn't do much diggin' here," said the Captain.

"Bones was so thick and scattered that they jes' took a few of 'em and called it quits. Didn't like diggin' here any more than Forney's niggers liked workin' here. Even in the daytime. Place that's got this much shame and anger in it . . . well, people *feel* it, don't they, Boy?"

"Yessir," I said automatically, although all I felt at that moment was sick and sleepy.

The Captain stopped. "Goddamnit, that house wasn't here before."

Through a break in the stone wall I could see a small house—more of a large shack, actually—made of wood so dark as to be almost black and set back in the shade of the trees. No driveway or wagon lane led to it, but I could see a faint trampling in Forney's field and the forest grass where horses might have passed through the break in the wall to gain access. The old man seemed deeply offended that someone had built a home so close to the field where his beloved 20th North Carolina had fallen. But the house was dark and silent and we moved away from that section of the wall.

The closer we came to the stone fence, the harder it was to walk. The grass grew twice as high as in the fields beyond and the wild grapevines marked a tangled area about the size of the football field where our Troop practiced its close order drill.

In addition to the tangled grass and thick vines there to hamper our progress, there were the holes. Dozens of them, scores of them, pockmarking the field and lying in wait under the matted foliage.

"Goddamn gophers," said Captain Montgomery, but the holes were twice as wide across the opening as any burrow I had seen made by mole or gopher or ground squirrel. There were no heaps of dirt at the opening. Twice the old man stepped into them, the second time ramming his wooden leg in so deeply that we both had to work to dislodge it. Tugging hard at his wool-covered leg, I suddenly had the nightmarish sense that someone or something was pulling at the other end, refusing to let go, trying to suck the old man underground.

The incident must have disconcerted Captain Montgomery as well, because as soon as his leg popped free of the hole he staggered back a few steps and sat down heavily with his back against the stone wall. "This is good enough, Boy," he panted. "We'll wait here."

It was a good place for an ambush. The vines and grass grew waist high there, allowing us glimpses of the field beyond but concealing us as effectively as a duck blind. The wall sheltered our backs.

Captain Montgomery removed his topcoat and canvas bag and commenced to unload, clean, and reload his pistol. I lay on the grass nearby, at first thinking about what was going on back at the Reunion, then wondering about how to get the Captain back there, then wondering what Iverson had looked like, then thinking about home, and finally thinking about nothing at all as I moved in and out of a strange, dream-filled doze.

Not three feet from where I lay was another of the ubiquitous holes, and as I fell into a light slumber I remained faintly aware of the odor rising from that opening: the same sickening sweetness I had smelled earlier, but thicker now, heavier, almost erotic with its undertones of corruption and decay, of dead sea creatures drying in the sun. Many years later, visiting an abandoned meat processing plant in Chicago with a real estate agent acquaintance, I was to encounter a similar smell; it was the stench of a charnel house, disused for years but permeated with the memory of blood.

The day passed in a haze of heat, thick air, and insect noises. I dozed and awoke to watch with the Captain, dozed again. Once I seem to remember eating hard biscuits from his bag and washing them down with the last water from his wineskin, but even that fades into my dreams of that afternoon, for I remember others seated around us, chewing on similar fare and talking in low tones so that the words were indistinguishable but the southern dialect came through clearly. It did not sound strange to me. Once I remember awakening, even though I was sitting up and staring and had thought I was already awake, as the sound of an automobile along the Mummasburg Road shocked me into full consciousness. But the trees at the edge of the field shielded any traffic from view, the sounds faded, and I returned to the drugged doze I had known before.

Sometime late that afternoon I dreamed the one dream I remember clearly.

I was lying in the field, hurt and helpless, the left side of my face in the dirt and my right eye staring unblinkingly at a blue summer sky. An ant walked across my cheek, then another, until a stream of them crossed my cheek and eye, others moving into my nostrils and open mouth. I could not move. I did not blink. I felt them in my mouth, between my teeth, removing bits of morning bacon from between two molars, moving across the soft flesh of my palate, exploring the dark tunnel of my throat. The sensations were not unpleasant.

I was vaguely aware of other things going deeper, of slow movement in the swelling folds of my guts and belly. Small things laid their eggs in the drying corners of my eye.

I could see clearly as a raven circled overhead, spiralling lower, landed nearby, paced to and fro in a wingfolding strut, and hopped closer. It took my eye with a single stab of a beak made huge by proximity. In the darkness which followed I could still sense the light as my body expanded in the heat, a hatchery to thousands now, the loose cloth of my shirt pulled tight as my flesh expanded. I sensed my own internal bacteria, deprived of other foods, digesting my body's decaying fats and rancid pools of blood in a vain effort to survive a few more hours.

I felt my lips wither and dry in the heat, pulling back from my teeth, felt my jaws open wider and wider in a mirthless, silent laugh as ligaments decayed or were chewed away by small predators. I felt lighter as the eggs hatched, the maggots began their frenzied cleansing, my body turning toward the dark soil as the process accelerated. My mouth opened wide to swallow the waiting Earth. I tasted the dark communion of dirt. Stalks of grass grew where my tongue had been. A flower found rich soil in the humid sepulcher of my skull and sent its shoot curling upward through the gap which had once held my eye.

Settling, relaxing, returning to the acid-taste of the

blackness around me, I sensed the others there. Random, shifting currents of soil sent decaying bits of wool or flesh or bone in touch with bits of them, fragments intermingling with the timid eagerness of a lover's first touch. When all else was lost, mingling with the darkness and anger, my bones remained, brittle bits of memory, forgotten, sharp-edged fragments of pain resisting the inevitable relaxation into painlessness, into nothingness.

And deep in that rotting marrow, lost in the loam-black acid of forgetfulness, I remembered. And waited.

"Wake up, Boy! It's him. It's Iverson!"

The urgent whisper shocked me up out of sleep. I looked around groggily, still tasting the dirt from where I had lain with my lips against the ground.

"Goddamnit, I *knew* he'd come!" whispered the Captain, pointing to our left where a man in a dark coat had come out of the woods through the gap in the stone wall.

I shook my head. My dream would not release me and I knuckled my eyes, trying to shake the dimness from them. Then I realized that the dimness was real. The daylight had faded into evening while I slept. I wondered where in God's name the day had gone. The man in the black coat moved through a twilight grayness which seemed to echo the eerie blindness of my dreams. I could make out the man's white shirt and pale face glowing slightly in the gloom as he turned in our direction and came closer, clearing a path for himself with short, sharp chops with a cane or walking stick.

"By God, it *is* him," hissed the Captain and raised his pistol with shaking hands. He thumbed the hammer back as I watched in horror.

The man was closer now, no more than twenty-five feet away, and I could see the dark mustaches, black hair, and deepset eyes. It did indeed look like the man whose visage I had glimpsed by starlight in the old tintype.

Captain Montgomery steadied his pistol on his left arm and squinted over the sights. I could hear hisses of breath from the man in the dark suit as he walked closer, whistling an almost inaudible tune. The Captain squeezed the trigger.

"No!" I cried and grabbed the revolver, jerking it down, the hammer falling cruelly on the web of flesh between my thumb and forefinger. It did not fire.

The Captain shoved me away with a violent blow of his left forearm and struggled to raise the weapon again even as I clung to his wrist. "No!" I shouted again. "He's too young! *Look.* He's too young!"

The old man paused then, his arms still straining, but squinting now at the stranger who stood less than a dozen feet away.

It was true. The man was far too young to be Colonel Iverson. The pale, surprised face belonged to a man in his early thirties at most. Captain Montgomery lowered the pistol and raised trembling fingers to his temples. "My God," he whispered. "My God."

"Who's there?" The man's voice was sharp and assured, despite his surprise. "Show yourself."

I helped the Captain up, sure that the mustached stranger had sensed our movement behind the tall grass and vines but had not witnessed our struggles nor seen the gun. The Captain squinted at the younger man even as he straightened his hat and dropped the pistol in the deep pocket of his coat. I could feel the old man trembling as I steadied him upright.

"Oh, a veteran!" called the man and stepped forward with his hand extended, batting away the grasping vines with easy flicks of his walking stick.

We walked the perimeter of the Pits in the fading light, our new guide moving slowly to accommodate the Captain's painful hobble. The man's walking stick served as a pointer while he spoke. "This was the site of a skirmish before the major battles began," he said. "Not many visitors come out here . . . most of the attention is given to more famous areas south and west of here . . . but those of us who live or spend summers around here are aware of some of these lesser-known spots. It's quite interesting how the field is sunken here, isn't it?"

"Yes," whispered the Captain. He watched the ground, never raising his eyes to the young man's face.

The man had introduced himself as Jessup Sheads and said that he lived in the small house we had noticed set back in the trees. The Captain had been lost in his confused reverie so I had introduced both of us to Mr. Sheads. Neither man paid notice of my name. The Captain now glanced up at Sheads as if he still could not believe that this was not the man whose name had tormented him for half a century.

Sheads cleared his throat and pointed again at the tangle of thick growth. "As a matter of fact, this area right along here was the site of a minor skirmish before the serious fighting began. The forces of the Confederacy advanced along a broad line here, were slowed briefly by Federal resistance at this wall, but quickly gained the advantage. It was a small Southern victory before the bitter stalemates of the next few days." Sheads paused and smiled at the Captain. "But perhaps you know all this, sir. What unit did you say you have had the honor of serving with?"

The old man's mouth moved feebly before the words could come. "20th North Carolina," he managed at last.

"Of course!" cried Sheads and clapped the Captain on the shoulder. "Part of the glorious brigade whose victory this site commemorates. I would be honored, sir, if you and your young friend would join me in my home to toast the 20th North Carolina regiment before you return to the Reunion Camp. Would this be possible, sir?"

I tugged at the Captain's coat, suddenly desperate to be away from there, lightheaded from hunger and a sudden surge of unreasoning fear, but the old man straightened his back, found his voice, and said clearly, "The boy and me would be honored, sir."

The cottage had been built of tar-black wood. An expensive-looking black horse, still saddled, was tied to the railing of the small porch on the east side of the house. Behind the house, a thicket of trees and a tumble of boulders made access from that direction seem extremely difficult if not impossible.

The house was small inside and showed few signs of being lived in. A tiny entrance foyer led to a parlor where sheets covered two or three pieces of furniture or to the dining room where Sheads led us, a narrow room with a single window, a tall hoosier cluttered with bottles, cans, and a few dirty plates, and a narrow plank table on which burned an old-style kerosene lamp. Behind dusty curtains there was a second, smaller room, in which I caught a glimpse of a mattress on the floor and stacks of books. A steep staircase on the south side of the dining room led up through a hole in the ceiling to what must have been a small attic room, although all I could see when I glanced upward was a square of blackness.

Jessup Sheads propped his heavy walking stick against the table and busied himself at the hoosier, returning with a decanter and three crystal glasses. The lamp hissed and tossed our shadows high on the roughly plastered wall. I glanced toward the window but the twilight had given way to true night and only darkness pressed against the panes.

"Shall we include the boy in our toast?" asked Sheads, pausing, the decanter hovering above the third wine glass. I had never been allowed to taste wine or any other spirits.

"Yes," said the Captain, staring fixedly at Sheads. The lamplight shone upward into the Captain's face, emphasizing his sharp cheekbones and turning his bushy, old-man's eyebrows into two great wings of hair above his falcon's beak of a nose. His shadow on the wall was a silhouette from another era.

Sheads finished pouring and we raised our glasses. I stared dubiously at the wine; the red fluid was dull and thick, streaked through with tendrils of black which may or may not have been a trick of the flickering lamp.

"To the 20th North Carolina Regiment," said Sheads and raised his glass. The gesture reminded me of Reverend Hodges lifting the communion cup. The Captain and I raised our glasses and drank.

The taste was a mixture of fruit and copper. It reminded me of the days, months earlier, when a friend of

Billy Stargill had split my lip during a schoolyard fight. The inside of my lip had bled for hours. The taste was not dissimilar.

Captain Montgomery lowered his glass and scowled at it. Droplets of wine clotted his white whiskers.

"The wine is a local variety," said Sheads with a cold smile which showed red-stained teeth. "Very local. The arbors are those which we just visited."

I stared at the thickening liquid in my glass. Wine made from grapes grown from the rich soil of Iverson's Pits.

Sheads' loud voice startled me. "Another toast!" He raised his glass. "To the honorable and valiant gentleman who led the 20th North Carolina into battle. To Colonel Alfred Iverson."

Sheads raised the glass to his lips. I stood frozen and staring. Captain Montgomery slammed his glass on the table. The old man's face had gone as blood red as the spilled wine. "I'll be goddamned to hell if I . . ." he sputtered. "I'll . . . *never*!"

The man who had introduced himself as Jessup Sheads drained the last of his wine and smiled. His skin was as white as his shirt front, his hair and long mustaches as black as his coat. "Very well," he said and then raised his voice. "Uncle Alfred?"

Even as Sheads had been drinking, part of my mind had registered the soft sound of footsteps on the stairs behind us. I turned only my head, my hand still frozen with the glass of wine half-raised.

The small figure standing on the lowest step was a man in his mid-eighties, at least, but rather than wearing the wrinkles of age like Captain Montgomery, this old man's skin had become smoother and pinker, almost translucent. I was reminded of a nest of newborn rats I had come across in a neighbor's barn the previous spring—a mass of pale-pink, writhing flesh which I had made the mistake of touching. I did not want to touch Iverson.

The Colonel wore a white beard very much like the one I had seen in portraits of Robert E. Lee, but there was no real resemblance. Where Lee's eyes had been sad and shielded under a brow weighted with sorrow, Iverson glared at us with wide, staring eyes shot through with yellow flecks. He was almost bald and the taut, pink scalp reinforced the effect of something almost infantile about the little man.

Captain Montgomery stared, his mouth open, his breath rasping out in short, labored gasps. He clutched at his own collar as if unable to pull in enough air.

Iverson's voice was soft, almost feminine, and edged with the whine of a petulant child. "You all come back sooner or later," he said with a hint of a slight lisp. He sighed deeply. "Is there no end to it?"

"You . . ." managed the Captain. He lifted a long finger to point at Iverson.

"Spare me your outrage," snapped Iverson. "Do you think you are the first to seek me out, the first to try to explain away your own cowardice by slandering me? Samuel and I have grown quite adept at handling trash like you. I only hope that you are the last."

The Captain's hand dropped, disappeared in the folds of his coat. "You goddamned, sonofabitching . . ."

"Silence!" commanded Iverson. The Colonel's wide-eyed gaze darted around the room, passing over me as if I weren't there. The muscles at the corners of the man's mouth twitched and twisted. Again I was reminded of the nest of newborn rats. "Samuel," he shouted, "bring your stick. Show this man the penalty for insolence." Iverson's mad stare returned to Captain Montgomery. "You will salute me before we are finished here."

"I will see you in hell first," said the Captain and pulled the revolver from his coat pocket.

Iverson's nephew moved very fast, lifting the heavy walking stick and slamming it down on the Captain's wrist before the old man could pull back the hammer. I stood frozen, my wine glass still in my hand, as the pistol thudded to the floor. Captain Montgomery bent and reached for it—awkward and slow with his false leg—but Iverson's nephew grabbed him by the collar and flung him backward as effortlessly as an adult would handle a child. The Captain struck the wall, gasped, and slid down it, his false leg gouging splinters from the uneven floorboards as his legs straightened. His face was as gray as his uniform coat.

Iverson's nephew crouched to recover the pistol and set it on the table. Colonel Iverson himself smiled and nodded, his mouth still quivering toward a grin. I had eyes only for the Captain.

The old man lay huddled against the wall, clutching at his own throat, his body arching with spasms as he gasped in one great breath after another, each louder and more ragged than the last. It was obvious that no air was reaching his lungs; his color had gone from red to gray to a terrible dark purple bordering on black. His tongue protruded and saliva flecked his whiskers. The Captain's eyes grew wider and rounder as he realized what was happening to him, but his horrified gaze never left Iverson's face.

I could see the immeasurable frustration in the Captain's eyes as his body betrayed him in these last few seconds of a confrontation he had waited for through half a century of single-minded obsession. The old man drew in two more ragged, wracking breaths and then quit breathing. His chin collapsed onto his sunken chest, the gnarled hands relaxed into loose fists, and his eyes lost their fixed focus on Iverson's face.

As if suddenly released from my own paralysis, I let out a cry, dropped the wine glass to the floor, and ran to crouch next to Captain Montgomery. No breath came from his grotesquely opened mouth. The staring eyes already were beginning to glaze with an invisible film. I touched the gnarled old hands—the flesh already seeming to cool and stiffen in death—and felt a terrible constriction in my own chest. It was not grief. Not exactly. I had known the old man too briefly and in too strange a context to feel deep sorrow so soon. But I found it hard to draw a breath as a great emptiness opened in me, a knowledge that sometimes there is no justice, that life was not fair. *It wasn't fair.* I gripped the old man's dead hands and found myself weeping for myself as much as for him.

"Get out of the way," Iverson's nephew thrust me aside and crouched next to the Captain. He shook the old man by his shirtfront, roughly pinched the bruise-colored cheeks, and laid an ear to the veteran's chest.

"Is he dead, Samuel?" asked Iverson. There was no real interest in his voice.

"Yes, Uncle." The nephew stood and nervously tugged at his mustache.

"Yes, yes," said Iverson in his distracted, petulant voice. "It does not matter." He flicked his small, pink hand in a dismissive gesture. "Take him out to be with the others, Samuel."

Iverson's nephew hesitated and then went into the back room to emerge a moment later with a pickaxe, a long-handled shovel, and a lantern. He jerked me to my feet and thrust the shovel and lantern into my hands.

"What about the boy, Uncle?"

Iverson's yellow gaze seemed absorbed with the shadows near the foot of the stairs. He wrung his soft hands. "Whatever you decide, Samuel," he whined. "Whatever you decide."

The nephew lighted the lantern I was holding, grasped the Captain under one arm, and dragged his body toward the door. I noticed that some of the straps holding the old man's leg had come loose; I could not look away from where the wooden peg dangled loosely from the stump of dead flesh and bone.

The nephew dragged the old man's body through the foyer, out the door, and into the night. I stood there—a statue with shovel and hissing lantern—praying that I would be forgotten. Cool, thin fingers fell on the nape of my neck. A soft, insistent voice whispered, "Come along, young man. Do not keep Samuel and me waiting."

Iverson's nephew dug the grave not ten yards from where the Captain and I had lain in hiding all day. Even if it had been daylight, the trees along the road and the grape arbors would have shielded us from view of anyone passing along the Mummasburg Road. No one passed. The night was brutally dark; low clouds occluded the stars and the only illumination was from my lantern and the faintest hint of light from Iverson's cabin a hundred yards behind us.

The black horse tied to the porch railing watched our strange procession leave the house. Captain Montgomery's

hat had fallen off near the front step and I awkwardly bent
to pick it up. Iverson's soft fingers never left my neck.

The soil in the field was loose and moist and easily excavated. Iverson's nephew was down three feet before
twenty minutes had passed. Bits of root, rock, and other
things glowed whitely in the heap of dirt illuminated by
the lantern's glare.

"That is enough," ordered Iverson. "Get it over with,
Samuel."

The nephew paused and looked up at the Colonel. The
cold light turned the young man's face into a white mask,
glistening with sweat, the whiskers and eyebrows broad
strokes of charcoal, as black as the smudge of dirt on his
left cheek. After a second to catch his breath, he nodded,
set down his shovel, and reached out to roll Captain Montgomery's body into the grave. The old man landed on his
back, eyes and mouth still open. His wooden leg had been
dragging loosely and now remained behind on the brink of
the hole. Iverson's nephew looked at me with hooded eyes,
reached for the leg, and tossed it onto the Captain's chest.
Without looking down, the nephew retrieved the shovel
and quickly began scooping dirt onto the body. *I* watched.
I watched the black soil land on my old veteran's cheek
and forehead. I watched the dirt cover the staring eyes,
first the left and then the right. I watched the open mouth
fill with dirt and I felt the constriction in my own throat
swell and break loose. Huge, silent sobs shook me.

In less than a minute, the Captain was gone, nothing
more than an outline on the floor of the shallow grave.

"Samuel," lisped Iverson.

The nephew paused in his labors and looked at the
Colonel.

"What is your advice about . . . the other thing?"
Iverson's voice was so soft that it was almost lost beneath
the hissing of the lantern and the pounding of pulse in my
ears.

The nephew wiped his cheek with the back of his
hand, broadening the dark smear there, and nodded slowly.
"I think we have to, Uncle. We just cannot afford to . . .
we cannot risk it. Not after the Florida thing . . ."

Iverson sighed. "Very well. Do what you must. I will abide by your decision."

The nephew nodded again, let out a breath, and reached for the pickaxe where it lay embedded in the heap of freshly excavated earth. Some part of my mind screamed at me to run, but I was capable only of standing there at the edge of that terrible pit, holding the lantern and breathing in the smell of Samuel's sweat and a deeper, more pervasive stench that seemed to rise out of the pit, the heap of dirt, the surrounding arbors.

"Put the light down, young man," Iverson whispered, inches from my ear. "Put it down carefully." His cool fingers closed more tightly on my neck. I set the lantern down, positioning it with care so that it would not tip over. Iverson's cold grip moved me forward to the very brink of the pit. His nephew stood waist-high in the hole, holding the pickaxe and fixing his dark gaze on me with a look conveying something between regret and anticipation. He shifted the pick handle in his large, white hands. I was about to say "It's all right" when his determined stare changed to wide-eyed surprise.

Samuel's body lurched, steadied, and then lurched again. It was as if he had been standing on a platform which had dropped a foot, then eighteen inches. Where the edges of the grave had come just to his waist, they now rose to his armpits.

Iverson's nephew threw aside the pickaxe and thrust his arms out onto solid ground. But the ground was no longer solid. Colonel Iverson and I stumbled backwards as the earth seemed to vibrate and then flow like a mudslide. The nephew's left hand seized my ankle, his right hand sought a firm grip on thick vines. Iverson's hand remained firm on my neck, choking me.

Suddenly there came the sound of collapsing, sliding dirt, as if the floor of the grave had given way, collapsing through the ceiling of some forgotten mine or cavern, and the nephew threw himself forward, half out of the grave, his chest pressed against the slippery edges of the pit, his fingers releasing my ankle to claw at loam and vines. He reminded me of a mountain climber on a rocky overhang,

using only his fingers and the friction of his upper body to
defy the pull of gravity.

"Help me." His voice was a whisper, contorted by effort and disbelief.

Colonel Iverson backed away another five steps and I
was pulled along.

Samuel was winning the struggle with the collapsing
grave. His left hand found the pickaxe where he had
buried it in the mound of dirt and he used the handle for
leverage, pulling himself upward until his right knee found
purchase on the edge of the pit.

The edge collapsed.

Dirt from the three-foot-high mound flowed past the
handle of the pick, over the nephew's straining arm and
shoulder, back into the pit. The earth had been moist but
solid where Samuel excavated it; now it flowed like fric-
tionless mud, like water . . . like black wine.

Samuel slid back into the pit, now filled with viscous
dirt, with only his face and upraised fingers rising out of
the pool of black, shifting soil.

Suddenly there came a sound from all around us as if
many large forms had shifted position under blankets of
grass and vines. Leaves stirred. Vines snapped. There was
no breeze.

Iverson's nephew opened his mouth to scream and a
wave of blackness flowed in between his teeth. His eyes
were not human. Without warning, the ground shifted
again and the nephew was pulled violently out of sight. He
disappeared as quickly and totally as a swimmer pulled
down by a shark three times his size.

There came the sound of teeth.

Colonel Iverson whimpered then, making the noise of
a small child being made to go to his room without a light.
His grip loosened on my neck.

Samuel's face appeared one last time, protruding eyes
filmed with dirt. Something had taken most of the flesh
from his right cheek. I realized that the sound I now heard
was a man trying to scream with his larynx and esophagus
half-filled with dirt.

He was pulled under again. Colonel Iverson took another three steps back and released my neck. I grabbed up the lantern and ran.

I heard a shout behind me and I looked over my shoulder just long enough to see Colonel Iverson coming through the break in the fence. He was out of the field, staggering, wheezing, but still coming on.

I ran with the speed of a terrified ten-year-old, the lantern swinging wildly from my right hand, throwing shifting patterns of light on leaves, branches, rocks. I had to have the light with me. There was a single thought in my mind: the Captain's pistol lying where Samuel had laid it on the table.

The saddled horse was pulling at its tether when I reached the house; its eyes were wild, alarmed at me, the swinging lantern, Iverson shouting far behind me, or the sudden terrible stench that drifted from the fields. I ignored the animal and slammed through the doorway, past the foyer, and into the dining room. I stopped, panting, grinning with terror and triumph.

The pistol was gone.

For seconds or minutes I stood in shock, not being able to think at all. Then, still holding the lantern, I looked under the table, in the hoosier, in the tiny back room. The pistol was not there. I started for the door, heard noises on the porch, headed up the stairs, and then paused in indecision.

"Is this . . . what you are after . . . young man?" Iverson stood panting at the entrance to the dining room, his left hand braced against the doorjamb, his right hand raised with the pistol leveled at me. "Slander, all slander," he said and squeezed the trigger.

The Captain had called the pistol a "double action." The hammer clicked back, locked into place, but did not fire. Iverson glanced at it and raised it toward me again. I threw the lantern at his face.

The Colonel batted it aside, breaking the glass. Flames ignited the ancient curtains and shot toward the ceiling, scorching Iverson's right side. He cursed and dropped the revolver. I vaulted over the stair railing, grabbed the kero-

sene lamp from the table, and threw it into the back room.
Bedding and books burst into flame as the lamp oil spread.
Dropping on all fours, I scrabbled toward the pistol but
Iverson kicked at my head. He was old and slow and I
easily rolled aside, but not before the burning curtain fell
between me and the weapon. Iverson reached for it, pulled
his hand back from the flames, and fled cursing out the
front door.

I crouched there a second, panting. Flames shot along
cracks in the floorboards, igniting pitch pine and the
framework of the tinder-dry house itself. Outside the horse
whinnied, either from the smell of smoke or the attempts
of the Colonel to gain the saddle. I knew that nothing
could stop Iverson from riding south or east, into the
woods, toward the town, away from Iverson's Pits.

I reached into the circle of flame, screaming silently as
part of my tunic sleeve charred away and blisters erupted
on my palm, wrist, and lower arm. I dragged the pistol
back, tossing the heated metal from hand to hand. Only
later did I wonder why the gunpowder in the cartridges did
not explode. Cradling the weapon in my burned hands, I
stumbled outside.

Colonel Iverson had mounted but had only one boot in
a stirrup. One rein dragged loosely while he tugged violently at the other, trying to turn the panicked horse back
toward the forest. Toward the burning house. The mare
had backed away from the flames and was intent on running toward the break in the wall. Toward the Pits. Iverson
fought it. The result was that the mare spun in circles, the
whites of its eyes showing at each revolution.

I stumbled off the porch of the burning cottage and
lifted the heavy weapon just as Iverson managed to stop
the horse's gyrations and leaned forward to grab the loose
rein. With both reins in hand and the mare under control,
he kicked hard to ride past me—or ride me down—on his
way into the darkness of the trees. It took all of my
strength to thumb the hammer back, blisters bursting on
my thumb as I did so, and fire. I had not taken time to
aim. The bullet ripped through branches ten feet above
Iverson. The recoil almost made me drop the gun.

The mare spun back toward the darkness behind it.

Iverson forced it around again, urged it forward with violent kicks of his small, black shoes.

My second shot went into the dirt five feet in front of me. Flesh peeled back from my burned thumb as I forced the hammer back the third time, aiming the impossibly heavy weapon between the mare's rolling eyes. I was sobbing so fiercely that I could not see Iverson clearly, but I could clearly hear him curse as his horse refused to approach the flames and source of noise a third time. I wiped at my eyes with my scorched sleeve just as Iverson wheeled the mare away from the light and gave it its head. My third shot went high again, but Iverson's horse galloped into the darkness, not staying on the faint path, jumping the stone wall in a leap which cleared the rocks by two feet.

I ran after them, still sobbing, tripping twice in the darkness but keeping possession of the pistol. By the time I reached the wall, the entire house was ablaze behind me, sparks drifting overhead and curtains of red light dancing across the forest and fields. I jumped to the top of the wall and stood there weaving, gasping for breath, and watching.

Iverson's mount had made it thirty yards or so beyond the wall before being forced to a halt. It was rearing now, both reins flying free as the white-bearded man on its back clung desperately with both hands in its mane.

The arbors were moving. Tall masses of vines rose as high as the horse's head, vague shapes seeming to move under a shifting surface of leaves. The earth itself was heaving into hummocks and ridges. And holes.

I saw them clearly in the bonfire light. Mole holes. Gopher holes. But as broad across the opening as the trunk of a man. And ribbed inside, lined with ridges of blood-red cartilage. It was like looking down the maw of a snake as its insides pulsed and throbbed expectantly.

Only worse.

If you have seen a lamprey preparing to feed you might know what I mean. The holes had teeth. Rows of teeth. They were ringed with teeth. The earth had opened to show its red-rimmed guts, ringed with sharp white teeth.

The holes moved. The mare danced in panic but the

holes shifted like shadows in the broad circle of bare earth
which had cleared itself of vines. Around the circumfer-
ence, dark shapes rose beneath the arbors.

Iverson screamed then. A second later his horse let out
a similar noise as a hole closed on its right front leg. I
clearly heard the bone snap and sever. The horse went
down with Iverson rolling free. There were more snapping
noises and the horse lifted its neck to watch with mad,
white eyes as the earth closed around its four stumps of
legs, shredding the ligament and muscle from bone as easily as someone stripping strands of dark meat from a
drumstick.

In twenty seconds there was only the thrashing trunk
of the mare, rolling in the black dirt and black blood in a
vain attempt to avoid the shifting lamprey teeth. Then
the holes closed on the animal's neck.

Colonel Iverson rose to his knees, then to his feet. The
only sounds were the crackling of flames behind me, the
rustling of vines, and the high, hysterical panting of
Iverson himself. The man was giggling.

In rows five hundred yards long, in lines as straight as
a dress parade and as precise as battle lines, the earth
trembled and furrowed, folding on itself, vines and grass
and black soil rising and falling, rippling like rats moving
under a thin blanket. Or like the furling of a flag.

Iverson screamed as the holes opened under him and
around him. Somehow he managed to scream a second
time as the upper half of his body rolled free across the
waiting earth, one hand clawing for leverage in the undu-
lating dirt while the other hand vainly attempted to tuck in
the parts of himself which trailed behind.

The holes closed again. There was no screaming now
as only the small, pink oval rolled in the dirt, but I will be
certain to my dying day that I saw the white beard move
as the jaws opened silently, saw the flicker of white and
yellow as the eyes blinked.

The holes closed a third time.

I stumbled away from the wall, but not before I had
thrown the revolver as far out into the field as I could
manage. The burning house had collapsed into itself but
the heat was tremendous, far too hot for me to sit so close.

My eyebrows were quickly singed away and steam rose from my sweat-soaked clothes, but I stayed as close to the fire as I could for as long as I could.

Close to the light.

I have no memory of the fire brigade that found me or of the men who brought me back to town sometime before dawn.

Wednesday, July 2, was Military Day at the Great Reunion. It rained hard all afternoon but speeches were given in the Great Tent. Sons and grandsons of General Longstreet and General Pickett and General Meade were present on the speakers' platform.

I remember awakening briefly in the hospital tent to the sound of rain on canvas. Someone was explaining to someone that facilities were better there than in the old hospital in town. My arms and hands were swathed in bandages. My brow burned with fever. "Rest easy, lad," said Reverend Hodges, his face heavy with worry. "I've cabled your parents. Your father will be here before nightfall." I nodded and stifled the urge to scream in the interminable seconds before sleep claimed me again. The beating of rain on the tent had sounded like teeth scraping bone.

Thursday, July 3, was Civic Day at the Great Reunion. Survivors of Pickett's brigade and ex-Union troops from the Philadelphia Brigade Association formed two lines and walked fifty feet north and south to the wall on Cemetery Ridge which marked the so-called high water mark of the Confederacy. Both sides lowered battle flags until they crossed above the wall. Then a bearer symbolically lifted the Stars and Stripes above the crossed battle flags. Everyone cheered. Veterans embraced one another.

I remember fragments of the train ride home that morning. I remember my father's arm around me. I remember my mother's face when we arrived at the station in Chestnut Hill.

Friday, July 4, was National Day at the Great Reunion. President Wilson addressed all of the veterans in the Great Tent at 11 A.M. He spoke of healing wounds, forgetting

past differences, of forgetting old quarrels. He spoke of
valor and courage and glory which the ages would not diminish. When he was finished, they played the National
Anthem and an honor guard fired a salute. Then all the old
men went home.

I remember parts of my dreams that day. They were
the same dreams I have now. Several times I awoke
screaming. My mother tried to hold my hand but I wanted
nothing to touch me. Nothing at all.

Seventy-five years have passed since my first trip to
Gettysburg. I have been back many times. The guides and
rangers and librarians there know me by name. Some flat-
ter me with the title historian.

Nine veterans died during the Great Reunion of
1913—five of heart problems, two of heatstroke, and one
of pneumonia. The ninth veteran's death certificate lists
the cause of death as "old age." One veteran simply disappeared sometime between his registration and the date he
was expected back at a home for retired veterans in Raleigh, North Carolina. The name of Captain Powell D.
Montgomery of Raleigh, North Carolina, veteran of the
20th North Carolina Regiment, was never added to the list
of the nine veterans who died. He had no family and was
not missed for some weeks after the Reunion ended.

Jessup Sheads had indeed built the small house southeast of the Forney farm, on the site where the 97th New
York regiment had silently waited behind a stone wall for
the advance of Colonel Alfred Iverson's men. Sheads designed the small house as a summer home and erected it
in the spring of 1893. He never stayed in it. Sheads was
described as a short, stout, redheaded man, cleanshaven,
with a weakness for wine. It was he who had planted the
grape arbors shortly before his death from a heart attack in
that same year of 1893. His widow rented the summer
house out through agents for the years until the cottage
burned in the summer of 1913. No records were kept of
the renters.

Colonel Alfred Iverson, Jr., ended the war as a Briga-
dier General despite being relieved of his command after

undisclosed difficulties during the opening skirmishes of the Battle of Gettysburg. After the war, Iverson was engaged in unlucky business ventures in Georgia and then in Florida, leaving both areas under unclear circumstances. In Florida, Iverson was involved in the citrus business with his grand-nephew, Samuel Strahl, an outspoken member of the KKK and a rabid defender of his grand-uncle's name and reputation. It was rumored that Stahl had killed at least two men in illegal duels and he was wanted for questioning in Broward County in relation to the disappearance of a 78-year-old man named Phelps Rawlins. Rawlins had been a veteran of the 20th North Carolina Regiment. Stahl's wife reported him missing during a month-long hunting trip in the summer of 1913. She lived on in Macon, Georgia, until her death in 1948.

Alfred Iverson, Jr., is listed in different sources as dying in 1911, 1913, or 1915. Historians frequently confused Iverson with his father, the Senator, and although both are supposed to be buried in the family crypt in Atlanta, records at the Oakland Cemetery show that there is only one coffin entombed there.

Many times over the years have I dreamt the dream I remember from that hot afternoon in the grape arbors. Only my field of view in that dream changes—from blue sky and a stone wall under spreading branches to trenches and barbed wire, to rice paddies and monsoon clouds, to frozen mud along a frozen river, to thick, tropical vegetation which swallows light. Recently I have dreamed that I am lying in the ash of a city while snow falls from low clouds. But the fruit and copper taste of the soil remains the same. The silent communion among the casually sacrificed and the forgotten-buried also remains the same. Sometimes I think of the mass graves which have fertilized this century and I weep for my grandson and great-grandchildren.

I have not visited the battlefields in some years. The last time was twenty-five years ago in the quiet spring of 1963, three months before the insanity of that summer's centennial celebration of the battles. The Mummasburg

Road had been paved and widened. John Forney's house had not been there for years but I did note a proliferation of iris where the foundation had once stood. The town of Gettysburg is much larger, of course, but zoning restrictions and the historical park have kept new houses from being built in the vicinity.

Many of the trees along the stone wall have died of Dutch elm disease and other blights. Only a few yards of the wall itself remain, the stones having been carried off for fireplaces and patios. The city is clearly visible across the open fields.

No sign of Iverson's Pits remains. No one I spoke to who lives in the area remembers them. The fields there are green when lying fallow and incredibly productive when tilled, but this is true of most of the surrounding Pennsylvania countryside.

Last winter a friend and fellow amateur historian wrote to tell me that a small archaeological team from Penn State University had done a trial dig in the Oak Hill area. He wrote that the dig had yielded a veritable goldmine of relics—bullets, brass buttons, bits of mess kits, canister fragments, five almost intact bayonets, bits of bone—all of the stubborn objects which decaying flesh leaves behind like minor footnotes in time.

And teeth, wrote my friend.

Many, many teeth.

Introduction to
"Shave and a Haircut, Two Bites"

My family moved frequently when I was a child. One of the problems of moving—at any age—is the tedious chore of finding a new doctor, dentist, favorite grocery store . . . and barber.

When I was about eight we moved to the small Illinois town of Brimfield, population less than a thousand, and although the town barely had one of everything—one store, one doctor, one school—it had two barbers. I remember my mother taking my younger brother Wayne and me downtown and entering the first barbershop we saw.

The wrong one.

I remember the desiccated cactus and the dead flies on the window ledge. I remember the musty, chewing-tobacco-and-old-sweat smell of the dark interior and the mirrors that seemed to absorb the light. I remember the old men in bib overalls who scurried away like cockroaches as we entered; I remember how startled the elderly barber was at out intrusion.

I had my hair cut that day, Wayne didn't. It was a terrible haircut. I wore my Cub Scout hat, indoors and out, for three weeks. Mom soon learned that the *real* barbershop was a block down the street. *No one* went to the shop we had blundered into. Even the old farmers who hung out there were bald or had never been seen in a barber chair.

The only interesting part to this anecdote is the epilogue: that same barbershop—or one just like it—has been in every town I've lived in since.

In Chicago, it was tucked away on an unnamed sidestreet just off Kildare Avenue.

In Indianapolis, it was a short block from the Soldiers and Sailors Monument.

In Philadelphia, it was on Germantown Avenue just across the street from a three-hundred-year-old haunted house named Grumblethorpe.

In Calcutta—where most people get their haircuts and shaves from sidewalk barbers who squat on the curb while the customer squats in the gutter—the old shop was just off Chowringhee Road, tucked under a hundred-trunked banyan tree which is said to be as old as the earth.

Out here where I live in Colorado, it is on Main Street, between Third and Fourth Avenues.

Of course it's not the *same* shop, it's just . . . well, the *same*.

Look around. You'll find it in your community. You don't get *your* hair cut there, and no one you know has ever had a haircut there . . . and the prices are from a previous decade if not century . . . but ask around. The locals will shake their heads as if trying to remember a dream, and then they'll say—"Oh, yeah, that place has *always* been here. That barber's always been here. Don't know nobody who goes to 'im anymore, though. Wonder how he gets by."

Go on. Work up the courage to go in. Ignore the mummified cactus and dead flies in the window. Don't be distracted by the old men who scurry out the back door when you come in the front.

Go ahead. Get your hair cut there.

I dare you.

Shave and a Haircut,
Two Bites

Outside, the blood spirals down.

I pause at the entrance to the barbershop. There is nothing unique about it. Almost certainly there is one similar to it in your community; its function is proclaimed by the pole outside, the red spiralling down, and by the name painted on the broad window, the letters grown scabrous as the gold paint ages and flakes away. While the most expensive hair salons now bear the names of their owners, and the shopping mall franchises offer sickening cutenesses—Hairport, Hair Today: Gone Tomorrow, Hair We Are, Headlines, Shear Masters, The Head Hunter, In-Hair-itance, and so forth, ad infinitum, ad nauseum—the name of this shop is eminently forgettable. It is meant to be so. This shop offers neither styling nor unisex cuts. If your hair is dirty when you enter, it will be cut dirty; there are no shampoos given here. While the franchises demand $15 to $30 for a basic haircut, the cost here has not changed for a decade or more. It occurs to the potential new customer immediately upon entering that no one could live on an income based upon such low rates. No one does. The potential customer usually beats a hasty retreat, put off by the too-low prices, by the darkness of the

place, by the air of dusty decrepitude exuded from both
the establishment itself and from its few waiting customers, invariably silent and staring, and by a strange sense of
tension bordering upon threat which hangs in the stale air.

Before entering, I pause a final moment to stare in the
window of the barbershop. For a second I can see only a
reflection of the street and the silhouette of a man more
shadow than substance—me. To see inside, one has to step
closer to the glass and perhaps cup hands to one's temples
to reduce the glare. The blinds are drawn but I find a crack
in the slats. Even then there is not much to see. A dusty
window ledge holds three desiccated cacti and an assortment of dead flies. Two barber chairs are just visible
through the gloom; they are of a sort no longer made:
black leather, white enamel, a high headrest. Along one
wall, half a dozen uncomfortable-looking chairs sit empty
and two low tables show a litter of magazines with covers
torn or missing entirely. There are mirrors on two of the
three interior walls, but rather than add light to the long,
narrow room, the infinitely receding reflections seem to
make the space appear as if the barbershop itself were a
dark reflection in an age-dimmed glass.

A man is standing there in the gloom, his form hardly
more substantial than my silhouette on the window. He
stands next to the first barber chair as if he were waiting
for me.

He *is* waiting for me.

I leave the sunlight of the street and enter the shop.

"Vampires," said Kevin. "They're both vampires."

"Who're vampires?" I asked between bites on my apple. Kevin and I were twenty feet up in a tree in his back
yard. We'd built a rough platform there which passed as a
treehouse. Kevin was ten, I was nine.

"Mr. Innis and Mr. Denofrio," said Kevin. "They're
both vampires."

I lowered the Superman comic I'd been reading.
"They're not vampires," I said. "They're *barbers*."

"Yeah," said Kevin, "but they're vampires too. I just
figured it out."

I sighed and sat back against the bole of the tree. It was late autumn and the branches were almost empty of leaves. Another week or two and we wouldn't be using the treehouse again until next spring. Usually when Kevin announced that he'd just figured something out, it meant trouble. Kevin O'toole was almost my age, but sometimes it seemed that he was five years older and five years younger than me at the same time. He read a lot. And he had a weird imagination. "Tell me," I said.

"You know what the red means, Tommy?"

"What red?"

"On the barber pole. The red stripes that curl down."

I shrugged. "It means it's a barbershop."

It was Kevin's turn to sigh. "Yeah, sure, Tommy, but why *red*? And why have it curling down like that for a barber?"

I didn't say anything. When Kevin was in one of his moods, it was better to wait him out.

"Because it's blood," he said dramatically, almost whispering. "Blood spiralling down. Blood dripping and spilling. That's been the sign for barbers for almost six hundred years."

He'd caught my interest. I set the Superman comic aside on the platform. "OK," I said, "I believe you. Why is it their sign?"

"Because it was their *guild sign*," said Kevin. "Back in the Middle Ages, all the guys who did important work belonged to guilds, sort of like the union our dads belong to down at the brewery, and . . ."

"Yeah, yeah," I said. "But why *blood*?" Guys as smart as Kevin had a hard time sticking to the point.

"I was getting to that," said Kevin. "According to this stuff I read, way back in the Middle Ages barbers used to be surgeons. About all they could do to help sick people was to bleed them, and . . ."

"Bleed them?"

"Yeah. They didn't have any real medicines or anything, so if somebody got sick with a disease or broke a leg or something, all the surgeon . . . the barber . . . could do was bleed them. Sometimes they'd use the same razor they shaved people with. Sometimes they'd bring bottles of leeches and let them suck some blood out of the sick person."

"Gross."

"Yeah, but it sort of worked. Sometimes. I guess when you lose blood, your blood pressure goes down and that can lower a fever and stuff. But most of the time, the people they bled just died sooner. They probably needed a transfusion more than a bunch of leeches stuck on them."

I sat and thought about this for a moment. Kevin knew some really weird stuff. I used to think he was lying about a lot of it, but after I saw him correct the teachers in fourth and fifth grade a few times . . . and get away with it . . . I realized he wasn't making things up. Kevin was weird, but he wasn't a liar.

A breeze rustled the few remaining leaves. It was a sad and brittle sound to a kid who loved summer. "All right," I said. "But what's all of this got to do with vampires? You think 'cause barbers used to stick leeches on people a couple of hundred years ago that Mr. Innis and Mr. Denofrio are *vampires*? Jeez, Kev, that's nuts."

"The Middle Ages were more than five hundred years ago, Niles," said Kevin, calling me by my last name in the voice that always made me want to punch him. "But the guild sign was just what got me thinking about it all. I mean, what other business has kept its guild sign?"

I shrugged and tied a broken shoelace. "Blood on their sign doesn't make them vampires."

When Kevin was excited, his green eyes seemed to get even greener than usual. They were really green now. He leaned forward. "Just think about it, Tommy," he said. "When did vampires start to disappear?"

"Disappear? You mean you think they were *real*? Cripes, Kev, my mom says you're the only gifted kid she's ever met, but sometimes I think you're just plain looney tunes."

Kevin ignored me. He had a long, thin face—made even thinner looking by the crewcut he wore—and his skin was so pale that the freckles stood out like spots of gold. He had the same full lips that people said made his two sisters look pretty, but now those lips were quivering. "I read a lot about vampires," he said. "A *lot*. Most of the se-

rious stuff agrees that the vampire legends were fading in
Europe by the Seventeenth Century. People still *believed*
in them, but they weren't so afraid of them anymore. A
few hundred years earlier, suspected vampires were being
tracked down and killed all the time. It's like they'd gone
underground or something."

"Or people got smarter," I said.

"No, think," said Kevin and grabbed my arm. "Maybe
the vampires were being wiped out. People knew they
were there and how to fight them."

"Like a stake through the heart?"

"Maybe. Anyway, they've got to hide, pretend they're
gone, and still get blood. What'd be the easiest way to do
it?"

I thought of a wise-acre comment, but one look at
Kevin made me realize that he was dead serious about all
this. And we were best friends. I shook my head.

"Join the barbers guild!" Kevin's voice was triumphant. "Instead of having to break into people's houses at
night and then risk others finding the body all drained of
blood, they *invite* you in. They don't even struggle while
you open their veins with a knife or put the leeches on.
Then they . . . or the family of the dead guy . . . *pay* you.
No wonder they're the only group to keep their guild
sign. They're vampires, Tommy!"

I licked my lips, tasted blood, and realized that I'd
been chewing on my lower lip while Kevin talked. "All of
them?" I said. "Every barber?"

Kevin frowned and released my arm. "I'm not sure.
Maybe not all."

"But you think Innis and Denofrio are?"

Kevin's eyes got greener again and he grinned.
"There's one way to find out."

I closed my eyes a second before asking the fatal question. "How, Kev?"

"By watching them," said Kevin. "Following them.
Checking them out. *Seeing* if they're vampires."

"And if they are?"

Kevin shrugged. He was still grinning. "We'll think of
something."

•   •   •

I enter the familiar shop, my eyes adjusting quickly to
the dim light. The air smells of talcum and rose oil and
tonic. The floor is clean and instruments are laid out on
white linen atop the counter. Light glints dully from the
surface of scissors and shears and the pearl handles of
more than one straight razor.

I approach the man who stands silently by his chair.
He wears a white shirt and tie under a white smock.
"Good morning," I say.

"Good morning, Mr. Niles." He pulls a striped cloth
from its shelf, snaps it open with a practiced hand, and
stands waiting like a toreador.

I take my place in the chair. He sweeps the cloth
around me and snaps it shut behind my neck in a single,
fluid motion. "A trim this morning, perhaps?"

"I think not. Just a shave, please."

He nods and turns away to heat the towels and prepare
the razor. Waiting, I look into the mirrored depths and see
multitudes.

Kevin and I had made our pact while sitting in our tree
on Sunday. By Thursday we'd done quite a bit of snoop-
ing. Kev had followed Innis and I'd watched Denofrio.

We met in Kevin's room after school. You could
hardly see his bed for all the heaps of books and comics
and half-built Heath Kits and vacuum tubes and plastic
models and scattered clothes. Kevin's mother was still
alive then, but she had been ill for years and rarely paid attention to little things like her son's bedroom. Or her son.

Kevin shoved aside some junk and we sat on his bed,
comparing notes. Mine were scrawled on scraps of paper
and the back of my paper route collection form.

"OK," said Kevin, "what'd you find out?"

"They're not vampires," I said. "At least my guy
isn't."

Kevin frowned. "It's too early to tell, Tommy."

"Nuts. You gave me this list of ways to tell a vampire,
and Denofrio flunks *all* of them."

"Explain."

"OK. Look at Number One on your stupid list. 'Vampires are rarely seen in daylight.' Heck, Denofrio and Innis are both in the shop all day. We both checked, right?"

Kevin sat on his knees and rubbed his chin. "Yeah, but the barbershop is *dark*, Tommy. I told you that it's only in the movies that the vampires burst into flame or something if the daylight hits them. According to the old books, they just don't *like* it. They can get around in the daylight if they have to."

"Sure," I said, "but these guys work all day just like our dads. They close up at five and walk home before it gets dark."

Kevin pawed through his own notes and interrupted. "They both live alone, Tommy. That suggests something."

"Yeah. It suggests that neither one of them makes enough money to get married or have a family. My dad says that their barbershop hasn't raised its prices in years."

"Exactly!" cried Kevin. "Then how come almost no one goes there?"

"They give lousy haircuts," I said. I looked back at my list, trying to decipher the smeared lines of pencilled scrawl. "OK, Number Five on your list. 'Vampires will not cross running water.' " Denofrio lives across the *river*, Kev. I watched him cross it all three days I was following him."

Kevin was sitting up on his knees. Now he slumped slightly. "I told you that I wasn't sure of that one. Stoker put it in *Dracula*, but I didn't find it too many other places."

I went on quickly. "Number Three—'Vampires hate garlic.' I watched Mr. Denofrio eat dinner at Luigi's Tuesday night, Kev. I could smell the garlic from twenty feet away when he came out."

"Three wasn't an essential one."

"All right," I said, moving in for the kill, "tell me *this* one wasn't essential. Number Eight—'All vampires hate and fear crosses and will avoid them at all cost.' " I paused dramatically. Kevin knew what was coming and slumped lower. "Kev, Mr. Denofrio goes to St. Mary's. *Your church, Kev.* Every morning before he goes down to open up the shop."

"Yeah. Innis goes to First Prez on Sundays. My dad

told me about Denofrio being in the parish. I never see him because he only goes to early Mass."

I tossed the notes on the bed. "How could a vampire go to your church? He not only doesn't run away from a cross, he sits there and stares at about a hundred of them each day of the week for about an hour a day."

"Dad says he's never seem him take Communion," said Kevin, a hopeful note in his voice.

I made a face. "Great. Next you'll be telling me that anyone who's not a priest has to be a vampire. Brilliant, Kev."

He sat up and crumpled his own notes into a ball. I'd already seen them at school. I knew that Innis didn't follow Kevin's Vampire Rules either. Kevin said, "The cross thing doesn't prove . . . or disprove . . . anything, Tommy. I've been thinking about it. These things joined the barber's guild to get some protective coloration. It makes sense that they'd try to blend into the religious community too. Maybe they can train themselves to build up a tolerance to crosses, the way we take shots to build up a tolerance to things like smallpox and polio."

I didn't sneer, but I was tempted. "Do they build up a tolerance to mirrors, too?"

"What do you mean?"

"I mean I know something about vampires too, Kev, and even though it wasn't in your stupid list of rules, it's a fact that vampires don't like mirrors. They don't throw a reflection."

"That's not right," said Kevin in that rushy, teacherish voice he used. "In the movies they don't throw a reflection. The old books say that they avoided mirrors because they saw their *true* reflection there . . . what they looked like being old or undead or whatever."

"Yeah, whatever," I said. "But *whatever* spooks them, there isn't any place worse for mirrors than a barbershop. Unless they hang out in one of those carnival funhouse mirror places. Do they have guild signs, too, Kev?"

Kevin threw himself backward on the bed as if I'd shot him. A second later he was pawing through his notes and back up on his knees. "There was one weird thing," he said.

"Yeah, what?"

"They were closed on Monday."

"Real weird. Of course, every darn barbershop in the entire *universe* is closed on Mondays, but I guess you're right. They're closed on Mondays. They've got to be vampires. QED, as Mrs. Double Butt likes to say in geometry class. Gosh, I wish I was smart like you, Kevin."

"Mrs. Doubet," he said, still looking at his notes. He was the only kid in our class who liked her. "It's not that they're closed on Monday that's weird, Tommy. It's what they do. Or at least Innis."

"How do you know? You were home sick on Monday."

Kevin smiled. "No, I wasn't. I typed the excuse and signed Mom's name. They never check. I followed Innis around. Lucky he has that old car and drives slow, I was able to keep up with him on my bike. Or at least catch up."

I rolled to the floor and looked at some kit Kevin'd given up on before finishing. It looked like some sort of radio crossed with an adding machine. I managed to fake disinterest in what he was saying even though he'd hooked me again, just as he always did. "So where did he go?" I said.

"The Mear place. Old Man Everett's estate. Miss Plankmen's house out on 28. That mansion on the main road, the one the rich guy from New York bought last year."

"So?" I said. "They're all rich. Innis probably cuts their hair at home." I was proud that I had seen a connection that Kevin had missed.

"Uh-huh," said Kevin, "the richest people in the county and the one thing they have in common is that they get their haircuts from the lousiest barber in the state. Lousiest barbers, I should say. I saw Denofrio drive off, too. They met at the shop before they went on their rounds. I'm pretty sure Denofrio was at the Wilkes estate along the river that day. I asked Rudy, the caretaker, and he said either Denofrio or Innis comes there most Mondays."

I shrugged. "So rich people stay rich by paying the least they can for haircuts."

"Sure," said Kevin. "But that's not the weird part. The weird part was that both of the old guys loaded their car trunks with small bottles. When Innis came out of Mear and Everett's and Plankmen's places, he was carrying *big* bottles, two-gallon jars at least, and they were heavy, Tommy. Filled with liquid. I'm pretty sure the smaller jars that they'd loaded at the shop were full too."

"Full of what?" I said. "Blood?"

"Why not?" said Kevin.

"Vampires are supposed to take blood *away*," I said, laughing. "Not *deliver* it."

"Maybe it was blood in the big bottles," said Kevin. "And they brought something to trade from the barber-shop."

"Sure," I said, still laughing, "hair tonic!"

"It's not funny, Tom."

"The heck it isn't!" I made myself laugh even harder. "The best part is that your barber vampires are biting just the rich folks. They only drink premium!" I rolled on the floor, scattering comic books and trying not to crush any vacuum tubes.

Kevin walked to the window and looked out at the fading light. We both hated it when the days got shorter. "Well, I'm not convinced," he said. "But it'll be decided tonight."

"Tonight?" I said, lying on my side and no longer laughing. "What happens tonight?"

Kevin looked over his shoulder at me. "The back entrance to the barbershop has one of those old-style locks that I can get past in about two seconds with my Houdini Kit. After dinner, I'm going down to check the place out."

I said, "It's dark after dinner."

Kevin shrugged and looked outside.

"Are you going alone?"

Kevin paused and then stared at me over his shoulder. "That's up to you."

I stared back.

·   ·   ·

There is no sound quite the same as a straight razor being sharpened on a leather strop. I relax under the wrap of hot towels on my face, hearing but not seeing the barber prepare his blade. Receiving a professional shave is a pleasure which modern man has all but abandoned, but one in which I indulge every day.

The barber pulls away the towels, dries my upper cheeks and temples with a dab of a dry cloth, and turns back to the strop for a few final strokes of the razor. I feel my cheeks and throat tingling from the hot towels, the blood pulsing in my neck. "When I was a boy," I say, "a friend of mine convinced me that barbers were vampires."

The barber smiles but says nothing. He has heard my story before.

"He was wrong," I say, too relaxed to keep talking.

The barber's smile fades slightly as he leans forward, his face a study in concentration. Using a brush and lather whipped in a cup, he quickly applies the shaving soap. Then he sets aside the cup, lifts the straight razor, and with a delicate touch of only his thumb and little finger, tilts my head so that my throat is arched and exposed to the blade.

I close my eyes as the cold steel rasps across the warmed flesh.

"You said two seconds!" I whispered urgently. "You've been messing with that darned lock for *five minutes*!" Kevin and I were crouched in the alley behind Fourth Street, huddled in the back doorway of the barbershop. The night air was cold and smelled of garbage. Street sounds seemed to come to us from a million miles away. *"Come on!"* I whispered.

The lock clunked, clicked, and the door swung open into blackness. *"Voilà,"* said Kevin. He stuck his wires, picks, and other tools back into his imitation-leather Houdini Kit bag. Grinning, he reached over and rapped 'Shave and a Haircut' on the door.

"Shut up," I hissed, but Kevin was gone, feeling his way into the darkness. I shook my head and followed him in.

Once inside with the door closed, Kevin clicked on a

penlight and held it between his teeth the way we'd seen
a spy do in a movie. I grabbed onto the tail of his windbreaker and followed him down a short hallway into the
single, long room of the barbershop.

It didn't take long to look around. The blinds were
closed on both the large window and the smaller one on
the front door, so Kevin figured it was safe to use the penlight. It was weird moving across that dark space with
Kevin, the penlight throwing images of itself into the mirrors and illuminating one thing at a time—a counter here,
the two chairs in the center of the room, a few chairs and
magazines for customers, two sinks, a tiny little lavatory,
no bigger than a closet, its door right inside the short hallway. All the clippers and things had been put away in
drawers. Kevin opened the drawers, peered into the
shelves. There were bottles of hair tonic, towels, all the
barber tools set neatly into top drawers, both sets arranged
the same. Kevin took out a razor and opened it, holding
the blade up so it reflected the light into the mirrors.

"Cut it out," I whispered. "Let's get out of here."

Kevin set the thing away, making sure it was lined up
exactly the way it had been, and we turned to go. His penlight beam moved across the back wall, illuminating a
raincoat we'd already seen, and something else.

"There's a door here," whispered Kevin, moving the
coat to show a doorknob. He tried it. "Drat. It's locked."

"Let's *go*!" I whispered. I hadn't heard a car pass in
what felt like hours. It was like the whole town was holding its breath.

Kevin began opening drawers again. "There has to be
a key," he said too loudly. "It must lead to a basement,
there's no second floor on this place."

I grabbed him by his jacket. "Come on," I hissed.
"Let's get out of here. We're going to get *arrested*."

"Just another minute . . ." began Kevin and froze. I felt
my heart stop at the same instant.

A key rasped in the lock of the front door. There was
a tall shadow thrown against the blind.

I turned to run, to escape, anything to get out of there,
but Kevin clicked off the penlight, grabbed my sweatshirt,
and pulled me with him as he crawled under one of the

high sinks. There was just enough room for both of us there. A dark curtain hung down over the space and Kevin pulled it shut just as the door creaked open and footsteps entered the room.

For a second I could hear nothing but the pounding of blood in my ears, but then I realized that there were *two* people walking in the room, men by the sounds of the heavy tread. My mouth hung open and I panted, but I was unable to get a breath of air. I was sure that any sound at all would give us away.

One set of footsteps stopped at the first chair while the other went to the rear wall. A second door rasped shut, water ran, and there came the sound of the toilet flushing. Kevin nudged me, and I could have belted him then, but we were so crowded together in fetal positions that any movement by me would have made a noise. I held my breath and waited while the second set of footsteps returned from the lavatory and moved toward the front door. *They hadn't even turned on the lights.* There'd been no gleam of a flashlight beam through our curtain, so I didn't think it was the cops checking things out. Kevin nudged me again and I knew he was telling me that it had to be Innis and Denofrio.

Both pairs of footsteps moved toward the front, there was the sound of the door opening and slamming, and I tried to breathe again before I passed out.

A rush of noise. A hand reached down and parted the curtain. Other hands grabbed me and pulled me up and out, into the dark. Kevin shouted as another figure dragged him to his feet.

I was on my tiptoes, being held by my shirtfront. The man holding me seemed eight feet tall in the blackness, his fist the size of my head. I could smell garlic on his breath and assumed it was Denofrio.

"Let us go!" shouted Kevin. There was the sound of a slap, flat and clear as a rifle shot, and Kevin was silent.

I was shoved into a barber chair. I heard Kevin being pushed into the other one. My eyes were so well adjusted to the darkness now that I could make out the features of the two men. Innis and Denofrio. Dark suits blended into black, but I could see the pale, angular faces that I'd been

sure had made Kevin think they were vampires. Eyes too
deep and dark, cheekbones too sharp, mouths too cruel,
and something about them that said *old* despite their
middle-aged looks.

"What are you doing here?" Innis asked Kevin. The
man spoke softly, without evident emotion, but his voice
made me shiver in the dark.

"Scavenger hunt!" cried Kevin. "We have to steal a
barber's clippers to get in the big kids' club. We're sorry.
Honest!"

There came the rifle shot of a slap again. "You're lying," said Innis. "You followed me on Monday. Your
friend here followed Mr. Denofrio in the evening. Both of
you have been watching the shop. Tell me the truth. *Now!*"

"We think you're vampires," said Kevin. "Tommy and
I came to find out."

My mouth dropped open in shock at what Kevin had
said. The two men took a half step-back and looked at
each other. I couldn't tell if they were smiling in the dark.

"Mr. Denofrio?" said Innis.

"Mr. Innis?" said Denofrio.

"Can we go now?" said Kevin.

Innis stepped forward and did something to the barber
chair Kevin was in. The leather armrests flipped up and
out, making sort of white gutters. The leather strops on either side went up and over, attaching to something out of
sight to make restraining straps around Kevin's arms. The
headrest split apart, came down and around, and encircled
Kevin's neck. It looked like one of those trays the dentist
puts near you to spit into.

Kevin made no noise. I expected Denofrio to do the
same thing to my chair, but he only laid a large hand on
my shoulder.

"We're not vampires, boy," said Mr. Innis. He went to
the counter, opened a drawer, and returned with the
straight razor Kevin had been fooling around with earlier.
He opened it carefully. "Mr. Denofrio?"

The shadow by my chair grabbed me, lifted me out of
the chair, and dragged me to the basement door. He held
me easily with one hand while he unlocked it. As he
pulled me into the darkness, I looked back and caught a

glimpse of my friend staring in silent horror as Innis drew the edge of the straight razor slowly across Kevin's inner arm. Blood welled, flowed, and gurgled into the white enamel gutter of the armrest.

Denofrio dragged me downstairs.

The barber finishes the shave, trims my sideburns, and turns the chair so that I can look into the closer mirror.

I run my hand across my cheeks and chin. The shave is perfect, very close but with not a single nick. Because of the sharpness of the blade and the skill of the barber, my skin tingles but feels no irritation whatsoever.

I nod. The barber smiles ever so slightly and removes the striped protective apron.

I stand and remove my suitcoat. The barber hangs it on a hook while I take my seat again and roll up my left sleeve. While he is near the rear of the shop, the barber turns on a small radio. The music of Mozart fills the room.

The basement was lighted with candles set in small jars. The dancing red light reminded me of the time Kevin took me to his church. He said the small, red flames were votive candles. You paid money, lit one, and said a prayer. He wasn't sure if the money was necessary for the prayer to be heard.

The basement was narrow and unfinished and almost filled by the twelve-foot slab of stone in its center. The thing on the stone was almost as long as the slab. The thing must have weighed a thousand pounds, easy. I could see folds of slick, gray flesh rising and falling as it breathed.

If there were arms, I couldn't see them. The legs were suggested by folds in slick fat. The tubes and pipes and rusting funnel led my gaze to the head.

Imagine a thousand-pound leech, nine or ten feet long and five or six feet thick through the middle as it lies on its back, no surface really, just layers of gray-green slime and wattles of what might be skin. Things, organs maybe, could be seen moving and sloshing through flesh as transparent as dirty plastic. The room was filled with the sound of its breathing and the stench of its breath. Imagine a huge sea creature, a small whale, maybe, dead and rotting on the beach for a week, and you've got an idea of what the thing itself smelled like.

The mass of flesh made a noise and the small eyes turned in my direction. Its eyes were covered with layers of yellow film or mucus and I was sure it was blind. The thing's head was no more defined than the end of a leech, but in the folds of slick fat were lines which showed a face which might once have been human. Its mouth was very large. Imagine a lamprey smiling.

"No, it was never human," said Mr. Denofrio. His hand was still firm on my shoulder. "By the time they came to our guild, they had already passed beyond hope of hiding amongst us. But they brought an offer which we could not refuse. Nor can our customers. Have you ever heard of symbiosis, boy? Hush!"

Upstairs, Kevin screamed. There was a gurgle, as of old pipes being tried.

The creature on the slab turned its blind gaze back to the ceiling. Its mouth pulsed hungrily. Pipes rattled and the funnel overflowed.

Blood spiralled down.

The barber returns and taps at my arm as I make a fist. There is a broad welt across the inner crook of my arm, as of an old scar poorly healed. It *is* an old scar.

The barber unlocks the lowest drawer and withdraws a razor. The handle is made of gold and is set about with small gems. He raises the object in both hands, holds it above his head, and the blade catches the dim light.

He takes three steps closer and draws the blade across my arm, opening the scar tissues like a puparium hatching. There is no pain. I watch as the barber rinses the blade and returns it to its special place. He goes down the basement stairs and I can hear the gurgling in the small drain tubes of the armrest as his footsteps recede. I close my eyes.

I remember Kevin's screams from upstairs and the red flicker of candlelight on the stone walls. I remember the red flow through the funnel and the gurgle of the thing feeding, lamprey mouth extended wide and reaching high, trying to encompass the funnel the way an infant seeks its mother's nipple.

I remember Mr. Denofrio taking a large hammer from its place at the base of the slab, then a thing part spike and part spigot. I remember standing alone and watching as he pounded it in, realizing even as I watched that the flesh beneath the gray-green slime was a mass of old scars.

I remember watching as the red liquid flowed from the spigot into the crystal glass, the chalice. There is no red in the universe as deeply red, as purely red as what I saw that night.

I remember drinking. I remember carrying the chalice—carefully, so carefully—upstairs to Kevin. I remember sitting in the chair myself.

The barber returns with the chalice. I check that the scar has closed, fold down my sleeve, and drink deeply.

By the time I have donned my own white smock and returned, the barber is sitting in the chair.

"A trim this morning, perhaps?" I ask.

"I think not," he says. "Just a shave, please."

I shave him carefully. When I am finished, he runs his hands across his cheeks and chin and nods his approval. I perform the ritual and go below.

In the candlelit hush of the Master's vault, I wait for the Purification and think about immortality. Not about the true eon-spanning immortality of the Master . . . of all the Masters . . . but of the portion He deigns to share with us. It is enough.

After my colleague drinks and I have returned the chalice to its place, I come up to find the blinds raised, the shop open for business.

Kevin has taken his place beside his chair. I take my place beside mine. The music has ended and silence fills the room.

Outside, the blood spirals down.

Introduction to
"The Death of the Centaur"

I was a teacher for eighteen years. Not a college pro-
fessor . . . not even a high school English teacher . . .
"just" an elementary teacher. Over the years I taught
third grade, fourth grade, and sixth grade, spent a year as
a "resource teacher," (sort of a lifeguard for kids in danger of going under because of learning problems) and
ended my career in education by spending four years
creating, coordinating, and teaching very advanced programs for "gifted and talented" (i.e., smart and able) students in a district with seven thousand elementary-aged
children.

I mention all this as background to the next story.

Teaching is a profession which is not quite a profession. As recently as twenty-five years ago, teachers balanced their low pay with whatever satisfaction they could
find in the job—and there is plenty for a good teacher—
and by enjoying a certain indefinable sense of status in the
eyes of the community.

Some years ago when I was a sixth grade teacher, I
stepped outside one winter evening to see the Colorado
skies ablaze with a disturbing light. It was the aurora bo-
realis, of course, in what may well be the most dramatic
display I'll ever see from these latitudes.

As I stood watching this incredible light show, a
young student of mine and her mother came down the
street and asked what was going on. I explained about
the aurora.

"Oh," said the mother. "I thought maybe it was the end of the world like it predicts in Revelation, but Jesse said you'd know if it was something else."

I think of that moment occasionally.

It used to be that teachers were—if not exactly the sages of society—at least respected as minor but necessary intellectual components in the community. Now, when parents go in to a parent/teacher conference, the odds are great that the parents are better educated than the teacher. Even if they're not, they almost certainly make significantly more *money* than the teacher.

Of course it's not just the low pay that is driving good people out of teaching; it's not even the combination of low pay, contempt from the community, contempt from school and district administrators who see master teachers as a liability (they would rather have beginning teachers whose *tabulas* are perfectly *rasa* and ready to be programmed with whatever new district fads the administration is pushing), and the fact that many children today are not pleasant to be around. Perhaps it's all this plus the reality that teaching is no longer a place for people with imagination. Creative people need not apply. Most don't.

The point of all this is that just at the time when we most desperately need quality teachers, just when our intellectual survival now demands men and women in the classroom who teach so well and make our children *think* so well that we'll have no choice but to pay that teacher the ultimate teacher's compliment—condemnation to death by hemlock or crucifixion; just at the time now when families and all the other traditional institutions are abdicating their responsibilities in everything from teaching ethics to basic hygiene, abandoning the effort it takes to turn young savages into citizens; surrendering and handing these duties to *schools* . . . that happens to be the time when the schools lack the small but critical mass of brilliant, creative, and dedicated people who've always made the system *work*.

To compensate, teachers hang signs in their faculty

lounges. The signs say things like—"A teacher's influence touches eternity."

It may. It may. But take it from somebody who was in there pitching for eighteen years—good teachers are invaluable, more precious than platinum or presidents, but a bad teacher's influence touches the same eternity.

The Death
of the Centaur

The teacher and the boy climbed the steep arc of lawn that overlooked the southernmost curve of the Missouri River. Occasionally they glanced up at the stately brick mansion that held the high ground. Its tiers of tall windows and wide French doors reflected the broken patterns of bare branches against a gray sky. Both the boy and the young man knew the big house was most likely empty—its owner spent only a few weeks a year in town—but approaching so close afforded them the pleasurable tension of trespass as well as an outstanding view.

A hundred feet from the mansion they stopped climbing and sat down, backs against a tree which shielded them from the slight breeze and protected them from the casual notice of anyone in the house. The sun was very warm, a false spring warmth which would almost surely be driven off by at least one more snowstorm before returning in earnest. The wide expanse of lawn, dropping down to the railroad tracks and the river two hundred yards below, had the faint, green splotchiness of thawing earth. The air smelled like Saturday.

The teacher took up a short blade of grass, rolled it in his fingers, and began to chew on it thoughtfully. The boy pulled a piece, squinted at it for a long second, and did likewise.

"Mr. Kennan, d'you think the river's gonna rise again this year and flood everythin' like it done before?" asked the boy.

"I don't know, Terry," said the young man. He did not turn to look at the boy, but raised his face to the sun and closed his eyes.

The boy looked sideways at his teacher and noticed how the red hairs in the man's beard glinted in the sunlight. Terry put his head back against the rough bark of the old elm but was too animated to shut his eyes for more than a few seconds.

"Do you figure it'll flood Main if it does?"

"I doubt it, Terry. That kind of flood only comes along every few years."

Neither participant in the conversation found it strange that the teacher was commenting on events which he had never experienced first hand. Kennan had been in the small Missouri town just under seven months, having arrived on an incredibly hot Labor Day just before school began. By then the flood had been old news for four months. Terry Bester, although only ten years old, had seen three such floods in his life and he remembered the cursing and thumping in the morning darkness the previous April when the volunteer firemen had called his father down to work on the levee.

A train whistle came to them from the north, the Dopplered noise sounding delicate in the warm air. The teacher opened his eyes to await the coming of the eleven a.m. freight to St. Louis. Both counted the cars as the long train roared below them, diesel throbbing, whistle rising in pitch and then dropping as the last cars disappeared toward town around the bend in the track where they had just walked.

"Whew, good thing we wasn't down there," said Terry loudly.

"Weren't," said Mr. Kennan.

"Huh?" said Terry and looked at the man.

"We *weren't* down there," repeated the bearded young man with a hint of irritation in his voice.

"Yeah," said Terry and there was a silence. Mr. Kennan closed his eyes and rested his head against the tree trunk once again. Terry stood to throw imaginary stones at the mansion. Sensing his teacher's disapproval, he stopped the pantomine and stood facing the tree, resting his chin against the bark and squinting up at the high branches. Far overhead a squirrel leaped.

"Twenty-six," said Terry.

"What's that?"

"Cars on that train. I counted twenty-six."

"Mmmmm. I counted twenty-four."

"Yeah. Me too. That's what I meant to say. Twenty-four, I meant."

Kennan sat forward and rolled the blade of grass in his hands. His thoughts were elsewhere. Terry rode an invisible horse around in tight circles while making galloping sounds deep in his throat. He added the phlegmy noise of a rifle shot, grabbed at his chest, and tumbled off the horse. The boy rolled bonelessly down the hill and came to a contorted, grass-covered stop not three feet from his teacher.

Kennan glanced at him and then looked out at the river. The Missouri moved by, coffee brown, complicated by never repeating patterns of swirls and eddies.

"Terry, did you know that this is the southernmost bend of the Missouri River? Right here?"

"Uh-uh," said the boy.

"It is," said the teacher and looked across at the far shore.

"Hey, Mr. Kennan?"

"Yes?"

"What's gonna happen on Monday?"

"What do you mean?" asked Kennan, knowing what he meant.

"You know, in the Story."

The young man laughed and tossed away the blade of grass. For a brief second Terry thought that his teacher threw like a girl, but he immediately banished that from his mind.

"You know I can't tell you ahead of the others, Terry. That wouldn't be fair, would it?"

"Awww," said the boy but it was a perfunctory whine, and something in the tone suggested that he was pleased with the response. The two stood up. Kennan brushed off the seat of his pants, and then pulled bits of grass from the child's tangled hair. Together they walked back down the hill in the direction of the rail line and town.

The centaur, the neo-cat, and the sorcerer-ape moved across the endless Sea of Grass. Gernisavien was too short to see above the high grass and had to ride on Raul's back. The centaur did not mind—he did not even notice her weight—and he enjoyed talking to her as he breasted the rippling waves of lemon-colored grass. Behind them came Dobby, ambling along in his comical, anthropoid stride and humming snatches of unintelligible tunes.

For nine days they waded the Sea of Grass. Far behind were the Haunted Ruins and the threat of the ratspiders. Far ahead—not yet in sight—was their immediate goal of the Mountains of Mist. At night Dobby would unsling his massive shoulder pack and retrieve the great silken umbrella of their tent. Intricate orange markings decorated the blue dome. Gernisavien loved the sound created as the evening wind came up and stirred a thousand miles of grass while rustling the silken canopy above them.

They were very careful with their fire. A single careless spark could ignite the entire Sea and there would be no escape.

Raul would return from his evening hunt with his bow over a shoulder and a limp grazer in one massive hand. After dinner they often talked softly or listened to Dobby play the strange wind instrument he had found in the Man Ruins. As the night grew later, Dobby would point out the constellations—the Swan, Mellam's Bow, the Crystal Skyship, and the Little Lyre. Raul would tell stories of courage and sacrifice handed down through six generations of Centaur Clan warriors.

One evening after they had carefully doused the fire, Gernisavien spoke. Her voice seemed tiny under the blaze of stars and was almost lost in the great sighing of wind in the grass.

"What are our chances of actually finding the farcaster?"

"We can't know that," came Raul's firm voice. "We just have to keep heading south and do our best."

"But what if the Wizards get there first?" persisted the tawny neo-cat.

It was Dobby who answered. "Best we not discuss the Wizards at night," he said. "Never talk about scaly things after dark, that's what my old Granmum used to say."

In the morning they ate a cold breakfast, looked at the magic needle on Dobby's direction finder, and once again picked up the journey. The sun was close to the zenith when Raul suddenly froze and pointed to the east.

"Look!"

At first Gernisavien could see nothing, but after taking a handful of Raul's mane to steady herself and standing on his broad back, she could make out—sails! Billowing white sails against an azure sky. And beneath the straining canvas she could see a ship—a huge ship—creaking along on wooden wheels that must have been twenty feet high.

And it was headed right for them!

The classroom was ugly and uncomfortable. For a long time it had been used as a storeroom and even now the walls were marked and gashed where boxes and metal map cases had been stored.

The room, like the school, was old but not picturesque. It evoked no Norman Rockwell twinges of nostalgia. The once-high ceilings had been lowered with ill-fitting accoustical tiles that cut off the top third of the windows. Tubular fluorescent lights hung from gray bars that emerged through holes in the ceiling tiles. The floors once had been smooth and varnished but were now splintered to the point that students could not risk taking off their soaked tennis shoes on wet days.

Twenty-eight plastic pink-and-tan metal desks filled a space designed for three rows of wooden schooldesks from a previous century. The desks were old enough that their tilted tops were carved and scratched and their ugly, tubular legs gouged new splinters from the floor. It was impossible to place a pencil on a desktop without it rolling noisily, and every time a child lifted the desktop to reach for a book, the little room echoed to the sound of screeching metal and notebooks falling to the floor.

The windows were high and warped and all but one refused to open. The previous September, when the temperature continued to hover near ninety degrees and children's sneakers sank into the asphalt playground, the little room was almost unlivable with only a rare stirring of breeze coming through the windows.

The chalkboard was four feet wide and had a crack running along the right side. Kennan had once used it to illustrate the San Andreas Fault. On his first day he had discovered that the room had no chalk, only one eraser, no yardstick, no globe, only one pull-down map (and that predating World War Two), no bookshelves, and a clock permanently frozen at one twenty-three. Kennan had requisitioned a wall clock on the third of September and an old one was mounted next to the door by the end of January. It stopped frequently so Kennan kept a cheap alarm clock on his desk. Its ticking had become background noise to all the other sounds in the room. Occasionally he set the alarm to signify the end of a quiz or silent reading period. On the last day before Christmas vacation, he had let the alarm go off at two o'clock to herald the end of work and the beginning of their hour-long Christmas party. The other classes reserved only the last twenty minutes of the day for their parties and although Kennan was reprimanded by the principal for not reading the school policy booklet, the incident confirmed the suspicion of most of the children in the school that Mr. Kennan's class was a fun place to be.

Kennan's memory of that Christmas season would always be linked with the musty, dimly lit basement of Reardon's Department Store, a faded and failing five and dime store on Water Street, where he had shopped for his fourth graders' presents late one evening. One by one he had selected the cheap rings, jars of bubble-blowing liquid, toy soldiers, balsa wood gliders, and model kits—each with a special message in mind—taking them home to wrap until the early morning hours.

Kennan had covered the chipped walls of the classroom with posters, including the illustrated map of Boston which had hung in his dorm room for three years. He changed the one bulletin board every three weeks. Now it boasted a huge map of the planet Garden on which the events of The Story were marked.

There was nothing he could do about the faint odor of rotting plaster and seeping sewage that permeated the room. Nor could he change the irritating buzz and flicker of the overhead lights. But he bought an old armchair at a fleamarket and borrowed an area rug from his landlord and every afternoon at one-ten, just after lunch period and just before language arts, Kennan sat in the sprung chair and twenty-seven children crowded into the carpeted corner and the tale resumed.

Gernisavien and Dobby paid their last two credit coins to enter the huge arena where Raul was scheduled to fight the Invincible Shrike. All around them were the dark alleys and gabled rooftops of legendary Carvnal. They pushed through the entrance tunnel with the crowd and came out in the tiered amphitheatre where hundreds of torches cast bizarre shadows up into the stands.

Around the circular pit were crowded all the races of Garden, or rather, all those races which had not been exterminated resisting the evil Wizards: the hooded Druids, brachiate tree dwellers from the Great Forest, a band of fuzzies in their bright orange robes, many lizard soldiers hissing and laughing and shouting, stubby little Marsh Folk, and hundreds of mutants. The night air was filled with strange sounds and stranger smells. Vendors bellowed over the noise to hawk their fried argot wings and cold beer. Out in the arena, work crews raked sand over the drying pools of blood that marked the spots where earlier Death Game contestants had lost to the Shrike.

"Why does he have to fight?" asked Gernisavien as they took their places on the rough bench.

"It's the only way to earn a thousand credits so we can take the Sky Galleon south tomorrow morning," Dobby answered in a low voice. A tall mutant sat down next to him on the bench, and Dobby had to tug to retrieve the end of his purple cape.

"But why can't we just leave the city or take the raft farther south?" persisted Gernisavien. The little neo-cat's tail was flicking back and forth.

"Raul explained all that," whispered Dobby. "The Wizards know that we're in Carvnal. They must already be covering the city gates and the docks. Besides, with their flying platforms we could never outdistance them on foot or by raft. No, Raul's right, this is the only way."

"But *no one* beats the Shrike! Isn't that right? The thing was genetically designed during the Wizard Wars as a killing machine, wasn't it?" Gernisavien said miserably. She squinted as if the light from the stadium torches hurt her eyes.

"Yes," said Dobby, "but he doesn't have to *beat* it to earn the thousand credits. Just stay alive for three minutes in the same arena."

"Has anyone ever done that?" Gernisavien's whisper was ragged.

"Well ... I think ..." began Dobby but was interrupted by a blare of trumpets from the arena. There was an immediate hushing of crowd noise. The torches seemed to flare more brightly and on one side of the wide pit a heavy portcullis drew up into the wall.

What's a portcullis?

It's like a big, heavy gate with spikes on the bottom. So every eye in the stadium was on that black hole in the wall. There was a long minute of silence so deep that you could hear the torches crackling and sputtering. Then the Shrike came out.

It was about seven and a half feet tall and it gleamed like polished steel in the light. Razor sharp spikes curled out like scythe blades from various parts of its smooth, metallic exoskeleton. Its elbows and knees were protected by rings of natural armor which also were covered by short spikes. There was even a spike protruding from its high forehead, just above where the red, multi-faceted eyes blazed like flaming rubies. Its hands were claws with five curved, metal blades that opened and closed so quickly that they were only a blur. The claws went snicker-snack, snicker-snack.

The Shrike moved out to the center of the arena slowly, lurching along like a sharp-edged sculpture learning how to walk. Its head lifted, the fighting beak snapped, and the red eyes searched the crowd as if seeking future victims.

Suddenly the stillness was broken as the hundreds of spectators began booing and jeering and throwing small items. Through it all the Shrike stood motionless and mute, seemingly unaware of the barrage of noise and missiles. Only once—when a large melon flew from the stands and headed straight for the Shrike's head—only then did it condescend to move. But how it moved! The Shrike leaped twenty feet to one side with a jump so incredibly fast that the terrible creature was invisible for a second. The crowd hushed in awe.

Then the trumpets sounded again, a tall wooden door opened, and the first contestant of the Late Games entered. It was a rock giant much like the one that had chased Dobby when they were crossing the Mountains of Mist. But this one was bigger—at least twelve feet tall—and it looked to be made of solid muscle.

"I hope he doesn't beat the Shrike and take the prize before Raul gets to fight," said Dobby. Gernisavien flashed the sorcerer-ape a disapproving glance.

It was over in twenty seconds. One moment the two opponents stood facing each other in the torchlight and an instant later the Shrike was back in the center of the ring and the rock giant was lying in various parts of the arena. Some of the pieces were still twitching.

There were four more contestants. Two were obvious suicides—whom the crowd booed loudly—one was a drunken lizard soldier with a high-powered crossbow, and the last was a fierce mutant with body armor of his own and a battle-axe twice as tall as Gernisavien. None of them lasted a minute.

Then the trumpets sounded again and Raul cantered into the arena. Gernisavien watched through her fingers as the handsome centaur, upper body oiled and glistening, moved toward the waiting Shrike. Raul was carrying only his hunting spear and a light shield. No—wait—there was a small bottle hanging from a thong around his neck.

"What's that?" asked Gernisavien, her voice sounding lost and quavery even to herself.

Dobby did not take his eyes off the arena as he answered. "A chemical I found in the Man Ruins. May the gods grant that I mixed it right."

Down in the arena the Shrike began its attack.

Dear Whitney,

Yes—you're right—this part of the country *is* the seventh circle of desolation. Sometimes I walk down the street (my "home" here is on a hill, if you can call furnished rooms in a rotting old brick house a home) and catch a glimpse of the Missouri River and remember those great days we had out on the Cape during spring break of our senior year. Remember the time we went riding along the beach and a thunderstorm came boiling in from the Bay and Pomegranate got so spooked? (And we had to . . . ahem . . . wait it out in the boathouse?)

Glad to hear that you enjoy working in the Senator's office. Do all you Wellesley girls ascend directly into jobs like that or do most end up at Katie Gibbs School for Future Secretaries? (Sorry about that—someone stuck in the Meerschaum Pipe Capital of the World as I am shouldn't throw stones . . . or stow thrones for that matter. *Did* you know that every corncob pipe in the western hemisphere comes from this town? I've got two inches of white soot on my windowsill and on the hood of my car to prove it!)

No—I *don't* get into St. Louis very much. It's about a fifty mile trip and the Volvo has been sitting by the curb for over a month. The head gasket is shot and it takes about ten years to get a part sent out here. I was lucky even to find a garage with metric tools. I did take the bus into the Big City three weeks ago. Went right after school Friday and got home Sunday evening in time to get depressed and to do my lesson plans. Ended up not seeing much except three movies and a lot of bookstores. Finally took a tour of the Gateway Arch. (No—I will *not* bore you with the details.) The best part of the weekend was enjoying the amenities of a good hotel for two nights.

To answer your question—I'm *not* totally sorry that I came out West to go to grad school in St. Louis. It was a good program (who can beat an 11-month Masters program?) but I hadn't anticipated that I'd be too poor to escape this goddamn state without teaching here for a year. Even that might have been OK if I could have found a position in Webster Groves or University City . . . but the Meerschaum Pipe Capital of the World? This place—and the people—are straight out of *Deliverance.*

Still—it's only a year, and if I get a job with Hovane Acad or the Experimental School (have you *seen* Fentworth recently?), this year could be invaluable background experience.

So you want to hear more about my students? What can you say about a bunch of bucolic fourth graders? I've already told you about some of the antics of Crazy Donald. If this podunk district had any real special ed or remedial programs he'd be in them all. Instead, I throw a lassoo on him and try to keep him from hurting anyone. So let's see, who does that leave to tell you about?

Monica—our resident nine-year-old sexpot. She has her eye on me but she'll settle for Craig Stears in the sixth grade if I'm not available.

Sara—a real sweet kid. A curly-haired, heart-faced little cutie. I like Sara. Her mother died last year and I think she needs an extra dose of affection.

Brad—Brad's the class moron. Dumber than Donald, if that's possible. He's been retained twice. (Yes . . . this district *does* flunk kids . . . *and* spank them.) Not a discipline problem, Brad's just a big, dumb cluck in bib overalls and a bowl haircut.

Teresa—Here's a girl after your own heart, Whit. A horse nut! Has a gelding which she enters in shows around here and in Illinois. But I'm afraid Teresa's into the Cowgirl Mystique. Probably wouldn't know an English riding saddle if she sat on it. The kid wears cowboy boots to school every day and keeps a currycomb in her desk.

And then there's Chuck & Orville(!) & William-call-me-Bill & Theresa (another one) & Bobby Lee & Alice & Alice's twin sister Agnes & etc. & etc . . .

Oh, I mentioned Terry Bester last time, but I do want to tell you more about him. He's a homely little kid—all overbite and receding chin. His hair hangs in his eyes and his mother must trim it with hedgeclippers. He wears the same filthy plaid shirt every day of the year and his boots have holes in them and one heel gone. (Get the picture? This kid's straight out of Tobacco Road!)

Still—Terry's my favorite. On the first day of school I was making some point and waving my arm around in my usual, histrionic fashion and Terry (who sits right up front, unlike most of the other boys) made a dive for the floor. I started to get mad at him for clowning around and then noticed his face. The kid was scared to death! Obviously he was getting the shit beat out of him at home and had ducked out of habit.

Terry seems determined to fit every poor-kid stereotype. He even drags around this homemade shoeshine box and makes a few quarters shining these hillbillies' boots down at the Dew Drop Inn and Berringer's Bar & Grill where his old man hangs out.

Anyway, to make a long story short, the little guy has been spending a lot of time with me. He often shows up at the back porch here about five-thirty or six o'clock. Frequently I invite him to stay for dinner—although when I tell him I'm busy and I have to write or something, he doesn't seem to resent it and he's back the next night. Sometimes when I'm reading I forget he's there until ten or eleven o'clock. His parents don't seem to care where he is or when he gets home. When I got back from my weekend in St. Louis, there was 'ol Terry sitting on my back steps with that absurd shoeshine kit. For all I know he'd been sitting there since Friday night.

Last weekend he calmly mentioned something that made my hair stand on end. He said that last year when he was in third grade "Ma and the Old Man got in a terrible fight." Finally Ma locked the front door when the drunken father stepped out onto the porch to scream at the neighbors or something. The guy just got madder and madder when he couldn't get back in and started shouting that he was going to kill them all. Terry says that he was hugging his six-year-old sister, his Ma was crying and screaming, and then the Old Man kicked in the door. He proceeded to hit Terry's mother in the mouth and drag the two kids out to his pickup truck. He drove them up Sawmill Road (in nearby Boone National Forest) and finally jerked the children out of the cab and pulled his shotgun off the rack. (*Everybody* carries guns in their pickups here, Whit. I've been thinking of getting a gun rack for the Volvo!)

You can imagine Terry telling me all of this. Every once in a while he'd pause to brush the hair out of his eyes, but his voice was as calm as if he were telling me the plot of a TV show he'd seen once.

So the father drags eight-year-old Terry and his little sister into the trees and tells them to get down on their knees and pray to God for forgiveness because he's got to shoot them. Terry says that the old drunk was waving the double-barreled shotgun at them and that his little sister, Cindy, just "went and wet her panties, then and there." Instead of shooting, Terry's father just lurched off into the woods and stood there cussing at the sky for several minutes. Then he stuck the kids back in the pickup and drove them home. The mother never filed charges.

I've seen Mr. Bester around town. He reminds me of whatshisname in the movie version of *To Kill A Mockingbird*. You know, the racist farmer that Boo Radley kills. Wait a minute, I'll look it up. (Bob Ewell!)

So you can see why I'm allowing Terry to spend so much time with me. He needs a positive male role model around . . . as well as a sensitive adult to talk to and learn from. I'd consider adopting Terry if that were possible.

So now you know a little bit of how the other half lives. That's one reason why this year's been so important even if it has been sheer purgatory. Part of me can't wait to get back to you and the sea and a real city where people speak correctly and where you can walk into a drugstore and order a frappe without being stared at. But part of me knows how important this year is—both for me and the kids I'm touching by being here. Just the oral tradition of the story that I'm telling them is something they would never get otherwise.

Well, I'm out of paper and it's almost one a.m. School tomorrow. Give my best to your family, Whit, and tell the Senator to keep up the good work. With any luck (and the head gasket willing) you'll be seeing me sometime in mid-June.

Take care. Please write. It's lonely out here in the Missouri woods.

Love,
Paul

The great Sky Galleon moved between high banks of stratocumulus that caught the last pink rays of sunset. Raul, Dobby, and Gernisavien stood on the deck and watched the great orb of the sun slowly sink into the layer of clouds beneath them. From time to time, Captain Kokus would bellow orders to the chimp-sailors who scampered through the rigging and sails far above the deck. Occasionally the captain turned and murmured quiet orders to the mate, who spoke into the metal speaking tube. Gernisavien could sense the fine adjustments to the hidden tanks of anti-gravity fluid.

Eventually the light faded except for the first twinkling of stars and the two minor moons hurtling above the cloud layer. Unseen sailors lit lantern running lights hanging from mast tops and spars. The climbing cloud towers lost the last of their glow and Dobby suggested that the three go below to prepare for the Spring Solstice party.

And what a party it was! The long Captain's Table was heaped with fine foods and rare wines. There was succulent roast bison from the Northern Steppes, swordfish from South Bay, and icy bellfruit from the far-off Equatorial Archipelago. The thirty guests—even the two dour Druids—ate and laughed as they never had before. The wine glasses continued to be refilled by the ship's stewards and soon the toasts began to flow as quickly as the wine. At one point Dobby rose to toast Captain Kokus and his splendid ship. Dobby referred to the grizzled old skysailor as a "fine fellow anthropoid" but stumbled a bit over the phrase and had to start again to general laughter. Captain Kokus returned the compliment by toasting the intrepid

trio and praising Raul for his courageous victory at the
Carvnal Death Games. Nothing was said about the Galleon's undignified departure from the city mooring tower
with two squads of lizard soldiers in hot pursuit of the last
three passengers. The diners applauded and cheered.

Then it was time for the Solstice Ball to begin. The table was cleared, the tablecloth was furled, and then the table itself was broken into pieces and carried away. Guests
stood around on the broad curve of the lowest deck and
accepted refills once more. Then the ship's orchestra filed
in and began their preparations.

When all was in readiness, Captain Kokus clapped his
hands and there was a silence.

"Once again I formally welcome you all aboard the
Benevolent Zephyr," rumbled the Captain, "and extend to
you all the best wishes of the Solstice season. And now
. . . let the dancing begin!"

And with a final clap of his hands the lantern light
dimmed, the orchestra began playing, and great wooden
louvers on the belly of the ship swung down so that nothing stood between the passengers and the depths of sky beneath them except crystal floor. There was a general
oohing and ahhing and everyone took an involuntary step
backward. Immediately this was followed by a burst of
laughter and applause and then the dancing began.

On sped the great, graceful Sky Galleon into the aerial
rivers of the night. Seen from above there would have
been only the glow of the running lanterns and the only
sound was the sigh and slap of wind in the sails and occasional calls of "All's Well!" from the lookout in the
crow's nest. But seen from below, the ship blazed with
light and echoed to tunes so ancient that they were said to
have come from legendary Old Earth. Forest nymphs and
demimen danced and pirouetted five thousand feet above
the night-shrouded hills. At one point sober Gernisavien
found herself in the undignified position of dancing with a
centaur—lifted high in Raul's strong arms as his hooves
tapped their own rhythm on the unscratchable crystal floor.

A storm came up before the party ended and the captain had the lights turned down so that the company could
look past their feet at the lightning that rippled through the

stormclouds far below. After a hushed moment, the orchestra began playing the Solstice Hymn and Gernisavien, much to her surprise, discovered herself singing the sentimental old ballad along with the others. Tears welled up in her eyes.

Then it was to bed, with revelers stumbling along the suddenly pitching corridors. Even the throes of an aerial storm could not prevent most of the tired passengers from dropping off to sleep. Dobby lay sprawled on his back, his purple beret on the pillow beside him, his great, smiling, simian mouth opened wide to release mighty snores. Gernisavien had found her bunk too large so she slept curled up in an open drawer which swung out slightly and then slid back to the ship's even rockings. Only Raul could not sleep, and after checking in on his friends he went above deck. There he stood huddled against the cold breeze and watched the first, false light of dawn touch the boiling cloudtops.

Raul was thinking grim thoughts. He knew that if they were not intercepted by the Wizard's flying machines, it was only a few more days' journey to South Bay. From there it would be a four or five day trek overland to the supposed Farcaster Site. They were already much too close to the Wizard's Stronghold. The odds were poor that the three friends would live out the week. Raul tapped at the dagger on his belt and watched the new day begin.

Mr. Kennan stood on the asphalt playground with fourth graders running and playing all around him and smiled up at the pleasant spring day. His army jacket, so frequently commented upon by the children, was not needed on such a warm day, but he wore it loosely along with his sports-car cap. Occasionally he would grin just for the hell of it and rub at his beard. It was a *beautiful* day!

The children's spirits reflected the promise of summer all around them. The little playground that had been such a grim exercise yard through the long months of winter now seemed to be the most pleasant of places. Discarded jackets and sweaters littered the ground as children swung

from the monkey bars, ran to the bordering alley and back,
or played kickball near the brick cliff of the school building. Donald and Orville were engrossed in floating some
tiny stick in a mud puddle, and even Terry entered into the
spirit of the day by galloping around with Bill and Brad.
Kennan overheard the boy say to Brad, "You be Dobby 'n
I'll be Raul an' we'll be fightin' the ratspiders." Bill began
to protest as the three boys ran toward the far end of the
playground and Kennan knew that he was resisting becoming a female neo-cat, even for the ten minutes left of the
recess.

Kennan breathed deeply and smiled once again. Life
seemed to be flowing again after months of frozen soli-
tude. Who would have dreamed that Missouri (hadn't it
been part of the Confederacy? . . . or *wanted* to be . . .)
could have such chill, gray, endless winters? There had
been five snow days when school had to be cancelled. After two such snow days followed by a weekend, Kennan
had realized with a shock that he had not spoken to anyone for four days. Would they have come looking for him
if he had died? Would they have found him in his furnished room, propped up at the jerry-rigged writing desk
surrounded by his manuscripts and shelves of silent paper-
backs?

Kennan smiled at the conceit now, but it had been a
grim thought during the darkest days of winter. The kickball eluded a fielder and rolled to where Kennan was
standing amid his inevitable flock of adoring girls. He
made a production of scooping up the ball and throwing it
to the shouting catcher. The throw went wide and bounced
off the basement window of the art room.

Kennan turned away to survey the apple blossoms filling the tree in a nearby yard. New grass was growing up
in the centerline of the alley. He could smell the river
flowing by only four blocks away. Thirteen days of school
left! He viewed the end of the year with self-conscious
sadness mixed with unalloyed elation. He couldn't wait to
be away—his car, newly resurrected, packed with his few
cartons of books and possessions, and the summer sunlight
warm on his arm as he headed east on Interstate 70.
Kennan imagined his leisurely escape from the Midwest—

the seemingly endless barrier of cornfields passed, the surge of traffic on the Pennsylvania Turnpike, the contraction of distance between cities, the familiar exit signs in Massachusetts, the smell of the sea . . . Still, this had been his first class. He would never forget these children and they would never forget him. He imagined them sharing with their children and grandchildren the long, epic tale he had forged for them. During the past weeks he had even toyed with the idea of another year in Missouri.

Sara came forward from the little pack of girls following their teacher. She slipped her arm through Mr. Kennan's and looked up at him with a practiced coquettishness. Kennan smiled, patted her absently on the part in her hair, and took a few steps away from the children. Reaching into his coat pocket he withdrew a crumpled letter and reread parts of it for the tenth time. Then he replaced it and stared north toward the unseen river. Suddenly he was roused by an explosion of noise from the kickball players. Kennan glanced irritably at his watch, raised a plastic whistle to his lips, and signaled the end of recess. The children grabbed at scattered coats and ran to line up.

It was much warmer near South Bay. Raul, Dobby, and Gernisavien headed along the coast toward the legendary Farcaster Site. According to the ancient map which Dobby had found in the Man Ruins so many months ago, their journey's end should be only a few days to the west. Around her neck Gernisavien wore the key that they had found in the Carvnal Archives and paid for with the death of their old friend Fenn. If the Old Books were right, that key would activate the long dormant farcaster and reunite Garden with the Web of Worlds. Then would the tyranny of the cruel Wizards finally be cast down.

It was under the shadow of these same Wizards that our trio of friends made their way west. The sharp Fanghorn Mountains lay to the north and somewhere in their shadowy reaches was the feared Wizards' Stronghold.

The friends kept watch on the skies, always on the

lookout for the Wizards' flying platforms as they moved
along under the cover of lush, tropical foliage. Gernisavien
marveled at the palm trees that rose two hundred feet high
along their march.

On the afternoon of the third day they made camp near
the mouth of a small river that fed into the South Sea.
Dobby arranged their silk tent under the trees so that the
warm breezes caused it to billow and ripple. Raul made
sure the tent would be invisible from the air and then they
sat down to their cold rations. By mutual consent they had
avoided a fire since landing at South Bay, subsisting on
biscuits and cold jerky purchased from the *Benevolent
Zephyr's* ship stores.

The tropical sunset was spectacular. The stars seemed
to explode into the night sky. Dobby pointed out the
Southern Archer, a constellation that was invisible from
their respective homes in the northern part of the continent. Gernisavien felt a stab of homesickness, but put off
the sadness by fingering the ancient key around her neck
and imagining the thrill of reopening the farcaster portals
to a hundred worlds. Which of those stars held other
worlds, other peoples?

Dobby seemed to read her thoughts. "It seems impossible that the journey is almost over, doesn't it?"

Raul rose, stretched, and moved away in the darkness
to reconnoiter the stream.

"I keep thinking of that Fuzzy's predictions," said
Gernisavien. "Remember, in Tartuffel's Treehouse?"

Dobby nodded his massive head. How could one forget
the frightening glimpses of the future which that strange
little creature had offered each of them?

"Most of them have come to pass," grumbled the
sorcerer-ape. "Even the Shrike is behind us."

"Yes, but not *my* dream—not the one with the Wizards
all around in that terrible little room," replied Gernisavien.
It was true. Of all the future-seeing dreams, the neo-cat's
had been the most frightening, the most ominous, and the
least discussed.

*Strapped down and helpless on a stainless steel oper-
ating table with the hooded Wizards looming over her.*

*Then the tallest stepping forward into the blood-red light
... slowly drawing back its hood ...*

Gernisavien shuddered at the memory. As if to change
the subject, Dobby stood and looked around in the darkness.

"Where's Raul?" His attention was captured by the rising of the two moons above the jungle canopy. Then he
realized that the moons did not rise this early ...

"Run!" cried Dobby and pushed the startled neo-cat toward the trees. But it was too late.

The air filled with the scream of flying platforms. Rays
of fire lanced out from the airborne machines and exploded the tops of trees into balls of flame. Knocked off
her feet, fur and eyebrow whiskers singed from the heat,
Gernisavien could see the hooded Wizards on the hovering
machines, could hear the screams of the lizard soldiers as
they leaped to the ground.

For a self-avowed coward, Dobby fought valiantly.
Dodging the first thrust of a lizard's pike, he grabbed the
long shaft and wrested it away. Dobby stabbed the startled
reptile through the throat and turned to hold off five more
of the hissing enemy. He had downed two lizards and was
lifting a third high into the air with his long, strong arms
when he was struck down by a blow from behind.

Gernisavien let out a yell and ran toward her friend,
but before she had taken five steps a tall, scaly form
loomed over her and something struck her on the skull.
The next few minutes were confused. She regained consciousness just after she and Dobby were loaded aboard
two platforms which lifted into the air.

Then came the stirring sound which had thrilled her so
many times before—Raul's war horn blown loud and
sweet and clear. Five pure notes of challenge broke
through the babble of noise and the crackle of flames.

Raul came charging across the clearing in a full gallop,
war spear leveled, shield high, with the cry of the Centaur
Clan on his lips. Lizard soldiers went down like tenpins. A
Wizard fired a shaft of flame, but Raul warded it off with
his shield of sacred metal. His long spear broke as it
pierced three lizards attempting to cower behind one another, but he cast it aside and pulled out his lethal short

sword. Once again he shouted his clan war cry and waded into a pack of hissing, sword-wielding lizards.

Gernisavien felt the platform shudder and stop at tree-top height. She heard the hooded Wizard at the controls rasp a command and thirty lizards fired their crossbows. The air was filled with the scream of feathered bolts and then filled again with lizard screams as the deadly shafts slammed into them and centaur alike. Gernisavien felt her heart stop as she saw at least six bolts strike home against Raul's chest and sides. The great centaur went down in a heap of lizard bodies. Green tails and scaled arms still twitched in that pile of death.

Gernisavien let out one high, mournful cry of rage and then the cuff of a Wizard's fist against her head sent her back into blessed darkness.

Thurs., May 20

Warmer today. Temp. in the high 70's all day. Evening seems to go on forever.

Spent some time in the library tonight. Mailed off my vita to three more places—Phillips-Exeter, the Latin School, and Green Mtn. No response yet from Whitney on the Exp. Sch. Sent her the forms almost two weeks ago & she was going to talk to Dr. Fentworth as soon as she received them.

Picked up some chicken at Col. Sanders. The neighborhood has really come alive—with the window open I can hear kids screaming and playing down on the 5th St. School playground. (It's after 9 p.m. but there's still a little light in the sky.) Late at night I can hear the deep rumble of the ships' engines as the barges move upriver & then the slosh of the waves against the concrete pilings down at the end of Locust Street.

Talked to Mr. Eppet and Dr. North (Asst. Supt.) about next year. Could still get a contract here if I wanted it. (Not much chance of that.) Other teachers are circling my room like buzzards. Mrs. Kyle has her name on a piece of tape on my file cabinet and Mrs. Reardon (the greedy old cow—why doesn't she just tend to her husband's store and keep shouting at the kids not to read the comics?) has staked out my chair, the globe, (the one we just got in March), and the paperback stand. She can't wait for me to be gone next year. (They'll only have two fourth grades again—) When I leave, the school can lapse back into the Dark Ages. (No wonder T.C. and the others called it the Menopause Foundation.)

Loud horn from the river. Ship's bells. Reminds me of the cowbells tinkling from the masts of the small craft at anchor in Yarmouth.

The story is right on schedule. Donna, Sara, and Alice were crying today. (So were some of the boys but they tried to hide it.) They'll be relieved to hear Monday's episode. It's not time for ol' Raul to die yet—when he does it will be in the finest epic tradition. If nothing else, this tale is a great lesson in friendship, loyalty, and honor. The ending will be sad—with Raul sacrificing himself to free the others—holding off the Wizards until his friends can activate the teleportation device. But hopefully the last episode where Gernisavien & Dobby bring the humans back to Garden to clobber the Wizards will offset the sad part. At least it'll be a hell of a finalé.

I've *got* to write this thing down! Maybe this summer.

Totally dark out now. The streetlight outside my second story window here is shining through the maple leaves. A breeze has come up. Think I'll go for a walk down to the river and then come back to do some work.

Gernisavien awoke to an icy wind whipping at her face. The nine Wizards' platforms were floating above mountaintops that glowed white in the starlight. The air was very thin. Gernisavien's arm hung over the side of the platform. If she rolled over she would fall hundreds of feet to her death.

The little neo-cat could dimly make out the other platforms silhouetted against the stars and could see the robed Wizard figures on each, but there was no sign of Dobby.

A hissing from a Wizard on her own platform, directed at the lizard at the controls, made Gernisavien look ahead. The platform was headed for a mountain that loomed up like a broken tooth directly ahead of them. The lizard made no attempt to change their course and Gernisavien realized that at their present speed they would crash into the rock and ice in less than thirty seconds. The neo-cat prepared to jump, but at the last second the lizard calmly touched a button on the panel and the platform began to slow.

Ahead of them the side of the mountain rose up into itself and revealed the entrance to a huge tunnel. Light as red as newly spilled blood poured out of the aperture. Then the platform was inside, the wall had lowered into place behind them, and Gernisavien was a prisoner in the Wizards' Stronghold.

On Saturday morning Mr. Kennan took Sara, Monica, and Terry on an all-day outing. Terry was not pleased with the presence of the two giggling girls, but he occupied the front seat with an air of proprietal indifference and ignored the silly outbursts of whispers emanating from the back. Mr. Kennan joked with all three children as he drove across the river into Daniel Boone National Forest. The girls dissolved into more giggles and frantic whispers whenever they were addressed, but Terry answered the jests with his usual humorless drawl.

Kennan parked near a picnic spot and the four spent an hour clambering around on a heap of boulders in among the trees. Then the teacher sent Terry back to the car and the boy returned with a wicker picnic hamper. Mr. Kennan had purchased sandwiches at the supermarket delicatessen and there were cans of soft drinks, bags of corn chips, and a pack of Oreo cookies. They sat on a high rock and ate in companionable silence. As always, Kennan marveled at the ravenous appetites of such little people.

In the early afternoon, he drove them back across the bridge and headed north along the state highway that soon headed back west again along the river. Fourteen miles and they were in Hermann, a picturesque little German community that had preserved all of the Victorian charm that nearby towns had either lost or never possessed. The *Maifest* was still underway and Kennan treated the kids to a ride on a wheezing Ferris wheel and to genuine chocolate ice cream at a sidewalk cafe. Women in bright peasant garb danced with older men who looked pleasantly ridiculous in *lederhosen*. A band sat in a white bandstand and gamely produced polka after polka for the small crowd.

It was almost dinnertime when Kennan drove them home. Monica whined and wheedled until the teacher told Terry to ride in the back and allowed Monica up front. This arrangement pleased no one. Terry and Sara sat in frozen silence while Monica fidgeted in paroxysms of nervousness whenever Kennan spoke to her or looked her way. Finally they stopped at a gas station under the pretext of a restroom break, and the old arrangement was restored for the last eight miles.

Both girls shouted their perfunctory "Thank-you-very-much-we-had-a-very-nice-time" while they ran pell mell for their respective front doors. Kennan heaved a melodramatic sigh after Monica was out of sight and turned to his last passenger.

"Well, Terry, where to? Shall we stop by the Dog'N'Suds for dinner?"

Surprisingly, the boy suggested an alternative. "How 'bout the fish fry?"

Kennan had forgotten about the fish fry. Held at the Elk's Lodge Recreation Area, three miles out of town, the annual event was evidently considered a big deal.

"OK," said Kennan, "let's go try the fish fry."

Half the town was there. Two huge tents sheltered tables where diners gorged themselves on fried catfish, French fries, and coleslaw. A few dilapidated carnival rides made up a midway in the high grass adjacent to the parking lot. Homemade booths sold pies, opportunities to throw a softball at weighted milk bottles, and raffle chances at a color television set. Out on the baseball diamond, the men's softball teams were playing their last tournament games. Deeper in the meadow, two opposing groups of volunteer firemen aimed their high pressure firehoses at a barrel suspended on a cable. They pushed it back and forth to the cheering of a small crowd.

Kennan and Terry sat at a long table and ate catfish. They strolled past the booths while townspeople greeted Kennan by name. The teacher recognized about one person in ten. Together they watched a ballgame, and by the time it was over the sun had set and strings of hanging lights had come on. The merry-go-round cranked out its four tunes of imitation calliope music while fireflies blinked along the edge of the woods. Some boys ran by in a pack and called to Terry. Kennan pressed two dollars into the surprised boy's hands, and Terry ran off with the others toward the rides and games.

Kennan watched the beginning of the next game under the yellow field lights and then wandered back to the tent for a beer. Kay Bennett, the district's school psychologist, was there and Kennan bought a second round of beers while the two sat talking. Kay was from California, was in her second year here, and felt as trapped as Kennan in this small, Missouri backwater. They took their plastic cups and wandered away from the lights. Broad paths ran from the Elk Lodge to small cabins in among the trees. The two walked the trails and watched as the full moon rose above the meadow. Twice they came upon high school students petting in the darkness. Both times they turned away with knowing smiles and amused glances. Kennan felt his own excitement rising as he stood near the young woman in the moonlight.

Later, as he was driving home, Kennan slammed the steering wheel and wished that he had gotten to know Kay earlier in the year. How different the winter would have been!

Back in his apartment, Kennan got out the bottle of Chivas Regal and sat reading Voltaire at the kitchen table. A gentle night breeze came in through the screen. Two drinks later he showered and crawled into bed. He decided not to make a journal entry but smiled at the fullness of the day.

"Shit!" said Kennan as he sat up in bed. He dressed quickly, ignoring his socks and pulling on a nylon windbreaker over his pajama tops.

The moon was bright enough that he could have driven without headlights as he pushed the Volvo around tight turns in the county road. The parking lot was empty and there were deep ruts and gouges in the field. The rides were still there, but folded and ready to be loaded on trailers. The meadow was moon-dappled and, to Kennan's first relieved glance, empty. But then he saw the shadowy figure on the top row of empty bleachers.

When he came close enough the moonlight allowed him to see the streaks on the boy's dusty face. Kennan stood on a lower level and started to speak, found no words, stopped, and shrugged.

"I knowed you'd come back," said Terry. His voice seemed cheerful. "I knowed you'd come back."

Raul was alive. He struggled to free himself from the pile of lizard bodies. It had been the shirt. Since Carvnal he had worn the brightly decorated tunic that Fenn had given him at Treetops. *It is more than decoration.* Isn't that what the strange little Fuzzy had said? Indeed it was. The shirt had stopped six high-velocity crossbow bolts from penetrating. Certainly it had been more effective than the loose-link armor that still adorned the lizard corpses all around.

Raul made it up onto all four legs and took a few shaky steps. He didn't know how long he had been unconscious. It hurt to breathe. Raul felt his upper torso and wondered if the impact had broken a rib.

No matter. He moved around the clearing, first picking up his bow and then retrieving as many arrows as he could. He found his short sword where it had cleft a lizard's shield, helmet, and skull. His clan warspear was broken, but he snapped off the sacred metal spearhead and dropped it in his quiver. When he had armed himself as well as he could, picking up a long lizard war lance, he galloped to the edge of the clearing.

Some of the palm trees were still smoldering. The Wizard platforms could not have been gone for long. And Raul knew where they must have gone.

To the north gleamed the high peaks of the Fanghorn Mountains. Wincing a bit, Raul strapped his shield and bow to his back. Then, breaking into an effortless, distance-devouring canter, he headed north.

•   •   •

Night. Bugs dance in agitated clouds around the mercury vapor lamps. Kennan is standing in a phone booth near a small grocery store. The store is closed and dark. The side street is empty.

"Yes, Whit, I *did* get it ..." Only Kennan's voice is audible in the darkness.

"No, I know what ... I *am* aware that it isn't easy to get to see Fentworth."

"Sure I do, but it isn't that simple, Whit. Not only do I ... I have a *contract*. It specifies that ..."

"Those last days *will* make a difference ..."

"So what did he say?"

"Look, I don't see what difference it makes if I see him now or when he gets back in August. If he has to decide on the position, they can't fill it 'til he gets back, can they? If I can just make arrangements to ..."

"Oh, yeah? Yeah, I see. *Before* he goes? Yeah. Yeah. Uh-huh, I see that ..."

"No, Whit, it *is* important that you're going to be there. It's just a matter of ... it's just that I don't have the money to fly. And then I'd have to fly back to get my stuff."

"Yeah. Yeah. That'd work out, but I can't afford to miss those last few ... I don't know. I suppose, why? Hell, Whitney, you've been to Europe before ... why don't you ... no, really, why don't you tell your folks you can't join them until late June or ..."

"Yeah. You did? Your folks won't be there? What about ... whatshername, the housekeeper, yeah, Millie ... Until when?"

"Damn. Yes, it *does* sound good."

"No, no, I *do* appreciate it, Whitney. You don't know how much it means to me ..."

"Yeah. Uh-huh, that all makes sense but, look, it's hard to explain. No, listen, there's tomorrow. Friday, yeah ... and then Monday's off because of Memorial Day. Then they go Tuesday and Wednesday and Thursday's their last day. No ... just report cards and stuff. Look, couldn't it be just a *week* later?"

"Uh-huh. Yeah. OK, I understand that. Well, look, let me think about it overnight, all right?"

"I *know* that ... but he's around on Saturday, isn't he?"

"OK, look, I'll call you tomorrow ... that's Friday night ... and I'll let you know what ... no, goddamn it, Whit, I'm poor but I'm not *that* poor, I don't want your parents getting billed for ... look, I'll call you about nine o'clock, that's ... uh ... eleven your time, OK?"

"Well, you could call him on Saturday then and tell him I'd be there Wednesday, or I can just wait and hope something else opens up. Uh-huh, uh-huh ... well, let's just ... just let me *think* about it, OK? Yes ... well, I *will* take that into consideration, don't worry."

"Look, Whit, I'm running out of quarters here. Yeah. About nine ... I mean eleven. No ... me too. It's real good to hear your voice ... Yeah. OK. I'll talk to you tomorrow then. Yeah ... I look forward to seeing you soon, too. Me too. Bye, Whit."

After Dobby's unsuccessful escape attempt, they hung him from chains on the wall. From where Gernisavien was strapped to the table, she could not see if he was still breathing. The red light made it look as if he had been flayed alive.

Tall, shrouded shapes moved through the bloody dimness. When the Wizards weren't turned her way, Gernisavien strained against the metal bands at her wrists and ankles. No use. The steel did not budge an inch. The neo-cat relaxed and inspected the steel table to which she was pinned. The smooth surface had metal gutters on the side and small drain holes. Gernisavien wondered at their purpose and then wished she hadn't. Her heart was racing so fast that she feared it would tear its way out of her chest.

At least Dobby's escape attempt the day before had distracted the guards long enough for Gernisavien to raise her hands, lift the key, and swallow it.

There was a movement in the shadows and the tallest of the hooded figures stepped forward into a shaft of red light. Slowly the Wizard drew back its hood. Gernisavien stared in horror at overlapping scales, a face like a mantis's skull, great eyes that looked like pools of congealed blood, and fangs which dripped a thick mucus.

The Wizard said something that Gernisavien did not understand. Slowly it raised its bony, scaly hand. Clenched in the foul claws was a scalpel ...

Less than half a mile away, Raul labored uphill through heavy snowdrifts. His hooves slipped on icy rocks. Twice he caught himself and only the strength of his massive arms allowed him to pull his body to safety. A fall now meant certain death.

The shirt Fenn had given him provided some warmth for his upper body, but the rest of him was freezing. His hands were quickly growing numb, and Raul knew that they would not save him again should he slip. What was worse, the sun was beginning to set. The centaur knew that he would not survive another night at these elevations.

If only he could find the opening!

Just as he was beginning to despair, Raul heard a rock fall below him and then a whispered curse came on the icy wind. Crawling to the edge of the snowy overhang, he looked down on two lizard guards no more than thirty feet away. They stood next to a heavy metal door that had been painted white to blend in with the snowy mountainside. The lizards wore white hoods and parkas and if it had not been for the curse, Raul would never have seen them.

The sun was down. A freezing wind swept the slopes and threw icy crystals against the centaur's quivering flanks. Raul crouched in the snow. His frozen fingers reached for his bow and arrows.

From the estate atop the hill, the view of the river had been largely occluded by late-spring foliage. But from the wide veranda doors one could easily watch the boy and the man climbing the verdant curve of lawn. They walked slowly. The man was talking; the boy was looking up at him.

The man sat down on the grass and beckoned for the boy to do likewise. The boy shook his head and took two steps backward. The man spoke again. His hands were stretched out, fingers splayed wide. He leaned forward in

an earnest gesture, but the boy took another two steps
back. When the man rose, the boy turned and began walking quickly down the hill. The man took a few steps after
him but stopped when the boy broke into a jog.

In less than a minute, the boy was out of sight around
the bend in the railroad tracks and the man stood alone on
the hill.

Kennan drove the Volvo down the narrow side street
and stopped opposite Terry's house. He sat in the car for
a long minute with his hands on the steering wheel. As
Kennan reached for the Volvo's door handle, Mr. Bester
came out of the house and stepped down from the high
porch into the side yard. The man wore baggy bib overalls
and no shirt. As he bent to peer under the house for something, his gray stubble caught the light. Kennan paused for
a second and then drove on.

At two a.m. Kennan was still loading the books into
cardboard cartons. As he passed in front of the screened
window he thought he heard a noise from across the street.
He put down the stack of books, walked to the screen, and
looked down through streetlight glare and leaf shadows.

"Terry?"

There was no response. The shadows on the lawn did
not move and a few minutes later Kennan resumed his
packing.

He had planned to leave very early Sunday morning,
but it was almost ten before the car was loaded. It was
strangely cold, and a few drops of rain fell from leaden
skies. His landlord was not home—in church probably—so
Kennan dropped the key in his mailbox.

He drove around the town twice and past the school
four times before he cursed softly and headed west on the
main highway.

Traffic was very light on Interstate 55 and the few cars
there tended to drive with their lights on. Occasionally rain

would spatter the windshield. He stopped for breakfast on the west side of St. Louis. The waitress said that it was too late for breakfast so he had a hamburger and coffee. The storm light outside made the café seem dark and cold.

It was pouring by the time he passed through downtown St. Louis. The tricky lane changes made Kennan miss seeing the Gateway Arch as he crossed the Mississippi. The river was as gray and turbulent as the sky.

Once in Illinois, the Volvo headed east on Interstate 70, the trip settled down to the hiss of tires on wet pavement and the quick metronome of the wipers. This soon depressed Kennan and he switched on the radio. It surprised him a bit to hear the roars and shouts of the Indianapolis 500 being broadcast. He listened to it as great trucks whooshed past him in the drizzle. Within half an hour the announcer in Indianapolis was describing the storm clouds coming in from the west, and Kennan turned off the radio in the sure knowledge that the race would be called.

In silence he drove eastward.

On the Tuesday after Memorial Day, Mr. Kennan's fourth graders filed into their classroom to find Mrs. Borcherding installed behind the teacher's desk. All of them knew her from times she had substituted for their regular teachers in years past. Some of the children had known her as their first grade teacher during her last year before retirement.

Mrs. Borcherding was a swollen mass of fat, wrinkles, and wattles. Her upper arms hung loose and flapped when she gestured. Her legs were bloated masses of flesh straining against support stockings. Her arms, hands, and face were liberally sprinkled with liver spots and her whole body gave off a faint aroma of decay that soon permeated the room. The children sat with their hands folded on their desks in unaccustomed formality and faced her silently.

"Mr. Kennan has been called away," said the apparition in a voice that seemed too phlegmy to be human. "I believe there was an illness in the family. At any rate, I will be your teacher for these last three days of school.

I want it understood that I expect everyone in this class to *work*. It does not matter to me whether there are three days of school left or three hundred. Nor am I interested in whether you've had to work as hard as you should have up to now. You will do your *best work* right up until the time you are dismissed on Thursday afternoon. Your report cards have already been filled out, but don't think that you can start fooling around now. Mr. Eppert has given me the authority to change grades as I see fit. And that includes conduct grades. It is still possible that some of you may have to be retained in fourth grade if I see the necessity during the next few days. Now, are there any questions? No questions? Very good, you may get out your arithmetic books for a drill."

During morning recess, Terry was besieged with kids demanding information. He stood as mute as a rock against the crashing waves of curiosity and desperation. The one piece of information he did impart caused the children to turn and babble at one another like extras in a melodramatic crowd scene.

It was mid-afternoon before someone worked up nerve to confront Mrs. Borcherding. Naturally it was Sara who went forward. In the thick stillness of the handwriting exercise, Sara's tiny voice was as high and urgent as a bee's distracting buzz. Mrs. Borcherding listened, frowned, and focused her scowl on the front row as Sara went back to her seat.

"Terry Bester."

"Yes'm," said Terry.

"Mmmmm . . . Sally says that you . . . ahh . . . have something to share with us," began Mrs. Borcherding. The class started to giggle at the mistake with Sara's name but then froze as Mrs. Borcherding's little eyes darted around to find the source of the noise. "All right, since the class evidently has been expecting this for some time, we will get this . . . *story* . . . out of the way right now and then go on to social studies."

"No, ma'm," said Terry softly.

"What was that?" Mrs. Borcherding looked long and

hard at the boy, obviously ready to rise out of her chair at any sign of defiance. Terry sat at polite attention, his hands folded on his notebook. Only in the firm set of the thin lips was there any sign of impertinence.

"It would be convenient to get this out of the way now," repeated the substitute.

"No, ma'am," repeated Terry and continued quickly before the shocked fat lady could say anything. "I was told that I was s'posed to tell it on the last day. That's Thursday. That's what he said."

Mrs. Borcherding stared down at Terry. She started to speak, closed her mouth with an audible snap, and then began again. "We'll use your regular Thursday recess time. Right before clean up. Those people who wish to *miss recess* can stay inside to listen. The others will be allowed to go outside and play."

"Yes, ma'am," said Terry and returned to his handwriting drill.

Wednesday morning was hot and thick with summer. The children entered the classroom with hopeful eyes that turned to downcast glances as they spied the bulk of Mrs. Borcherding behind the desk. She rarely rose from her chair, and, as if to balance her immobility, the children were confined to their desks, Mr. Kennan's assignment check-out cards and independent work centers abandoned.

At each recess Terry was mobbed with children seeking some small preview. Uncharacteristically for him, the attention did not seem to please him. He sought the far reaches of the playground and stood throwing pebbles at a picket fence.

Before school on Thursday, the rumor spread that Mr. Kennan's Volvo had been seen on Main Street the night before. Monica Davis had been eating downtown at the Embers Restaurant when she was sure she had seen Mr. Kennan drive by. Sara took it upon herself to call her classmates with the information and happily accepted the reprimands from irate parents who did not appreciate early morning phone calls from fourth graders. By eight-fifteen, forty-five minutes before the bell rang, most of the class was on the playground. It was Bill who volunteered to go into the school and check out the situation.

Three minutes later he returned. One look at his crestfallen face told most of them what they needed to know.

"Well?" insisted Brad.

"It's Borcherding," said Bill.

"Maybe he's not here yet," ventured Monica, but few believed it and the girls wilted under their reprimanding stares.

When it came time to file in, reality sat before them in the same strained, purple-print dress that she had worn on Tuesday. The day dragged by with that indescribable, open-windowed languor that only the last day of school can engender. The morning was filled with busy work made all the more maddening by the echoing emptiness of the rest of the school. Most classes were gone on class picnics. Mr. Kennan had long ago outlined his plan of hiking all the way to Riverfront Park to spend the entire day in "an orgy of playing softball and eating goodies." Specific children had volunteered to bring specific goodies. But there was no question of that now. When the students glanced up from their work to acknowledge a command from Mrs. Borcherding, there was a common look in their eyes. They shared a dawning realization that the world was not stable; that there were trapdoors to reality which could be sprung without warning. It was a lesson that all of the children instinctively had known once, but had been foolish enough to forget temporarily while encircled with the protective ring of magic.

The day crawled to noon. The class ate in the almost empty lunchroom, sharing it with only a first grade class being punished and five slobbering members of Miss Carter's self-contained EMR class.

Shouts on the playground were strangely subdued. No one approached Terry. If he was nervous, he did not show it as he stood leaning against a tetherball pole with his arms folded.

In the afternoon they checked in their rented books—Brad and Donald had to pay for their lost or damaged books—and sat in silent rows as Mrs. Borcherding laboriously took inventory. They knew that the last hour and a half of school would consist of scrubbing desks, clearing the walls of posters, and covering the bookshelves with paper. All these activities were useless, the children knew, because in a week or two the custodians would move everything out of the room to clean again anyway. They knew that Mrs. Borcherding would wait until the last possible moment to hand out their report cards, hinting all the while that some of them did not pass—or certainly did not *deserve* to. They also knew that everyone would pass.

At five minutes past two, Mrs. Borcherding ponderously stood and looked at the twenty-seven children sitting silently in their strangely clean desks. Tall stacks of books surrounded them like defensive sandbags.

"All right," said Mrs. Borcherding, "you may go out to recess."

No one moved except Brad who stood up, looked around in confusion at his seated classmates, and then sat back down with a foolish grin. Mrs. Borcherding flushed, started to speak, checked herself, and dropped heavily into her chair.

"Terry, I believe that you had something to say," she wheezed. She glanced up at the clock on the wall—it was not running—and then down at the alarm clock which the children had covertly continued to wind. "You have thirteen minutes, young man. Try not to waste their entire recess time."

"Yes'm," said Terry and stood. He crossed to the long bulletin board and raised his hand to the triangular pattern of magic marker mountains which ran near the southern coast of the sketched-in continent. He said nothing. The children nodded silently. Terry dropped his hand and went to the front of the room. His corduroy pants made a *whik-wik* sound as he walked.

Once at the front of the room, he turned and faced his classmates. Sluggish currents of heat, the drone of insects, and distant shouts came through the open windows. Terry cleared his throat. His lips were white but his high, soft voice was firm as he began to speak.

· · ·

Raul was up the hill from the two lizards who're guarding the door to that place where the Wizards was keeping Dobby and Gernisavien. Remember, this was about the time that that big Wizard was getting his knife out to maybe cut Gernisavien open to get the key. Anyway, Raul's fingers was froze, but he knew he'd have to kill the lizards real quick or he wouldn't get a second chance. The snow was blowing all around him and it was getting dark real fast.

The lizards were hunkered over and sort of mumbling to each other. They were wearing these real thick parka-like coats and Raul knew that if he didn't shoot just right that the arrow wouldn't get through all that stuff. Especially if they was wearing armor too.

So Raul got two arrows out. One he stuck point first in the snow and the other he goes and notches. His hands feel like he's wearing thick gloves but he ain't. He's worried that he can't feel nothing with his fingers and maybe the arrow'll let go too soon and that'll tip off the lizards. But he tries not to think about that and he draws the bowstring back as far as he can. Remember, this is a special bow—it come down the clan line from his old man who was war chief of all the centaurs and nobody 'cept for Raul can pull it all the way back.

He does. And he has to hold it that way while he takes aim. His muscles are freezing and for a second he begins to shake up and down, but he takes a big, deep breath and holds it steady . . . the bow . . . on that first lizard, the one who's standing closest to the door. It's real dark now but there's a little bit of red light coming from around that door.

Swiish! Raul lets her go. And no sooner than he lets the first one fly but than he's notchin' the second arrow and pulling back on it. The first lizard—the one nearest the door?—he makes a funny little sound as the arrow gets him smack dab in the throat and sticks out the other side. But the other lizard, he's looking out the other way and when he turns to see what's going on—*swiish*—there's an arrow growin' out of the back of *his* neck too and then he falls, but he slides over the edge and keeps on going down to the frozen ice about two miles below, but neither one of them made no sound.

And then Raul's coming down the hill on all four legs, sort of slipping and sliding and making straight for the door. Well, it's a real big metal door and there ain't no doorknob or nothing and it's locked. But the first lizard— the one who's laying dead in the snow—he's got this ring of keys with about sixteen big keys on it. And one of them fits. But it's lucky that he wasn't the one who fell over the edge, is all.

So Raul sticks this key in and the door slides back sideways and there's this long tunnel going off straight ahead 'til it turns and it's all lit with red light and sort of spooky. He walks into the tunnel and maybe he done something wrong or maybe there's an electric eyeball or something 'cause suddenly these bells are going off like an alarm.

"Well, I done it now," Raul thinks to hisself and takes off galloping down the hallway full speed. He'd put his bow back by this time and he's got his sword out.

Meanwhile, you remember that Gernisavien was all strapped down to this steel table and there was a Wizard standing over her fixing to slit open her belly to get at that farcaster key? He had the knife out—it was sort of like a doctor's knife, it was so sharp you could cut butter with it—and he was standing there just sort of deciding where to make the cut when all the bells went off.

"It's Raul!" yells Dobby who's hanging there on the wall and who's still alive.

The Wizard, he turns real fast and throws some switches and all these TV screens light up. On some of the screens you see lizard soldiers running and others you see a couple of Wizards sort of looking around and on one you see Raul running down this hallway.

The Wizard says something in Wizard talk to these other guys in robes in the room and then they go running out of the room together. So now Dobby and Gernisavien are all alone in there, but there ain't nothing they can do except to watch the TV because they're all tied up.

Raul, he's coming around this bend and all of the sudden here are a bunch of lizards in front of him and they've got crossbows and he's just got his sword. But they're more surprised than he is and he puts his head down and charges full speed into them and before they can get their crossbows loaded and everything he's in there swinging and there are lizard heads and tails and stuff flying around.

Now Gernisavien can see this on the TV and she and Dobby are cheering and everything but they can see the other TVs too, and the halls is full of lizards and the Wizards are coming too. So Dobby, he begins to pull and pull against the chains as hard as he can. Remember, his arms are stronger than they look like we found out when he held up part of Tartuffel's Treehouse that time.

"What're you doing?" goes Gernisavien.

"Tryin' to get at that!" goes Dobby and he points at the table full of test tubes and bottles and all the chemical stuff where the Wizards had been working.

"What for?" goes Gernisavien.

"It's nucular fuel," Dobby says, "and that blue stuff is anti-gravity stuff like in the sky galleon. If it gets all mixed up . . ." And Dobby keeps pulling and pulling until the veins stood up out of his head, but finally one of the chain things breaks and Dobby's hanging down by one arm but he's too tired to keep going.

"Wait a minute," goes Gernisavien. She's watching the TV.

Raul was killing lizards this way and that and he got to within maybe a hundred feet or so to where Dobby and Gernisavien's being kept, but he don't know that and suddenly here come these four or five Wizards with their fire guns. Raul, he barely gets his shield up in time. As it is they scorched off some of his hair and mane and burned up all of his arrows and stuff on his back. And they burned up his daddy's bow, too.

So Raul starts going backwards and he knows they're trying to cut him off 'cause he can see the lizards running down these side hallways. So he turns and gallops as fast as he can but the Wizards are coming down the main way and when they get a clear shot he'll be a goner. So Raul stops and picks up a crossbow and he sort of keeps them back by shooting their way.

All of the sudden he's in this big room where the Wiz-

ards keep their flying platforms. And Raul goes and jumps
the railing and lands on one and starts to look at the controls. He pushes this button and the wall rolls up—it's the
door on the side of the mountain. Raul looks outside and
sees the fresh air and stars and everything. And when he
looks back all he can see is doorways full of lizards and
here come the Wizards with their fire guns and everything
and Raul knows that if he stays he can't dodge them all.
Raul's not so much afraid of getting killed as he is of getting hurt real bad and having to stay there all chained up
like Gernisavien and Dobby.

So Raul, he pushes the buttons until the flying platform starts flying and the Wizards are blasting away with
their fire guns, but he's already outside in the night air and
they can't get a good shot at him as he flies away sort of
zig-zagging.

Now back up the hallway, Gernisavien and Dobby've
been watching all this on the TV. Dobby's face, it always
looks kind of sad but now it looks sadder than ever.

"Can you get your other arm loose?" goes
Gernisavien.

Dobby just shakes his head no. He ain't got no leverage.

Gernisavien, she knows that the key's still in her stomach. And she knows that the Wizards're planning to use it
to get at all those other worlds in the Web of Worlds. And
maybe the humans could fight them off but it looks like
it'd be real hard what with the Wizards coming on them
by surprise and all. Gernisavien remembers all the times
they talked about when they would get to the farcaster and
all the planets they'd go to together and all the people
they'd see.

"It's been fun, hasn't it?" goes Dobby.

"Yeah," says Gernisavien. And then she says. "Go
ahead. Do it."

Dobby knows what she means. He smiles and the
smile, it's sort of sad and sort of happy at the same time.
Then he leans out real far until he's standing on the wall
sideways. That's when they hear the Wizard's footsteps in
the hallway. So Dobby starts swinging his right arm—the
one with the chain hanging loose from it—and then he

brings it down on the nucular fuel and other things on the table and smashes them all together.

Raul is five or six miles away when he sees the mountain blow up. The top just sort of came off and the whole thing went up in the air like a volcano. Raul's just high enough and just far enough away that he didn't get blown all to pieces with it. And he knew who did it. And why.

Now I don't know what else he was thinking about. But he was all by himself now. And he flew around up there alone while all the lava runs down the mountains and sparks shoot up into the air. And there's nowhere for him to go now. He can't get the farcaster to work all by himself. Gernisavien had the key and Dobby was the only one who knew how to turn it on.

Raul stayed up there in the dark for a long time. Then he turned the platform around and flew away. And that's the end.

There was a silence. Children sat stone still and watched as Terry went back to his desk. His corduroys went *whik-wik*. As he sat down, several of the girls began to sob. Many of the boys looked down or raised their desk lids to hide their own tears.

Mrs. Borcherding was at a loss. Then she turned to the wall clock, turned back angrily to the alarm clock, and raised it between her and the class.

"See what you did, young man," she snapped. "You've wasted the class's entire recess and put us behind schedule on our clean-up. Quickly everyone, get ready to scrub your desks!"

The children rubbed at their eyes, took deep breaths, and obediently set to the final tasks that stood between them and freedom.

Introduction to
"Two Minutes Forty-Five Seconds"

One of my favorite people in publishing—if not the world—is Ellen Datlow, fiction editor of OMNI. For awhile they were calling Ellen the Mother of Cyberbunk, but I think they were getting her mixed up with Mother Teresa.

One day Ellen phoned me, announced that she was commissioning a bunch of very short horror-SF pieces for OMNI and asked if I would be interested.

"Ellen, is this so you can pay three grand for seven or eight of us rather than the same amount for one story?" I ask.

"Sure," she says.

"And is it so you can say you ran *eight* pieces of fiction in the issue instead of the one measly story they allow you that month?" I persist.

"Of course," says Ellen. "What else?"

"And are you calling me because you know I work cheap, write fast, and essentially worship the ground you walk on?"

"Sure," says Ellen. "Plus you're behind on payments from the deal where we let you sit at the OMNI table at the World Fantasy Con banquet two years ago, and I figure I can deduct most of your fee for this to get you caught up."

"Count me in," I said.

She had only one condition. The other contributors (their stuff was already in, but there was room for one more story because layout had moved a Trojan ad) had written horror stories that were *horror*. "They forgot it was horror/SF," said Ellen. "Make sure yours is high-tech horror."

"High-tech horror," I said. "Right. No problem."

I hung up the phone, warmed up the computer, flexed nimble fingers over the keyboard, turned off the computer, and said to myself, "What the hell is high-tech horror?"

Now I know. "Two Minutes Forty-five Seconds" is high-tech horror.

As a footnote, I should mention that I spent several hours on the phone with OMNI's lawyers about this story. A partial transcript of one conversation follows:

OMNI LAWYER: Is this story really about the Challenger explosion?

ME: Of course it's really about the Challenger explosion.

O.L.: No, *it is not about the Challenger explosion.*

ME: Of course it's not about the Challenger explosion. Uh . . . what's it about?

O.L.: Obviously it's about an *alternate reality* . . . one in which a certain unnamed shuttle exploded, possibly related to alleged negligence by an unnamed and/or fictional corporation which *bears no resemblance* to any corporation, individual, and or planet in this universe. Correct?

ME: Uh, right. That's what I had in mind.

O.L.: One more thing. You'll have to change your working title for this story.

ME: Right! Sure. Why?

O.L.: We think "Love Song to J. M*rt*n Th**k*l" is . . . ah . . . inadvisable.

ME: OK. How about . . . "The Day Corporate Greed and Malfeasance Killed Seven of Our Astronauts and Almost Killed Our Space Program?"

O.L.: Let us think about that. We'll get back to you.

• •   •

Epilogue to the Footnote:
Recently Ellen Datlow chose "Two Minutes Forty-five
Seconds" to be in the second annual edition of *The Year's
Best Fantasy*, a collection she co-edits with Terry Windling.
Ellen wrote the introduction to the story, and in it she says:

> It's a compact and chilling tale about guilt, based
> in part on a very well-publicized event in our re-
> cent past—the Challenger disaster.

Excuse me, I have to go now. The phone's ringing,
there's a process-server at the door, and a corporate helicopter has just landed in the back yard.

Two Minutes
Forty-Five Seconds

Roger Colvin closed his eyes and the steel bar clamped down across his lap and they began the steep climb. He could hear the rattle of the heavy chain and the creek of steel wheels on steel rails as they clanked up the first hill of the rollercoaster. Someone behind him laughed nervously. Terrified of heights, heart pounding painfully against his ribs, Colvin peeked out from between spread fingers.

The metal rails and white wooden frame rose steeply ahead of him. Colvin was in the first car. He lowered both hands and tightly gripped the metal restraining bar, feeling the dried sweat of past palms there. Someone giggled in the car behind him. He turned his head only far enough to peer over the side of the rails.

They were very high and still rising. The midway and parking lots grew smaller, individuals growing too tiny to be seen and the crowds becoming mere carpets of color, fading into a larger mosaic of geometries of streets and lights as the entire city became visible, then the entire county. They clanked higher. The sky darkened to a deeper blue. Colvin could see the curve of the earth in the haze-blued distance. He realized that they were far out over the edge of a lake now as he caught the glimmer of light on wavetops miles below through the wooden ties. Colvin closed his eyes as they briefly passed through the cold breath of a cloud, then snapped them open again as the pitch of chain rumble changed, as the steep gradient lessened, as they reached the top.

And went over.

There was nothing beyond. The two rails curved out and down and ended in air.

Colvin gripped the restraining bar as the car pitched forward and over. He opened his mouth to scream. The fall began.

"Hey, the worst part's over." Colvin opened his eyes to see Bill Montgomery handing him a drink. The sound of the Gulfstream's jet engines was a dull rumble under the gentle hissing of air from the overhead ventilator nozzle. Colvin took the drink, turned down the flow of air, and glanced out the window. Logan International was already out of sight behind them and Colvin could make out Nantasket Beach below, a score of small white triangles of sail in the expanse of bay and ocean beyond. They were still climbing.

"Damn, we're glad you decided to come with us this time, Roger," Montgomery said to Colvin. "It's good having the whole team together again. Like the old days." Montgomery smiled. The three other men in the cabin raised their glasses.

Colvin played with the calculator in his lap and sipped his vodka. He took a breath and closed his eyes.

Afraid of heights. *Always* afraid. Six years old and in the barn, tumbling from the loft, the fall seemingly endless, time stretching out, the sharp tines of the pitchfork rising toward him. Landing, wind knocked out of him, cheek and right eye against the straw, three inches from the steel points of the pitchfork.

"The company's ready to see better days," said Larry Miller. "Two and a half years of bad press is enough. Be good to see the launch tomorrow. Get things started again."

"Here, here," said Tom Weiscott. It was not yet noon but Tom had already had too much to drink.

Colvin opened his eyes and smiled. Counting himself, there were four corporate vice presidents in the plane. Weiscott was still a Project Manager. Colvin put his cheek to the window and watched Cape Cod Bay pass below. He guessed their altitude to be eleven or twelve thousand feet and climbing.

Colvin imagined a building nine miles high. From the carpeted hall of the top floor he would step into the elevator. The floor of the elevator would be made of glass. The elevator shaft drops away 4,600 floors beneath him, each floor marked with halogen lights, the parallel lights drawing closer in the nine miles of black air beneath him until they merged in a blur below.

He looks up in time to see the cable snap, separate. He falls, clutching futilely at the inside walls of the elevator, walls which have grown as slippery as the clear glass floor. Lights rush by, but already the concrete floor of the shaft is visible miles below—a tiny blue concrete square, growing as the elevator car plummets. He knows that he has almost three minutes to watch that blue square come closer, rise up to smash him. Colvin screams and the spittle floats in the air in front of him, falling at the same velocity, hanging there. The lights rush past. The blue square grows.

Colvin took a drink, placed the glass in the circle set in the wide arm of his chair, and tapped away at his calculator.

Falling objects in a gravity field follow precise mathematical rules, as precise as the force vectors and burn rates in the shaped charges and solid fuels Colvin had designed for twenty years, but just as oxygen affects combustion rates, so air controls the speed of a falling body. Terminal velocity depends upon atmospheric pressure, mass distribution, and surface area as much as upon gravity.

Colvin lowered his eyelids as if to doze and saw what he saw every night when he pretended to sleep; the billowing white cloud, expanding outward like a time-lapse film of a slanting, tilting stratocumulus blossoming against a dark blue sky, the reddish brown interior of nitrogen tetroxide flame, and—just visible below the two emerging, mindless contrails of the SRBs—the tumbling, fuzzy square of the forward fuselage, flight deck included. Even the most amplified images had not shown him the closer details—the intact pressure vessel that was the crew compartment, scorched on the right side where the runaway SRB had played its flame upon it, tumbling, falling free, trailing wires and cables and shreds of fuselage behind it like an umbilical and afterbirth. The earlier images had not shown these details, but Colvin had seen them, touched them, after the fracturing impact with the merciless blue sea. There were layers of tiny barnacles growing on the ruptured skin. Colvin imagined the darkness and cold waiting at the end of that fall; small fish feeding.

"Roger," said Steve Cahill, "where'd you get your fear of flying?"

Colvin shrugged, finished his vodka. "I don't know."

In Viet Nam—not "Nam" or "in-country"—a place Colvin still wanted to think of as a place rather than a condition, he had flown. Already an expert on shaped charges and propellants, Colvin was being flown out to Bong Son Valley near the coast to see why a shipment of standard C-4 plastic explosive was not detonating for an ARVN unit when the Jesus nut came off their Huey and the helicopter fell, rotorless, 280 feet into the jungle, tore through almost a hundred feet of thick vegetation, and came to a stop, upside down, in vines ten feet above the ground. The pilot had been neatly impaled by a limb that smashed up through the floor of the Huey. The co-pilot's skull had smashed through the windshield. The gunner was thrown out, breaking his neck and back, and died the next day. Colvin walked away with a sprained ankle.

Colvin looked down as they crossed Nantucket. He estimated their altitude at eighteen thousand feet and climbing steadily. Their cruising altitude, he knew, was to be thirty-two thousand feet. Much lower than forty-six thousand, especially lacking the vertical thrust vector, but so much depended upon surface area.

When Colvin was a boy in the 1950's, he saw a photograph in the "old" *National Enquirer* of a woman who had jumped off the Empire State Building and landed on the roof of a car. Her legs were crossed almost casually at the ankles; there was a hole in the toe of one of her nylon stockings. The roof of the car was flattened, folded inward, almost like a large goosedown mattress, molding itself to the weight of a sleeping person. The woman's head looked as if it were sunk deep in a soft pillow.

Colvin tapped at his calculator. A woman stepping off the Empire State Building would fall for almost fourteen seconds before hitting the street. Someone falling in a metal box from 46,000 feet would fall for two minutes and forty-five seconds before hitting the water.

What did she think about? What did *they* think about?

Most popular songs and rock videos are about three minutes long, thought Colvin. It is a good length of time; not so long one gets bored, long enough to tell a complete story.

"We're damned glad you're with us," Bill Montgomery said again.

"Goddammit," Bill Montgomery had whispered to Colvin outside the company teleconference room twenty-seven months earlier, "are you with us or against us on this?"

A teleconference was much like a séance. The group sat in semi-darkened rooms hundreds or thousands of miles apart and communed with voices which came from nowhere.

"Well, that's the weather situation here," came the voice from KSC. "What's it to be?"

"We've seen your telefaxed stuff," said the voice from Marshall, "but still don't understand why we should consider scrubbing based on an anomaly that small. You assured us that this stuff was so fail-safe that you could kick it around the block if you wanted to."

Phil McGuire, the chief engineer on Colvin's project team, squirmed in his seat and spoke too loudly. The four-wire teleconference phones had speakers near each chair and could pick up the softest tones. "You *don't* understand, do you?" McGuire almost shouted. "It's the *combination* of these cold temperatures and the likelihood of electrical activity in that cloud layer that causes the problems. In the past five flights there've been three transient events in the leads that run from SRB linear shaped charges to the Range Safety command antennas . . ."

"Transient events," said the voice from KSC, "but within flight certification parameters?"

"Well ... yes," said McGuire. He sounded close to tears. "But it's within parameters because we keep signing wavers and rewriting the goddamn parameters. We just don't *know* why the C-12B shaped range safety charges on the SRBs and ET record a transient current flow when no enable functions have been transmitted. Roger thinks maybe the LSC enable leads or the C-12 compound itself can accidentally allow the static discharge to simulate a command signal ... Oh, hell, *tell* them, Roger."

"Mr. Colvin?" came the voice from Marshall.

Colvin cleared his throat. "That's what we've been watching for some time. Preliminary data suggests that temperatures below 28 degrees Fahrenheit allow the zinc oxide residue in the C-12B stacks to conduct a false signal ... if there's enough static discharge ... theoretically ..."

"But no solid database on this yet?" said the voice from Marshall.

"No," said Colvin.

"And you did sign the Critically One waiver certifying flight readiness on the last three flights?"

"Yes," said Colvin.

"Well," said the voice from KSC, "we've heard from the engineers at Beaunet-HCS, what do you say we have recommendations from management there?"

Bill Montgomery had called a five-minute break and the management team met in the hall. "Goddammit, Roger, are you with us or against us on this one?"

Colvin had looked away.

"I'm serious," snapped Montgomery. "The LCS division has brought this company 215 million dollars in *profit* this year, and your work has been an important part of that success, Roger. Now you seem ready to flush that away on some goddamn transient telemetry readings that don't mean *anything* when compared to the work we've done as a team. There's a vice-presidency opening in a few months, Roger. Don't screw your chances by losing your head like that hysteric McGuire."

"Ready?" said the voice from KSC when five minutes had passed.

"Go," said Vice-President Bill Montgomery.

"Go," said Vice-President Larry Miller.

"Go," said Vice-President Steve Cahill.

"Go," said Project Manager Tom Weiscott.

"Go," said Project Manager Roger Colvin.

"Fine," said KSC. "I'll pass along the recommendation. Sorry you gentlemen won't be here to watch the lift-off tomorrow."

Colvin turned his head as Bill Montgomery called from his side of the cabin, "Hey, I think I see Long Island."

"Bill," said Colvin, "how much did the company make this year on the C-12B redesign?"

Montgomery took a drink and stretched his legs in the roomy interior of the Gulfstream. "About four hundred million, I think, Rog. Why?"

"And did the Agency ever seriously consider going to someone else after . . . after?"

"Shit," said Tom Weiscott, "where else could they go? We got them by the short hairs. They thought about it for a few months and then came crawling back. You're the best designer of shaped range safety devices and solid hypergolics in the country, Rog."

Colvin nodded, worked with his calculator a minute and closed his eyes.

The steel bar clamped down across his lap and the car he rode in clanked higher and higher. The air grew thin and cold, the screech of wheel on rail dwindling into a thin scream as the rollercoaster lumbered above the six mile mark.

In case of loss of cabin pressure, oxygen masks will descend from the ceiling. Please fasten them securely over your mouth and nose and breath normally.

Colvin peeked ahead, up the terrible incline of the rollercoaster, sensing the summit of the climb and the emptiness beyond.

The tiny air tank-and-mask combinations were called PEAPs—Personal Egress Air Packs. PEAPs from four of the five crew-members were recovered from the ocean bottom. All had been activated. Two minutes and forty-five seconds of each five-minute air supply had been used up.

Colvin watched the summit of the rollercoaster's first hill arrive.

There was a raw metallic noise and a lurch as the rollercoaster went over the top and off the rails. People in the cars behind Colvin screamed and kept on screaming.

Colvin lurched forward and grabbed the restraining bar as the rollercoaster plummeted into nine miles of nothingness. He opened his eyes. A single glimpse out the Gulfstream window told him that the thin lines of shaped charges he had placed there had removed all of the port wing cleanly, surgically. The tumble rate suggested that enough of a stub of the starboard wing was left to provide the surface area needed to keep the terminal velocity a little lower than maximum. Two minutes and forty-five seconds, plus or minus four seconds.

Colvin reached for his calculator but it had flown free in the cabin, colliding with hurtling bottles, glasses, cushions, and bodies that had not been securely strapped in. The screaming was very loud.

Two minutes and forty-five seconds. Time to think of many things. And perhaps, just perhaps, after two and a half years of no sleep without dreams, perhaps it would be time enough for a short nap with no dreams at all.

Colvin closed his eyes.

Introduction to "Carrion Comfort"

Some of you reading this may know that "Carrion Comfort" the story has since led to *Carrion Comfort* the massive novel.

I've always been a bit uncomfortable with short stories or novellas that evolve into novels. It makes me wonder—"Was the story incomplete?" or "Is the novel a mere stretching of the shorter piece?"

In this case, I'm in a position to answer.

"Carrion Comfort" the story stands alone as my inquiry into the psychology of absolute power corrupting absolutely. *Carrion Comfort* the novel—all half-million words of it—is my once and final exploration of the effect of such absolute power on people who refuse to be victims of it.

The story included here deserves, I believe, to continue to exist . . . and to be read . . . for its own merit, not only because it was the seed crystal to a larger solution, but because it is the pure thing. Undistilled.

This is the Scotch without the water or ice.

This is the Borgia potion without the antidote.

Drink deep.

Enjoy.

Carrion Comfort

Nina was going to take credit for the death of the Beatle, John. I thought that was in very bad taste. She had her scrapbook laid out on my mahogany coffee table, newspaper clippings neatly arranged in chronological order, the bald statements of death recording all of her Feedings. Nina Drayton's smile was as radiant as ever, but her pale-blue eyes showed no hint of warmth.

"We should wait for Willi," I said.

"Of course, Melanie. You're right, as always. How silly of me. I know the rules." Nina stood and began walking around the room, idly touching the furnishings or exclaiming softly over a ceramic statuette or piece of needlepoint. This part of the house had once been the conservatory, but now I used it as my sewing room. Green plants still caught the morning light. The light made it a warm, cozy place in the daytime, but now that winter had come the room was too chilly to use at night. Nor did I like the sense of darkness closing in against all those panes of glass.

"I love this house," said Nina. She turned and smiled at me. "I can't tell you how much I look forward to coming back to Charleston. We should hold all of our reunions here."

I knew how much Nina loathed this city and this house.

"Willi would be hurt," I said. "You know how he likes to show off his place in Beverly Hills—and his new girlfriends."

"And boyfriends," Nina said, laughing. Of all the changes and darkenings in Nina, her laugh has been least affected. It was still the husky but childish laugh that I had first heard so long ago. It had drawn me to her then—one lonely, adolescent girl responding to the warmth of another like a moth to a flame. Now it served only to chill me and put me even more on my guard. Enough moths had been drawn to Nina's flame over the many decades.

"I'll send for tea," I said.

Mr. Thorne brought the tea in my best Wedgwood china. Nina and I sat in the slowly moving squares of sunlight and spoke softly of nothing important: mutually ignorant comments on the economy, references to books that the other had not gotten around to reading, and sympathetic murmurs about the low class of persons one meets while flying these days. Someone peering in from the garden might have thought he was seeing an aging but attractive niece visiting her favorite aunt. (I drew the line at suggesting that anyone would mistake us for mother and daughter.) People usually consider me a well-dressed if not stylish person. Heaven knows I have paid enough to have the wool skirts and silk blouses mailed from Scotland and France. But next to Nina I've always felt dowdy.

This day she wore an elegant, light-blue dress that must have cost several thousand dollars if I had identified the designer correctly. The color made her complexion seem even more perfect than usual and brought out the blue of her eyes. Her hair had gone as gray as mine, but somehow she managed to get away with wearing it long and tied back with a single barrette. It looked youthful and chic on Nina and made me feel that my short, artificial curls were glowing with a blue rinse.

Few would suspect that I was four years younger than Nina. Time had been kind to her. And she had Fed more often.

She set down her cup and saucer and moved aimlessly

around the room again. It was not like Nina to show such signs of nervousness. She stopped in front of the glass display case. Her gaze passed over the Hummels and the pewter pieces and then stopped in surprise.

"Good heavens, Melanie. A pistol! What an odd place to put an old pistol."

"It's an heirloom," I said. "A Colt Peacemaker from right after the War Between the States. Quite expensive. And you're right, it *is* a silly place to keep it. But it's the only case I have in the house with a lock on it and Mrs. Hodges often brings her grandchildren when she visits—"

"You mean it's *loaded*?"

"No, of course not," I lied. "But children should not play with such things . . ." I trailed off lamely. Nina nodded but did not bother to conceal the condescension in her smile. She went to look out the south window into the garden.

Damn her. It said volumes about Nina that she did not recognize that pistol.

On the day he was killed, Charles Edgar Larchmont had been my beau for precisely five months and two days. There had been no formal announcement, but we were to be married. Those five months had been a microcosm of the era itself—naive, flirtatious, formal to the point of preciosity, and romantic. Most of all, romantic. Romantic in the worst sense of the word: dedicated to saccharine or insipid ideals that only an adolescent—or an adolescent society—would strive to maintain. We were children playing with loaded weapons.

Nina, she was Nina Hawkins then, had her own beau—a tall, awkward, but well-meaning Englishman named Roger Harrison. Mr. Harrison had met Nina in London a year earlier, during the first stages of the Hawkins' Grand Tour. Declaring himself smitten—another absurdity of those times—the tall Englishman had followed her from one European capital to another until, after being firmly reprimanded by Nina's father (an unimaginative little milliner who was constantly on the defensive about his doubtful social status), Harrison returned to London to "settle his affairs." Some months later he showed up in New York just as Nina was being packed off to her aunt's home in Charleston in order to terminate yet another flirtation. Still undaunted, the clumsy Englishman followed her south, ever mindful of the protocols and restrictions of the day.

We were a gay group. The day after I met Nina at Cousin Celia's June ball, the four of us were taking a hired boat up the Cooper River for a picnic on Daniel Island. Roger Harrison, serious and solemn on every topic, was a perfect foil for Charles's irreverent sense of humor. Nor did Roger seem to mind the good-natured jesting, since he was soon joining in the laughter with his peculiar *haw-haw-haw*.

Nina loved it all. Both gentlemen showered attention on her, and although Charles never failed to show the primacy of his affection for me, it was understood by all that Nina Hawkins was one of those young women who invariably becomes the center of male gallantry and attention in any gathering. Nor were the social strata of Charleston blind to the combined charm of our foursome. For two months of that now-distant summer, no party was complete, no excursion adequately planned, and no occasion considered a success unless we four merry pranksters were invited and had chosen to attend. Our happy dominance of the youthful social scene was so pronounced that Cousins Celia and Loraine wheedled their parents into leaving two weeks early for their annual August sojourn in Maine.

I am not sure when Nina and I came up with the idea of the duel. Perhaps it was during one of the long, hot nights when the other "slept over"—creeping into the other's bed, whispering and giggling, stifling our laughter when the rustling of starched uniforms betrayed the presence of our colored maids moving through the darkened halls. In any case, the idea was the natural outgrowth of the romantic pretensions of the time. The picture of Charles and Roger actually dueling over some abstract point of honor relating to *us* thrilled both of us in a physical way that I recognize now as a simple form of sexual titillation.

It would have been harmless except for our Ability. We

had been so successful in our manipulation of male behavior—a manipulation that was both expected and encouraged in those days—that neither of us had yet suspected that there was anything beyond the ordinary in the way we could translate our whims into other people's actions. The field of parapsychology did not exist then; or rather, it existed only in the rappings with whispered fantasies and knockings of parlor-game séances. At any rate, we amused ourselves for several weeks, and then one of us—or perhaps both of us—used the Ability to translate the fantasy into reality.

In a sense, it was our first Feeding.

I do not remember the purported cause of the quarrel, perhaps some deliberate misinterpretation of one of Charles's jokes. I cannot recall who Charles and Roger arranged to have serve as seconds on that illegal outing. I do remember the hurt and confused expression on Roger Harrison's face during those few days. It was a caricature of ponderous dullness, the confusion of a man who finds himself in a situation not of his making and from which he cannot escape. I remember Charles and his mercurial swings of mood—the bouts of humor, periods of black anger, and the tears and kisses the night before the duel.

I remember with great clarity the beauty of that morning. Mists were floating up from the river and diffusing the rays of the rising sun as we rode out to the dueling field. I remember Nina reaching over and squeezing my hand with an impetuous excitement that was communicated through my body like an electric shock.

Much of the rest of that morning is missing. Perhaps in the intensity of that first, subconscious Feeding I literally lost consciousness as I was engulfed in the waves of fear, excitement, pride—of *maleness*—emanating from our two beaus as they faced death on that lovely morning. I remember experiencing the shock of realizing *this is really happening* as I shared the tread of high boots through the grass. Someone was calling off the paces. I dimly recall the weight of the pistol in my hand—Charles's hand, I think, I will never know for sure—and a second of cold clarity before an explosion broke the connection and the acrid smell of a gunpowder brought me back to myself.

It was Charles who died. I have never been able to forget the incredible quantities of blood that poured from the small, round hole in his breast. His white shirt was crimson by the time I reached him. There had been no blood in our fantasies. Nor had there been the sight of Charles with his head lolling, mouth dribbling saliva onto his bloodied chest while his eyes rolled back to show the whites like two eggs embedded in his skull.

Roger Harrison was sobbing as Charles breathed his final, shuddering gasps on that field of innocence.

I remember nothing at all about the confused hours that followed. The next morning I opened my cloth bag to find Charles's pistol lying with my things. Why would I have kept that revolver? If I had wished to take something from my fallen lover as a sign of remembrance, why that alien piece of metal? Why pry from his dead fingers the symbol of our thoughtless sin?

It said volumes about Nina that she did not recognize that pistol.

"Willi's here."

It was not Mr. Thorne announcing the arrival of our guest, but Nina's 'amanuensis', the loathsome Miss Barrett Kramer. Kramer's appearance was as unisex as her name: short-cropped, black hair, powerful shoulders, and a blank, aggressive gaze that I associated with lesbians and criminals. She looked to be in her mid-thirties.

"Thank you, Barrett dear," said Nina.

Both of us went out to greet Willi, but Mr. Thorne had already let him in, and we met in the hallway.

"Melanie! You look marvellous! You grow younger each time I see you. Nina!" The change in Willi's voice was evident. Men continued to be overpowered by their first sight of Nina after an absence. There were hugs and kisses. Willi himself looked more dissolute than ever. His alpaca sport coat was exquisitely tailored, his turtleneck sweater successfully concealed the eroded lines of his wattled neck, but when he swept off his jaunty sports-car cap the long strands of white hair he had brushed forward to hide his encroaching baldness were knocked into disarray.

Willi's face was flushed with excitement, but there was also the telltale capillary redness about the nose and cheeks that spoke of too much liquor, too many drugs.

"Ladies, I think you've met my associates, Tom Reynolds and Jensen Luhar?" The two men added to the crowd in my narrow hall. Mr. Reynolds was thin and blond, smiling with perfectly capped teeth. Mr. Luhar was a gigantic Negro, hulking forward with a sullen, bruised look on his coarse face. I was sure that neither Nina nor I had encountered these specific catspaws of Willi's before. It did not matter.

"Why don't we go into the parlor?" I suggested. It was an awkward procession ending with the three of us seated on the heavily upholstered chairs surrounding the Georgian tea table that had been my grandmother's. "More tea, please, Mr. Thorne." Miss Kramer took that as her cue to leave, but Willi's two pawns stood uncertainly by the door, shifting from foot to foot and glancing at the crystal on display as if their mere proximity could break something. I would not have been surprised if that had proved to be the case.

"Jensen!" Willi snapped his fingers. The Negro hesitated and then brought forward an expensive leather attaché case. Willi set it on the tea table and clicked the catches open with his short, broad fingers. "Why don't you two see Mrs. Fuller's man about getting something to drink?"

When they were gone Willi shook his head and smiled at Nina. "Sorry about that, Love."

Nina put her hand on Willi's sleeve. She leaned forward with an air of expectancy. "Melanie wouldn't let me begin the Game without you. Wasn't that *awful* of me to want to start without you, Willi dear?"

Willi frowned. After fifty years he still bridled at being called Willi. In Los Angeles he was Big Bill Borden. When he returned to his native Germany—which was not often because of the dangers involved—he was once again Wilhelm von Borchert, lord of dark manor, forest, and hunt. But Nina had called him Willi when they had first met in 1925 in Vienna, and Willi he had remained.

"You begin, Willi dear," said Nina. "You go first."

I could remember the time when we would have spent the first few days of our reunion in conversation and catching up with one another's lives. Now there was not even time for small talk.

Willi showed his teeth and removed news clippings, notebooks, and a stack of cassettes from his briefcase. No sooner had he covered the small table with his material than Mr. Thorne arrived with the tea and Nina's scrapbook from the sewing room. Willi brusquely cleared a small space.

At first glance one might see certain similarities between Willi Borchert and Mr. Thorne. One would be mistaken. Both men tended to the florid, but Willi's complexion was the result of excess and emotion; Mr. Thorne had known neither of these for many years. Willi's balding was a patchy, self-consciously concealed thing—a weasel with mange—Mr. Thorne's bare head was smooth and unwrinkled. One could not imagine Mr. Thorne ever having *had* hair. Both men had gray eyes—what a novelist would call cold, gray eyes—but Mr. Thorne's eyes were cold with indifference, cold with a clarity coming from an absolute absence of troublesome emotion or thought. Willi's eyes were the cold of a blustery North Sea winter and were often clouded with shifting curtains of the emotions that controlled him—pride, hatred, love of pain, the pleasures of destruction.

Willi never referred to his use of the Ability as *Feedings*—I was evidently the only one who thought in those terms—but Willi sometimes talked of The Hunt. Perhaps it was the dark forests of his homeland that he thought of as he stalked his human quarry through the sterile streets of Los Angeles. Did Willi dream of the forest, I wondered. Did he look back to green loden hunting jackets, the applause of retainers, the gouts of blood from the dying boar? Or did Willi remember the slam of jackboots on cobblestones and the pounding of his lieutenants' fists on doors? Perhaps Willi still associated his Hunt with the dark European night of the ovens that he had helped to oversee.

I called it Feeding. Willi called it The Hunt. I had never heard Nina call it anything.

"Where is your VCR?" Willi asked. "I have put them all on tape."

"Oh, Willi," said Nina in an exasperated tone. "You know Melanie. She's *so* old-fashioned. You know she wouldn't have a video player."

"I don't even have a television," I said. Nina laughed.

"Goddamn it," muttered Willi. "It doesn't matter. I have other records here." He snapped rubber bands from around the small, black notebooks. "It just would have been better on tape. The Los Angeles stations gave much coverage to the Hollywood Strangler, and I edited in the . . . Ach! Never mind."

He tossed the videocassettes into his briefcase and slammed the lid shut.

"Twenty-three," he said. "Twenty-three since we met twelve months ago. It doesn't seem that long, does it?"

"Show us," said Nina. She was leaning forward, and her blue eyes seemed very bright. "I've been wondering since I saw the Strangler interviewed on *Sixty Minutes*. He *was* yours, Willi? He seemed so—"

"*Ja, ja*, he was mine. A nobody. A timid little man. He was the gardener of a neighbor of mine. I left him alive so that the police could question him, erase any doubts. He will hang himself in his cell next month after the press loses interest. But this is more interesting. Look at this." Willi slid across several glossy black-and-white photographs. The NBC executive had murdered the five members of his family and drowned a visiting soap-opera actress in his pool. He had then stabbed himself repeatedly and written 50 SHARE in blood on the wall of the bathhouse.

"Reliving old glories, Willi?" asked Nina. "DEATH TO THE PIGS and all that?"

"No, goddamn it. I think it should receive points for irony. The girl had been scheduled to drown on the program. It was already in the script outline."

"Was he hard to Use?" It was my question. I was curious despite myself.

Willi lifted one eyebrow. "Not really. He was an alcoholic and heavily into cocaine. There was not much left. And he hated his family. Most people do."

"Most people in California, perhaps," said Nina primly. It was an odd comment from Nina. Years ago her father had committed suicide by throwing himself in front of a trolley car.

"Where did you make contact?" I asked.

"A party. The usual place. He bought the coke from a director who had ruined one of my . . ."

"Did you have to repeat the contact?"

Willi frowned at me. He kept his anger under control, but his face grew redder. "*Ja, ja.* I saw him twice more. Once I just watched from my car as he played tennis."

"Points for irony," said Nina. "But you lose points for repeated contact. If he were as empty as you say, you should have been able to Use him after only one touch. What else do you have?"

He had his usual assortment. Pathetic skid-row murders. Two domestic slayings. A highway collision that turned into a fatal shooting. "I was in the crowd," said Willi. "I made contact. He had a gun in the glove compartment."

"Two points," said Nina.

Willi had saved a good one for last. A once-famous child star had suffered a bizarre accident. He had left his Bel Air apartment while it filled with gas and then returned to light a match. Two others had died in the ensuing fire.

"You get credit only for him," said Nina.

"*Ja, ja.*"

"Are you absolutely sure about this one? It *could* have been an accident."

"Don't be ridiculous," snapped Willi. He turned toward me. "*This* one was very hard to Use. Very strong. I blocked his memory of turning on the gas. Had to hold it away for two hours. Then forced him into the room. He struggled not to strike the match."

"You should have had him use his lighter," said Nina.

"He didn't smoke," growled Willi. "He gave it up last year."

"Yes," smiled Nina. "I seem to remember him saying that to Johnny Carson." I could not tell whether Nina was jesting.

The three of us went through the ritual of assigning
points. Nina did most of the talking. Willi went from being
sullen to expansive to sullen again. At one point he
reached over and patted my knee as he laughingly asked
for my support. I said nothing. Finally he gave up, crossed
the parlor to the liquor cabinet, and poured himself a tall
glass of bourbon from Father's decanter. The evening light
was sending its final, horizontal rays through the stained-
glass panels of the bay windows, and it cast a red hue on
Willi as he stood next to the oak cupboard. His eyes were
small, red embers in a bloody mask.

"Forty-one," said Nina at last. She looked up brightly
and showed the calculator as if it verified some objective
fact. "I count forty-one points. What do you have,
Melanie?"

"*Ja*," interrupted Willi. "That is fine. Now let us see
your claims, Nina." His voice was flat and empty. Even
Willi had lost some interest in the Game.

Before Nina could begin, Mr. Thorne entered and motioned that dinner was served. We adjourned to the dining
room—Willi pouring himself another glass of bourbon and
Nina fluttering her hands in mock frustration at the inter-
ruption of the Game. Once seated at the long, mahogany
table, I worked at being a hostess. From decades of tradition, talk of the Game was banned from the dinner table.
Over soup we discussed Willi's new movie and the purchase of another store for Nina's line of boutiques. It
seemed that Nina's monthly column in *Vogue* was to be
discontinued but that a newspaper syndicate was interested
in picking it up.

Both of my guests exclaimed over the perfection of the
baked ham, but I thought that Mr. Thorne had made the
gravy a trifle too sweet. Darkness had filled the windows
before we finished our chocolate mousse. The refracted
light from the chandelier made Nina's hair dance with
highlights while I feared that mine glowed more bluely
than ever.

Suddenly there was a sound from the kitchen. The
huge Negro's face appeared at the swinging door. His
shoulder was hunched against white hands and his expression was that of a querulous child.

". . . the hell you think we are sittin' here like goddamned—" The white hands pulled him out of sight.

"Excuse me, ladies." Willi dabbed linen at his lips and stood up. He still moved gracefully for all of his years.

Nina poked at her chocolate. There was one sharp, barked command from the kitchen and the sound of a slap. It was the slap of a man's hand—hard and flat as a small-caliber rifle shot. I looked up and Mr. Thorne was at my elbow, clearing away the dessert dishes.

"Coffee, please, Mr. Thorne. For all of us."

He nodded and his smile was gentle.

Franz Anton Mesmer had known of it even if he had not understood it. I suspect that Mesmer must have had some small touch of the Ability. Modern pseudosciences have studied it and renamed it, removed most of its power, confused its uses and origins, but it remains the shadow of what Mesmer discovered. They have no idea of what it is like to Feed.

I despair at the rise of modern violence. I truly give in to despair at times, that deep, futureless pit of despair that the poet Gerard Manley Hopkins called carrion comfort. I watch the American slaughterhouse, the casual attacks on popes, presidents, and uncounted others, and I wonder whether there are many more out there with the Ability or whether butchery has simply become the modern way of life.

All humans feed on violence, on the small exercises of power over another. But few have tasted—as we have—the ultimate power. And without the Ability, few know the unequaled pleasure of taking a human life. Without the Ability, even those who do feed on life cannot savor the flow of emotions in stalker and victim, the total exhilaration of the attacker who has moved beyond all rules and punishments, the strange, almost sexual submission of the victim in that final second of truth when all options are canceled, all futures denied, all possibilities erased in an exercise of absolute power over another.

I despair at modern violence. I despair at the impersonal nature of it and the casual quality that has made it

accessible to so many. I had a television set until I sold it
at the height of the Vietnam War. Those sanitized snippets
of death—made distant by the camera's lens—meant nothing to me. But I believe it meant something to these cattle
that surround me. When the war and the nightly televised
body counts ended, they demanded more, *more*, and the
movie screens and streets of this sweet and dying nation
have provided it in mediocre, mob abundance. It is an addiction I know well.

They miss the point. Merely observed, violent death is
a sad and sullied tapestry of confusion. But to those of us
who have Fed, death can be a *sacrament*.

"My turn! My turn!" Nina's voice still resembled that
of the visiting belle who had just filled her dance card at
Cousin Celia's June ball.

We had returned to the parlor. Willi had finished his
coffee and requested a brandy from Mr. Thorne. I was embarrassed for Willi. To have one's closest associates show
any hint of unplanned behavior was certainly a sign of
weakening Ability. Nina did not appear to have noticed.

"I have them all in order," said Nina. She opened the
scrapbook on the now-empty tea table. Willi went through
them carefully, sometimes asking a question, more often
grunting assent. I murmured occasional agreement although I had heard of none of them. Except for the Beatle,
of course. Nina saved that for near the end.

"Good God, Nina, that was you?" Willi seemed near
anger. Nina's Feedings had always run to Park Avenue suicides and matrimonial disagreements ending in shots fired
from expensive, small-caliber ladies' guns. This type of
thing was more in Willi's crude style. Perhaps he felt that
his territory was being invaded. "I mean ... you were
risking a lot, weren't you? It's so ... damn it ... so *public*."

Nina laughed and set down the calculator. "Willi *dear*,
that's what the Game is *about*, is it not?"

Willi strode to the liquor cabinet and refilled his
brandy snifter. The wind tossed bare branches against the

leaded glass of the bay window. I do not like winter. Even in the South it takes its toll on the spirit.

"Didn't this guy ... what's his name ... buy the gun in Hawaii or someplace?" asked Willi from across the room. "That sounds like his initiative to me. I mean, if he was *already* stalking the fellow—"

"Willi dear." Nina's voice had gone as cold as the wind that raked the branches. "No one said he was *stable*. How many of yours are stable, Willi? But I made it *happen*, darling. I chose the place and the time. Don't you see the irony of the *place*, Willi? After that little prank on the director of that witchcraft movie a few years ago? It was straight from the script—"

"I don't know," said Willi. He sat heavily on the divan, spilling brandy on his expensive sport coat. He did not notice. The lamplight reflected from his balding skull. The mottles of age were more visible at night, and his neck, where it disappeared into his turtleneck, was all ropes and tendons. "I don't know." He looked up at me and smiled suddenly, as if we shared a conspiracy. "It could be like that writer fellow, eh, Melanie? It could be like that."

Nina looked down at the hands in her lap. They were clenched and the well-manicured fingers were white at the tips.

The Mind Vampires. That's what the writer was going to call his book.

I sometimes wonder if he really would have written anything. What was his name? Something Russian.

Willi and I received telegrams from Nina: COME QUICKLY YOU ARE NEEDED. That was enough. I was on the next morning's flight to New York. The plane was a noisy, propeller-driven Constellation, and I spent much of the flight assuring the overly solicitous stewardess that I needed nothing, that, indeed, I felt fine. She obviously had decided that I was someone's grandmother who was flying for the first time.

Willi managed to arrive twenty minutes before me. Nina was distraught and as close to hysteria as I had ever seen her. She had been at a party in lower Manhattan two days before—she was not so distraught that she forgot to tell us what important names had been there—when she found herself sharing a corner, a fondue pot, and confidences with a young writer. Or rather, the writer was sharing confidences. Nina described him as a scruffy sort with a wispy little beard, thick glasses, a corduroy sport coat worn over an old plaid shirt—one of the type invariably sprinkled around successful parties of that era, according to Nina. She knew enough not to call him a beatnik, for that term had just become passé, but no one had yet heard the term *hippie*, and it wouldn't have applied to him anyway. He was a writer of the sort that barely ekes out a living, these days at least, by selling blood and doing novelizations of television series. Alexander something.

His idea for a book—he told Nina that he had been working on it for some time—was that many of the murders then being committed were actually the result of a small group of psychic killers, he called them *mind vampires*, who used others to carry out their grisly deeds.

He said that a paperback publisher had already shown interest in his outline and would offer him a contract tomorrow if he would change the title to *The Zombie Factor* and put in more sex.

"So what?" Willi had said to Nina in disgust. "You have me fly across the continent for this? I might buy that idea to produce myself."

That turned out to be the excuse we used to interrogate this Alexander Somebody during an impromptu party given by Nina the next evening. I did not attend. The party was not overly successful according to Nina, but it gave Willi the chance to have a long chat with the young would-be novelist. In the writer's almost pitiable eagerness to do business with Bill Borden, producer of *Paris Memories*, *Three on a Swing*, and at least two other completely forgettable Technicolor features touring the drive-ins that summer, he revealed that the book consisted of a well-worn outline and a dozen pages of notes.

He was sure, however, that he could do a treatment for Mr. Borden in five weeks, perhaps even as fast as three weeks if he were flown out to Hollywood to get the proper creative stimulation.

Later that evening we discussed the possibility of Willi simply buying an option on the treatment, but Willi was short on cash at the time and Nina was insistent. In the end the young writer opened his femoral artery with a Gillette blade and ran screaming into a narrow Greenwich Village side street to die. I don't believe that anyone ever bothered to sort through the clutter and debris of his remaining notes.

"It could be like that writer, *ja*, Melanie?" Willi patted my knee. I nodded. "He was mine," continued Willi, "and Nina tried to take credit. Remember?"

Again I nodded. Actually he had been neither Nina's nor Willi's. I had avoided the party so that I could make contact later without the young man noticing he was being followed. I did so easily. I remember sitting in an overheated little delicatessen across the street from the apartment building. It was not at all difficult. It was over so quickly that there was almost no sense of Feeding. Then I was aware once again of the sputtering radiators and the smell of salami as people rushed to the door to see what the screaming was about. I remember finishing my tea slowly so that I did not have to leave before the ambulance was gone.

"Nonsense," said Nina. She busied herself with her little calculator. "How many points?" She looked at me. I looked at Willi.

"Six," he said with a shrug. Nina made a small show of totaling the numbers.

"Thirty-eight," she said and sighed theatrically. "You win again, Willi. Or rather, you beat *me* again. We must hear from Melanie. You've been so quiet, dear. You must have some surprise for us."

"Yes," said Willi, "it is your turn to win. It has been several years."

"None," I said. I had expected an explosion of questions, but the silence was broken only by the ticking of the clock on the mantelpiece. Nina was looking away from me, at something hidden by the shadows in the corner.

"None?" echoed willi.

"There was . . . one," I said at last. "But it was by accident. I came across them robbing an old man behind . . . but it was completely by accident."

Willi was agitated. He stood up, walked to the window, turned an old straight-back chair around and stradled it, arms folded. "What does this mean?"

"You're quitting the Game?" Nina asked as she turned to look at me. I let the question serve as the answer.

"Why?" snapped Willi. In his excitement it came out with a hard *v*.

If I had been raised in an era when young ladies were allowed to shrug, I would have done so. As it was, I contented myself with running my fingers along an imaginary seam on my skirt. Will had asked the question, but I stared straight into Nina's eyes when I finally answered. "I'm tired. It's been too long. I guess I'm getting old."

"You'll get a lot *older* if you do not Hunt," said Willi. His body, his voice, the red mask of his face, everything signaled great anger just kept in check. "My God, Melanie, you *already* look older! You look terrible. This is *why* we Hunt, woman. Look at yourself in the mirror! Do you want to die an old woman just because you're tired of using *them*? *Ach!*" Willi stood and turned his back on us.

"Nonsense!" Nina's voice was strong, confident, in command once more. "Melanie's *tired*, Willi. Be nice. We all have times like that. I remember how *you* were after the war. Like a whipped puppy. You wouldn't even go outside your miserable little flat in Baden. Even after we helped you get to New Jersey you just sulked around feeling sorry for yourself. Melanie *made up* the Game to help you feel better. So quiet! *Never* tell a lady who feels tired and depressed that she looks terrible. Honestly, Willi, you're such a *Schwachsinniger* sometimes. And a crashing boor to boot."

I had anticipated many reactions to my announcement, but this was the one I feared most. It meant that Nina had also tired of the game. It meant that she was ready to move to another level of play.

It had to mean that.

"Thank you, Nina darling," I said. "I knew you would understand."

She reached across and touched my knee reassuringly. Even through my wool skirt, I could feel the cold of her white fingers.

My guests would not stay the night. I implored. I remonstrated. I pointed out that their rooms were ready, that Mr. Thorne had already turned down the quilts.

"Next time," said Willi. "Next time, Melanie, my little love. We'll make a weekend of it as we used to. A week!" Willi was in a much better mood since he had been paid his thousand-dollar prize by each of us. He had sulked, but I had insisted. It soothed his ego when Mr. Thorne brought in a check already made out to WILLIAM D. BORDEN.

Again I asked him to stay, but he protested that he had a midnight flight to Chicago. He had to see a prizewinning author about a screenplay. Then he was hugging me good-bye, his companions were in the hall behind me, and I had a brief moment of terror.

But they left. The blond young man showed his white smile, and the Negro bobbed his head in what I took as a farewell. Then we were alone.

Nina and I were alone.

Not quite alone. Miss Kramer was standing next to Nina at the end of the hall. Mr. Thorne was out of sight behind the swinging door to the kitchen. I left him there.

Miss Kramer took three steps forward. I felt my breath stop for an instant. Mr. Thorne put his hand on the swinging door. Then the husky little brunette went to the hall closet, removed Nina's coat, and stepped back to help her into it.

"Are you sure you won't stay?"

"No, thank you, darling. I've promised Barrett that we would drive to Hilton Head tonight."

"But it's late . . ."

"We have reservations. Thank you anyway, Melanie. I *will* be in touch."

"Yes."

"I mean it, dear. We must talk. I understand *exactly* how you feel, but you have to remember that the Game is still important to Willi. We'll have to find a way to end it without hurting his feelings. Perhaps we could visit him next spring in Karinhall or whatever he calls that gloomy old Bavarian place of his. A trip to the Continent would do wonders for you, dear."

"Yes."

"I *will* be in touch. After this deal with the new store is settled. We need to spend some time together, Melanie . . . just the two of us . . . like old times." Her lips kissed the air next to my cheek. She held my forearms tightly for a few seconds. "Good-bye, darling."

"Good-bye, Nina."

I carried the brandy glass to the kitchen. Mr. Thorne took it in silence.

"Make sure the house is secure," I said. He nodded and went to check the locks and alarm system. It was only nine forty-five, but I was very tired. *Age,* I thought. I went up the wide staircase—perhaps the finest feature of the house—and dressed for bed. It had begun to storm, and the sound of the cold raindrops on the window carried a sad rhythm to it.

Mr. Thorne looked in as I was brushing my hair and wishing it were longer. I turned to him. He reached into the pocket of his dark vest. When his hand emerged, a slim blade flicked out. I nodded. He palmed the blade shut and closed the door behind him. I listened to his footsteps recede down the stairs to the chair in the front hall where he would spend the night.

I believe I dreamed of vampires that night. Or perhaps I was thinking about them just prior to falling asleep, and a fragment had stayed with me until morning. Of all mankind's self-inflicted terrors, of all their pathetic little monsters, only the myth of the vampire had any vestige of dignity. Like the humans it feeds on, the vampire must respond to its own dark compulsions. But unlike its petty human prey, the vampire carries out its sordid means to the only possible ends that could justify such actions—the goal of literal immortality. There is a nobility there. And a sadness.

Before sleeping I thought of that summer long ago in

Vienna. I saw Willie young again—blond, flushed with youth, and filled with pride at escorting two such independent American ladies.

I remembered Willi's high, stiff collars and the short dresses that Nina helped to bring into style that summer. I remembered the friendly sounds of crowded *Biergartens* and the shadowy dance of leaves in front of gas lamps.

I remembered the footsteps on wet cobblestones, the shouts, the distant whistles, and the silences.

Willi was right; I had aged. The past year had taken a greater toll than the preceding decade. But I had not Fed. Despite the hunger, despite the aging reflection in the mirror, despite the dark compulsion which had ruled our lives for so many years *I had not Fed*.

I fell asleep trying to think of that writer's last name. I fell asleep hungry.

I awoke to bright sunlight through bare branches. It was one of those crystalline, warming winter days that makes living in the South so much less depressing than merely surviving a Yankee winter. I had Mr. Thorne open the window a crack when he brought in my breakfast tray. As I sipped my coffee I could hear children playing in the courtyard. Once Mr. Thorne would have brought the morning paper with the tray, but I had long since learned that to read about the follies and scandals of the world was to desecrate the morning. In truth I was growing less and less interested in the affairs of men. I had done without a newspaper, telephone, or television for twelve years and had suffered no ill effects unless one were to count a growing self-contentment as an ill thing. I smiled as I remembered Willi's disappointment at not being able to play his videocassettes. He was such a child.

"It is Saturday, is it not, Mr. Thorne?" At his nod I gestured for the tray to be taken away. "We will go out today," I said. "A walk. Perhaps a trip to the fort. Then dinner at Henry's and home. I have arrangements to make."

Mr. Thorne hesitated and half-stumbled as he was leaving the room. I paused in the act of belting my robe. It was not like Mr. Thorne to commit an ungraceful movement. I realized that he too was getting old. He straightened the tray and dishes, nodded his head, and left for the kitchen.

I would not let thoughts of aging disturb me on such a beautiful morning. I felt charged with a new energy and resolve. The reunion the night before had not gone well but neither had it gone as badly as it might have. I had been honest with Nina and Willi about my intention of quitting the Game. In the weeks and months to come, they—or at least Nina—would begin to brood over the ramifications of that, but by the time they chose to react, separately or together, I would be long gone. Already I had new (and old) identities waiting for me in Florida, Michigan, London, southern France, and even in New Delhi. Michigan was out for the time being. I had grown unused to the harsh climate. New Delhi was no longer the hospitable place for foreigners it had been when I resided there briefly before the war.

Nina had been right about one thing—a return to Europe would be good for me. Already I longed for the rich light and cordial *savoir vivre* of the villagers near my old summer house outside of Toulon.

The air outside was bracing. I wore a simple print dress and my spring coat. The trace of arthritis in my right leg had bothered me coming down the stairs, but I used my father's old walking stick as a cane. A young Negro servant had cut it for Father the summer we moved from Greenville to Charleston. I smiled as we emerged into the warm air of the courtyard.

Mrs. Hodges came out of her doorway into the light. It was her grandchildren and their friends who were playing around the dry fountain. For two centuries the courtyard had been shared by the three brick buildings. Only my home had not been parceled into expensive town houses or fancy apartments.

"Good morning, Miz Fuller."

"Good morning, Mrs. Hodges. A beautiful day."

"It is that. Are you off shopping?"

"Just for a walk, Mrs. Hodges. I'm surprised that Mr. Hodges isn't out. He always seems to be working in the yard on Saturdays."

Mrs. Hodges frowned as one of the little girls ran between us. Her friend came squealing after her, sweater flying. "Oh, George is at the marina already."

"In the daytime?" I had often been amused by Mr. Hodges's departure for work in the evening; his security-guard uniform neatly pressed, gray hair jutting out from under his cap, black lunch pail gripped firmly under his arm.

Mr. Hodges was as leathery and bowlegged as an aged cowboy. He was one of those men who was always on the verge of retiring but who probably realized that to be inactive would be a form of death sentence.

"Oh, yes. One of those colored men on the day shift down at the storage building quit, and they asked George to fill in. I told him that he was too old to work four nights a week and then go back on the weekend, but you know George."

"Well, give him my best," I said. The girls running around the fountain made me nervous.

Mrs. Hodges followed me to the wrought-iron gate. "Will you be going away for the holidays, Miz Fuller?"

"Probably, Mrs. Hodges. Most probably." Then Mr. Thorne and I were out on the sidewalk and strolling toward the Battery. A few cars drove slowly down the narrow streets, tourists staring at the houses of our Old Section, but the day was serene and quiet. I saw the masts of the yachts and sailboats before we came in sight of the water as we emerged onto Broad Street.

"Please acquire tickets for us, Mr. Thorne," I said. "I believe I would like to see Fort Sumter."

As is typical of most people who live in close proximity to a popular tourist attraction, I had not taken notice of it for many years. It was an act of sentimentality to visit the fort now. An act brought on by my increasing acceptance of the fact that I would have to leave these parts forever. It is one thing to plan a move; it is something altogether different to be faced with the imperative reality of it.

There were few tourists. The ferry moved away from the marina and into the placid waters of the harbor. The combination of warm sunlight and the steady throb of the diesel caused me to doze briefly. I awoke as we were putting in at the dark hulk of the island fort.

For a while I moved with the tour group, enjoying the catacomb silences of the lower levels and the mindless singsong of the young woman from the Park Service. But as we came back to the museum, with its dusty dioramas and tawdry little trays of slides, I climbed the stairs back to the outer walls. I motioned for Mr. Thorne to stay at the top of the stairs and moved out onto the ramparts. Only one other couple—a young pair with a cheap camera and a baby in an uncomfortable-looking papoose carrier—were in sight along the wall.

It was a pleasant moment. A midday storm was approaching from the west and it set a dark backdrop to the still-sunlit church spires, brick towers, and bare branches of the city. Even from two miles away I could see the movement of people strolling along the Battery walkway. The wind was blowing in ahead of the dark clouds and tossing whitecaps against the rocking ferry and wooden dock. The air smelled of river and winter and rain by nightfall.

It was not hard to imagine that day long ago. The shells had dropped onto the fort until the upper layers were little more than protective piles of rubble. People had cheered from the rooftops behind the Battery. The bright colors of dresses and silk parasols must have been maddening to the Yankee gunners. Finally one had fired a shot above the crowded rooftops. The ensuing confusion must have been amusing from this vantage point.

A movement down below caught my attention. Something dark was sliding through the gray water—something dark and shark silent. I was jolted out of thoughts of the past as I recognized it as a Polaris submarine, old but obviously still operational, slipping through the dark water without a sound. Waves curled and rippled over the porpoise-smooth hull, sliding to either side in a white wake. There were several men on the dark tower. They were muffled in heavy coats, their hats pulled low. An improbably large pair of binoculars hung from the neck of one man, whom I assumed to be the captain. He pointed at something beyond Sullivan's Island. I stared at him. The periphery of my vision began to fade as I made contact. Sounds and sensations came to me as from a distance.

Tension. The pleasure of salt spray, breeze from the north-northwest. Anxiety of the sealed orders below. Awareness of the sandy shallows just coming into sight on the port side.

I was startled as someone came up behind me. The dots flickering at the edge of my vision fled as I turned. Mr. Thorne was there. At my elbow. Unbidden. I had opened my mouth to command him back to the top of the stairs when I saw the cause of his coming closer. The youth who had been taking pictures of his pale wife was now walking toward me. Mr. Thorne moved to intercept him.

"Hey, excuse me, ma'am. Would you or your husband mind taking our picture?"

I nodded and Mr. Thorne took the proffered camera. It looked minuscule in his long-fingered hands. Two snaps and the couple were satisfied that their presence there was documented for posterity. The young man grinned idiotically and bobbed his head. Their baby began to cry as the cold wind blew in.

I looked back to the submarine, but already it had passed on, its gray tower a thin stripe connecting the sea and sky.

We were almost back to town, the ferry was swinging in toward the slip, when a stranger told me of Willi's death.

"It's awful, isn't it?" The garrulous old woman had followed me out onto the exposed section of deck. Even though the wind had grown uncomfortably chilly and I had moved twice to escape her mindless chatter, the foolish woman had obviously chosen me as her conversational target for the final stages of the tour. Neither my reticence nor Mr. Thorne's glowering presence had discouraged her. "It must have been terrible," she continued. "In the dark and all."

"What was that?" A dark premonition prompted my question.

"Why, the airplane crash. Haven't you heard about it? It must have been awful, falling into the swamp and all. I told my daughter this morning . . ."

"What airplane crash? When?" The old woman cringed a bit at the sharpness of my tone, but the vacuous smile stayed on her face.

"Why last night. This morning I told my daughter . . ."

"Where? What aircraft?" Mr. Thorne came closer as he heard the tone of my voice.

"The one last night," she quavered. "The one from Charleston. The paper in the lounge told all about it. Isn't it terrible? Eighty-five people. I told my daughter . . ."

I left her there by the railing. There was a crumpled newspaper near the snack bar, and under the four-word headline were the sparse details of Willi's death. Flight 417, bound for Chicago, had left Charleston International Airport at twelve-eighteen A.M. Twenty minutes later the aircraft had exploded in midair not far from the city of Columbia. Fragments of fuselage and parts of bodies had fallen into Congaree Swamp, where night fishermen had found them. There had been no survivors. The FAA, NTSB and FBI were investigating.

There was a loud rushing in my ears, and I had to sit down or faint. My hands were clammy against the green vinyl upholstery. People moved past me on their way to the exits.

Willi was dead. Murdered. Nina had killed him. For a few dizzy seconds I considered the possibility of a conspiracy—an elaborate ploy by Nina and Willi to confuse me into thinking that only one threat remained. But no. There would be no reason. If Nina had included Willi in her plans, there would be no need for such absurd machinations.

Willi was dead. His remains were spread over a smelly, obscure marshland. It was all too easy to imagine his last moments. He would have been leaning back in first-class comfort, a drink in his hand, perhaps whispering to one of his loutish companions. Then the explosion. Screams. Sudden darkness. A brutal tilting and the final fall to oblivion. I shuddered and gripped the metal arm of the chair.

How had Nina done it? Almost certainly not one of Willi's entourage. It was not beyond Nina's powers to Use Willi's own catspaws, especially in light of his failing Ability, but there would have been no reason to do so. She could have Used anyone on that flight. It *would* have been difficult. The elaborate step of preparing the bomb. The supreme effort of blocking all memory of it, and the almost unbelievable feat of Using someone even as we sat together drinking coffee and brandy.

But Nina could have done it. Yes, she *could* have. And the timing. The timing could mean only one thing.

The last of the tourists had filed out of the cabin. I felt the slight bump that meant we had tied up to the dock. Mr. Thorne stood by the door.

Nina's timing meant that she was attempting to deal with both of us at once. She obviously had planned it long before the reunion and my timorous announcement of withdrawal. How amused Nina must have been. No wonder she had reacted so generously! Yet, she had made one great mistake. By dealing with Willi first, Nina had banked everything on my not hearing the news before she could turn on me. She knew that I had no access to daily news and only rarely left the house anymore. Still, it was unlike Nina to leave anything to chance. Was it possible that she thought I had lost the Ability completely and that Willi was the greater threat?

I shook my head as we emerged from the cabin into the gray afternoon light. The wind sliced at me through my thin coat. The view of the gangplank was blurry, and I realized that tears had filled my eyes. For Willi? He had been a pompous, weak old fool. For Nina's betrayal? Perhaps it was only the cold wind.

The streets of the Old Section were almost empty of pedestrians. Bare branches clicked together in front of the windows of fine homes. Mr. Thorne stayed by my side. The cold air sent needles of arthritic pain up my right leg to my hip. I leaned more heavily upon Father's walking stick.

What would her next move be? I stopped. A fragment of newspaper, caught by the wind, wrapped itself around my ankle and then blew on.

How would she come at me? Not from a distance. She was somewhere in town. I knew that. While it is possible to Use someone from a great distance, it would involve great rapport, an almost intimate knowledge of that person, and if contact were lost, it would be difficult if not impossible to reestablish at a distance. None of us had known why this was so. It did not matter now. But the thought of Nina still here, nearby, made my heart begin to thud.

Not from a distance. Whoever she used to come at me, I would see my assailant. If I knew Nina at all, I knew that. Certainly Willi's death had been the least personal Feeding imaginable, but that had been a mere technical operation. Nina obviously had decided to settle old scores with *me*, and Willie had become an obstacle to her, a minor but measurable threat that had to be eliminated before she could proceed. I could easily imagine that in Nina's own mind her choice of death for Willi would be interpreted as an act of compassion, almost a sign of affection. Not so with me. I felt that Nina would want me to know, however briefly, that she was behind the attack. In a sense, her own vanity would be my warning. Or so I hoped.

I was tempted to leave immediately. I could have Mr. Thorne get the Audi out of storage, and we could be beyond Nina's influence in an hour—away to a new life within a few more hours. There were important items in the house, of course, but the funds that I had stored elsewhere would replace most of them. It would be almost welcome to leave everything behind with the discarded identity that had accumulated them.

No. I could not leave. Not yet.

From across the street the house looked dark and malevolent. Had *I* closed those blinds on the second floor? There was a shadowy movement in the courtyard, and I saw Mrs. Hodges's granddaughter and a friend scamper from one doorway to another. I stood irresolutely on the curb and tapped father's stick against the black-barked tree. It was foolish to dither so—I knew it was—but it had been a long time since I had been forced to make a decision under stress.

"Mr. Thorne, please check the house. Look in each room. Return quickly."

A cold wind came up as I watched Mr. Thorne's black coat blend into the gloom of the courtyard. I felt terribly exposed standing there alone. I found myself glancing up and down the street, looking for Miss Kramer's dark hair, but the only sign of movement was a young woman pushing a perambulator far down the street.

The blinds on the second floor shot up and Mr. Thorne's face stared out whitely for a minute. Then he turned away and I remained staring at the dark rectangle of window. A shout from the courtyard startled me, but it was only the little girl—what was her name?—calling to her friend. Kathleen, that was it. The two sat on the edge of the fountain and opened a box of animal crackers. I stared intently at them and then relaxed. I even managed to smile a little at the extent of my paranoia. For a second I considered using Mr. Thorne directly, but the thought of being helpless on the street dissuaded me. When one is in complete contact, the senses still function but are a distant thing at best.

Hurry. The thought was sent almost without volition. Two bearded men were walking down the sidewalk on my side of the street. I crossed to stand in front of my own gate. The men were laughing and gesturing at each other. One looked over at me. *Hurry.*

Mr. Thorne came out of the house, locked the door behind him, and crossed the courtyard toward me. One of the girls said something to him and held out the box of crackers, but he ignored her. Across the street the two men continued walking. Mr. Thorne handed me the large front-door key. I dropped it in my coat pocket and looked sharply at him. He nodded. His placid smile unconsciously mocked my consternation.

"You're sure?" I asked. Again the nod. "You checked all of the rooms?" Nod. "The alarms?" Nod. "You looked in the basement?" Nod. "No sign of disturbance?" Mr. Thorne shook his head.

My hand went to the metal of the gate, but I hesitated. Anxiety filled my throat like bile. I was a silly old woman, tired and aching from the chill, but I could not bring myself to open that gate.

"Come." I crossed the street and walked briskly away

from the house. "We will have dinner at Henry's and return later." Only I was not walking toward the old restaurant; I was heading away from the house in what I knew was a blind, directionless panic. It was not until we reached the waterfront and were walking along the Battery wall that I began to calm down.

No one else was in sight. A few cars moved along the street, but to approach us someone would have to cross a wide, empty space. The gray clouds were quite low and blended with the choppy, white-crested waves in the bay.

The open air and fading evening light served to revive me and I began to think more clearly. Whatever Nina's plans had been, they almost certainly had been thrown into disarray by my day-long absence. I doubted that Nina would stay if there were the slightest risk to herself. No, she would be returning to New York by plane even as I stood shivering on the Battery walk. In the morning I would receive a telegram. I could almost imagine the precise wording: MELANIE ISN'T IT TERRIBLE ABOUT WILLI? TERRIBLY SAD. CAN YOU TRAVEL WITH ME TO THE FUNERAL? LOVE, NINA.

I began to realize that my hesitation had come from a desire to return to the warmth and comfort of my home. I simply had been afraid to shuck off this old cocoon. I could do so now. I would wait in a safe place while Mr. Thorne returned to the house to pick up the one thing I could not leave behind. Then he would get the car out of storage, and by the time Nina's telegram arrived I would be far away. It would be *Nina* who would be starting at shadows in the months and years to come. I smiled and began to frame the necessary commands.

"Melanie."

My head snapped around. Mr. Thorne had not spoken in twenty-eight years. He spoke now.

"Melanie." His face was distorted in a rictus grin that showed his back teeth. The knife was in his right hand. The blade flicked out as I stared. I looked into his empty gray eyes, and I knew.

"Melanie."

The long blade came around in a powerful arc. I could do nothing to stop it. It cut through the fabric of my coat sleeve and continued into my side. But in the act of turning, my purse had swung with me. The knife tore through the leather, ripped through the jumbled contents, pierced my coat, and drew blood above my lowest left rib. The purse had saved my life.

I raised Father's heavy walking stick and struck Mr. Thorne squarely in his left eye. He reeled but did not make a sound. Again he swept the air with the knife, but I had taken two steps back and his vision was clouded. I took a two-handed grip on the cane and swung again, bringing the stick around in an awkward chop. Incredibly, it again found the eye socket. I took three more steps back.

Blood streamed down the left side of Mr. Thorne's face and the damaged eye protruded onto his cheek. The rictus grin remained. His head came up, he raised his left hand slowly, plucked out the eye with a soft snapping of a gray cord, and threw it into the water of the bay. He came toward me. I turned and ran.

I *tried* to run. The ache in my right leg slowed me to a walk after twenty paces. Fifteen more hurried steps and my lungs were out of air, my heart threatening to burst. I could feel a wetness seeping down my left side and there was a tingling—like an ice cube held against the skin— where the knife blade had touched me. One glance back showed me that Mr. Thorne was striding toward me faster than I was moving. Normally he could have overtaken me in four strides. But it is hard to make someone run when you are Using him. Especially when that person's body is reacting to shock and trauma. I glanced back again, almost slipping on the slick pavement. Mr. Thorne was grinning widely. Blood poured from the empty socket and stained his teeth. No one else was in sight.

Down the stairs, clutching at the rail so as not to fall. Down the twisting walk and up the asphalt path to the street. Street lamps flickered and went on as I passed. Behind me Mr. Thorne took the steps in two jumps. As I hurried up the path, I thanked God that I had worn low-heel shoes for the boat ride. What would an observer think seeing this bizarre, slow-motion chase between two old people? There were no observers.

I turned onto a side street. Closed shops, empty warehouses. Going left would take me to Broad Street, but to the right, half a block away, a lone figure had emerged from a dark storefront. I moved that way, no longer able to run, close to fainting. The arthritic cramps in my leg hurt more than I could ever have imagined and threatened to collapse me on the sidewalk. Mr. Thorne was twenty paces behind me and quickly closing the distance.

The man I was approaching was a tall, thin Negro wearing a brown nylon jacket. He was carrying a box of what looked like framed sepia photographs. He glanced at me as I approached and then looked over my shoulder at the apparition ten steps behind.

"Hey!" The man had time to shout the single syllable and then I reached out with my mind and *shoved*. He twitched like a poorly handled marionette. His jaw dropped, his eyes glazed over, and he lurched past me just as Mr. Thorne reached for the back of my coat.

The box flew into the air and glass shattered on the brick sidewalk. Long, brown fingers reached for a white throat. Mr. Thorne backhanded him away, but the Negro clung tenaciously and the two swung around like awkward dance partners. I reached the opening to an alley and leaned my face against the cold brick to revive myself. The effort of concentration while Using this stranger did not afford me the luxury of resting even for a second.

I watched the clumsy stumblings of the two tall men and resisted an absurd impulse to laugh.

Mr. Thorne plunged the knife into the other's stomach, withdrew it, plunged it in again. The Negro's fingernails were clawing at Mr. Thorne's good eye now. Strong teeth were snapping in search of Mr. Thorne's jugular. I distantly sensed the cold intrusion of the blade for a third time, but the heart was still beating and he was still usable. The man jumped, scissoring his legs around Mr. Thorne's middle while his jaws closed on the muscular throat. Fingernails raked bloody streaks across white skin. The two went down in a tumble.

Kill him. Fingers groped for an eye, but Mr. Thorne reached up with his left hand and snapped the thin wrist. Limp fingers continued to flail. With a tremendous exertion, Mr. Thorne lodged his forearm against the other's

chest and lifted him bodily; the black man looking like a
child being tossed above his reclining Father. Teeth tore
away a piece of flesh, but there was no vital damage. Mr.
Thorne brought the knife between them, up, left, then
right. He severed half the Negro's throat with the second
swing, and blood fountained over both of them. The
smaller man's legs spasmed twice, Mr. Thorne threw him
to one side, and I turned and walked quickly down the alley.

Out into the light again, the fading evening light, and
I realized that I had run myself into a dead end. Backs of
warehouses and the windowless, metal side of the Battery
Marina pushed right up against the waters of the bay. A
street wound away to the left, but it was dark, deserted,
and far too long to try.

I looked back in time to see the black silhouette enter
the alley behind me.

I tried to make contact, but there was nothing there.
Nothing. Mr. Thorne might as well have been a hole in the
air. I would worry later how Nina had done this thing.

The side door to the marina was locked. The main
door was almost a hundred yards away and would also be
locked. Mr. Thorne emerged from the alley and swung his
head left and right in search of me. In the dim light his
heavily streaked face looked almost black. He began
lurching toward me.

I raised Father's walking stick, broke the lower pane of
the window, and reached in through the jagged shards. If
there was a bottom or top bolt I was dead. There was a
simple doorknob lock and crossbolt. My fingers slipped on
the cold metal, but the bolt slid back as Mr. Thorne
stepped up on the walk behind me. Then I was inside and
throwing the bolt.

It was very dark. Cold seeped up from the concrete
floor and there was a sound of many boats rising and falling at their moorings. Fifty yards away, light spilled out of
the office windows. I had hoped there would be an alarm
system, but the building was too old and the marina too
cheap to have one. I began to move toward the light as Mr.
Thorne's forearm shattered the remaining glass in the door
behind me. The arm withdrew. A tremendous kick broke

off the top hinge and splintered wood around the bolt. I glanced at the office, but only the sound of a radio talk show came out of the impossibly distant door. Another kick.

I turned to my right and stepped to the bow of a bobbing inboard cruiser. Five steps and I was in the small, covered space that passed for a forward cabin. I closed the flimsy access panel behind me and peered out through the streaked Plexiglas.

Mr. Thorne's third kick sent the door flying inward, dangling from long strips of splintered wood. His dark form filled the doorway. Light from a distant streetlight glinted off the blade in his right hand.

Please. Please hear the noise. But there was no movement from the office, only the metallic voices from the radio. Mr. Thorne took four paces, paused, and stepped down onto the first boat in line. It was an open outboard and he was back up on the concrete in six seconds. The second boat had a small cabin. There was a ripping sound as Mr. Thorne kicked open the tiny hatch door and then he was back up on the walkway. My boat was the eighth in line. I wondered why he couldn't just hear the wild hammering of my heart.

I shifted position and looked through the starboard port. The murky Plexiglas threw the light into streaks and patterns. I caught a brief glimpse of white hair through the window, and the radio was switched to another station. Loud music echoed in the long room. I slid back to the other porthole. Mr. Thorne was stepping off the fourth boat.

I closed my eyes, forced my ragged breathing to slow, and tried to remember countless evenings watching a bow-legged old figure shuffle down the street. Mr. Thorne finished his inspection of the fifth boat, a longer cabin cruiser with several dark recesses, and pulled himself back onto the walkway.

Forget the coffee in the thermos. Forget the crossword puzzle. Go look!

The sixth boat was a small outboard. Mr. Thorne glanced at it but did not step onto it. The seventh was a low sailboat, mast folded down, canvas stretched across the cockpit. Mr. Thorne's knife slashed through the thick material. Blood-streaked hands pulled back the canvas like a shroud being torn away. He jumped back to the walkway.

Forget the coffee. Go look! Now!

Mr. Thorne stepped onto the bow of my boat. I felt it rock to his weight. There was nowhere to hide, only a tiny storage locker under the seat, much too small to squeeze into. I untied the canvas strips that held the seat cushion to the bench. The sound of my ragged breathing seemed to echo in the little space. I curled into a fetal position behind the cushion as Mr. Thorne's leg moved past the starboard port. *Now.* Suddenly his face filled the Plexiglas strip not a foot from my head. His impossibly wide grimace grew even wider. *Now.* He stopped into the cockpit.

Now. Now. Now.

Mr. Thorne crouched at the cabin door. I tried to brace the tiny louvered door with my legs, but my right leg would not obey. Mr. Thorne's fist slammed through the thin wooden strips and grabbed my ankle.

"Hey there!"

It was Mr. Hodges's shaky voice. His flashlight bobbed in our direction.

Mr. Thorne shoved against the door. My left leg folded painfully. Mr. Thorne's left hand firmly held my ankle through the shattered slats while the hand with the knife blade came through the opening hatch.

"Hey!" cried Mr. Hodges and then my mind shoved. Very hard. The old man stopped. He dropped the flashlight and unstrapped the safety strap over the grip of his revolver.

Mr. Thorne slashed the knife back and forth. The cushion was almost knocked out of my hands as shreds of foam filled the cabin. The blade caught the tip of my little finger as the knife swung back again.

Do it. Now. Do it.

Mr. Hodges gripped the revolver in both hands and fired. The shot went wide in the dark as the sound echoed off concrete and water. *Closer, you fool. Move!*

Mr. Thorne shoved again and his body squeezed into the open hatch. He released my ankle to free his left arm, but almost instantly his hand was back in the cabin, grasping for me. I reached up and turned on the overhead light. Darkness stared at me from his empty eye socket. Light through the broken shutters spilled yellow strips across his ruined face. I slid to the left, but Mr. Thorne's hand, which had my coat, was pulling me off the bench. He was on his knees, freeing his right hand for the knife thrust.

Now! Mr. Hodges's second shot caught Mr. Thorne in the right hip. He grunted as the impact shoved him backward into a sitting position. My coat ripped, and buttons rattled on the deck.

The knife slashed the bulkhead near my ear before it pulled away.

Mr. Hodges stepped shakily onto the bow, almost fell, and inched his way around the starboard side. I pushed the hatch against Mr. Thorne's arm, but he continued to grip my coat and drag me toward him. I fell to my knees. The blade swung back, ripped through foam, and slashed at my coat. What was left of the cushion flew out of my hands. I had Mr. Hodges stop four feet away and brace the gun on the roof of the cabin.

Mr. Thorne pulled the blade back and poised it like a matador's sword. I could sense the silent scream of triumph that poured out over the stained teeth like a noxious vapor. The light of Nina's madness burned behind the single, staring eye.

Mr. Hodges fired. The bullet severed Mr. Thorne's spine and continued on into the port scupper. Mr. Thorne arched backward, splayed out his arms, and flopped onto the deck like a great fish that had just been landed. The knife fell to the floor of the cabin, while stiff, white fingers continued to slap nervelessly against the deck. I had Mr. Hodges step forward, brace the muzzle against Mr. Thorne's temple just above the remaining eye, and fire again. The sound was muted and hollow.

There was a first-aid kit in the office bathroom. I had the old man stand by the door while I bandaged my little finger and took three aspirin.

My coat was ruined, and blood had stained my print

dress. I had never cared very much for the dress—I
thought it made me look dowdy—but the coat had been a
favorite of mine. My hair was a mess. Small, moist bits of
gray matter flecked it. I splashed water on my face and
brushed my hair as best I could. Incredibly, my tattered
purse had stayed with me although many of the contents
had spilled out. I transferred keys, billfold, reading glasses,
and Kleenex to my large coat pocket and dropped the
purse behind the toilet. I no longer had Father's walking
stick, but I could not remember where I had dropped it.

Gingerly I removed the heavy revolver from Mr.
Hodges's grip. The old man's arm remained extended, fingers curled around air. After fumbling for a few seconds I
managed to click open the cylinder. Two cartridges remained unfired. The old fool had been walking around
with all six chambers loaded! *Always leave an empty
chamber under the hammer.* That is what Charles had
taught me that gay and distant summer so long ago when
such weapons were merely excuses for trips to the island
for target practice punctuated by the shrill shrieks of our
nervous laughter as Nina and I allowed ourselves to be
held, arms supported, bodies shrinking back into the firm
support of our so-serious tutors' arms. *One must always
count the cartridges*, lectured Charles, as I half-swooned
against him, smelling the sweet, masculine shaving soap
and tobacco smell rising from him on that warm, bright
day.

Mr. Hodges stirred slightly as my attention wandered.
His mouth gaped open and his dentures hung loosely. I
glanced at the worn leather belt, but there were no extra
bullets there and I had no idea where he kept any. I
probed, but there was little left in the old man's jumble of
thoughts except for a swirling tape-loop replay of the muzzle being laid against Mr. Thorne's temple, the explosion,
the . . .

"Come," I said. I adjusted the glasses on Mr. Hodges's
vacant face, returned the revolver to the holster, and let
him lead me out of the building.

It was very dark out. We moved from streetlight to
streetlight. We had gone six blocks before the old man's
violent shivering reminded me that I had forgotten to have

him put on his coat. I tightened my mental vise, and he stopped shaking.

The house looked just as it had ... my God ... only forty-five minutes earlier. There were no lights. I let us into the courtyard and searched my overstuffed coat pocket for the key. My coat hung loose and the cold night air nipped at me. From behind lighted windows across the courtyard came the laughter of little girls, and I hurried so that Kathleen would not see her grandfather entering my house.

Mr. Hodges went in first, with the revolver extended. I had him switch on the light before I entered.

The parlor was empty, undisturbed. The light from the chandelier in the dining room reflected off polished surfaces. I sat down for a minute on the Williamsburg reproduction chair in the hall to let my heart rate return to normal. I did not have Mr. Hodges lower the hammer on the still-raised pistol. His arm began to shake from the strain of holding it. Finally I rose and we moved down the hall toward the conservatory.

Miss Kramer exploded out of the swinging door from the kitchen with the heavy iron poker already coming down in an arc. The gun fired harmlessly into the polished floor as the old man's arm snapped from the impact. The gun fell from limp fingers as Miss Kramer raised the poker for a second blow.

I turned and ran back down the hallway. Behind me I heard the crushed-melon sound of the poker contacting Mr. Hodges's skull. Rather than run into the courtyard I went up the stairway. A mistake. Miss Kramer bounded up the stairs and reached the bedroom door only a few seconds after me. I caught one glimpse of her widened, maddened eyes and of the upraised poker before I slammed and locked the heavy door. The latch clicked just as the brunette on the other side began to throw herself against the wood. The thick oak did not budge. Then I heard the concussion of metal against the door and frame. Again. Again.

Cursing my stupidity, I turned to the familiar room, but there was nothing there to help me, not even a telephone. There was not as much as a closet to hide in, only the antique wardrobe. I moved quickly to the window and threw up the sash. My screams would attract attention but not before that monstrosity had gained access. She was prying at the edges of the door now. I looked out, saw the shadows in the windows across the way, and did what I had to do.

Two minutes later I was barely conscious of the wood giving away around the latch. I heard the distant grating of the poker as it pried at the recalcitrant metal plate. The door swung inward.

Miss Kramer was covered with sweat. Her mouth hung slack and drool slid from her chin. Her eyes were not human. Neither she nor I heard the soft tread of sneakers on the stairs behind her.

Keep moving. Lift it. Pull it back—all the way back. Use both hands. Aim it.

Something warned Miss Kramer. Warned Nina, I should say, for there was no more Miss Kramer. The brunette turned to see little Kathleen standing on the top stair, her grandfather's heavy weapon aimed and cocked. The other girl was in the courtyard shouting for her friend.

This time Nina knew she had to deal with the threat. Miss Kramer hefted the poker and turned into the hall just as the pistol fired. The recoil tumbled Kathleen backward down the stairs as a red corsage blossomed above Miss Kramer's left breast. She spun but grasped the railing with her left hand and lurched down the stairs after the child. I released the ten-year-old just as the poker fell, rose, fell again. I moved to the head of the stairway. I had to *see*.

Miss Kramer looked up from her grim work. Only the whites of her eyes were visible in her spattered face. Her masculine shirt was soaked with her own blood, but still she moved, functioned. She picked up the gun in her left hand. Her mouth opened wider, and a sound emerged like steam leaking from an old radiator.

"Melanie . . ." I closed my eyes as the thing started up the stairs for me.

Kathleen's friend came in through the open door, her small legs pumping. She took the stairs in six jumps and wrapped her thin, white arms around Miss Kramer's neck in a tight embrace.

The two went over backward, across Kathleen, all the way down the wide stairs to the polished wood below.

The girl appeared to be little more than bruised. I went down and moved her to one side. A blue stain was spreading along one cheekbone, and there were cuts on her arms and forehead. Her blue eyes blinked uncomprehendingly.

Miss Kramer's neck was broken. I picked up the pistol on the way to her and kicked the poker to one side. Her head was at an impossible angle but she was still alive. Her body was paralyzed, urine already stained the wood, but her eyes still blinked and her teeth clicked together obscenely. I had to hurry. There were adult voices calling from the Hodges's town house. The door to the courtyard was wide open. I turned to the girl. "Get up." She blinked once and rose painfully to her feet.

I shut the door and lifted a tan raincoat from the coatrack. It took only a minute to transfer the contents of my pockets to the raincoat and to discard my ruined spring coat. Voices were calling in the courtyard now.

I knelt down next to Miss Kramer and seized her face in my hands, exerting strong pressure to keep the jaws still. Her eyes had rolled upward again, but I shook her head until the irises were visible. I leaned forward until our cheeks were touching. My whisper was louder than a shout.

"I'm coming for you, Nina."

I dropped her head onto the wood and walked quickly to the conservatory, my sewing room. I did not have time to get the key from upstairs, so I raised a Windsor side chair and smashed the glass of the cabinet. My coat pocket was barely large enough.

The girl remained standing in the hall. I handed her Mr. Hodges's pistol. Her left arm hung at a strange angle and I wondered if she had broken something after all. There was a knock at the door and someone tried the knob.

"This way," I whispered, and led the girl into the dining room.

We stepped across Miss Kramer on the way, walked through the dark kitchen as the pounding grew louder, and then were out, into the alley, into the night.

• • •

There were three hotels in this part of the Old Section. One was an expensive but modern motor hotel some ten blocks away, comfortable but commercial. I rejected it immediately. The second was a small, but homey lodging house only a block from my home. It was a pleasant but nonexclusive little place, exactly the type I would choose when visiting another town. I rejected it also. The third was two and a half blocks farther on, an old Broad Street mansion done over into a small hotel, expensive antiques in every room, absurdly overpriced. I hurried there. The girl moved quickly at my side. The pistol was still in her hand, but I had her remove her sweater and carry it over the weapon. My leg ached and I frequently leaned on the girl as we hurried down the street.

The manager of the Mansard House recognized me. His eyebrow went up a fraction of an inch as he noticed my disheveled appearance. The girl stood ten feet away in the foyer, half-hidden in the shadows.

"I'm looking for a friend of mine," I said brightly. "A Mrs. Drayton."

The manager started to speak, paused, frowned without being aware of it, and tried again. "I'm sorry. No one under that name is registered here."

"Perhaps she registered under her maiden name," I said. "Nina Hawkins. She's an older woman but very attractive. A few years younger than me. Long gray hair. Her friend may have registered for her . . . a young, dark-haired lady named Barrett Kramer . . ."

"No, I'm sorry," said the manager in a strangely flat tone. "No one under that name has registered. Would you like to leave a message in case your party arrives later?"

"No," I said. "No message."

I brought the girl into the lobby, and we turned down a corridor leading to the restrooms and side stairs. "Excuse me, please," I said to a passing porter. "Perhaps you can help me."

"Yes, ma'am." He stopped, annoyed, and brushed back his long hair. It would be tricky. If I was not to lose the girl, I would have to act quickly.

"I'm looking for a friend," I said. "She's an older lady but quite attractive. Blue eyes. Long, gray hair. She travels with a young woman who has dark, curly hair."

"No, ma'am. No one like that is registered here."

I reached out and held his forearm tightly. I released the girl and focused on the boy. "Are you sure?"

"Mrs. Harrison," he said. His eyes looked past me. "Room 207. North front."

I smiled. *Mrs. Harrison.* Good God, what a fool Nina was. Suddenly the girl let out a small whimper and slumped against the wall. I made a quick decision. I like to think that it was compassion, but I sometimes remember that her left arm was useless.

"What's your name?" I asked the child, gently stroking her hair. Her eyes moved left and right in confusion. "Your *name*," I prompted.

"Alicia." It was only a whisper.

"All right, Alicia. I want you to go home now. Hurry, but don't run."

"My *arm* hurts," she said. Her lips began to quiver. I touched her forehead again and *pushed.*

"You're going home," I said. "Your arm does not hurt. You won't remember anything. This is like a dream that you will forget. Go home. Hurry, but do not run." I took the pistol from her but left it wrapped in the sweater. "Bye-bye, Alicia."

She blinked and crossed the lobby to the door. I handed the gun to the bellhop. "Put it under your vest," I said.

"Who is it?" Nina's voice was light.

"Albert, ma'am. The porter. Your car's out front and I'm ready to carry your bags down."

There was the sound of a lock clicking and the door opened the width of a still-secured chain. Albert blinked in the glare, smiled shyly, and brushed his hair back. I pressed against the wall.

"Very well." She undid the chain and moved back. She had already turned and was latching her suitcase when I stepped into the room.

"Hello, Nina," I said softly. Her back straightened, but even that move was graceful. I could see the imprint on the bedspread where she had been lying. She turned slowly. She was wearing a pink dress I had never seen before.

"Hello, Melanie." She smiled. Her eyes were the softest, purest blue I had ever seen. I had the porter take Mr. Hodges's gun out and aim it. His arm was steady. He pulled back the hammer until it locked in place. Nina folded her hands in front of her. Her eyes never left mine.

"Why?" I asked.

Nina shrugged ever so slightly. For a second I thought she was going to laugh. I could not have borne it had she laughed—that husky, childlike laugh that had touched me so many times. Instead she closed her eyes. Her smile remained.

"Why Mrs. Harrison?" I asked.

"Why, darling, I felt I owed him *something*. I mean, poor Roger. Did I ever tell you how he died? No, of course I didn't. And you never asked, Melanie dear." Her eyes opened. I glanced at the porter, but his aim was steady. It only remained for him to exert a little more pressure on the trigger.

"He *drowned*, darling," said Nina. "Poor Roger threw himself from that steamship—what was its name?—the one that was taking him back to England. So strange. And he had just written me a letter promising marriage. Isn't that a *terribly* sad story, Melanie? Why do you think he did a thing like that? I guess we'll never know, will we?"

"I guess we never will," I said. I silently ordered the porter to pull the trigger.

Nothing.

I looked quickly to my right. The young man's head was turning toward me. *I had not made him do that.* The stiffly extended arm began to swing in my direction. The pistol moved smoothly like the tip of a weather vane swinging in the wind.

No! I strained until the cords in my neck stood out. The turning slowed but did not stop until the muzzle was pointing at my face. Nina laughed now. The sound was very loud in the little room.

"Good-bye, Melanie *dear*," Nina said, and laughed again. She laughed and nodded at the porter. I stared into the black hole as the hammer fell.

On an empty chamber. And another. And another.

"Good-bye, Nina," I said as I pulled Charles's long pistol from my raincoat pocket. The explosion jarred my wrist and filled the room with blue smoke. A small hole, smaller than a dime but as perfectly round, appeared in the precise center of Nina's forehead. For the briefest second she remained standing as if nothing had happened. Then she fell backward, recoiled from the high bed, and dropped face forward onto the floor.

I turned to the porter and replaced his useless weapon with the ancient but well-maintained revolver. For the first time I noticed that the boy was not much younger than Charles had been. His hair was almost exactly the same color. I leaned forward and kissed him lightly on the lips.

"Albert," I whispered, "there are four cartridges left. One must always count the cartridges, mustn't one? Go to the lobby. Kill the manager. Shoot one other person, the nearest. Put the barrel in your mouth and pull the trigger. If it misfires, pull it again. Keep the gun concealed until you are in the lobby."

We emerged into general confusion in the hallway.

"Call for an ambulance!" I cried. "There's been an accident. Someone call for an ambulance!" Several people rushed to comply. I swooned and leaned against a white-haired gentleman. People milled around, some peering into the room and exclaiming. Suddenly there was the sound of three gunshots from the lobby. In the renewed confusion I slipped down the back stairs, out the fire door, into the night.

Time has passed. I am very happy here. I live in southern France now, between Cannes and Toulon, but not, I am happy to say, too near St. Tropez.

I rarely go out. Henri and Claude do my shopping in the village. I never go to the beach. Occasionally I go to the townhouse in Paris or to my pensione in Italy, south of

Pescara, on the Adriatic. But even those trips have become less and less frequent.

There is an abandoned abbey in the hills behind my home, and I sometimes go there to sit and think among the stones and wild flowers. I think about isolation and abstinence and how each is so cruelly dependent upon the other.

I feel younger these days. I tell myself that this is because of the climate and my freedom and not as a result of that final Feeding. But sometimes I dream about the familiar streets of Charleston and the people there. They are dreams of hunger.

On some days I rise to the sound of singing as girls from the village cycle by our place on their way to the dairy. On those days the sun is marvelously warm as it shines on the small white flowers growing between the tumbled stones of the abbey, and I am content simply to be there and to share the sunlight and silence with them.

But on other days—cold, dark days when the clouds move in from the north—I remember the shark-silent shape of a submarine moving through the dark waters of the bay, and I wonder whether my self-imposed abstinence will be for nothing. I wonder whether those I dream of in my isolation will indulge in their own gigantic, final Feeding.

It is warm today. I am happy. But I am also alone. And I am very, very hungry.

- Here is a preview of

THE HOLLOW MAN
by Dan Simmons

Coming in hardcover in August 1992

• • • • • • •

Dan Simmons has tried something different—and succeeded—with every book he has written. From *Song of Kali*, which won the World Fantasy Award, to *Hyperion*, which received the Hugo Award for Best Science Fiction Novel, to *Carrion Comfort*, named best novel of the year by the Horror Writers of America, he has explored new landscapes and won new readers with every book.

Now comes *The Hollow Man*, which draws together elements of fantasy, science fiction, horror, and some of the world's finest literature. Here is what Mr. Simmons has to say about his upcoming novel:

"*The Hollow Man* is a labor of love which—like so many labors of love—proved to be back-breaking, gut-wrenching, and mind-bending. On the surface, the story is a simple one about a traumatized telepath wandering America after the death of his wife. *"Wandering between two worlds, one dead/ The other powerless to be born"* which so obsessed Dante, Thomas Aquinas, T.S. Eliot, and Joseph Conrad. Besides committing the hubris of dealing with themes suggested by these literary geniuses, I found myself wrestling with such contemporary concepts as chaos mathematics and how it applies to the human mind. The result was a unique, exhilarating, and often terrifying intellectual ride for the writer, and I hope it will prove such for the reader."

• • • • • •

At the Violet Hour

A little over half of Bremen's remaining money would buy him a bus ticket to Denver. He bought it and slept in the park across from the Hyatt where he had dumped the Goofy suit. The bus departed Orlando at 11:15 that night. He waited until the last minute to board, coming in through a maintenance entrance and walking straight to the bus, his head down and collar up. He saw no one who looked like a gangster; more importantly, the surge and rasp of neurobabble had not been punctuated by the shock of recognition from any of the bystanders.

By one A.M. they were halfway to Gainesville and Bremen began to relax, watching out the window at the closed stores and mercury vapor lamps lining the streets of Ocala and a dozen smaller towns. The neurobabble was less this late at night. For years Bremen and Gail had been convinced that much of the effect of the so-called circadian rhythm on human beings was nothing more than nascent telepathy in most people sensing the national dream sleep around them. It was very hard to stay awake this night, although Bremen's nerves were jumping and twitching with the ricocheting thoughts of those two dozen or so people still awake aboard the bus. The dreams of the others added to the mental din, although dreams were deeper, more private theaters of the mind, and not nearly so accessible.

Bremen thanked God for that.

They were on Interstate 75 and headed north out of Gainesville when Bremen began to ponder his situation.

Why hadn't he gone back to the fishing shack? Somehow his home of the past three days seemed like the only haven in the world for him now. Why hadn't he returned ... for his money if nothing else?

Bremen knew that part of it was that it seemed almost certain that Vanni Fucci or Sal Empori or some of their cronies would be watching the place. And Bremen had no desire to get Norm Sr. or the old man Verge in trouble with gangsters on his account.

He thought of the rental car parked there. But Verge or Norm Sr. would have found him missing by now. And found the money in the cabin. That would certainly settle the bill with the rental people. Would Norm Sr. call the police about his disappearance? Unlikely. And what if he did? Bremen had never given his name, never shown his driver's license. The two men had respected Bremen's privacy to the extent that there was little they could tell the police about him other than his description.

A more practical reason for Bremen not returning there was simply that he did not know the way. He knew only that the fishing shack was somewhere closer to Miami than to Orlando, on the edge of a lake and a swamp. Bremen thought about phoning Norm Sr. from Denver, asking that the bulk of the money be wired to a P.O. box in Denver, but he remembered seeing no name on the little store and Norm Sr. had never thought of his own last name when Bremen was eavesdropping. The refuge of the fishing shack was lost forever.

It was only two hundred and fifty–some miles from Orlando to Tallahassee, but it was after five A.M. by the time the bus pulled through the rain-silent streets of the capital and hissed to a stop. "Rest break!" called the driver, and quickly disembarked. Bremen lay back in his seat and dozed until the others reboarded. He already knew his fellow passengers very well and their return echoed in his skull like shouts in a metal pipe. The bus pulled out at 5:42 A.M. and leisurely found its way back to Interstate 10 West while Bremen squeezed his temples and tried to concentrate on his own dreams.

Two rows behind him sat a young marine, Burk Stemens, and a young WAF sergeant named Alice Jean Dernitz. They had not met until boarding the bus in Orlando, but they were quickly becoming more than friends. Neither had slept much during the past seven hours; each had told the other more about his or her life than either had ever revealed to their mates, past or present. Burk had just gotten out of fourteen months in the brig for assaulting a noncommissioned officer with a knife. He had traded a dishonorable discharge from the marines for the final four months of his sentence and was now on his way home to Fort Worth to see his wife, Debra Anne, and his two infants. He did not tell Alice Jean about Debra Anne.

Sergeant Dernitz was two months away from a quite honorable discharge from the air force and was spending the bulk of that time on leave. She had been married twice, the last time to the brother of her first husband. She had divorced the first brother, Warren Bill, and lost the second, William Earl, four months ago; he had been killed when his Mustang went off a Tennessee mountain road at eighty-five miles per hour. Alice Jean hadn't cared too much by then. She and brother number two had been separated for almost a year before the accident. She did not tell Burk about either Warren Bill or the late William Earl.

Burk and Alice Jean had been inching toward intimacy since Gainesville, and by Lake City, just before I-75 encountered I-10, they had ceased swapping barracks stories and gotten down to the business at hand. As they passed Lake City Alice Jean was pretending to nap and had let her head fall on Burk's shoulder, while Burk had put his arm around her and let his hand "accidently" fall to her left breast.

By the suburbs of Tallahassee both were breathing shallowly, Burk's hand was inside her blouse, and Alice Jean's hand was on Burk's lap under the jacket he had spread like a robe across both of them. She had just unzipped his pants when the driver announced the rest break.

Bremen had been prepared to spend the rest break in the tiny bus station rather than suffer the next stage of their slow and painful foreplay, but luckily Burk had whispered in Alice Jean's ear and both had left the bus, Burk holding his jacket rather clumsily in front of himself. They had thoughts of trying their luck in a storeroom or . . . if all else failed . . . in the ladies' rest room.

Bremen tried to doze with the other sleeping passengers aboard the bus, but Burk and Alice Jean's contortions—it had been the ladies' rest room—assaulted him even from a distance. Their love-making was as banal and short-lived as their loyalty to their current and former mates.

By the time the bus was approaching Pensacola it was almost ten A.M. and everyone aboard was awake and the highway sounds had taken on a new timbre. Storm clouds lay heavy in the west, the direction they were headed, but a thick, low light from the east painted the fields on either side in rich hues and threw the shadow of their bus ahead of them. The neurobabble was much louder than the hiss of tires on asphalt.

Across the aisle and three rows ahead of Bremen were a couple from Missouri. As far as Bremen could sort out, their names were Donnie and Donna. He was very drunk; she was very pregnant. Both were in their early twenties, although from the glimpses Bremen got through the seats ahead—and occasionally from Donnie's perception—Donna looked at least fifty. The two were not married, although Donna considered their four-year relationship a common-law marriage. Donnie didn't think of it that way.

The couple had been on a seventeen-day odyssey across the nation trying to find the best place to have the baby and while having welfare pay for it. They had ricocheted east from St. Louis to Columbus, Ohio, on the advice of a Missouri friend, had found Columbus no more generous in its welfare policies than St. Louis, and then had started on an endless series of bus trips—charging it all to Donna's sister's husband's borrowed credit card—going from Columbus to Pittsburgh, Pittsburgh to Washington, D.C. . . . where they were shocked at how poorly the nation's capital treated its deserving citizens . . . and then from Washington to Huntsville because of something they had read in the *National Enquirer* about Huntsville being one of the ten friendliest cities in America.

Huntsville had been terrible. The hospitals would not even *admit* Donna unless it was an emergency or proof of their ability to pay was shown in advance. Donnie had started drinking in earnest in Huntsville and had dragged Donna out of the hospital while shaking his fist and hurling curses at doctors, administrators, nurses, and even at a cluster of patients staring from their wheelchairs.

The trip to Orlando had been bad, with the credit card approaching its max and Donna saying that she was definitely feeling contractions now, but Donnie had never seen Walt Disney World and he figured that they were close, so what the hell?

Brother-in-law Dickie's card lasted long enough to get them into the Magic Kingdom, and Bremen noticed through Donnie's drunken memories that the two had been there while he had been fleeing Vanni Fucci. Small world. Bremen pressed his cheek and temple to the glass hard enough to drive thoughts away, to form a barrier between these new wavelengths of foreign thoughts and his own bruised mind.

It did not work.

Donnie hadn't enjoyed the Magic Kingdom much, even though he'd waited his whole life to go there, because goddamn spoilsport Donna refused to go on any of the real rides with him. She'd ruined his fun by standing, ponderous as a cow heavy with two heifers, and waving as he'd boarded Space Mountain and Splash Mountain and all the fun rides. She'd said it was because her water broke an hour after coming into the park, but Donnie knew it was mostly to spite him.

She'd insisted on going into Orlando that evening, saying the pains were starting in earnest now, but Donnie had left her wedged in one of the TV chairs in the bus station while he checked out the hospitals by phone. They were worse than Huntsville or Atlanta or St. Louis about their payment policies.

Donnie had used the last of Dickie's credit card to get them tickets from Orlando to Oklahoma City. A toothless old fart sitting near the phone banks in the bus station had overheard Donnie's angry queries on the phone and—after Donnie had slammed the phone down for the last time—had suggested Oklahoma City. "Best goddamn place in the goddamn country to get born for free," the old fart had said, showing an expanse of gums. "Had me two sisters and one of my wives who calved there. Them Oklahoma City hospitals just put it on Medicare and don't bother you none."

So they were off to Houston with connecting tickets for Fort Worth and Oklahoma City. Donna was whimpering more than a little now, saying that the contractions were just a few minutes apart, but as Donnie drank more sour mash he grew increasingly certain that she was lying just to ruin his trip.

Donna was not lying.

Bremen felt her pain as if it were his own. He had timed the contractions with his watch, and they had moved from almost seven minutes apart in Tallahassee to less than two minutes separating them by the time they crossed the state line into Alabama. Donna would whimper at Donnie, tugging at his sleeve in the dark and hissing invective, but he would shove her away. He was busy talking with the man across the aisle, Meredith Soloman, the toothless old fart who had suggested Oklahoma City. Donnie had shared his sour mash until Gainesville, and Meredith Soloman had shared his own flask of something even stronger from there onward.

Just before the tunnel to Mobile, Donna had said, loud enough for the entire bus to hear, "Goddamn you to hell, Donnie Ackley, if you're gonna make me drop this goddamn kid here on this bus, at least give me a swig of what you're drinkin' with that toothless old fart."

Donnie had shushed her, knowing they'd be thrown off the bus if the driver heard too much about the drinking, had apologized to Meredith Soloman, and had let her drink heavily from the flask. Incredibly, her contractions slowed and returned to pre-Tallahassee intervals. Donna fell asleep, her dimmed consciousness rising and falling on the waves of cramping that flowed through her for the next few hours.

Donnie continued to apologize to Meredith Soloman, but the old man had shown his gums again, reached into his soiled ditty bag, and brought out another unlabeled bottle of white lightning.

Donnie and Meredith took turns drinking the fierce booze and sharing views on the worst way to die.

Meredith Soloman was sure that a cave-in or gas explosion was the worst way to go. As long as it didn't kill you right away. It was the layin' there and waitin', in the cold and dank and dark a mile beneath the surface with the helmet lights fadin' and the air getting foul . . . that had to be the worst way to go. He should know, Meredith Soloman explained, since he'd worked in the deep mines of West Virginia as man and boy long before Donnie'd been born. Meredith's pap had died down in the mines, as had his brother Tucker and his brother-in-law Phillip P. Argent. Meredith allowed as how it was a terrible shame about his pap and brother Tucker, but no cave-in had served humanity better than the one that took that low-life, foulmouthed, mean-spirited Phillip P. in 1972. As for sixty-eight-year-old Meredith Soloman, he'd been caved in on three times and blown up twice, but they'd always dug him out. Each time, though, he'd sworn he was never goin' down again . . . no one could make him go down again. Not his wives . . . he'd had four, one after the other, y'understand, even the young things don't last too long back in the hollers of West Virginia, what with pneumonia and childbirth and all . . . not his wives, or his kin . . . real kin, not bastards-in-law like Phillip P. . . . nor even his own children, them grown up nor them still in bare feet, could talk him into goin' back down.

But he did, finally, talk himself into goin' back down. And he'd continued goin' down until the company its own self made him retire early at age fifty-nine just because his lungs were filling up with coal dust. Well, *hell*, he explained to Donnie Ackley as they passed the bottle back and forth, everybody who worked down there had lungs clogged black like one of them old Hoover vacuum bags that hadn't been changed in years, everyone knew that.

Donnie disagreed. Donnie thought that dying underground in a cave-in or gas explosion wasn't nearly the worst way to go. Donnie started listing terrible ways he'd seen and been around. The time when that biker, Jack Coe, the one him and the others called the Hog, had been working for the highway department and had rolled backward off his mower on an incline and gone under the blades. Jack Coe'd lived on in the hospital for another three months until pneumonia'd got *him*, but Donnie didn't hardly call it living what with the paralysis and the drooling and all the tubes carrying stuff into him and carrying stuff out.

Then there'd been Donnie's first girlfriend, Farah, who'd gone down into niggertown to a bar and gotten gang-raped by a bunch of black bucks who ended up using things other than their dicks on her—their fists and broom handles and Coke bottles and even the sharp end of a tire iron, according to Farah's sister—and . . .

"Don't tell me she died a gettin' raped," said Meredith Soloman, leaning across the aisle and taking the bottle back. His voice was soft and slurry, but Bremen could hear him as if in an echo chamber . . . first the slow, drunken structuring of the words in Meredith's mind, then the slow, drunken words themselves. "Hell no, she didn't die of getting raped," said Donnie, and laughed at the idea. "Farah killed herself with Jack Coe's sawed-off shotgun a couple of months later . . . she was living with the Hog then . . . and that's what made Jack go and get a job with the highway people. Neither one of them never had no luck."

"Well, a shotgun ain't a bad way to go," whispered Meredith Soloman, wiping the mouth of the bottle, drinking, and then wiping his own mouth as some of the moonshine dribbled out onto his sharp chin. "The tire iron an' stuff don't count 'cause none of that ain't what killed her. And none of the shit you're talkin' about's near as bad as layin' there in the dark a mile underground with your air runnin' out. It's like bein' buried alive an' lastin' for days."

Donnie started to protest but Donna whimpered and tugged at his arm. "Donnie, hon, these pains're coming real close now."

Donnie handed her the bottle, pulled it back after she had taken a long drink, and leaned across the aisle to get back to his conversation. Bremen noticed that the pains were only a minute or so apart now.

Meredith Soloman, it turned out, was on a quest not terribly dissimilar from Donnie and Donna's. The old man was trying to find a decent place in the country to die: someplace where the authorities would give his old bones a decent burial at county expense. He'd tried going home, back to West Virginia, but most of his kin were dead or moved away or didn't want to see him. His children—all eleven if you counted the two illegitimate ones by little Bonnie Maybone—fell into the last category. So Meredith Soloman had been on a quest to find some hospitable state and county where an old boy with his lungs clogged as thick as two Glad bags full of black dust could spend a few weeks or months duty free in a hospital somewhere and . . . when the time came . . . have his bones treated with the respect due to bones belonging to a white Christian man.

Donnie began an argument about what happens to the soul once you die . . . he had specific views on reincarnation that he'd got from Donna's cousin with the credit card . . . and the two men's urgent whispers turned into urgent shouts as Meredith explained that heaven was heaven, no niggers or animals or insects allowed.

Four rows in front of the arguing drunks, a quiet man named Kushwat Singh sat reading a paperback by the light of the small reading light above him. Singh was not concentrating on the words in the book; he was thinking about the slaughter at the Golden Temple a few years before—the rampage of Indian government troops that had killed Singh's wife, twenty-three-year-old son, and his three best friends. The officials had said that the radical Sikhs had been planning to overthrow the government. The officials had been right. Now Kushwat Singh's mind, tired from twenty hours of traveling and sleepless nights before that, ran over the list of things he was going to buy at that certain warehouse near the

Houston airport: Semtex plastic explosive, fragmentation grenades, Japanese electronic timing devices, and . . . with a little luck . . . several Stinger-type, shoulder-launched ground-to-air missiles. Enough matériel to level a police station, to cut down a gaggle of politicians like a sharp blade scything wheat . . . enough killing technology to bring down a fully loaded 747 . . .

Bremen stuffed his fists tight against his ears, but the babble continued and grew louder as the mercury vapor lamps switched on along the darkening interstate exchanges. Donna went into labor in earnest just as they crossed the Texas line and Bremen's last glimpse of the couple was in the Beaumont bus station just after midnight, Donna curled up on a bench in great pain as the contractions racked her, Donnie standing with boots planted wide apart, weaving, the empty bottle of Meredith's moonshine still in his right fist. Bremen actually looked into Donnie's mind then, extending his telepathic probe through the surrounding neurobabble, but pulled it back quickly. Except for the drunken fragments of the earlier argument with Meredith still rattling around in there, there was nothing in Donnie Ackley's mind. No plan. No suggestion of what to do with his wife and the infant trying to be born. Nothing.

Bremen actually sensed the panic and pain of the baby itself as it . . . she . . . approached her final struggle to be born. The infant's consciousness burned through the gray shiftings of the bus station neurobabble like a searchlight through a thin fog.

Bremen stayed aboard the bus again, too exhausted to flee the cauldron of images and emotions boiling around him. At least Burk and Alice Jean, the horny marine just out of the brig and the equally horny WAF, had disembarked to find a room somewhere near the bus station. Bremen wished them well.

Meredith Soloman was snoring, his gums gleaming in the reflection from sodium vapor lamps as they pulled out of Beaumont at midnight. The old man was dreaming of the mines, of men shouting in the cold damp air, and of a clean, white, painless death. Donna's birthing pains receded in Bremen's mind as they left the downtown and climbed onto the interstate access ramp. Kushwat Singh touched his money belt where the hundred and thirty thousand dollars in Sikh cash waited to be converted into vengeance.

The seat next to Bremen's was empty. He pulled the arm-rest back and curled up in a fetal position, drawing his legs up onto the seats and hugging his fists against his temples. At that second he wished that he had his brother-in-law's .38 back; he wished that Vanni Facci had succeeded in delivering him to Sal and Bert and Ernie.

Bremen wished—with no melodrama, with no shred of self-consciousness or regret—that he was dead. The silence. The peacefulness. The perfect stillness.

But, for now, trapped in his living body and tortured mind, the roar and onslaught of mindrape continued, even as the bus moved southwest on causeways above swampland and pine forest, tires hissing on wet pavement now as the late-night rains came down in earnest. Bremen felt himself slowly being released to sleep now that the others slept, the small universe of sleeping humanity within the bus falling with him in the night, their muted dreams flickering like snippets of old film projected on an unwatched wall, the entire sealed cabin of them tumbling like the shattered *Challenger* shuttle in mid-night free-fall together toward Houston and Denver and the deeper regions of darkness that Bremen knew that he was, for some reason he could not fathom, condemned to live to see.

EYES

Of all the new concepts that Jeremy has brought to me, the two most intriguing are love and mathematics.

These two sets would seem to have few common elements, but, in truth, the comparisons and similarities are powerful to someone who has experienced neither. Both pure mathematics and pure love are completely observer dependent—one might say observer generated—and although I see in Jeremy's memory the assertion by a few mathematicians like Kurt Gödel that mathematical entities exist independently of the human mind, rather like stars that would persist in shining even if there are no astronomers to study them—I choose to reject Gödel's *Platonism* in favor of Jeremy's stance of *formalism*: i.e., numbers and their mathematical relationships are merely a set of human-generated abstracts and the rules with which to manipulate these symbols. Love seems to me to be a similar set of abstracts and relation-of-abstracts, despite their frequent relationship with things in the real world. (2 apples + 2 apples did indeed = 4 apples, but the apples are not needed for the equation to be true. Similarly, the complex set of equations governing the flow of love do not seem dependent upon either the giver or recipient of that love. In a real sense I have rejected the *Platonic* idea of love, in its original sense, in favor of a *formalist* approach to the topic.)

Numbers are an astonishing revelation to me. In my former existence, prior to Jeremy, I understand the concept of *thing* but never dream that a thing—or several things—have the ghost echo of numerical values sewn to them like Peter Pan's shadow. If I am allowed three glasses of apple juice at lunch, for instance, for me there is only juice ... juice ...

juice, and no hint of quantification. My mind no more counts the juices than my stomach would. Similarly, the shadow of *love*, so attached to a physical object yet simultaneously so separate, never occurs to me. I find that property connected to only one thing in my universe—my teddy bear—and my reaction to that one thing has been in the form of pleasure/pain response with the bias toward the pleasurable, so that I "miss" teddy when he is lost. The concept of "love" simply never enters the equation.

Jeremy's worlds of mathematics and love, so often overlapped before he comes to me, strike me like powerful lightning bolts, illuminating new reaches to my world.

From simple one-to-one correspondence and counting, to basic equations such as $2 + 2 = 4$, to the equally basic (for Jeremy) Schrodinger wave equation that had been the starting point for his evaluation of Goldmann's neurological studies:

$$i\hbar\partial\psi/\partial t = \hbar^2/2\mu\nabla^2\psi + V(r,t)\psi \text{ or } i\hbar\partial\psi/\partial t = H\psi$$

All is revealed to me simultaneously. Mathematics descends upon me like a thunderclap, like the Voice of God in the biblical story of Saul of Tarsus being knocked off his horse. More importantly, perhaps, is that I can use what Jeremy knows to learn things that Jeremy does not consciously know. Thus, Jeremy's basic knowledge of the logical calculus of neural nets, almost too elementary for him to remember, allows me to understand the way that neurons can "learn":

$$N_3(+) = .SN[_1(t)VN_b(t)] \equiv .S\{N_1(t)VS[SN_2(t).\sim N_2(t)]\}$$

Not my neurons, perhaps, given Jeremy's rather frightening understanding of holographic learning functions in the human mind, but the neurons of ... let's say ... a laboratory rat: some simple form of life that responds almost exclusively to pleasure and pain, reward and punishment.

Me. Or at least me, pre-Jeremy.

Gail does not care about mathematics. No, that is not quite accurate, I realize now, because Gail cares immeasurably about Jeremy, and much of *Jeremy*'s life and personality and deepest musings are about mathematics. Gail loves that aspect of *Jeremy*'s love of mathematics, but the realm of numbers itself holds no innate appeal for her. Gail's perception of the universe is best expressed through language and music, through dance and photography, and through her thoughtful and often forgiving appraisal of other human beings.

Jeremy's appraisal of other people—when he takes time to appraise them at all—is frequently less forgiving and often downright dismissive. Other people's thoughts, on the whole, bore him . . . not out of innate arrogance or self-interest, but due to the simple fact that most people think about boring things. Back when his mindshield—his and Gail's combined mindshields—could separate him from the random neurobabble around them, he did so. It was no more a value judgment on his part than if another person in deep and fruitful concentration had risen to close a window to shut out distracting street sounds.

Gail once shared her analysis of Jeremy's distance from the common herd of thoughts. He is working up in his study on a summer evening; Gail is reading a biography of Bobby Kennedy down on the couch by the front window. The thick evening light comes through the white cotton curtains and paints rich stripes on the couch and hardwood floor.

Jerry, here's something I want you to see.

? ? ? Mild irritation at being removed from the flow of the equation he is scrawling on the chalkboard. He pauses.

Bobby Kennedy's friend Robert McNamara said that Kennedy thought the world was divided into three groups of people—

The world's divided into two groups of people, Jeremy interrupts. *Those who think the world's divided into groups, and those who are smart enough to know better.*

Shut up, a minute. Images of the pages fluttering and Gail's left hand as she searches for her place again. The breeze through the screen smells of newly mown grass. The thick light deepens the flesh tones of her fingers and gleams on her simple gold band. *Here it is . . . no, don't read it!* She closes the book.

Jeremy reads the sentences in her memory as she begins to structure her thoughts into words.

Jerry, stop it! She concentrates fiercely on the memory of rootcanal work she'd suffered the summer before.

Jeremy retreats a bit, allows the slight fuzziness of perception that passes for a mindshield between them, and waits for her to finish framing her message.

McNamara used to go to those evening "seminars" at Hickory Hill . . . you know, Bobby's home? Bobby runs them. They were sort of like informal discussion sessions . . . bull sessions . . . only Kennedy would have some of the best people in whatever field there when they talked about things.

Jeremy glances back at his equation, holding the next transform in his mind.

This won't take long, Jerry. Anyway, Robert McNamara said that Bobby used to sort of separate people into three groups. . . .

Jeremy winces. *There are two groups, kiddo. Those who—*

Shut up, wise guy. Where was I? Oh, Yes, McNamara said that the three groups were people who talked mostly about things, people who talked mostly about people, and people who talked mostly about ideas.

Jeremy nods and sends the image of a hippo yawning broadly.

That's deep, kiddo, deep. What about those people who talk about people talking about things? Is that a special sub-set, or can we create a whole new—

Shut up. The point is that McNamara said that Bobby Kennedy didn't have any time for people in the first two groups. He was only interested in people who talked about . . . and thought about . . . ideas. Important ideas.

Pause. *So?*

So that's you, silly.

Jeremy chalks the transform in before he forgets the equation that follows it. *That's not true.*

Yes, it is. You—

Spend most of my waking hours teaching students who haven't had an idea in their heads since infancy. QED.

No . . . Gail opens the book again and taps long fingers against the page. *You teach them. You move them into the world of ideas.*

I can barely move them into the hall at the end of the class period.

Jerry, you know what I mean. Your removal from things . . . from people . . . it's more than shyness. It's more than your work. It's just that people who spend most of their thinking time on anything lower than Cantor's Incompleteness Theorem is boring to you . . . irrelevant . . . you want things to be cosmological and epistemological and tautological, not the clay of the everyday.

Jeremy sends, *Gödel.*

What?

Gödel's Incompleteness Theorem. It's Cantor's Continuum Problem. He chalks some transfinite cardinals onto his blackboard, frowns at what they have done to his wave equation, erases them, and scrawls the cardinals onto a mental blackboard instead. He begins framing a description of Gödel's defense of Cantor's Continuum Problem.

No, no, interrupts Gail, *the point is only that you're sort of like Bobby Kennedy that way ... impatient ... expecting everyone to be interested in the abstract things that you are ...*

Jeremy is growing impatient. The transforms he holds in his mind are slipping slightly. Words do that to clear thinking. *The Japanese at Hiroshima didn't think that $E = mc^2$ was particularly abstract.*

Gail sighs. *I give up. You're not like Bobby Kennedy. You're just an insufferable, arrogant, eternally distracted snob.*

Jeremy nods and fills in the transform. He goes on to the next equation, seeing precisely now how the probability wave will collapse into something looking very much like a classical eigenvalue. *Yeah,* he sends, already fading, *but I'm a nice insufferable, arrogant, eternally distracted snob.*

Gail does not comment, but gazes out the window at the sun setting behind the line of woods beyond the barn. The warmth of the view is echoed by the warmth of her wordless thoughts as she shares the evening with him.

Bantam Spectra Special Editions

A program dedicated to masterful works of fantastic fiction by many of today's most visionary writers.

◆

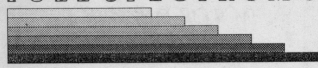